BOMB

A NOVEL

LES EDGERTON

www.gutterbooks.com

Printed in the United States of America

First Printing, 2016

ISBN: 978-1-939751-20-1

Raves for Les Edgerton and BOMB

"Les Edgerton has swiftly become my favorite crime writer. Original voice, uncompromising attitude and a pure hardboiled style leap him to the front ranks of my reading list. He will become legendary."

–Joe R. Lansdale, *Paradise Sky*, *The Bottoms*, *Edge of Dark Water*, *The Thicket*, the *Hap and Leonard* series, the books behind the TV series of the same name, and many others

"Les Edgerton is the new High King of Noir."

—Ken Bruen, *The Emerald Lie*, *The Guards*, *Pimp* and many others

"Les Edgerton is the perfect reason for both of my favorite maxims: Don't trust anyone over thirty and: Don't trust crime fiction from anyone under thirty. The weight of experience behind Les's books is my anchor in the choppy waters of criminal literature."

—Jedidiah Ayres, *Peckerwood* and others

"Edgerton commits the perfect crime story."

—Dietrich Kalteis, *Triggerfish*, *The Deadbeat Club* and *Ride the Lightning*

"I'm not sure which is more fascinating, Les Edgerton's IED of a suspense novel, BOMB! or the convoluted, heartbreaking story of its journey to publication. Both had me hooked. The good news is that you get it all with this fine new release from

Gutter Books . . . With multiple story lines (each burning like a fuse), an authentic New Orleans setting, flawed good guys, and seriously—seriously—flawed bad guys, BOMB! is the work of a gifted writer who knows how to ratchet up the suspense. If you're high strung, this is not the book for you. Adrenaline junkies won't be disappointed. "

—Grant Jerkins, *Abnormal Man: A Novel, A Very Simple Crime, The Ninth Step* and others

"With the flavor of Elmore Leonard at his peak, Les Edgerton's Bomb! is a sumptuous crime fiction feast. Rich in characterization, plot, dialogue and with a great sense of place."

—Paul D. Brazill, author of *Cold London Blues, The Last Laugh,* and *Kill Me Quick!*

"Les Edgerton is a writing hero of mine. Every time I read one of his novels, I feel like I'm being schooled all over again. All crime fiction fans should take a chance on BOMB! and see what it means to read the real deal instead of the pretenders."

—Anthony Neil Smith, *Holy Death, Yellow Medicine, All the Young Warriors, Worm* and others

"Les Edgerton cements his place at the crime fiction chessboard with *Bomb*, a delicious and intricate mix of whodunit and cat-and-mouse. Masterful and engrossing."

—Liam Sweeny, author of *Welcome Back, Jack*

DEDICATION

For my readers. Without readers, writing is like having sex with yourself. The feedback you get for your performance is ultimately flawed.

For my late friend, Bob Parker, my guy on all things electronic and explosive.

For my brothers and sisters behind bars, particularly the ones in Pendleton—this one's for you.

For Tom Pitts and the gang at Gutter Books, who got behind the new version of this book and did yeoman work on it. You guys rock!

For librarians like Robin Deffendall and her counterparts at libraries everywhere, booksellers like Scotty Montgomery and Mauro Falciani, and literary show hosts and hostesses like Livius Needin, Robb Olson, and Pam Stack—all of whom are the best friends possible for writers and largely underappreciated and underacknowledged. Not in my house!

And, as always, for my wife ~~Eye Candy~~ er, Mary and my three wonderful kids—Britney, Sienna and Mike—I love you guys!

A Background for *BOMB*

by Les Edgerton

THIS NOVEL HAS a history. I wrote it back in the nineties and at the time my agent, Jimmy Vines, was arguably the hottest guy in agenting. If you've ever seen the movie, *Jerry Maguire*, the title character played by Tom Cruise was Jimmy to a T. A slick-talking (in machine-gun bursts), expensively-dressed, stereotypical polished New Yorker smart-ass type, Jimmy could easily have been the originator of the phrase, "Show me the money." Lots of publishers did just that for his writers.

Jimmy received so much initial excitement from publishers when he first sent out feelers on what was then titled THE PERFECT CRIME that he decided that even though this was a first novel, this was a book that needed to go to auction. For those writers here who've had a book go to auction, you know that's one of the biggest thrills for a writer to be had, up there almost with getting a nomination for the National Book Award, or a travel agent calling to check on your drink preferences for your flight to Stockholm, or, even getting a message on your unlisted cell phone from Kim Khardashian giving you her private number and inviting you to a "personal and up-close" slumber party and something she called a "sesh" with her and her sisters, ending her message with a cheery, "Call me, ya big lug!"

In other words, a literary auction is a big deal.

It was… what's the word?… *exciting*. I'm sitting here in the Great

Flyover in Fort Hooterville, Indiana, and every three or four minutes, Jimmy was phoning me breathlessly from the Big Apple, giving me up-dates. Between his calls, I'm screaming at my wife Mary to "Don't go near that phone!" and ignoring the withering looks she was shooting my way. Offers were being messengered to Jimmy every couple of minutes, and he'd be calling to tell me who'd offered what, what the bidding was up to, who'd joined the fray and who'd dropped out.

Finally, everyone had dropped out except two players, Random House and St. Martin's. Both made their final bids. Random House offered $45,000 for their advance and St. Martin's offered $50,000.

"It's your call," Jimmy said. "We'll go with whoever you want."

We talked about it and I tried to weigh the offers. Both were big, well-known, respected presses. Both were talking about a probable three-book deal, a series based on the same characters, and depending on how the first book did, the advances for the next two would most likely go way up. Jimmy figured the final tally would be in the healthy six-figure range. Enough money that I would be able to achieve my version of true wealth—being able to fill the gas tank up completely each time on my car instead of the normal two buck purchase. He talked about the excellent chances he saw for a future movie deal.

Finally, I made my decision.

Worst decision of my life, bar none. The financial fall-out from that decision destroyed me at the time and actually, I've never recovered. More about that later...

"Random House," I told Jimmy. "Why them?" he asked. "Because," I said. "They're *Random House.*" The House of Bennett Cerf and all those legends of literature. I didn't care it was for less money than St. Martin's was offering. This was *Random House.*

Jimmy understood. He called St. Martin's, told them my decision, and the editor who had been doing the bidding, Charlie Spicer, was disappointed, but before he hung up, told Jimmy, "If

Edgerton ever has another book and is looking for a publisher, we want first crack at it." Just a pure gentleman. I just wish...

Next, he contacted Scott Moyers, the senior editor who had been doing the bidding for Random House. Scott had just come over from Villard Press and been appointed a senior editor. Mine was the first book he'd signed for his new publisher.

The day I signed the contract was one of the happiest of my life.

I was at a crossroads in life. Up to that point, I had made a terrific living for thirty-plus years as a hairstylist. My wife Mary and I had our own salon, Bold Strokes Hair Design, and we were booked solid for six months in advance. But, our lease was up and we had to make a decision. To sign a new 5-year lease or close the salon. Up until then, even though I had sold several books, I had never considered quitting my day job. I'd heard and listened to all the advice about not doing so until one was absolutely certain he'd be able to make his entire living from writing.

Now seemed the time. I'll relate the rest of what turned out to be a horror story by including the gist of an exchange of emails between myself and one of the most respected agents in the business a couple of years ago. I won't name the agent as I don't want to reveal his identity as he was honest with me about what had probably happened but didn't want to be identified for clear reasons.

Here's is the email I sent this agent:

Dear＿＿＿＿＿＿;

I'll try to be as concise as I can be. A few years ago, when I was a client of Jimmy Vines, I wrote a crime thriller that he was ecstatic about. So ecstatic that he took it to auction, which, as you know is a rarity for a first novel. It was an exciting time—phone calls and emails every few minutes for several days—you know the drill. The upshot was that it came down to two houses, Random House and St. Martin's. St. Martin's offered $50,000 and RH offered $45,000. Jimmy said we'd go with whoever I wanted. I decided on RH because... well, it was Random House. The company that Bennett Cerf built and with all that glorious history. I was going to be a Random House author!

The editor who took it was Scott Moyers who had just that week come over from Villard to become a senior editor at RH and this was the very first book he signed. They were going to bring it out simultaneously in hard and soft cover, from Ballantine and RH. Jimmy told me that Ann Godoff, who was the president at the time, personally phoned him and raved about the book, telling him how much she loved it. She said they were going to guarantee me that not only would it come out on the *NY Times* bestseller list; it would come out as #1 the first week. She said she could guarantee that because the lists weren't derived from sales but from copies printed, etc. She and Scott then asked that I change the title as they saw a trilogy in the future and they wanted the name to be one that would lend itself to that. The original title I had was *The Perfect Crime* and they asked that it be changed to *Over Easy*, a play on the "Big Easy" since it was set in New Orleans and they wanted the other two to be as well. As soon as it came out, they wanted to create a new contract for a new two-book deal. But, my God—I couldn't believe what she was telling me—that my book was going to be Number One. That's a cloud I'm probably never going to reach again. From the lips of the president of Random House, that's something you can take to the bank. Or so I thought. (I'm bad on dates, but it seems to me this was around '97.)

I know this is all very interesting and all, but so far everything's going well and why am I telling you all this you're probably thinking. Well, that's when the bottom dropped out. The time period here is crucial as you'll see. A week after I took RH's offer, Bertlesmann took over Random House. Being out here in the "great flyover" I had no clue as to what was probably going on in NY and London, in the power centers of publishing, but it's obvious to me now that the Bertlesmann takeover is what impacted my deal.

For the next several months I rewrote the book entirely for Scott four times. I'd already rewritten it twice for Jimmy before he'd sent it out and I had no problem with either guy requesting rewrites. I'm a firm believer that writing is rewriting and I do it cheerfully and professionally. At the end of the last rewrite, Scott emailed me and said he was regretfully going to have to turn it down. During the process, he had me eliminate a major character and do some other things. In his notes for the last rewrite, he said he wished I would write like Russell Banks! For the first time I got mad. I told him if he wanted Russell Banks, why didn't he just sign him? Just weird stuff. I told him I'd done everything he'd said without question as I didn't want to "be that guy" editors talked about--the difficult writer. To that he said, "You should have pushed back." My bad, I guess... I talked to Jimmy and he was furious with Scott and RH and said he'd never ever do another deal with Random House the rest of his life—that he'd never heard of a major publisher treating someone this way, etc. At this remove, I confess I'm a bit skeptical now of what he was saying, considering I was this little guy out here in Indiana and he was claiming he'd never again deal with the biggest publisher in the business because of what they'd done to me. Lots of things I thought at the time have changed the more I think about it. I have a strong suspicion that he was... how do you say it? Blowing smoke up my ass? Yeah, that's a good way to describe what I think happened.

What was the kicker was that St. Martin's had offered $5,000 more and wanted to publish it without changing as much as a comma and they wanted an additional 2- or 3-book deal after it came out. The editor who participated for them was Charlie Spicer and Jimmy told me that after they lost out in the auction, Charlie told him that "if Edgerton ever wanted to leave RH, we'd take him in a minute." He said later, that if "Edgerton wrote another novel like that that they wanted first crack at it."

Which made what transpired next hard for me to get the logical part of my brain around. After the RH fiasco, I asked Jimmy if he could take it to St. Martin's as only a handful of people had even read it—RH and St. Martin's and maybe a dozen others who had participated early in the auction. No, Jimmy said, it's a dead issue now, but as soon as we sell your next one, then we can get it published. That never made sense to me being as no one had read the book except the ones mentioned above. It wasn't as if the public was aware of it or had read it or anything.

Anyway, Scott was very apologetic and said he'd make sure I would never have to repay the part of the advance I'd already received ($12,500). Sometime after that, he left RH and I've never heard from him again. About two years later, I got a bill from RH for the 12.5 and I wrote them back, relaying what Scott had told me. Nothing happened until a couple of years after that and I got another bill and I told them the same thing and again, haven't heard from them since.

This whole thing really impacted my life in ways that are still happening. At the time, my wife and I owned a very successful hairstyling business. At the exact time I signed with RH, our lease for our shop was up and we had to make a decision to sign a new 5-year lease or not. I'd always tried to be realistic and practical and even though I'd sold a number of books before the RH thing, never succumbed to the temptation of quitting my day job. Well, this seemed to be the perfect time to do so. I was given enough money to live on for the next year while I rewrote; Ann Godoff had guaranteed Jimmy (according to him anyway) my book would be #1; they wanted at least two more books after this one, etc. She could guarantee it would come out as #1 simply because they were publishing 50,000 copies in paperback from Ballantine and 5,000 copies in hardcover from Random House to be released simultaneously. I felt it was time to become a truly full-time writer. So we closed the business and my wife went to work at another salon and I settled down to all that I've related above. The upshot was that after a year of all that, our business was gone and I was jobless and went through some health problems that wiped out our savings and put us heavily into debt, etc. We've never caught up since. You can't go back and regain your clients--they're gone forever, for the most part. I feel pretty sure that Bertlesmann taking over probably put all this into action—there was probably some sort of house cleaning and lots of books like mine were probably thrown overboard, and people jettisoned, etc. I have no way of knowing this—just a strong suspicion.

I'm not a whiner and I don't blame the world for the bad things that happen to me—it's just part of the deal of life and usually because of bad choices I'd made on my own. The reason I wanted to share this with you is that I still have this novel and it's a good one and I'd like your opinion as to if I should send it out.

Mr. _____, thank you for reading this and taking your valuable time to do so. If any of this intrigues you and you'd like a look at it, I'd be very happy to send it to you. Also, if you know Charlie Spicer and run into him you might ask him about the deal. We don't get "do-overs" in live as a rule, but that's one guy I wish I'd gone with. He really liked my work and in every dealing with him I always felt he was a true gentleman.

Thank you so much for taking time for someone who isn't even earning any money for you.

Blue skies,
Les

The agent's reply to this was:

Les-
You don't owe Random House squat. Having "won" you at auction, followed up by having you rewrite the book multiple times, what they did is completely shitty behavior. And it happens every day. I'm actually surprised they bothered to send you two bills. For Das Random Haus, $12,500 is pocket change and they probably cleared

it from their books as a write-off years ago.

When Rupert Murdoch's NewsCorp Inc bought a company, (name deleted), they cancelled a lot of contracts... only they found other ways of saying it so CEO Jane Friedman could be quoted in the press saying, "*We didn't cancel any contracts.*"

I do business with Random House every day, and would sell them one of my represented books in a heartbeat. To booksellers and book reviewers that little house on the spine, or even better, that little Borzoi dog, still carries a lot of cachet and helps get reviews and in-store display space. The fact is, though, the Random House of Bennet Cerf, or even Bob Bernstein is long gone. They do some books brilliantly. Most others are little more than putting a cover on the barely edited manuscript and shipping it out the door. Sadly, that's true most places. The hard part for old grizzlies is that they remember what Random House used to be -- before it was a division of an arm of a media conglomerate and expected to cough up 15% quarterly profits to the Mother Ship. The old souls have either fled the building (actually "the building" is gone too) or sit in their offices, bitterly waiting for the day they can full advantage of a fat 401K.

Ann Godoff is over at Penguin now. She "might" view this as an opportunity to do right by a book and an author she once seduced with fantasies of a #1 New York Times best seller ** or she might want to slink away in embarrassment. Plus, who knows what portraits of you as a madman had to be painted by Scott or others in order for them to look less evil.

I'm actually surprised Ann would do such an amateur thing. She is a total pro and I think brilliant publisher. I love the way she works between the cracks. Who could have predicted the huge best selling audience for *Orchid Thief* or *Midnight in the Garden of Good & Evil before* they were published? All those previous best sellers about Savannah or orchids? What was the obvious category for these books? They are not typical true crime or travel or anything but extremely well written. I love Ann for that. But I would NEVER promise an author a best seller. The fates are too fickle. Why is *Marley & Me* a massive and ongoing seller, where Mark Doty's version of the same book (only MUCH better) a quiet success and no one reads Willie Morris' classic *My Dog Skip*. I'm not even sure the Morris is still in print.

There is a great essay by E.B. White called *Here is New York*. White wrote it in 1949 and it is absolutely relevant to this day. In writing about New York City, I think he nailed the right attitude for anyone aspiring to be a writer. He wrote (and I paraphrase badly, having not read the piece for ten years), "*If you come to New York, you having to be willing to be lucky.*"

So yeah, dust off *Over Easy* and send it in. I am even more surprised than Ann's promised best seller that your agent would say it's a dead book and not resubmit it to St. Martin's. This happens all the time. After David Ulin had post-Harper Morrow back away from his book, he resold it to Viking. And heck, what's gotten more press this last year than the passed around *If I Did It* by O.J. Simpson?

Best,

Mr. _____

Mr. _____ and I ended up not hooking up, as I have other forms of work he doesn't represent, such as sports books, a YA, etc. He's a great guy, though, and very generous in sharing his advice and wisdom with me as he did with the above. I just thought it'd be easier to show our correspondence about the PERFECT CRIME/OVER EASY/BOMB! book as it contains all the pertinent facts about what happened so you'd know the history.

I had some other worries about this novel. When I wrote it, the idea behind the crime was truly original. Such a crime had never been committed. My worry was that some outlaw would eventually come up with the same idea and even though I had thought of it first, his effort would trump mine in the public's eye. Well, a couple of years ago that very thing happened. And then again. The good thing is that neither were really the "perfect crime." They'd made some mistakes—which is why they were caught. Mistakes I'd foreseen and hadn't had my character make. So, while yes, there have been a couple of instances where the basic idea has been used, they still haven't reached the "perfect" level mine has.

This was written upon the occasion of obtaining a new publisher for the book, Aaron Patterson of StoneGate Books. About a year ago, Aaron graciously gave me back the rights to it and Tom Pitts of Gutter Press signed it. This version, under the new title BOMB! is based on the original version sold to Random House and re-edited a bit more. This to alert readers who may have read the StoneGate version—this is a different version but some of the core remains.

I hope this little saga proves of interest to the writers out there. This isn't stuff that's reported on in English class or even your MFA workshops as a rule. . . . The Cosa Nostra has very little on publishing.

Blue skies,
Les

BOMB

The New Orleans Times-Picayune
February 13, 1961—City Edition
Bulletin

BANKER MURDERED BY OWN SON
Grisly Scene at Spanish Fort
By Donald R. Noles
STAFF WRITER

Prominent New Orleans banker Bradford Charles Derbigny, and his wife Mary were found dead in their Queen Anne-style mansion at 3323 Robert E. Lee Boulevard in the section of town commonly known as Spanish Fort. It has been confirmed that Mary Derbigny, 36, was the victim of a broken neck, while Bradford Derbigny, 42, president of the Derbigny State Bank, was bludgeoned to death with a baseball bat.

The chief suspect in the slayings, according to police, is the couple's fourteen-year-old son, Charles, a freshman at Isidore Newman School. Captain Jimmy Fauvounette of the Abita Springs police department stated the Derbigny's seven-year-old daughter Sarah, also a Newman student, reported the murders to New Orleans police, who contacted them. Shortly afterwards Charles was arrested by Abita Springs uniformed officers who were waiting for him as he drove up to Titus Fuller Derbigny's estate just outside of that town. Titus Derbigny is Charles Derbigny's grandfather. Allegedly, the boy had gone there with the intent of murdering his grandfather as well, although police cautioned that this was only speculation.

"The girl is in family custody at this time, with her grandfather," said Captain Fauvounette, referring to Sarah Derbigny. "She's in intense shock, as you can imagine."

Due to the violent nature of the crime, Charles Derbigny was taken to the New Orleans parish jail, where he is being held in a private cell, instead of a juvenile facility. New Orleans Parish Assistant District Attorney William Agee has confirmed that a motion has already been filed in Superior Court to try the youth as an adult and arraignment is set for 10:00 A.M. for February 15.

The killings, according to New Orleans police detective Randall Harte, were, "among the most vicious I've seen in sixteen years, and I was a beat cop in the French Quarter for six years. Mr. Derbigny was struck at least sixteen times in the face alone and [was] virtually unrecognizable. This is one rich, sick, spoiled kid. I personally know Mr. Derbigny and one finer gentleman cannot be found in this city."

Bradford Derbigny was involved in many local business pursuits, and, in addition to being president of the bank founded by his father, Titus Fuller Derbigny, he also sat on the boards of Covington Lumber, Inc., Phoenix Oil, Inc., and Hazelton Industries. In 1969, he was Chairman of the United Fund Drive in New Orleans Parish and over the years has been involved in many various civic and charitable activities as well as being an officer of the Knights of the Kross Krewe during Mardi Gras. *New Orleans* Magazine listed him as one of "100 People to Watch" in the July, 1956 issue. Mary Derbigny was a member of the Pontchartrain Women's Club.

Titus Derbigny was unavailable for comment. A spokesman for Mr. Derbigny stated that he was "overwhelmed by the savage attack on his son and daughter-in-law," and that his only concern was for his granddaughter at this time.

More_ Society Section, Page 32

CHARLES "READER" KINCAID'S temper was running just a bit short. He'd stop at one more booth and if this guy didn't have what he was looking for, then he'd say fuck it, get in his car and find a bar, work out another plan. A week and a half out of prison and he was mucking around with this shit up here in this freezing-ass state. Ohio. Who the hell would want to live in Ohio anyway? He should have sent Eddie is what he should have done. Yeah. Except Eddie would probably screw it up. He sighed, moved down the line looking for the booth some guy had suggested. What should have been something simple was already turning into a pain in the butt.

He was poking through the items on the table when the man standing behind it asked, "Looking for anything in particular?" The guy had on a hearing aid, one of those old-fashioned ones looked like the prototype of the first one invented. Must have been why he spoke so loudly, Reader figured. Guy ought to get something that worked. Electronics expert with something half a step up from a hearing trumpet. The thought brought a half-smile to his lips.

Jack Fogarty, was printed on the man's name tag, stuck on his lapel at a crooked angle. It was one of the blue tags, the ones dealers wore. His own tag was red, the color assigned to everyone else, except the show personnel, who wore green ones. He'd scrawled the name *Joe Witucki* on it, but anyone who tried to make it out would have to stand toe to toe and guess at what it said.

They were standing in a huge open-air tent with dozens of tables crowded together in long rows, interspersed at intervals with the large booths of the top manufacturers and dealers. The sign at the entrance read "Midwest Electronic Swap Meet—Dayton, Ohio" in large Caligula print, red on black.

"Yeah," he said. "Some warm weather would be nice. You always keep it this cold in this town?"

"Not from Dayton, eh? It *is* nippy, isn't it? Who woulda thought we'd get this weather in the middle of May! If we'd known, believe me, this thing'd be indoors. Too late to reschedule and find something inside I guess is what they figured. Who knows what they figured? Bunch of screwups. Gave me the lousiest spot in the place. T'hell with 'em next year. Where you from, partner? I've heard your accent before." He smiled, in a friendly way. The neighborly kind, Reader thought, forcing a smile. He hated the type.

Reader ignored the man's question. He didn't want him to know anything about him. Especially where he was from. That was the whole point of this trip. He regretted that weather bit. In a week, the guy might pick up the papers and read about something that happened in New Orleans and put two and two together.

Acquaintances of Reader wouldn't recognize him. He was wearing a windbreaker and hat. Also, a blonde wig, a beard and eyeglasses, your basic windowpane glass.

"I'm looking for something in particular. I need a remote control for a model plane. Big-ass thing. Guy over there said you were the man to see. He said you'd have what I'm looking for."

"Well, pal, maybe I do. All you have to do is tell me what it is and I'll tell you if I have it."

"A Futaba. Nine-channel crystal-controlled receiver and transmitter. I want one goes a mile, at least. And some R/C switches. At least six. No, make it eight. Some other things, odds and ends."

The crowd jostled around them, someone bumping against Reader and causing him to lose his balance slightly. He ignored whoever it was, heard an "excuse me" as he went by.

"Well, I don't have all that here. Back at the store, I do. Got a nice

Futaba, newest thing. Nine channel, PCM 1024, lists for twenty-five hundred. I can let it go for twenty-three and tax. You should have been here earlier. Sold one, not half an hour ago. Day late, pal. Didn't figure I'd sell the one I brought. Some businessman, huh? I guess I shoulda brought both of them. Come around to the store in the morning." He handed Reader a business card. "Jack's Hobbies, Crafts And Electronics" it read. The address and phone number were in smaller print below. Reader looked at it and stuck it in his shirt pocket. He leaned across the table closer to the man.

"My problem . . . Jack . . . is I have to leave town tonight. Could I get you to sell it to me when you get done? I need a few other things, too. I'll pay extra." In an attempt at charm, he gave the man a wry grin.

The dealer cocked his head slightly and looked thoughtful. He said, "Louis Armstrong. That's it."

"Louis Armstrong?"

"Yeah. I'm a big fan. Got all his records. That's who you sound like. You're from . . . man, you're from the Big Easy! That's it! Man, I been there! Best fucking food in the world! You're a long way from home, old son. Hell, if you're from New Orleans, just get this stuff when you get home. Any hobby shop'll have it. Go to a Radio Shack."

"It's Jack, isn't it?" Reader looked at the guy's name tag then back to his face. "Well, Jack, I would but I can't. I'm up in Ohio on business and I've got to leave for Europe. My kid's in school in Switzerland and he's a nut over those remote controlled boats. This is a present for him. I get on the plane tomorrow morning at six and I don't know if I can find this stuff when I hit Switzerland. He's meeting me at the Zurich airport and I want to have it for him when he meets me. I thought sure I could pick it up at this show."

The man looked at him. "I thought you said he has a *plane*. You want this for a boat or a plane? Not that it matters. Works on either."

"Look," Reader said, making a show of glancing at his watch, ignoring the question. "It's after six. All the places in town are closed where I might find this stuff. Can't I get you to stop by your store after you're done and sell it to me? Look, I've asked every dealer in the place and nobody else has one. This would mean a lot to my kid. I'll be glad to pay you extra. How 'bout I add a C-note to whatever it costs? Charge me the list and make a little extra. Have a heart, pal. I only get to see my kid once a year. The old lady swung a hell of a one-way fucking deal when we split up. You got any kids?" He leaned in closer to Jack. "You ever married to a fucking cunt who kept you away from your only fucking son 'cept one week a year?"

Fuck. *Two* mistakes. He must be slipping. First, the guy pegs him from New Orleans and he ended up messing up his goddamned story trying to ad-lib. This wasn't good. Not good at all. This changed things. All this way to remain incognito and that blown all to hell. The guy didn't push the discrepancy any further, but Reader didn't want to take the chance he'd start thinking about it again. Especially a few weeks down the road when there was going to be one hell of an explosion in New Orleans and the Fibbies got themselves involved, as he was sure they would. First thing they'd do is contact all electronics dealers in the country, see who their suspicious customers were. He could try and find another source, but that would only give them two more people to quiz. No, the best thing to do was to get what he needed from this guy and take care of business. Sorry Jack, he thought. My mistake, but looks like you're the bozo that's gonna have to pay for it. The thought of killing the man didn't particularly trouble him. It just made what should have been a simple thing more complicated.

"Okay," the dealer said. "I'd be crazy to pass up a deal like that. Tell you what. Give me some time to clean up here and grab a bite. Meet me at my store at nine. Hey, lemme tell you a story about New Orleans. I'm walking through the French Quarter one morning and this little black kid comes up and says—"

"Betcha I can tell you where you got your shoes."

Jack Fogarty looked at the man in amazement. "How the hell'd you know that?"

Reader grimaced. "They been using that one on tourists since *I* was a kid. Paid him a buck to hear him say, 'in a shoe store', didn't you?"

"I'll be damned!" He smacked his leg with the open side of his hand. "One born every minute, isn't there!"

Reader grinned. "You see those pickaninnies break-dancing down there?"

The man stared at him, searching his memory. "Little black kids dancing on a sheet of cardboard t'rap music? Those kids?"

"Yeah." Might as well give this guy a story, close the sale. "About twelve years ago, some reporter from the *Times-Picayune* did a story on them. Some nasty shit. Seems this ol' boy had kidnapped pretty near every one of them. Picked 'em up at the bus station, places like that. Runaways. He kept them over across the lake in this cabin way out in the boonies. Old slave cabin. That's what they were. Slaves. He even chained them to their beds at night. Every morning, he'd throw 'em in a pickup, haul them over to the Quarters, set them down on some street corner. One of the older kids was in charge. Kid he'd picked up years ago, promoted to foreman. This kid's job was to see none of them ran for it. Like . . . where the hell would they go anyway?"

The electronics dealer's jaw had dropped six inches. "You're shittin' me!"

"Nope. Real deal. Kept these little niggers half-starved and beat half to death. Making the guy a fortune. All the happy tourists standing around, giggling to each other how cute they were, stuffing dollar bills in the cup. This reporter figured they took in a five hundred, maybe a thousand a day, easy."

"My God! So what happened? They arrest this guy?"

Reader was enjoying this. He couldn't wait to see the guy's face when he told him the rest. "Sure. Made a big deal over it, too. Made the front page. Pictures, the whole bit. The paper put the reporter up for one of those Pulitzer prizes. Quite a story."

"Well, at least it ended up all right. They got the kids back to their families, right?"

A smile spread over Reader's face, slow and easy. "Not exactly. A week later, the same kids were back down in the Quarters, dancing their little black asses off, tourists oohing and ahhing like nothing ever happened."

"You're shittin' me!"

A chuckle escaped Reader's throat. "Not a bit. We're talking about New Orleans, friend. Town runs on graft. Guy making a couple of thousand bucks a day from cheap labor like that can afford to make a real healthy donation to the sheriff."

He liked the look on the bozo's face when he said that. Probably nothing like that ever happened up here in fucking Mayberry, he thought. Taking a slowhead lame like this off was going to be a piece of cake. Fun, too. Hell, if it wasn't for the weather and the cardboard-tasting food, he might want to settle down here. A town full of lames like this one could get a guy rich quick.

An hour later and luck was with him, he found the store right away and the setup looked perfect. An alley in back and nothing open on either side of it at this hour. He drove around until he found a twenty-four hour supermarket two blocks up and parked in the lot.

There was a coffee shop directly across the street from Jack's Hobbies, Crafts and Electronics. As dinky and run-down as Jack's place looked from the storefront, he figured this character must make most of his money doing trade shows. He took a sip of coffee and winced. Fucking Cadillac coffee. I'd give ten bucks for some Community Blend dark roast, he thought. You gotta be a Yankee to drink this shit. Bandy's Grill. He needed to remind himself not to order coffee any place with "grill" in the name as long as he was in the north. This stuff tasted like they *fried* it on the grill.

The weather didn't help his mood. He hadn't seen the sun since he'd been up north. Everything was . . . gray. How anybody lived in this place was beyond him.

It was too bad ol' Jack'd placed his accent. He knew what he had to do now, but it wasn't something he was exactly crazy about. Added a layer of complexity.

He ordered another cup and waited. The waitress asked how the coffee was and he told her. Come back tomorrow and maybe they'd get the good stuff in by then, she retorted. He was close to making a mistake, he realized, drawing attention to himself, so he toned down his conversation with the woman. She was a looker. Great red hair. Like that old-time actress, what's-her-name. Rita Hayworth.

When it was time, he walked out of the coffee shop and down the street. A block over, he crossed and came back up the alley behind the electronics store. He was sure nobody saw him. A knock and Jack was letting him in the back door. He followed him to the front and they went down the rows of shelves, the dealer removing the items Reader told him he wanted and placing them in a red plastic shopping basket.

"That it?"

"Yeah. I think so. Let's see, transmitter, receiver, crystals . . . say, give me five, six more crystals. Different frequencies. I don't know if he has a preference so I might as well get a bunch. And yeah. All the stuff's here. How much? Add a hundred to that for your trouble. No, add a couple hundred. You been a real sport. My kid's gonna be thrilled."

He thumbed through the items spread out on the counter mentally cataloging them, making sure everything was there. He looked up at the guy, Jack, showed him some teeth.

"Say, Jack, you know I saw Louis Armstrong once. Live, in person. When I was a kid. Over on Rampart Street. Helluva thing. On a Second Line. Lead trumpet. Cat was whaling some stuff, I tell you!"

Might as well have him go out with a stupid grin on his kisser, fucking citizen with an ear for accents. Major mistake on his part. He should have used his Spanish accent up here. Who would have thought some clown in Ohio would recognize a New Orleans inflection?

The store they stood in was jam-packed to the ceiling with every possible inch of shelf space stuffed with electronic parts and accessories. Some of the things Reader could see were right out of Star Wars. It'd be fun to find out what some of these items were.

"This is what it comes to. Plus what you said." Jack tore an invoice out of the pad he was writing on and pushed it across the glass counter to Reader. "What kind of boat did you say you have?"

"Looks fair, Jack. Say, what's this?" He pointed with his right hand to one of the figures near the bottom of the sheet. Jack leaned over and Reader pulled the hand swiftly to the hunting knife sheathed behind his back. His other hand grabbed Jack's hair and slammed his face down on the counter. The glass shattered from the force of the man's head. "Here you go, partner," Reader said softly, and plunged the knife into the back of his neck. He twisted, tearing gristle and cartilage. There was no sound other than a soft grunt. Reader waited several seconds for the tenseness to leave the man's back muscles, all the time working the blade slowly and methodically. While he let the knife work, Reader's mind went back to when he was a kid. He'd spend hours outside with a sewing needle, a length of thread attached to it and a clear jelly glass full of water. He'd sit on the sidewalk and wait for the ants to come by. One by one, he'd stab the needle through their heads, impaling them, and then drop them into the water, holding on by the thread. Watch their legs wiggle. Sometimes, it took ten minutes for one of them to drown. Sometimes, he'd wait until the instant they quit moving their feet and take them out, let them revive. Then do it all over again. It wasn't glee he felt, any more than he felt glee at the feel of the man pinioned beneath his knife now. It was just a semi-hypnotic state that just kind of felt good. If somebody would have happened along to interrupt him, he wouldn't feel anger that they'd ruined his pleasure, but more a minor feeling of irritation. He sometimes wondered why he didn't get more out of killing than he did.

When the man relaxed, Reader withdrew the knife and wiped it clean on Jack's back as his body slid to the floor.

He got busy. First, he put on a pair of tight-fitting driving gloves and placed the items on the counter into a large supermarket shopping bag he took out from under his shirt. The invoice was lying on the counter, and he picked that up and put it in his pocket along with the carbon and the copy. He left the bag on the counter while he methodically walked around the store tipping over shelves and scattering merchandise. He found the burglar alarm and checked it. It was activated, pretty much as he'd thought. When Jack had opened the door and let him in earlier, he'd excused himself after rebolting the back door and hurried to the front. *A cautious fuck,* Reader thought, glad he was paying attention. *Fucking deaf bastard.*

The alarm was one of those combination deals.

He considered the situation. Let's hope he wrote the combination down somewhere, he thought. He went to the cash register, careful not to step in any of the blood, and lifted up the coin receptacle. Under it was a hundred dollar bill, which he stuck in his pocket. There was a mass of other papers, bills and notes, mostly names of various electronic gadgets and numbers, probably order or serial numbers. At the very bottom of the stack, so small he came close to missing it, was a torn scrap with a series of four numbers written in pencil and faded to where it was barely legible.

Bingo. This is it.

It was. He entered the numbers and the green light went off.

Last thing he did was to go back to the cash register. There was only silver, no green in the slots. He took the coins out, throwing some on the floor and scattering some of them onto Jack's body.

Slipping out the back door, he made sure the alley was deserted. Once he was sure no eyes were on him, he picked up the brick he'd seen an hour earlier during his casing and slammed it against the plate glass. It took two more blows before it shattered. It would look like somebody broke in. He stepped very quickly to the end of the alley and slowed his walk to a casual stroll until he reached his car parked in the supermarket parking lot.

A block away, he happened to glance at the gas gauge and saw that it registered half-full. He was going to fill it up earlier only it slipped his mind. Slipshod work like this got you caught. He always kept his car full of gas. He knew a guy in the joint who had gotten caught because he ran out of fuel during a high-speed chase.

He spotted a station up the street. He pulled in, pumped his own gas and checked the oil, which turned out to be a quart low. While he was there he picked up some food for the trip back—potato chips, hard candies and a jumbo pack of cinnamon gum. He paid with the hundred dollar bill. The sour look the attendant gave him made it plain he wasn't happy about depleting his stock of change.

Reader went back out to his car and pulled it over to the side of the station by the restroom. From under the front seat he retrieved a large sack and took it into the restroom, locking the door behind him. Quickly, he shucked the clothes he'd been wearing and changed into the white sports shirt and khakis that he took out of the bag. He removed the wig and the beard, wincing as the spirit gum tore loose from his cheeks. He stuffed the items into the bag and washed his face with cold water to reduce the redness, then splashed his hair with water until it was sopping and combed it straight back.

Back in his car he picked up his knife from where he'd laid it on the floor and put it in the bag with the suit and wig and other items. He hated to lose a good knife, but he knew he should in this case. He wouldn't need that particular wig any more. He had another one at home, a white one, for the last part of the job.

He stayed to county roads, heading south, and when he came to the first good-sized stream he pulled off and threw the bag into it, weighted down by a large rock. Twenty minutes later he was on the Interstate heading south. Heading for problems he couldn't begin to anticipate. Problems that would have their origin in the town he was leaving behind.

2

A FEW YEARS back, before the routine "burglary in progress" call that cost Grady Fogarty his eye, his compadres on the Dayton police force would tease him about his weakness for expensive suits. Internal Affairs might even have shown a little interest in his wardrobe if it wasn't widespread knowledge that he obtained most of it from a grateful clothier, a store owner whose daughter Grady had saved from certain rape one night, responding to screams coming from an alley off Grafton Avenue. It was positively amazing what a little chunk of lead that weighed less than half an ounce could do to a man's life.

The biggest change wasn't his wardrobe, though. It was his physical appearance. Plastic surgery had reconstructed his crushed left cheekbone, but he refused to wear the glass eye the doctor recommended, opting instead for what, in black, self-deprecating humor, he called his pirate patch. Three months after he was forced into medical retirement, an old friend from the department walked right past Grady without recognizing him. It wasn't so much that his features had changed radically—all that was different was the addition of the eyepatch, which made him look somewhat rakish, actually—it was the look in his good eye, and his posture. A fever seemed to burn behind the remaining gray-green iris—not the fever of excitement, but the confused temperature illness sometimes brings. His dark hair, once carefully coifed, was dull and mussed. And he seemed smaller: a big man, a tad over 6'3", he appeared diminished by inches. Holding himself in, slump-shouldered, head bent slightly forward, as if something in his gut was on fire and the muscles in his back had softened.

For a while, the change in Grady Fogarty was the talk of the station house, but soon he was mentioned less and less in their conversations until in time he was largely forgotten. Just another cop the job had fucked up. You didn't want to think about something like that too much. It could happen to you.

Squinting through the bottles into the dingy bar mirror, Grady considered the subject of the present conversation.

The woman sitting on the stool next to him leaned forward. "Come on, so how'd it happen?"

He sighed. He wondered if he really needed this shit. He knew what was going to happen next. He'd answer her silly-ass question, take her drunken ass out on the dance floor, and an hour later they'd be doing the horizontal cha-cha. Not the worst fate, he supposed.

"How'd I lose my eye? That what you mean?"

She wasn't too bad-looking. Actually, she was the best-looking woman in the joint. It was his pirate patch, he knew. Always got them. It was the pity-factor. Only they always called it something else.

"Tragic," was how one had put it. "You look tragic, Grady."

Somebody was over at the Wurlitzer, feeding coins into it. Sam Cooke began singing "You Send Me."

"Yeah. Oh! Dance with Susie!" the woman exclaimed. "That's Susie's favorite song!"

Great, Grady thought. She refers to herself in the third person. First person I ever heard of that did that who wasn't a basketball superstar or a World Series hero. Or some air-brained movie star.

"Can you dunk it?" he asked, following the blonde out onto the dance floor.

"Never mind," he said to her puzzled look, her hands going up around his neck, her body settling into his in such a way that the only place for his own hands was on her ass. That wasn't all bad. She did have a nice ass. Nice everything, in fact.

"Come on," she slurred, her face buried in his chest and her hips doing interesting things with his own. "Tell Susie."

"It was a hearing problem," he said. Might as well have some fun.

"Huh?" she said, picking her head up to look into his eyes before nestling back into his chest.

"Yeah," he went on. "Somebody said 'shut up' and I thought they said 'stand up.'"

She cocked her head to look up at him again.

"Really?" She processed what he'd said. "Oh, you! Come on, what really happened?"

The song ended and they stood there a minute until Willie Nelson began singing "On The Road Again", and he steered her to a table, holding her chair out for her.

"Can't dance to that stuff," he said, grabbing another chair and pulling it next to hers where he could catch her if she decided to go out. She was that drunk.

They got new drinks and he resumed. "I guess you want the real deal."

"Uh-huh." Her chin was resting on her hand and when she spoke she slipped. Grady caught her before she crashed to the floor. This time, she propped up her chin with both hands and gazed into his eyes.

"What happened was I was pitching in the World Series . . . for Cleveland . . . seventh game, bottom of the ninth, score tied 2-2, two outs, 3-2 count on the batter and I brought my heat."

One of Susie's eyes started to cross slightly. Grady could see her losing focus.

"Heat?" she said, glomming onto the word.

"Yeah," he said. "Smoke. You know . . . *heat*."

She twisted her mouth into a smile.

"I got heat . . . you want some heat, baby?"

Grady said, "Yeah, well, let me finish this." He took a long drink to loosen up his pipes.

"Anyway, I wind up and put everything I got into it. They told me later the gun got me at 96. The batter was Hack Wilson, remember him?"

"Sure," she said.

"Yeah, there's gonna be a test later, babe. Hack Wilson and the Chicago Cubs. Three years ago in the Series. You remember this, Susie, and we're a romance."

His drink gone, Grady signaled the bartender for another. Susie's was barely touched. He doubted if she could hold another drop.

Susie said, "I remember. Jack Wilson and the Chicago Cubs."

The bartender put his drink in front of him and took three singles off the stack he had out.

"Yeah, well, you passed the test, Susie. You know your baseball, that's for sure. Anyway, Hack nailed the best pitch I've ever thrown. He just crushed that ol' pea."

He looked at her to see if she was still buying this and went on. "Hit me smack in the eye. Here." He pointed to his patch. "Three runs scored."

Susie's eyes widened and her hand flew to her mouth.

"Hey!" he said. "Don't be throwing up on me here!"

She nodded her head and swallowed hard. "I'm okay." She surprised him then, leaning over and pulling his face to hers, planting a wet kiss on him. When her lips left his, he murmured, "Someday I'll tell you about the time I got kicked in the nuts in the NBA championship game and my dick grew a foot."

Later, in her apartment, they pulled their sweaty bodies apart. "Wake me up at five, will you?" Grady whispered. "I promised my brother Jack I'd help him out in the morning."

He was talking to himself. She was already snoring. He thought about waking her, or trying to figure out her alarm and setting it himself, but before he did any of that he was nodding off himself.

3

THE SUN WAS just coming up in Dayton when a hungover Grady Fogarty discovered the bloody body. He'd come by to help Jack unload a truckload of merchandise scheduled to arrive that morning . . . only he'd overslept.

He knew something was wrong as soon as he unlocked the door. For starters, it should have been open. His brother was never late. As soon as he walked in he saw that something terrible had happened. Not a single shelf was standing. Electronic parts were everywhere on the floor.

"Jack!" he yelled, his voice shrill and harsh. "Oh, man, no. *No!*" He pushed on into the store, not bothering to step over boxes and the other debris, just plowing through them as he ran. He didn't realize he was holding his breath until he reached the counter and saw his brother's hand, twisted and bloody, sticking out from behind the edge of the counter.

"Oh, God," Grady whispered hoarsely, expelling pent-up breath. "Jack . . . " He inhaled deeply, got a lung full of air . . . and stepped forward.

It was a miracle that his brother was still alive. Barely. He'd lost a lot of blood. His face lacerated by glass shards and he'd been stabbed in the back of the neck. Gore was everywhere, soaking Jack's shirt and pooled on the floor around him, making it difficult for Grady to keep his balance as he knelt to place his finger on the carotid artery to confirm what was horribly certain. That his brother was dead.

But he wasn't. Grady couldn't believe it at first, thought the faint pulse he felt was nothing more than idiotic hope. No one could look like this and be alive. He fought to calm himself, steel his shaking fingers and apply them again to Jack's neck. He bent close, his ear to his brother's mouth and then he was sure he felt the faint pressure of a fluttery breath. He got to the phone fast, dialed.

It wasn't the first blood-splattered victim in Grady's experience, not from sixteen years on the Dayton police force, just the first one he'd been related to. He discovered that made a significant difference in his reaction.

In his years on the police force he'd witnessed hundreds of victims, but his brother's wounds were barbaric beyond anything he remembered. His intuition told him that the person who did this wasn't just desperate to get what he wanted, but took a savage glee in his attack. He felt an excruciating stab of guilt. Maybe if he'd been there when he was supposed to . . . although, from most of the signs, this had gone down many hours before. His guess would be the night before.

Just as he was figuring out this logic, beginning to assuage his guilt, the thought occurred that if he had been there on time, his brother would have been taken to the hospital that much sooner. If he died when another hour might have saved him . . .

The emergency technicians found Grady tenderly picking glass splinters from Jack's face. He didn't notice that he was cutting his own fingers.

On their heels came the police, uniformed officers from two squad cars and a detective who pulled up in a blue Taurus. Grady could see all this from the window and then from the front door as they rushed in, picking their way over and around the thousands and thousands of electronic parts and boxes littering the floor.

"Grady? That you? Grady Fogarty?"

Looking down at him was a detective Grady knew from his days on the force. Marty Sprague. He'd come in directly behind the white-coated E.T.'s and ahead of the uniformed cops.

"Marty."

"Jesus, man! This a friend of yours?"

Grady nodded. His voice was husky. "My brother."

"Christ!" He shook his head from side to side. "I'm sorry, Grady. Man."

Grady let the E.T.'s take his brother and watched as they moved him carefully into the ambulance, already looking alien with an IV in his arm, oxygen mask over his nose and mouth.

"I'm going with him."

One of the emergency technicians looked at Detective Sprague, who nodded his okay. As they wheeled the stretcher toward the door, Sprague said, "Grady! I'll need to talk to you later." Grady glanced back, squinted in the white sun. He nodded agreement, turned, and hurried to the ambulance. Behind him, uniforms strung up yellow tape to secure the crime site. Car radios crackled and people coming out of storefronts and apartments started to form a crowd. More sirens in the distance and the sound of a dog barking barely entered Grady's awareness as the driver slammed the doors and trotted around to the front of the vehicle.

In spite of the circumstance, his mind shot back to the last time he'd ridden in an ambulance. That time he'd been the one lying on the gurney, his left eye socket shattered by a burglar's bullet.

He could trace a lot of shit from that moment. *Bad karma*, the New Age folks would say.

Somewhere during all that—the lost eye, his forced retirement from the force, the drinking that began—something snapped. It was a soft little thing—a *click*—but ever since, Grady's take on life had been altered along with his physical view of the world. It was like a man with 20/20 eyesight wakes up one day with astigmatism. Grady's internal vision became slightly skewed along with the external. Nothing seemed to matter as much anymore. He settled into a new life that could more accurately be termed a mere existence.

Speeding in an ambulance through a light mist down Dayton's downtown streets, Grady didn't spend much time thinking about the past. What he was involved with was dabbing the seeping blood from Jack's face and concentrating all his energy on willing his brother to stay alive. It had been a long time since his pulse had raced like this. He focused on his brother's face.

The friend who failed to recognize him that time would be surprised to see the change in his body language now.

4

TWENTY-ONE YEARS BEFORE he attacked and killed the man in Dayton, Ohio, and ten days after the passage of his twenty-second birthday, Charles "Reader" Kincaid walked past the razor-wired outer fence of Louisiana's maximum security prison at Angola and stepped onto a bus bound for New Orleans. He got on the Greyhound with a hundred and thirty-three dollars in his state issue trousers, a new name and an attitude. The acrid odor of diesel exhaust was the first thing he smelled as a free man and the smell was sweet.

Because he'd been behind bars from the age of fourteen when he'd taken a Louisville slugger to his father's skull, he had only one acquired skill. He could kill a human being in any number of ways. He had another attribute as well. He didn't much care who it was he killed. Once you've done your own father, it doesn't matter a whole lot who it is you ease into the afterlife. That's a spiritual mountain that looks down on everything else.

He'd had two bats to choose from for his bloody at-bat, a Roger Maris 32-ouncer and a lighter, 29-ounce Richie Ashburn that more resembled a fungoe bat than a major leaguer's. The barrel of the Ashburn model was almost as thick as the rest of the bat, but then, Ashburn was a spray hitter, known for his singles and doubles. Charles was after a home run, not a single, so he grabbed the Maris. It just felt better in his hands. More balanced.

A couple of weeks before his release Charles had his last name changed legally. To Kincaid. The name meant nothing to him—he just liked the sound of it. An old lifer who specialized as a jailhouse lawyer filed the necessary papers for him for a retainer of five cartons of Camels. He figured that returning home with the surname of Derbigny would cause more problems than he could use, and besides, there were still plenty of people in town who remembered the crime he'd gone to jail for. The Derbigny's weren't exactly a low-profile family, even though two-fifths of them had been eliminated when Charles was fourteen.

His first week out of the joint, he discovered how hard it was for an ex-con to locate a decent job, especially if all you've been doing for the past eight years is man the card catalogue in a prison library. Even with a bright, shiny new name that didn't have the baggage his original name carried. Besides, he had a pretty good idea he wouldn't be happy leading a straight life. He'd had a glimpse of it and what he saw wasn't attractive.

Sitting in the Absinthe House in the French Quarter, nursing a beer he'd purchased with the last of his release money and contemplating holding the place up, he overheard the two men at the table behind him talking about some guy one of them wished was dead. Some guy who was fucking the man's wife. Sounded like a pretty common story in the sexually-relaxed milieu of the Big Easy, but an opportune one to be overhearing at this particular time, with Reader sitting there with a pressing need to come up with some hard cash.

"Five hundred," Reader said, walking over and sitting at their table. "And keep your voices down. Let's move to that back table, boys."

It was the beginning of a career. An hour and a half's actual work and he was five hundred richer. More, it turned out. It had been easy. He did it that night. His wife was with the boyfriend at that very moment, at a motel out in Metairie, according to the man being cuckolded, guy name of Maxwell. Maxwell wanted to kill his wife's lover himself, only he lacked the cojones. That wasn't the reason he gave, but Reader figured that out on his own. Maxwell ended up driving Reader to where his wife and her lover went on their regular Thursday night tryst, just to show Reader where his wife would be if he were to take the job. He didn't have any idea that Reader was going to do the job right then. On the way to the motel, Reader did two things. Three things. One, he made Maxwell leave his buddy behind at the Absinthe House, and two, he made a pit stop at a variety store, where he bought a package of Ping-Pong balls, a roll of Scotch tape, and a small container of Draino. He needed one other item which he couldn't buy in any store. A rig. A hypodermic. He got that off a hype he spotted mush-footing it down Pirate's Alley. Just took it off his bony, junkie ass. Third thing: When they got to the motel, Maxwell pointed out the boyfriend's car and then started to pull out of the parking lot.

"Wait," Reader said, putting his hand on the man's arm.

Forty-five minutes later, the door to one of the rooms opened and Maxwell's wife and her boyfriend walked out, arm in arm, and got in the man's car, a lemon-yellow Ford Fairlane. It was misting, making for poor visibility, ideal for what Reader had in mind.

"Wait here," Reader said. "You're gonna enjoy this." He got out of the car and walked across the parking lot in the mist. He could see the outline of the two inside locked in an embrace through the fogged-over rear window. They weren't aware of him or anything else in the universe. He walked casually up to the rear of the Fairlane, bent down and pulled down the license plate where the gas cap was. Unscrewing it, he dropped the Ping-Pong ball into the tank, screwed the cap back on and sauntered back to Maxwell's car. The Ping-Pong ball was filled with Draino, the needle hole he'd used to fill it taped over. Just as he was opening the passenger door, he felt the thump of the explosion and turned to see the Fairlane in a ball of flame. Metal, glass and debris flew everywhere and in addition to the smell of burning upholstery wafted up a faint odor akin to that of a barbecue. Flash-fried human flesh smelled a lot like roast pork, Reader noted. He was glad to observe that the Draino trick worked just as his cellmate back in Angola had insisted it would. Sodium hydroxide was the key ingredient, Tommy had told him. Doesn't mix well with gasoline. He eased into the seat, closed the door, and said to the wide-eyed Maxwell, "I'd pull on out if I was you. I don't think you want to be around when the fire trucks and cops get here. Chances are, they're gonna see this as one of those unfortunate mechanical malfunctions, but if you're seen here they might change their thinking. Cops are lazy, as a rule—most of 'em—but I wouldn't push it, give them something they might want to look at closer."

Nodding dumbly, Maxwell put his car into gear and fishtailed out of the parking lot onto the slick black pavement. Later, back at a Kenner bar, he handed Reader five hundred dollars, all in hundred dollar bills, and Reader gave the man a stare.

"Five hundred was for one hit, friend. I did two. You owe me another five. I've still got two more Ping-Pong balls. You might want to consider that. Plus, you might want to think about all the enjoyment you got tonight, watching your old lady become shish-kebob."

Maxwell started to argue, then saw the look in Reader's eyes and hesitated for only the smallest part of a second before reaching down and easing off his shoe. He reached up into the toe and pulled out a folded-up wad of bills, all hundreds it looked like to Reader. He peeled five of them off and handed them to Reader. It hardly made a dent in the roll.

It was the last job Reader was to do for less than $10,000.

A month later, he met a woman who wanted her husband dead. She was slurring-words-drunk when Reader happened on her in a patio bar over in Marrerro at eleven o'clock on a Tuesday morning, the sick-sweet perfume of bougainvillea in the late spring air. Reader discovered that if you hung out in the right places and used your ears, there were all kinds of people out there who had someone in their life they wished wasn't there. He also found he had a gift for thinking up unusual ways to hide a murder, make it look like an accident. Which you had to do to collect insurance or inherit a business or a fortune, which was usually what the client had in mind.

The second hit was even more fun than the first. Not only did he get to bang the client, but the job ended up paying twenty-five large. He got very creative on this one. He sat in his room for a week, toying with various ideas until he got the perfect one. It required a disguise. Not a problem in New Orleans, the home of costume stores. There were costume rental shops on more corners than there were gas stations in the town that lived to dress up and party.

For this hit, he used an Afro wig—one that looked exactly like the "do"

O.J. Simpson was currently sporting. Simpson and five million other Super Fly wannabes. Topped off with a Big Apple hat, a tangerine-colored jump suit with wide lapels, and of course, Stacy-Adams shoes, the kind that came out of the box with a spitshine you could see your face in. Getting the right stain for his skin tones was a bit harder, but he finally found what he was looking for in a theatrical supply shop over in Elysian Fields.

Her husband always made a stop for extra crispy fried chicken at the Popeye's outlet on Metairie Road by the country club on his way home. His wife gave him that bit of information at the same time she was giving him a blow job. Popeye's would work, Reader decided, after checking it out.

There were two other people standing behind his mark in line—both women—when Reader came in and threw down on all of them for their purses, the guy's billfold and the cash in the register. They all acquiesced and then Reader started laughing and capped the guy he was after four times, giggling all the time like he was a loon. He was in the car he'd stolen for the job, parked over on Mildred Avenue, a block away, before the survivors came out of shock and started screeching for the cops. He could hear them hollering clear over to where he was getting into the car. It was that kind of quiet neighborhood where you could pick out a scream.

Later, in the Times-Picayune, it said, "An unidentified black" had held up the place, killed a "prominent businessman." "High on drugs," was how one of the two women customers had described the bandit. The police artist's rendition of the murderer was fairly close.

What was particularly nice about that hit was that both customers and the register clerk were all black and had taken him for the same. That's when he knew it was a dynamite disguise. He'd used it often since, even though it took a lot of time to prepare, especially the skin tones.

Over the years, Reader had come up with one scheme better than the next. Not that he had to, always. Some of his targets he could have just whacked the old-fashioned way, but he liked to use his mind. The one he was the proudest of, was the one he'd done in Baton Rouge. The woman who hired him to kill her husband made it clear it absolutely had to look like an accident.

What he did was break into a lab at the LSU campus over in Baton Rouge, where they were holding a dog suspected of having rabies—he was in luck—it did—and then extract a hypodermic full of the diseased animal's blood. The break-in was never discovered. The next day, Reader injected half a dozen wild mice he'd trapped earlier with the dog's blood, and a week later the furry little mammals all began shunning their water dish.

Satisfied, he made a phone call and two nights later, his client had him over for dinner with her and her husband. He posed as a buyer from a South American company interested in a line of shoewear the firm she repped for manufactured. That was a bonus, as he got to use the Spanish he'd studied during his stay in Angola. He went as a dark-skinned Brazilian, and the husband never suspected he was anything but an expert samba dancer who knew expensive footwear. He was getting good at disguises and accents came easily to Reader. Spanish had been his best class in high school and he'd had plenty of chances to polish it in the joint, chinning with the Latinos.

During the course of the meal, when the maid served the rice pudding, Reader took the opportunity to present the gift he'd brought—a bottle of Poully-Fousse—and pour them all a glass. His host's glass was the only one that also had Dalinane mixed with it.

An hour later, the servants dismissed, he and the missus made love on a highly-polished oak floor. Harvest moonlight streamed through the open bay windows on two glistening bodies a few feet from where the woman's husband snored happily. While she retired to the bathroom to freshen up, Reader took another hypodermic, this one filled with dark mice blood, and injected a few milligrams of the liquid into a spot he selected between the man's left big toe and the middle one. The mark the needle left was scarcely noticeable. Looked like a harmless spider bite.

A week later, Mr. Anthony Marguary, of the Baton Rouge Marguary's and of Marguary's Textiles, came down with a rare case of rabies. It was, unfortunately, too late to save his life. He lingered another week, locked in a special room at University Hospital, and passed away in what could only be described as an unseemly and hideous death. If they'd only caught the disease in time, Mr. Marguary could have been given anti-rabies serum, but by the time the symptoms appeared it was too late. The grieving Crystal Marguaray told the newspaper she had smelled something rotten in the house for days and days and sure enough, a handyman had found several dead mice behind a pantry wall, which she'd had him bury in her rose garden. She thought they'd make good fertilizer, she told the sympathetic investigator. A veterinarian professor at LSU confirmed the mice were rabid after he performed a rodent autopsy.

To her credit, the widow Marguaray donated a hundred thousand dollars to the university, with the proviso it be used for rabies research. "Maybe Jeffrey's death wasn't in vain. Maybe his passing can accomplish some good," she said, a lone tear running down her cheek. The reporter who was taking all this down was astute enough to quickly instruct his photographer to get a shot of the tear, which ran in the next day's edition.

That was twenty-one years back and Reader had managed to carve a substantial career out of the largesse of clients he'd helped become wealthy since then. He'd even done a job for the New Orleans godfather, Frank Cabrini, only that time there was no insurance or inheritance money at stake. It was a vengeance hit on Cabrini's daughter-in-law. The *capo* had just learned of an infidelity she was guilty of, and he knew his son would never divorce the bitch. His son was disgustingly weak that way. Because of who the client was, and the respect he had for him, Reader'd decided to take on the job for only half his normal fee. He also thought there might come a day when he'd need a favor. As it turned out, he made a wise move, even though the payoff didn't come until many years later. One thing he did gain immediately. The man's friendship. The one thing Reader missed in his successful life of crime was someone to talk about it to. It wasn't nearly as much fun being a criminal genius if no one knew. Because of who the godfather was, Reader knew he could keep a secret. After the kindness he did the old man, he began to call him after hits to chat with him about the cleverness he'd displayed. The old man always welcomed his calls. Cabrini's own *mafia* world was composed of mostly straight-ahead killings done the old-fashioned way with garrotes, knives, and .22 shorts at the base of the skull, and Reader's finesse amused him. He'd also known not only Reader but his father and grandfather for years, having done a considerable amount of business with both men, neither of whom he liked half as much as he did Reader.

Reader had also suffered a few reversals in his career, being busted twice for crimes which he allowed were "stupid." Both times, he got nailed for armed robberies. Neither of which were done for the money, but, as he admitted, "for the excitement." Sometimes it was months between suitable gigs and he just plain got bored. "My downfall," he admitted freely and with a cheerful sense of fatalism, but he really didn't mind jail time. It was almost like coming home.

Armed robberies were stupid, but he was addicted to them. He fought off doing any for as long as he could, but eventually the gut-check thrill drew him back. His bread and butter operation, executing citizens and making the hit look like an accident, satisfied his cerebral side, but every now and then an overwhelming desire overtook him for the more visceral pleasure of standing in front of a checkout counter with a sawed-off in his hands, hoping the guy would go for the .357 Magnum Reader just knew the chump had stashed under the counter. It was Wild West stuff, mano a mano, and what he loved was the uncertainty of it all. Would the guy go for his piece, would he be faster than Reader? It was all about control. See who was the best, who was in charge. Who was the smartest, the quickest, the one with the most balls. Control.

Reader had successfully pulled off thirty-one armed robberies over the years, four of which ended in shoot-outs, Reader the one who walked out of the store. He could remember every single detail of those, the ones ending in a killing. The others, the ones in which he hadn't fired his weapon, were more vague in his memory. After a job where the clerk had meekly handed over the money and laid down on the floor as per Reader's instructions, he was alternately morose and angry for days. He felt cheated, swindled out of his nut. Yes, that's what it was. His nut. Very nearly sexual. The four times he'd gotten the justification to take the storekeeper out, when he'd reached for a weapon and he'd blown him away—*that* was a glorious moment. He never felt more alive than at that instant when the shopkeeper made his move and his lips curled up, and he remembered to pull, not jerk, his trigger finger, and the best thing of all, the look of shock and surprise on the asshole's face when the load hit him full in the chest and punched him off his feet. The look of surprise was the reward. There was fear there, too, in the action. Mouth dry-as-dust, hands clammy on the stock of the scatter-gun, an urge to urinate mounting as he stood there and waited to see what his victim would do in the next instant. The thought that maybe this would be the time when the guy would beat him. The arrogance that said *nobody* could beat him. The feeling that he was challenging death itself, daring the gods to defeat him, knowing they couldn't.

When he walked into a place, his shotgun hidden under a raincoat, his mind was a whirl of activity. Look where the customers are, look where the clerk is, check out the mirrors. See the street, who might be coming in. Were there surveillance cameras. All this and a hundred other details. He liked it when there were customers. It added to the challenge. Who knew if an off-duty cop might be in there, buying a six-pack? Possibilities like that only heightened the excitement, brought on the adrenaline. While others in this line of work would normally wait until the target establishment was empty of shoppers, Reader always did the opposite. Waited until a rush, customers lined up ten-deep at the checkout. His mind would be going a thousand miles a minute, checking this, figuring that, estimating this. And then, when he stepped up, brought that bad boy out from where it was hidden, told the guy behind the register to hand it over, at that precise moment, he shut everything off. At that point, he went into a kind of out-of-body trance where all conscious thought faded away and it was just the two of them, him and the man behind the counter. It was like diving off into unknown water from a great height. You didn't think, you just did it. You dove, shot into the water and that's where he was, from that second on. In the water. Everything, sound, motion, all else was muffled, distorted, leaving only instinct. He was the caveman ten feet from the mastodon, the soldier coming over the rise and looking at the man in the other uniform.

The two times he'd been caught had been the only two times he'd taken a partner along. Bad mistakes. Both times, they'd gotten away with the crime, but his partner each time had taken a fall down the line and ended up giving up all the jobs he'd done. Including the one with Reader. The first time that happened, Reader swore off partners forever. The second time, the one he'd just done a bit for, he remembered his previous vow and laughed. There wouldn't be a next time, he knew.

He was doing well in his life, except for the occasional stretch in the graybar hotel, but always, at the back of his mind like a festering sore, lay unfinished business from that time with his father. His grandfather. He'd planned to take Grandfather out the same day he killed his father, but when he drove across the lake to his place, he'd no sooner pulled up in the driveway than the Abita Springs police whipped up behind him. Seemed his little sister had called the police on her Princess phone and told them Charles might be heading out to Grandfather's. She'd found their mother with her neck broken in their parents' bathroom. Screaming, she ran into Charles' room to tell him and found him standing over their father, Louisville slugger in hand. Charles wasn't responsible for their mother's death, but Sarah mistakenly thought he had been. It was a natural error as it was plain from the scene before her that Charles had wielded the instrument that felled their father. She was ignorant of the fact that their father had been the one responsible for their mother's death a few minutes earlier. Which was why Charles had dented his father's head in. For that and for other sundry crimes, mostly involving sexual and physical abuse over most of his young life. He hadn't bothered to stick around and tell his sister any details. He'd just grinned at her in a funny way and told her to go eat her breakfast. He was going to go see Grandfather, he said. *You know why,* he said to her, patting her head. *It all gets taken care of now.* It wasn't until the police came that she found out her hair had streaks of her father's blood in it. From her brother's hand when he patted her.

For the next two decades plus, the only regret Reader had in life was that he'd been unable to kill his grandfather that day. The "other crimes" his father had died for had been inherited from that man. Both men liked to fondle little Charles from the time he was a baby. Neither knew the other did, but Charles knew. After all, he was the one being fondled.

5

MIDWAY THROUGH HIS second stretch for armed robbery at the Louisiana state prison at Angola, Charles "Reader" Kincaid got what he considered the luckiest break of his life. Dewey Fortney was assigned as his assistant in the prison library. At Reader's request.

Dewey Fortney was a famous dude. The papers had been full of his exploits. His specialty was department store safes. Guys who could blow safes were considered to be in the top tier of criminality and everyone at Angola was anxious to get a look at a guy who had the kind of expertise Dewey Fortney obviously possessed. He was clever at circumventing alarm systems and being in a different time zone before the robberies were even noticed. His real genius, though, was in blowing safes. It was a precise science with Dewey. He had pulled off sixteen successful such robberies in six states, getting caught on the seventeenth only because a partner had given him up and assisted the New Orleans police in setting a trap in exchange for immunity. The partner had been caught a week earlier on another job he had unwisely tried to pull off as an independent. The police were waiting on Dewey and came into the Maison Blanche Canal Street store office, weapons drawn, while the smoke was still hanging in the air from the charge he had just set off.

"Fucker hadn't gotten stupid, we'd both still be free men," Dewey growled, following Reader past the stacked shelves to the tiny space that served as the library office in the back. "He's in the Witness Protection Program but I'll find him."

"Yeah," Reader laughed, sitting down behind his desk, indicating with a wave that Dewey was to take the chair in front. "When you get out, right? What's that? Twenty-five years?"

That sobered the other man. "I'll still find him," he muttered. "I don't care if I'm a hundred and one. I'll find the bastard."

"That's important to you, right?" Reader said, shaking out a couple of Camels and rolling one over the desk toward Dewey. "I guessed as much," he said, lighting his own from a match and lighting Dewey's when he leaned over. "Which is why I had you transferred here. You give me what I want, I'll take care of this guy for you. I have my own ways to find him."

"That's how I got this job?" He got up, went over to thumb through some of the books stacked in piles, awaiting transfer to the shelves. "Man! You get anything in here but Zane Grey paperbacks? Some library!" He sniffed and sat back down.

Reader smiled. He really didn't know. Jobs like this weren't available to new inmates. Not without a lot of pull, plus a decent-sized bribe to the hack in charge.

"You thought you got this gig on your looks, Fortney? I guess you figure that's how you got put in Ash-1 Dorm, too. There's sixty-four guys in Ash-1 and the waiting list, last time I looked, was over three hundred. Don't you know they had you slated for Camp J? You know where the guys in Camp J are right now? They're out picking onions. Acres and acres of them. It's called stoop labor. That sound like fun to you? I don't know about you, but I'd rather be playing pinochle nights than picking open my bloody-ass blisters. We got everything in the dorm. Cards, TV, magazines. The best thing is you get to walk around, 'stead of laying in a six by eight, staring at your trouser worm, teaching it tricks, trying to hold a conversation with your cellmate who doesn't share your enthusiasm for Tolstoy."

"Hell, I didn't know." Dewey said, and then he stared at the cigarette Reader'd given him, with a funny look. He held it away from him as if he couldn't decide quite what to do with it. "Say . . . I'm no punk." He looked up at Reader, his eyes widening as if he was just realizing something.

"Relax." Reader got up, walked around and put his hand on the man's shoulder, felt him flinch beneath his touch. "It's nothing like that. If I wanted a punk, there're easier ways to get one. Cheaper, too. I want something all right, but it doesn't involve your fucking virginity."

He explained how he'd gone to all this trouble to secure a cushy job for the man and why.

"Well, shit," Dewey said, visibly relaxing. "That's no big deal. What is it you want to know, specifically? Say, Reader, you mind if I ask you something?"

Reader indicated permission with a nod.

"You seem a lot brighter than most of the guys I've seen in here. How come you're in here rather than a federal joint? You seem like . . . well, you come across like a guy out of place in here. More like a guy who maybe got caught embezzling from the company coffers, not holding up Takee Outee's like most of these misfits. No offense, but how'd you end up in a shithole like this? I met you on the street, I'd figure you for a lawyer or something. Don't tell me you steal cars!" He grinned, nervously, as if he wasn't sure if he'd just insulted the man or not.

Reader didn't return the smile. "I didn't grow up in a trailer park, if that's what you mean. I'm equipped to live on both sides of the street. Look. Let's get something straight. What I am or what I was isn't any of your fucking business." He swiveled his chair around to stare out the window. Cool it, Reader, he told himself. Don't get him scared of you, where he won't tell you what you need to know.

He turned back around, this time with a smile on his face. If Fortney had been a bit more observant, he would have seen the smile didn't extend to Reader's eyes. "Fuck, kid," he said. "I've been in here too long. Starting to get like these other assholes, playing Clint Eastwood all the time. Hell, I grew up rich, if you want to know. Silver spoon brat, the whole bit. Didn't quite make it to college—something happened—but I've read a bit. Self-educated, I guess you'd say. I did go to Newman, which means I don't drop my g's much, 'cept when it's useful. You speak to rats, you need to know how to squeak."

"Newman. That's the school in New Orleans, right? The one for rich kids?"

"I guess. One of them, anyway. My father—everybody in my family went to Isodore Newman. My grandfather's picture hangs in the main foyer. His father's. My choice would have been public school. The kids in my family weren't given choices, though. We didn't have much of a football team at Newman. Lacrosse. That was the big sport. Field hockey for the girls. Nice little plaid uniforms that are long enough they don't show their cunts when they run." The other man joined his laughter. "Newman girls don't even have cunts," Reader said, and this time his eyes joined his lips in his smile. "They're sewn shut by their nannies every morning before school." Both men laughed again, harder.

Reader wanted to get this done right, which is why he'd called in another favor. The guy wanted a hundred green to do the job, "green" being the term used for real money, *greenbacks*. Green was considered contraband by the prison administration, the possession of which was guaranteed to cost you a month in the hole. Worse, it would mean the loss of the librarianship and that Reader would find his own ass out pulling weeds or shoveling cow shit should he get nailed with it. It was a chance worth taking and it came off without a hitch.

The job was a simple one, albeit requiring a special person. All Reader wanted the guy to do was torch the library, paying particular attention to the electrical wiring and fuse box. That was the simple part. It called for a certain kind of person though, because whoever it was who did it was probably going to get caught. Prison authorities took arson very seriously, even to the extent of calling in the state police crime unit in such situations. Which meant whoever lit the match was going to be sent to the fields or the dairy or worse. And to a cellhouse, losing his comfortable dorm. After a stretch in solitary. A lot to ask, but Reader knew the perfect guy. A doofus named Murphy who was actually rumored to be bored by dorm life and, more importantly, was known to be missing his little punk over in Camp J. But it was going to cost.

He explained all that to Dewey and the man was puzzled. "Why you doing all that?" he asked. And, "Why don't they want us to have green?"

"I need the bulb snatcher," was Reader's reply. "I need him for at least a week. This'll get him here. When you start giving me the information I want, I want his input, too. What he doesn't know about electronics isn't worth knowing. I figure between the two of you, I'll learn everything I need."

He answered his other question. "They don't want inmates to have green because of escapes."

"Escapes?"

"Yeah. Lots of guys walk off, especially the trustees who work outside. Fucking civilians would have nightmares if they knew how many guys escape from here all the time. They catch 'em mostly because they don't have any money when they walk. Which means they end up trying to steal a car and get busted. With money, they could grab a bus. Without it, they're sitting ducks. The Man gets real nervous when he finds green on anybody."

"What's a 'bulb snatcher'?" Dewey wanted to know.

They were sitting in the chow hall, eating supper. They were having beans this meal. That wasn't news—when they *didn't* have beans, that was news. Reader's main concern was not biting down on a rock. There were rocks all the time in the beans. When he looked around, he could see everyone else eating the way he was. Carefully, so as not to bite down on a rock.

There were long rows of inmates eating, just shy of five hundred at most meals. Twenty to a table, ten on each side. Five rows of tables, five tables to a row. There weren't any tablecloths on the tables, just the metal, painted gray, gloss finish. They were fed in shifts. Reader knew why. They didn't want the inmates all together. That could lead to trouble.

Not every table was full this night. Here and there was an empty seat for the ones who didn't feel like beans tonight or the ones who stayed in their cell or dorm for another reason. Reader could see a few spots where there were two vacant seats right next to each other and he could guess why they skipped supper. There were more absent than usual but that was because it was payday—when the state issues your monthly pay chit—and everybody had been to the commissary, buying bags of cookies and Pall Malls. Because of their length. More smoke for the buck. If he hadn't owed all his money out, Reader would've been back in Ash-1 himself, eating Oreos and not worrying if he was going to bust a tooth with these beans.

The man across from Reader and Dewey said, "Hey, look at that." Then he kicked Reader under the table.

Reader looked where the guy was looking and saw one of the inmate cooks walking fast from the steam tables and he had a meat cleaver in his hand, held down, blade up. He was walking like a man with a mission, in a straight line. He walked with even, precise steps, each stride the same length as the previous and at the same speed. Not slow, not fast, just the same. He walked in a line that could have been marked off with a carpenter's plumb line chalked on the concrete, up to the head table. His last three steps were like this: On one, the hand with the cleaver went back, like a pendulum; it swung forward in an underhand arc on two; sank into this inmate's white cotton belly on three. It was as smooth a thing as Reader had ever seen. The man whose belly had received the cleaver cooperated, as if they'd practiced their little dance together for hours. He stiffened in awareness on the first of those last three steps, began to rise on the second and was fully risen on the third, in perfect position.

Somebody slow-walking a debt just went to trial, Reader figured.

From a sudden, complete silence, there erupted a general hubbub of noise and the noise made Reader forget the spoonful of beans he'd just put in his mouth and he bit down hard on a rock. He was almost done with the meal and he did that.

"Damn," breathed Dewey. "Did you see that?"

"I broke my fucking tooth," Reader said, sticking his finger in his mouth to touch the gum around it and withdrawing it to see if there was any blood on it. "Henry Jefferson," he said, wiping his finger on his trousers.

"Huh?" Dewey had a bewildered look on his face. He looked back and forth between Reader's face and the man who'd just been gutted, as if trying to figure out the connection of what Reader was saying and the event that had just transpired. There was a crowd of guards and inmates gathered around the fallen man, a couple of the guards beginning to push back inmates. They already had the cook down and cuffed, one of the bigger hacks sitting on him.

"Henry Jefferson," Reader repeated. "He's the inmate electrician. Bulb snatcher's what everybody calls him. He probably knows more than you do about electronics. I need you for the explosives part."

That night, back in the dorm, Dewey was still going on about the disembowelment at the chow hall earlier.

"My God!" he said, coming over to sit on the bunk next to Reader's. "Can you believe that shit that went down at supper?"

Reader grimaced and closed the tablet he was writing in and stuck it under his pillow. "Kid," he said, "Welcome to the joint. What'd you think it was like in here? Like that?" He waved his arm in the direction of the table up front where four men were playing poker and seven-eight more were standing around watching and kibitzing. Cards were being slammed down, jokes were being cracked, seemingly harmless wolf tickets were being sold. One guy had his arm around another as they leaned over to see what one of the players was holding. It could have been a card game anywhere. A regular weekly get-together at a friend's house out in Kenner between guys who all worked second shift at the local fertilizer plant. The only thing missing was the beer and chips—and a mad wife slamming drawers back in the bedroom—but there were two or three bags of cookies, which is what they were playing for, and, as they watched, one of the players suddenly reached into the pot and snatched a cookie and popped it in his mouth. That caused a good-natured hubbub, another player slapping the miscreant's hand and others yelling at him to replace the "chip".

"Looks harmless, doesn't it?" Reader said.

Dewey shook his head, a puzzled look on his face.

"Yeah, well, see that guy over along the wall?"

A beefy inmate stood a few feet away, leaning back, arms crossed, a cigarette hanging from his lips. He seemed intent on the game, even though he wasn't in any position to see anyone's cards. In particular, he seemed to be watching one man, a young guy seated with his back to Reader and Dewey. The guy who had snatched the cookie from the ante.

"See the guy he's mugging on?"

"Yeah? So? He's just interested in the game."

"Ha!" Reader couldn't believe this clown. "You got a lot to learn, pal. "That's Donny Schiffler, the guy standing over there. The dude he's watching is a new guy, came in a week before you did. I forget his name. Later on tonight, along about one in the morning, just when you're getting your first wet dream, Schiffler is going to be fucking that kid he's watching. Schiffler and two of the guys in the game with the kid. They set it up earlier this afternoon. That's a brother-in-law game."

"What's a 'brother-in-law' game?"

Reader snorted. "This really is your first stretch, isn't it? You never hustled on the street, either, did you? Just went out and pulled jobs, got your ideas from TV." He sneered. "What happens is a couple of players get somebody like this kid in a game and they just keep raising each other on every hand, until everybody drops out and one of them wins. Oh, the mark catches a monster hand now and then and stays in and they lose a few on account of that, but they're not worried. It's two to one that one of them will have the better hand anyway. In the long run, they wipe the poor sucker out. The fourth guy in there's in on it, too. He's gonna lose his shirt, but not really. He'll get paid back for whatever he loses. He won't be fucking the kid later on, since that's not his thing, but he owes Schiffler money and this is how he's repaying him. Did you see the kid grab that cookie and eat it?"

Dewey's face was pale. "Yeah."

"You think if this wasn't a setup, if this was a game on the up-and-up, he'd get away with that?"

"He wouldn't?" Dewey looked downright uncomfortable. He was learning more than he wanted to.

"Fuck no! Guy reaches in like this clown did, he'd draw back a stub. Cookies are money, fool!" Reader shook his head in disgust. "Pay attention, learn something. This poor idiot thinks these are all his buds, that he's just made some nice new friends in the joint. Probably already writing the letter to his mom and dad in his head about all the swell guys he's just met at camp, that just like him so darned much. What he doesn't know is that there's a payback at the end of this game. What he doesn't know is that he's going to owe a bunch of cookies when this winds up and he's going to be real surprised when they ask him for his losses and he shines them his huckleberry smile and they turn surly on his ass. What he doesn't know now, but he's gonna learn real quick, is how he's going to pay them back. With his sweet little bootie."

"My God," Dewey whispered. He looked ill, like he might have to throw up. "That's . . . that's barbaric!"

"No," Reader chuckled. "That's the joint. Look, kid, this isn't a TV show or some fucking silly-ass movie with Tony Curtis and Sydney Poitier. This is the *joint*. The only thing you can count on in here is violence. I've done three stretches, my friend—that's a lot of days in here—and you know what? I can't think of a single day during any one of those stretches when somebody didn't get shanked, fucked, or had his teeth knocked out for drill. You think that shit at the chowhall was unique? Fuck! That's just another day here at the O.K. Corral. You walk in here and see some guys playing cards and you think you're at Boy Scout camp or something. Looks peaceful, doesn't it? Shit! It's never peaceful in here. It just looks that way, sometimes. There's always shit going on in here. We're *criminals*, Jack, and that's what we do. We think up shit like this all the time. You can bet somebody in this dorm is already checking you out, figuring if he can get your brown eye or take your shit from you. It's what most of us do on the outside. You think it ends when we get in here? You think that, you seen too many movies. Nobody in here's your friend. And that includes me. You think I'd even be talking to you or do you the favor of getting you into this dorm and the library if I didn't want something? You give me what I want and we're okay. You don't, and I'll burn you worse than those assholes are going to burn that punk-ass mama's boy sitting over there shuckin' and jivin' with his 'friends'."

Reader reached back under his pillow, took out his notebook. He opened the page he'd been writing on and took out the pen he'd placed there to mark his spot.

"Take a hike, kid," he said, suddenly weary of snotnose punks like this who thought they were some kind of criminal. "I got things to do."

Later, when the lights went out, he looked over at Dewey, lying on his back, six bunks away, and he could see the whites of his eyes as he stared at the ceiling. *Not gonna get much sleep tonight, are you, kid?* He chuckled softly, closed his eyes. *Better you learn a little reality now,* he thought, just before he drifted off. *Might save your ass down the line.*

In the morning, when they rolled out for chow, Reader noticed one of the inmates wasn't leaving the dorm. In a bunk down at the end of his row, a man lay hunkered down, knees drawn up to his belly, blanket over him, even though it was already a scorcher. When they came back from chow, the bunk was empty, and a hack was escorting another inmate to it. The inmate threw down the bundle of bedding he was carrying and flipped the mattress over and began to remake the bed with the sheets he'd brought in.

On the way out to their job assignments, Reader came up behind Dewey, whose hair was uncharacteristically uncombed. Reader smiled into his assistant's eyes, which he noticed were bloodshot. "He's in the hospital, kid. Lost some teeth is what I heard at breakfast, but he's not in that bad of shape. He'll live."

He brushed by him. Looking back, seeing him just standing there while other inmates walked around him, he called out, "Hey! Don't be late now. We got a lot of work to do."

And not a lot of time to do it in.

6

HE WAS SO mean that wherever he was standing became the bad part of town.

That's the way Reader Kincaid heard himself being described at a Mardi Gras party one time, years ago. The woman providing the description was someone to whom he had made a rather vulgar sexual proposition to five minutes earlier. She hadn't replied, only moved quickly away to a group of masked men standing by the wetbar. She was drunk, so she probably didn't realize her voice carried. Even over the noise in the room and the parade passing by down amongst the drunken revelers below on Bourbon Street. You could just see the tops of the floats from the second-floor room, the Endimion Krew's float rolling by at that moment, tossing their throw-things to the massed crowd and blowing on kazoos and other noise-makers.

"See that asshole?" she said, holding her hand in front of her mouth. She was twenty feet away, standing in the center of a knot of masked partiers. She delivered her description and they all laughed. Reader left the party shortly thereafter and made pretty much the same proposition to a whore he bumped into on Conti an hour later and she took it with a much more charitable spirit. For a fee.

Since then, he'd often thought of what the woman had said. He decided he kind of liked what she'd said.

Even though from where he stood at the moment, he could see at least ten guys about whom she might have made the same comment had she been present. Where he was standing being the main exercise yard outside

Ash-1 Dorm. Near the basketball court, where he was chatting with the bulb snatcher.

"Nuttin' to it," Henry was saying. "If you kin work a TV remote control, you kin run one of those. They simple. Cost a lot, though. Two-three grand, if you get a Futaba. Top of th' line, Futaba's. Go a mile, easy. Yassir. What you want's a Futaba. Best thing is just steal you one."

"Yeah, and get caught doing some punk B&E. You got good advice, Henry. Ever wonder why you're in here? I got another idea, thank you."

Reader fished around in his mouth with his tongue, touching the tooth that had been bothering him since last night. It'd go on bothering him, too. No way he was going to let that Third World quack over at the infirmary get hold of it.

"Whatcha got in mind 'zactly, Reader-man?"

Reader just shook his head. No way he was going to do what most of these clowns would do—tell everybody and their brother your plan just to show what a smart fuck you were. Besides, he already had an audience for this one, his best one so far if things worked out. Frank Cabrini. The godfather. They were in the same dorm and Reader talked to him almost every day. Cabrini was helping him with another part of his plan.

An inmate mowing grass with an old-fashioned push mower came clacking their way and they stepped back to let him pass. They watched him work his way up to the concrete square where the weight-lifters were straining against the iron in their hands. The mower was one of the old handkerchief-heads who were mostly ignored. He kept a steady pace with the mower, head down, concentrating on the grass beneath his feet, seeing who-knows-what busted dreams in the shorn blades.

"Look, Henry, when they get that mess cleared up at the library, you're going to have to come in and rewire it. Make the job last a week. I got this new assistant I want you to meet and I want enough time to go over everything with the two of you." Henry already had possession of four cartons of Pall Malls, delivered that morning by one of the hacks who Reader'd told to keep a carton for himself for the errand, but had kept two of the original six.

"'Kay," Henry said. "Y'all don't wanna tell me, fu'get I ast, Reader. One thing ya might keep in mind. Watch where y'all get it." He grinned. "Feds track shit lak dat."

They moved back again as the lawn mower approached. Reader loved to be in the yard when it was being mowed. The smell always reminded him of watermelon. Cut right through the constant odor of male sweat that hung in the air. The stink of fear that seemed to cling to every man jack in here. He nodded to the mower but the man passed, too busy concentrating on the grass just in front of him to notice.

"I already thought of that," Reader said. "Say, you ever been to the dentist here?"

Henry laughed and as he did he revealed his open mouth, perhaps even wider than usual to show Reader that his own dental inventory consisted only of back teeth, nothing in the front but pink.

Reader nodded and scratched his back where it itched. He was glad laundry day was tomorrow. Three days in this stinking shirt. "Yeah. Guess you have, haven't you."

"Fucka don't use no Nov'caine."

"He doesn't?"

"Naw, man. He got him a connection—one of the Bartholomew brothers from Bozier City over at Camp Aitch—sells the shit to them."

"He doesn't use *any*?"

Henry showed his gums again. "Not much. Mebbe half what he's s'posed'ta. Muhfucka's a user hisself. Got to sell the Nov'caine in here so's he can afford the good stuff on the outside. You know that big guy air'body call Big Rufus? Thass his assistant. Holds you down when de doctah gets in your mout'. Muhfucka *mean*, Reader."

"Yeah." Reader'd heard that about him. The main reason he hadn't yet gone to the trouble of getting a pass to go see Dr. Fahib.

"Fucka look like a brutha, but he ain't no brutha. Got funky-lookin' skin. An' honky-ass features. Straight-ass hair an' it ain't been conked. What kinda setup's that? Foreign-ass nigger! Shee!" He spat in front, accurately nailing a nightcrawler that had just wriggled up in the new-cut grass.

"He's Indian, Henry."

"Yo, Reader. *Ah'm* Indian; part anyways. Dude don't look like no muhfuckin' Indian *I* ever seen."

"Different kind, Henry. He's an Indian Indian. From India. And you don't look like any Indian to me. You look pure-d slave-times descendant. Bet you highsteppin' on Juneteenth."

"That so? Well, he don't look like no Indian's all ah can say 'bout that bitch."

As Henry limped away on arthritic knees, Reader heard him growl, "Cherry-*kee*. Ah'm part Cherry-kee."

He couldn't keep his tongue off his tooth the rest of the day. He could feel where it had cracked, and all day long he thought about going to that dentist, but in the end decided against it. He only had ten more days until his release date. He could hold out that long, go see the real dentist he used to go to over in Metry.

It was all he could do to concentrate on the information he was gathering from Dewey and the bulb snatcher. They'd already had quite a session between the three of them, Reader asking questions and the other two providing answers. By eleven that morning the library had been washed down of the soot and mess of the fire and the firefighter's efforts and Henry Jefferson had been dispatched to fix the wiring, install a new fuse box. Which, it turned out, had to be special ordered. Henry saw to that, telling Reader the vendor the prison used for such things was notoriously slow. That bit of information got a smile from Reader.

For the next nine days, Reader went to school. For hour upon hour, he asked question after question of both Dewey and Henry, accumulating his master's degree in electronics and materials that explode. From time-to-time, they were interrupted by inmates coming in to check out books and scan the shelves for something to read, and Henry had to actually do a bit of work to justify his presence, but Reader was relentless in his search for information from him and Fortney.

He also felt an obligation to pass on his own wisdom to the new man.

"Dewey, you have a wife or girlfriend?" he said one morning, taking a break from "school."

His assistant gave him a funny look before answering that he did, indeed. You could see he was proud of his little bride. "She's coming to visit in two weeks. I can't wait to see her. This has been hard on both of us." He made the classic gesture of pulling out his wallet to show Reader a picture of the missus, when he made the equally classic double-take that signaled that he just realized he didn't have a wallet anymore.

"When you see her," Reader said, "tell her to forget you."

"Excuse me?"

"Get rid of her. The last thing you need in here is a wife. How long you in for, Dewey?"

"Twenty-five flat."

"You got some kind of idea she's going to wait for you?" Reader gave a rough laugh. Henry, working a few feet from them, and seemingly engrossed in a length of wire he was running through a section of conduit, chuckled himself.

Dewey's face reddened. "Well . . . I don't know. I . . . we—"

Reader's voice softened. "Yeah. Exactly. You haven't really thought about it, have you? You keep putting it off in your mind, don't you?"

Without waiting for the other man's response, he said, "On the outside, you can play these little mind games, Fortney. Not in here. In here, your mind's the only thing you got. You start fucking around inventing Magic Kingdoms, you're fucked. They'll have you down in Mandeville, walking around in a straitjacket like the other zombies, eating your own shit and thinking it's a Hershey bar you got for a reward for not cutting your own pecker off."

"Maybe I'll get a pardon," Dewey said, glaring down at his shoes, his voice angry and low. "There's guys get pardons."

"Sure, Dewey. The governor shits out about twenty pardons a week. It's a big secret, but I can see you got inside information the rest of us poor chumps don't. C'mon, Dewey. Get right, man. You got to get your head on straight. You look up your asshole, that's where you're gonna find it. Look." Reader got up, walked over to a shelf where a book was sticking out a bit more than the other, perfectly-aligned tomes, and pushed it back to where it was even with the rest. He came back, put his foot up on his chair and stared down at the man. "She's gonna leave you, sucker. Done deal. Sooner or later. I *promise* you she will. It's going to be a long, slow, *painful-ass* process. Cut her loose now and in a month you won't even remember what she looks like. Am I right, Henry?"

Henry stared intently at the length of wire he was holding, slid his thumb to a spot and cut it in half. "Y'all betta listen to dis man, boy. He's tellin' Gospel. This ain't no place to be holdin' onto no woman. She gohn break your heart. Betta t'cut her loose now, get dat sad shit outta th' way. Longer you wait, harder it's gonna be, bro. Gone be like you drunk bat'ry acid, shit goin' on inside."

"Dewey, how long you been locked up now? With your trial and all. Six months? Hell. She's already screwing somebody. Don't you know that?"

Fortney stood up, fists clenched, his jaw muscles twitching. He looked like he wanted to fight the both of them.

"Bring it on if you want," Reader said to the man, reading his anger. "Sorry I hurt your little punk-ass feelings. But you think about it, you're going to know I'm giving you good advice. You want to drag this out another six months, a year, go ahead. I could give a fuck."

"But . . . I . . . we love each other." Reader saw the abject look on the man's face and it made him sick. He looked away from the pitiful sight of a man realizing for the first time he was really in prison. He couldn't even remember his own moment of truth, it was so long ago, but he knew he'd had one. He also knew he'd handled it better. Fucker wasn't cut out for this. He shrugged his shoulders. Asshole shoulda thought of the consequences before he started pulling his genius little crimes, he thought to himself, wondering why he was wasting his time with a punk like this. Part of him wanted to feel sorry for the man, but his main response was derision.

"Look, Fortney. Do whatever the fuck you want. You want to put yourself through that kind of misery, go ahead. Be my guest. You cut her loose, though, you're gonna thank me in the end."

Reader looked at the man and thought he saw moisture in his eyes. Tears! If he didn't need what Fortney had, he'd have his ass sent over to J right this minute. Fucking pussy.

"How do I . . . cut her loose?" The words came haltingly.

"Piece'a cake," Reader said. He was already tired of the subject. Try and do a guy a favor . . . "You imagine her dead. Put her in a casket and throw flowers on top. Kick some dirt in. Hell, pick her favorite flowers. Carnations, whatever. Give her a good send-off and then every time she tries to come up in your mind, remember she's dead. It's easy. You got an imagination, don't you? You imagine that pussy picture you keep in your pocket is in bed with you, don't you? You supposed to be some kind of criminal whiz kid, you oughta be able to do that. Don't be a punk, man. This is the joint. Ain't no place to be holding onto something you ain't never gonna have any more. Hell, the state doesn't have to punish you. You doing a good job your own simple self. Do the time; don't let the time do you."

"Easy . . . " Fortney slumped in the chair, hands dangling in front of him like he'd just been sentenced to the same casket Reader was suggesting for his beautiful wife. He turned away from the two men and walked in the direction of the head.

Reader looked at Henry and they both shook their heads.

"I gi'm a month," Henry said.

"Fuck, Henry!" Reader giggled, picturing something in his mind. "You're a mighty generous cocksucker! I say a week and the fucker's trading cigarettes for a rope to hang himself. He starts thinking about the AIDS somebody's probably going to end up giving him, it'll be sooner. I was you, I'd keep a close watch and get his shit before somebody else cops it."

He'd seen the type before. A few thousand were resting out at Point Lookout and Point Lookout II. The look on Forney's face when he'd realized fully he was in prison told Reader he needed to hurry up, get the information he needed from the man. Before he decided to cheat the state out of their time.

7

FOR A LONG time, Reader Kincaid had been putting together a plan. For the caper of all capers. The big enchilada. The one he could retire on. Actually, he'd had the main frame of it figured out a long time ago, but didn't have a clue when or where he was going to use it. Until a week ago, that is. The week before Dewey Fortney arrived. And why Dewey's arrival turned out to be the luckiest day of his life. It was like Dewey had been sent to him by God or the gods or whoever was in charge of shit like that, at the perfect time.

Over the years he'd taken a germ of an idea, and, like a master jeweler, had cut and carved and polished it until it was a perfect gem. By asking questions—both of himself and of others, then answering them. Angola University. You could learn a lot from your fellow "students."

Pushing his library cart down one of Angola's long corridor walks, the one between Ash-1 and the laundry on his way to the dorms, he'd stopped to say hi to a hack escorting a batch of new inmates. Wide-eyed men clutched their bags of prison issue clothing, the numbers newly stamped, the ink barely dry. The number that would be their identity for the rest of the time they'd be here. The guard was in no hurry and the five guys he was shepherding were obviously happy to not get to wherever they were going. The old-timers in the group knew they were just going to be sitting in a cell in Quarantine and the new ones caught a case of nerves whenever they were headed to any new place, expecting the worst from all the stories they'd heard. Being worried was smarter than they realized.

"How's it going, Jonesy?" he said. "New meat, eh?"

They chatted awhile, mostly about the yearly prison rodeo, and Reader turned to leave when he overheard one of the new guys say something to the guy he was shackled to, using a name that caught his attention immediately.

"Who'd you say?" he said, going up to the man, a tall, muscular Hispanic, with a Simon Legree mustache.

"Sorry, Kincaid," Officer Jones said, stepping between him and the prisoner. "You can talk to the Frito Bandito here after he's processed. Not now. Rules."

The name the man had spoken so aroused Reader's curiosity that he couldn't wait until the man was released into general population. He called in a favor and that night he was stepping into the man's cell in Quarantine during their recreation period.

The Cuban sat on his bunk, smoked one cigarette after another while another guy put the finishing touches on a tattoo. A teardrop on his left temple. The blood was really running and the man's mouth was running right along with it, cursing steadily in a monotone. In Spanish.

"You earn that?" Reader said, stepping into the cell, a package of Oreos in his hand.

"Fuck you want, puta?" This from the artist.

Reader didn't say anything to the guy, just took a casual step forward and with a flash of his hand, jabbed his finger into the man's eye. The guy didn't even have a chance to yell or moan or any of that. He just went out, from the pain, crumpled on the bunk. Thing like that caused a lot of hurt.

The man receiving the artwork, the man Reader'd come to see, backed up closer on the bunk to the wall, but kept his calm. "Fuck, yes, I earned it, you fuck. Maybe I get another one tomorrow, eh? In your memory. You wanna try *me*, chinga? You think you can get your finger in *my* eye?" He wiped the meat of his palm against his temple, looked at the blood smeared on it. Stood up casually, knees flexed, hands down and open. He was a big fuck, Reader saw. Filled up half the cell, it seemed. "Bring it on, amigo." The man's voice was low, confident. "I'm not a pussy like that one." He spat in the direction of the other man, who was now coming to and moaning.

Just then a guard walked by, looked in and sized up the situation.

"Friend of yours, Reader?" he said.

"Yeah," Reader said. "This one got something in his eye. You might want to take him over to the infirmary. A thing like that could be serious."

"C'mon," the guard said, went over and grabbed the wounded inmate by the back of his shirt and lifted him up. The man was coming to, moaning and rubbing his eye with the back of his hand.

The guard shoved him in front of him and as he was going out, he said, "Twenty minutes, Reader. That's what you get. Then I want you out of here. And don't be fucking up any more of my boys."

When the guard and the inmate disappeared, the Cuban sat down on his bunk, reached under his pillow and pulled out a deck of smokes. He tossed them down on the far end of his bunk toward Reader and said, "You're Reader? Reader Kincaid? I hearda you. I hearda you in New Orleans, man. Shit, man, you're a fucking legend! I didn't mean nothin' by that shit, man. Man, you're okay, in my book."

Turned out the guy was Cuban, one of the boat people who'd left Miami as soon as he was processed and released. He'd quickly made his way to New Orleans to work for another Cuban, a drug dealer.

"Yeah," Reader said. He sat down on the bunk and tapped out a cigarette from the pack lying there. "I'm so smart I'm in here with you. We're both a couple of brainy dudes, aren't we?" He tossed the man the Oreos. "I heard you use a name earlier today. By the laundry. I want you to tell me what you have to do with this guy. That okay with you?"

"Sure, Reader. Anything you want to know. He don't mean nothing to me, man. I just do a job for him is all. My boss, he do a job for him. I'm just one of the peons. Fuck do I care about this guy. He just some rich fucker. You gonna fuck him up?"

He felt his temple again, looked at his hand and seemed satisfied it had quit bleeding. He picked up his prison-issue steel mirror and peered at it. "What you think? This punk did good work?" He turned so Reader could get a good look at his new tattoo.

"Yeah," said Reader. "He's a regular Rembrandt. You might wait till you get out in population before you get your next one. You know, the one in my memory. Look up a guy named Billy Scrugs. He's the best in here. Doesn't make it bleed so much, either. You don't have to worry about AIDS with Billy, either. I was you, I'd keep a watch out for sores. Less you know for sure your friend sterilized that ballpoint."

"AIDS?" The man got a stricken look on his face and began rubbing the fingers he'd touched the tattoo with on his pants leg.

When he left the man's cell, Reader knew then where he was going to use the plan he'd been putting together for years.

The name he'd overheard the Cuban mention? *C.J. St. Ives*. Electricity passed through Reader's body and he'd literally stopped in his tracks at the sound of that name.

That's when it all started rolling.

The creme de la creme of scams.

Things were looking up. He had one more thing to do. Get financed. The last of his stash had gone for lawyers. It'd been worth it. The judge could easily have slapped the bitch on him. The "bitch" was what a judge was supposed to give a three-time loser. Life without parole. Ha-*bitch*-ual criminal is where the term came from. All he got was three Mickey Mouse years. Good lawyers. They'd cleaned him out, but it was worth it. But now he needed money. He had a pretty good idea where he could get it.

These last days, Reader chose to remain in his dorm evenings when most of the other inmates headed out to the main prison exercise yard. More weird shit went down there than any other single place in Angola. With a release date in a few days, the last thing he wanted was to be standing next to some asshole who decided to go apeshit. Try to avoid the guy who just sucked glue fumes up his nose. Try to avoid the psychopath who suddenly realizes you look just like the stepfather who took turns smacking him and his floozy mother around. Or listen to all the sports nuts talking about the Saints and their sorry-ass quarterback all the time. He couldn't care less about the Saints. All he cared about now was getting the hell out of the joint and gaining control of his life once more. Get someplace where people listened to something other than yippy-yi-yo music. He was sick to death of Tom Jones and his fucking "Green, Green Grass of Home" they played over and over on KLSP, the prison radio station. Or hear another jackleg prison preacher damning him to hell on the in-house "Incarceration Radio Station" as it proudly billed itself.

Yet here he was, standing outside in the sultry central Louisiana sun, watching the weightlifters grunting over their iron. He could smell their sweat from twenty feet away. Sweat was what you smelled the most in the joint and not just from the weightlifters.

The old man standing next to him was talking. "You got a parole, Reader, or are you walking free?"

Parole. Right.

"When I walk, I walk free, Mr. Cabrini. I coulda had a parole a year ago. Turned it down cold. Fucking parole's worse than being in here."

The old man nodded.

"Yeah. I been there. What they say these days, 'Been there, done that'?" He snorted. "I'm with you. Fuck a bunch of paroles. Sissies go out on paroles. Fucking parole officer fucking with my shit ain't the kind of freedom I want either. Freedom's in here. I go, do what I want."

And he did. Fucking guy owned the joint.

He was saying, "You go out in what? A week?"

"Yessir. Nine days. I need something. A favor. Money."

"Ah." The old man grunted, an understanding look on his wizened face. "I always wondered when you were going to ask. For Carla, right? Reader, that was a long time ago. You got some memory, friend."

Reader looked around the yard. Weightlifters here, black motherfuckers over there in a group, rednecks over there, smaller group. Guys sitting in little gangs on the grass, smoking, laughing, playing chess or checkers, doing deals. Deals going on all over the place. For dope, punks, applejack, whatever. More trading, dealing went on in here than on Wall Street. He could see a group of eight, ten guys, standing in a circle and a pair of prison issue shoes sticking out, heels up. Somebody's getting hummed, he thought. Bet it's Maggie, the Yard Bitch, making her rounds for tightrolls. On the basketball court, nine blacks and one white raced up and down the court, half a dozen more watched from the sidelines, kneeling or flopped down, catching their breath from their turn.

"I'm hoping you have, too."

"A long memory? You know the answer to that. Thing is, I gotta know what it's for." He didn't say anything about how much he wanted. Reader knew that didn't matter. He just wanted him to play the game. The right hand should always know what the left hand was doing. He told him his plan.

The old capo listened, never interrupted once. When Reader was done, he looked into Cabrini's eyes and saw something he liked. Respect. Cabrini dug in his shirt pocket, pulled out a pack of Camels and shook out a couple, handed one to Reader. They both lit up and stared out at the activity in the yard. Neither said anything right away, just enjoyed their smokes. Cabrini still hadn't spoken, but Reader knew his problem was taken care of. The money was his.

Cabrini finished his cigarette, threw it on the ground. He didn't bother to step on it. Then he spoke. "Reader, I been knowing you a long time. All this time, we been friends, I know about all the things you done. Those jobs! The rabies one, that was the best." He smiled. "But, one thing I don't know about you."

"What's that?" Reader couldn't figure out where this was going.

"I don't invest in jobs. I invest in people. And you know what I don't know about you? I don't know your philosophy of life." He took out a new cigarette, picked up the still burning one from the grass and put the ember to the new one. "I like you, Reader. I like your plan. For a lot of reasons. Both these guys, they cause me a lotta trouble for a long time. No skin off my ass, you burn them. Fact is, you do this thing, it's good for me, too. Opens up a lotta things. I like that. But this could backfire. It ever comes out I helped you . . . " He let the sentence trail off, the implication clear to Reader what he was saying. "What I gotta know is what your vision of life is. I gotta be happy with that or I don't do this for you. That's gonna be my price. You don't even have to pay me back. I'm just returning a favor. We're even, you and I. If I grant it."

"This a character check?"

Cabrini's eyes were deadly serious. "The only kind worth a damn, my friend," he said softly. "Something like this, you don't back the plan. You back the man. You want to see what he's made of."

Reader looked out over the yard, saw the hack Jonesy making his way across the compound, stop and say something to the basketball players who all stopped and then laughed at whatever he said. One of them handed him the ball and he stepped up and fired it at the hole. When it swished, they all applauded.

"You see these guys?" he said to the old man. He was looking back at the weightlifters. He had to be careful here. He'd read between the lines. What the old man was saying—*wasn't saying*—was that if his answer didn't satisfy him, not only wouldn't he get the money, Cabrini would feel he had to take him out. What he'd told him was serious shit. Something that could backfire, get the old man himself killed, should Reader fuck up. These were powerful men he was going up against. As powerful as Cabrini himself. His answer had to be nothing but the truth. Even if it displeased the old man. No bullshit here. He had to lay it out on the line, hope the old man respected it. Make him see he was different from the others in here, that he had something besides criminal smarts. Something deeper.

"Yeah, I see 'em. Big motherfuckers. Big *stupid* motherfuckers."

"Yeah. You know why they do this shit? Work their ass off with those weights?"

The old man shook his head and waited.

"Control."

"Control?"

"Yeah. Just like you. They want control. Their way is to get muscles. They figure muscles are the ticket. Nobody's gonna fuck with someone big as a house, they figure."

The old man laughed. "Yeah, maybe. That's bullshit, though."

Reader looked at him.

"To you, that's bullshit. It's their way. You have another way, is all. You're the bossman, right?"

The old man's eyes narrowed. "What kinda crapola you givin' me,

Reader? I own this fucking place. Fuck!" His lips stretched into a broad smirk. "Half of these clowns work for me. The other half wishes they did."

"Then you ought to understand. It's always about control. That's why we're all here. It isn't because we got a fucked-up daddy who used to ram it up our butts when we were kids."

Nobody had it right. Nobody but Reader. Psychologists, sociologists, welfare workers, they were all wrong. Arguing all the time about what made a criminal, the environment or the heredity. It wasn't either. It was always about control. Sure, the environment played a part, but not like they thought. Reader had studied the subject carefully. He wanted to know why he was the person he was. All the times in the joint, he'd listened to the other inmates and their bullshit stories. They thought he was just interested in their tall tales—fuckers were all Jesse James, John Dillinger, according to their stories—but what he was really after was their motivation. To gain a clue into his own. He'd discovered something. At the root of every one of the choices they'd made was one common denominator. Each and every one of them felt a deep lack of control in their existence. It didn't matter if it was because a father or mother or foster parent or institution had dominated them in any of a dozen ways. It didn't matter if they felt powerless because of an inferior education or the lack of any number of social skills. Each man's story had eventually revealed the sense of not being in control at some point in his particular universe. Reader recognized a similar lack in his own makeup. It wasn't because your father beat you when you were six years old that made you go out and rob a 7-11. That was just the epiphany that made you realize in your soul that you were never going to be big enough or smart enough or lucky enough to be in charge of your own pathetic life. Which was why it didn't matter what social class you came from. Somewhere along the line, whether you grew up on St. Charles Avenue in a mansion or in a trailer park in Marerro, something occurred to drive home the fact that you were powerless. It just happened more in poorer circumstances because there was more evidence of your impotence, but it happened in virtually every environment because a lack of control over your destiny was just a basic fact of life. Once you realized you were at the mercy of another person, you experienced a profound feeling of powerlessness. The most frightening feeling in the world. The only way to overcome it was by seizing command in whatever way your imagination could come up with. Every situation in life was a situation of control. The winners seized it every time.

When you walked into a liquor store and held a sawed-off on the guy behind the counter, you were in control.

When you knocked a woman down and raped her, they were right—it wasn't about sex—it was about control.

Same with the perverts who abused children sexually, mentally, or emotionally.

Same with the guy who embezzled funds from his company.

Same with every single variety of crime committed. Usually you reacted with a variety of the same force that had been used on you.

For at least a moment, you were in charge of your destiny. Somewhere in the back of your mind, no matter how stupid you were, you knew the moment would pass. Knew you'd get caught and once again relinquish control of your corner of the universe. But hey, that was all right. You never had control anyway. The high one achieved, no matter how brief, when you held that gun or knife on another, or took something from another through stealth or cunning, was so incredible, it was worth it. It was the only shot a person had. Or thought they had.

The more Reader had explored his theory, the more he knew he was right. Almost everything a person did—criminal or not—was about power. Even the "God-squadders," the Jesus freaks, were after the same thing. Cloaking themselves in the "omnipotence" of God gave them that feeling of power. Which was why there was so much "backsliding" in the religious community, Reader figured. The veil would come down and the convert would realize Jesus was as much bullshit as anything else.

And control was nothing but a word that meant life. All of it, all that a man did, legal or illegal, was only a pathetic attempt to beat the ultimate master. Death. A guy holding up a bank seemed on the surface to be inviting someone to shoot him, but what he was doing was challenging the Reaper. He was daring the thing he feared worst—his own extinction—and if he succeeded in the challenge—got away with the loot—for a second, anyway, he'd beaten the inevitable and it gave him a sense of power. Made him feel invincible, even if it was a bullshit feeling and in his heart of hearts knew it was bullshit. It was all you had, all fate had given you. Name virtually any action a human being engaged in and it all came down to the same thing. A battle for control, which was really only a battle for immortality.

He was amazed nobody but himself had ever grasped this. It explained almost everything about human behavior.

That's what he laid out to Cabrini in so many words. For the first and only time in his life, he bared himself to another human being. The way he saw things. The truth of it all. He could only hope this man would see that.

"And that's what it's all about, Frank," he said. "Control. It's about being in charge. That's what was taken from me as a kid. What I have to regain."

There was a stretch of silence when he finished. Reader stood wondering what was going through Cabrini's mind, not realizing he was holding his breath.

"You got the money, Reader." The godfather turned to Reader, put his hand on his shoulder and gave it a gentle squeeze. "I knew you were smart and I knew you had balls. What I didn't know, I do now. The important thing."

"What's that, Mr. Cabrini?" A wave of relief washed over him, nearly nauseating it was so intense.

"You got wisdom. A man who has wisdom is a man to put your faith in. You see more than just the score. Not like most of these nitwits."

Nine days later, his gear all packed in a bundle on his bunk, Reader picked up a green carton of Salems and walked to the front of the dorm where the old man was sitting on a bunk, chatting with the guard just outside. Frank Cabrini looked up at Reader and then over at the guard. A raised eyebrow was enough to signal the guard to get up and take a hike, go play with his keys. Reader glanced at the movie poster of Sophia Loren taped up over the wall behind the old man's bed. He was going to miss ol' Sophia. It was the only poster up. Not allowed. Except for the godfather, of course. Most of the other guys had Playboy bunnies stashed under their pillows, a few Hustler centerfolds with the beavers exposed. There wasn't anything under Reader's pillow. He didn't much go in for that self-torture shit. But, the old man sure knew class when he saw it. Sophia was the only girl on the wall or under a mattress in the dorm who still had her clothes on and, in Reader's estimation, was the sexiest for that reason.

"So. You going now."

"I am. The hack'll be here in a few minutes. Here." Reader handed him the carton of cigarettes he had in one hand. "Going-away present. Last of my stash. Think of it as lagniappe."

The old man nodded his thanks, took the carton and tossed it behind him on the blanket.

"This job you been bustin' your hump figuring out—it isn't about money, is it?"

Reader smiled. "No, sir. It isn't about money. It never is. Not really."

He turned, looked out the window. The shutter was open and he could just see a patch of brown grass beyond it.

"It's about family."

"I understand. I been in a few vendettas. This is like the old days, watching you. That control thing, I been thinking about that. You're right, Reader. I learn something from you."

The old man got up, picked up the carton Reader had given him and took it over to an inmate who had just appeared at the dorm door bars. The inmate accepted it, nodded and disappeared beyond the concrete wall.

"You remember the name?" Cabrini said.

"Yessir," Reader said. "Eddie Delahousie." He held out his hand and the old man held out limp fingers and gave him the kind of squeeze you give a tomato, checking for freshness. "We're going to have a get-acquainted next week down at the Mockingbird Cafe. The old one down on Rampart, not the new one."

"I guess you gonna see Bobby Rodriguez too, aintcha? You got a good plan, Reader. I'm wishing you luck. Get that old bastard for me, okay? I figure he owes me plenty. Every time I dealt with him I got fucked." He snorted, grabbed up a handkerchief from his pocket when phlegm began dripping. "I already started praying for your success. Soon as you told me. Every night I light a candle."

"I appreciate that and yeah, I'm gonna see Bobby."

"Remember me to him. Good man. I remember that shit he did for you that time."

"Saved my ass. Lost some teeth over that shit, he did."

"Yeah." The old man let out a fart, so soft Reader almost didn't catch it. He turned his head slowly enough to not show disrespect.

"Good man." He farted again, louder this time. Reader looked away, trying not to smile. Even his farts smelled like garlic. "Watch this Eddie, Reader. He'll do what you want him to do, but he's the kind of guy thinks he's smarter than he is. You know?"

Reader nodded. "I know, Mr. Cabrini. He's exactly the kind I want."

He got up to go.

"And watch your back, Reader. You fucking with the big boys here. You're tough and you're smart, but these guys . . . these guys are in a different league than you used to playing in. Believe me, I know. It's *my* league. I don't know if I'd have the balls to do what you you're gonna do. Maybe I just need a good reason. Like the one you got." He looked at Reader, squinting his rheumy eyes. "Ha!" He began hacking and coughing. "Fucking lungs," he said, gaining control, attempting a watery smile and jabbing a finger at his chest. "All this shit in here is wearin' out."

Reader shook his head up and down slowly. "I will, sir. Don't worry. Thanks for everything. The advice. The loan. I couldn't do this without a stake."

"Yeah. It's already in a safety deposit in your name. You know which bank. Pick up the key from Leon. You need more, you give me a call." He squinted up at Reader. "I been knowin' you since you a kid, Reader. I hope it works out like you want. I'll be watching the papers." The old man reached under his butt with his hand, scratched, brought his fingers up and smelled them. This time, Reader had to turn to hide his grin, pretending to flick something off the back of his trousers.

There was a click of hard leather heels on the concrete walk outside the dorm and a guard appeared.

"Quarter to eight, Kincaid," he said, approaching the barred door with his set of keys. "Time to go. This is your big day, boy. Trailways coming to *take . . . you . . . home.*" He falsettoed the last part like it was a spiritual and laughed at his own witticism.

About time, Reader thought. That tooth was killing him. Soon's he got off the bus, he was heading out to Metry, look up that dentist. Even before he got a drink or withdrew the money the old man had loaned him.

Even before he began part one of his plan. That's how bad that tooth hurt.

8

NEW ORLEANS, TO Reader, was everything. It was good to be home.

He was thinking exactly that as he left the dentist's office in Metairie, the throbbing over, at least until the Novocain wore off, and forever, if Doctor Whitehall had done a good job repairing his tooth.

Riding in a cab over to Rampart Street, he sat back and let the city's smells and sights wash over him. It had been three years since he'd been locked up this last time, not a long time, but in most cities there would have been significant changes in that period. Not here. It seemed the buildings on Jefferson Highway were still painted the same pastel colors as when he'd left and he swore the same women were standing in front of their houses, yelling at kids who hadn't grown an inch.

New Orleans had everything, he thought, slumping back in the cab's seat, enjoying the streets they were rolling through. Juicy, hot, gorgeous, sexy weather. Lots of folks, even native New Orleanians, hated the weather, but not Reader. He loved it, basked in it, fondled it, let it pour over him, soak him, drench him. It was like returning to the womb. His insides just plain felt good in the New Orleans heat. No muscle aches, no bones that creaked in that weather. Walk outside at midnight in New Orleans, your balls don't shrivel up in anticipation of Jack Frost like they do in Chicago or New York. Your balls turn into raisins in Chicago at midnight, he remembered from his one trip there. Even in August. Not in New Orleans. In New Orleans, if you walked outside at midnight, your gonads expanded and grew like they were on cojones steroids. They became coconuts. Your balls in New Orleans grow twice as big as anywhere else on the planet as not only do they have a warm, moist climate to grow in, they get fed hot, spicy food all the time. They feel so good, Reader was thinking, that you just have to reach down and massage them every five minutes, in appreciation, let them know how fantastic the rest of your body feels in all that heat, all the parts and organs and limbs and juices, rejoicing, giving thanks and hosannas for their good fortune. That's some weather, brother!

He must have said that last aloud, as the cabbie turned, gave him a dirty look. He was already pissed as Reader had told him to turn the A/C off and roll down the windows instead. Reader ignored the look, felt too good at being back home and rid of the pain in his jaw to be bothered by a little piss-ant like that. They passed by The Oriental Triangle and Reader's mouth began to water and his cigarette hand tremble with hunger, recalling meals he'd had there. He'd planned to get something at the Mockingbird, but thinking about Triangle Tony's bulgogee, quick-fried strips of meat so thin you could read a newspaper through them, almost caused him to tell the driver to turn around. And Tony's red beans and rice.

The chow! Reader's stomach growled at the thought. That's what he'd missed the most. Louisiana's washday Monday's red beans and rice were so tangy and spicy you can't wait for Sunday to end. Is there any place on earth (Reader mused) that has a meal like red beans and rice? So blistering fiery you can only slew down two, three, maybe four bites before you have to reach for and gulp down a whole, ice-cold longneck in one, long, bone-aching draught to cool the back of your throat, and can you imagine anything half as good as gazing across your plate at a black-haired, green-eyed Cajun sorceress with her round, white, quivering breasts falling plumb out of her red, red teddy as she leans toward you and shines you her wicked, sparkling, white-toothed smile, and hands you the basket of for-real French bread; the evil beautiful goddess who brewed up this exquisite feast, laced with spices that you can feel speeding toward your sex—*can you imagine this, cabbie*—he hurled the thought at the back of the man's head—and can you go away from this place at the bottom of the country once you've seen this and live in Boston or Minneapolis or Chicago or Salt Lake City, ever again?

He thought not.

He couldn't.

New Orleans was a beautiful, enchanting, malignant, terrible mistress. It'll suck a man in, put a hex on him, make a slave of him.

It's wonderful.

And, as soon as he met the man the old capo in Angola had hooked him up with, he was going to have to leave for awhile, go up north to a town in Ohio.

The thought brought a frown to his face.

"You heard me say the Mockingbird Cafe, didn't you?" he asked the cabbie, sliding forward to catch his reflection in the mirror.

"Yeah. One on Rampart, yo?"

They drove in silence for another block, now heading up St. Charles Avenue toward downtown. Reader was watching the mansions, dozens of them, one flashing by right after the other, when he sensed the cabbie was staring at him. He was.

"You got a problem, buddy?" Reader asked.

The cabbie, a black man, pushed the toothpick he'd been gnawing on the whole trip around to the other side of his mouth. "How long y'all been out, brother?" he said, finally, after his toothpick business was finished.

"You were there?" Might as well talk to the guy. Talk didn't hurt anything.

"Been fo' years, September nine," was the reply, words around the toothpick. "Won the calf-roping, my second year. Got my picture in the Angolite." They were approaching Rampart from luscious Esplanade with its courtly mansions. The most recent French Quarter facelift had again avoided Rampart, looked like to Reader as they turned onto the street. Same crumbling stucco buildings, faded wooden storefronts. Same winos lying on the same spots on the sidewalk. Hustlers, pimps, whores strolled the pavement, studying each car that passed with a practiced eye to see if it contained the Man or a potential customer.

"You happen to know a guy named Eddie Delahousie?" He didn't know why he'd asked that, it just came out. "He was there about then, I hear. He used to be in the rodeo, I heard. One of the clowns." From what Reader'd heard about the man, that was appropriate.

"Little squirrely kinda mutt? Likes t'wear them high-shines them old-time Super Fly pimps usta wear? Yeah. I know'm. Y'all don't enjoy yore freedom, Mistah Angola?" He cackled and slapped the side of the steering wheel with the palm of his hand with great glee. "Shee-it!"

"Why do you say that?"

The cabbie sounded like a thoroughbred after a warm-up run, the way he snorted. "'Cause, man. That monkey's an accident waitin' t'happen! He's the unluckiest chump I ever seen!" He snorted again.

That's my man, Reader thought. Just the guy I want.

The cabby's tune changed. "Say, man, if the dude's a friend of yours, I—"

"No friend," Reader interrupted. "I'd say you're talking about the same guy. Don't worry, buddy. I'm not going back to the joint. Not in this lifetime."

He had the cabbie drop him off in the back, in the alley.

"Say, Angola," the cabbie said through the window as Reader started toward the building. "You ain't got hooked up a crib yet, I got an auntie over in Algiers has a place she rents out. Right price, man in your situation. You want, I can give you the address. You don't got to thank me, neither. I been where you are."

Reader hadn't even thought about that. In the back of his mind, he guessed, he'd just assumed he'd flop at some cheap hotel, but the thought of his own bed, a key to a door that only *he* owned, appealed to him more than he would have realized even a minute ago.

A bath. That was what he wanted more than anything. All the hot water he could stand, lay in it long as he wanted. No motherfuckers standing around, watching his ass. Heaven.

Reader stared at him. "I used to live in Algiers, last time I was out. Algiers is fine. You want to give me that address?"

A couple of minutes later, he was walking through the Mockingbird

Cafe's kitchen. Two ancient black men clad in soiled whites sat around a pail shucking mudbugs for the lunchtime bisque. One looked up at him and nodded. There was a radio going on the floor next to him. *Please . . . somebody . . . won't you take me to the city beneath the sea . . .* He recognized the singer. *. . . where the night outshines the day—you can hear the tap of soda caps and smell the etoufee . . .*

He walked past them, through the swinging Dutch doors and out into the bar. Behind him, the melodic stylings of Harry Connick, Jr. crooned on over the tinny speaker of the cheap radio, *Pork Chops dances all night long, but he won't dance for free. Please . . . somebody . . .*

He was back in New Orleans. For better or worse.

9

A WEEK AND a half later and a lot of shit had already gone down in Reader Kincaid's life. Got his tooth fixed, hooked up with this Eddie Delahousie character who'd turned out to be the punk he'd expected, drove up to Ohio, got the parts he needed. Killed a guy. In fact, Dayton was at this very minute disappearing in his rear-view mirror and good riddance as far as he was concerned. What should have been a simple thing had turned into a complicated mess.

Reader headed south and kept to county roads until he got on the Interstate about thirty miles from Dayton. Whacking out that electronics store owner wasn't part of his original plan but once it was done, he forgot it. People in the way, you eliminated them and got on with the job.

In Memphis he checked into a Motel Six, paying cash and signing a false name. The clerk barely glanced up from reading his *Motor Trend* to look at the name and the license plate number, which was a fiction as well. After finding a restaurant and polishing off most of a steak he found barely tolerable, Reader drove around until he found an outside pay phone at a Quik Mart. He used the change taken from the cash register at the electronics store.

The phone rang ten times before it was answered. Reader counted every ring and each trill without an answer got him more and more pissed.

"Yeah? Whozit?"

He was drunk, Reader thought. Figures. Guy was juiced the first time they'd met.

"In a couple of days," Reader spoke softly into the phone. "Sunday. We're going to take a ride in the country, show you something. I've got everything I need. I want you to get something. A dog. Try and get a large one. A German shepherd. I like German shepherds. And try and stay sober, Eddie. Get it together. I don't want a fuckup on my hands. How come you didn't answer right away? You stroking your trouser worm?"

It rained all the way back to New Orleans. Reader was deep in the state of Mississippi before he switched license plates on the Caprice, frisbeeing the stolen tag far out into a field of sorghum. He made a total of four brief stops, twice each for gas and twice more to relieve his bladder alongside the road.

All the way back he played the same CD. Miles Davis's *Sketches of Spain.* Whenever it reached the end, he hit the restart button. It was the same record he played after killing his daddy. He liked it more than any other of his jazz tapes and CD's. Miles had made it during his flamenco period, saying to the world he was done with bop and cool. Miles was the Man.

The tune Reader liked the most was Concierto de Aranjuez. It reminded him of the bullfights he enjoyed going to in Mexico. The bullfights and jazz, those were Reader's loves. He learned a lot, observing the way the matador thrust the sword into the bull's neck, knowing precisely when and where to apply the blade. He would rather be the matador who made the initial thrust than the torero with his short little dagger who came on for the final kill, the coup de grace, although he admired both for their skill.

He, too, was a matador. He was one of the blessed ones, the ones with the skill and the nerve. His opponent, though not possessing the brute strength of *el toro,* owned another strength more formidable—the strength of intelligence.

That is the way he saw himself and it filled him with pride. He reached over and turned up the volume. He made sure not to exceed the speed limit. Mississippi cops were a bitch, especially on these little lousy state highways out in the middle of nothing, with only miles of brown, sad-looking cotton fields and tarpaper shacks. Occasionally he saw a mansion sitting far back up a lane. Who the fuck wants to live in Mississippi, he thought, playing the CD over and over as he sped down the cracked ribbon of concrete, keeping his speed a safe five miles over the limit and an eye out for Smokey.

There was something. Reader rubbed his eyes. One loose end that kept nagging at him. The waitress. He'd briefly considered going back and acing her after he left Jack's, but figured there wasn't much chance she'd identify him even if the cops put two and two together and fingered him as the man having coffee across the street earlier. No, he decided. He was in disguise. She wasn't a loose end. She wasn't anything but a bimbo waitress in a lousy diner.

He got up and put his shorts back on and went into the kitchen, rummaging through cabinets until he found the bottle of Jack Daniels. He poured a good three fingers in a glass, walked back to the living room, sat down on the couch, from where he could see both his bed and the refrigerator in the kitchen. This house was similar to almost all the houses he had ever rented whenever he wasn't in the joint. A three-room shotgun. Open the back door and see all the way to the front, which was the whole idea. Catch what breeze might flow in the sultry New Orlean's climate. The poor man's bungalow. A house style no longer needed since the advent of air conditioning, they were slowly becoming extinct. And usually found in poorer neighborhoods, which suited Reader just fine. Even during those periods when he was flush, he preferred such a house. They made him feel more comfortable. In his youth, before all that happened with his parents, he'd lived with them in the *faux* antebellum mansion his father had built early in his marriage, just off Canal on Robert E. Lee Boulevard, a five-minute stroll from the lake. That house had many rooms. Large, airy sitting rooms and a cavernous dining area which doubled as a ballroom for parties. Also small, darkened rooms that were almost caves, found along narrow passageways. His father's contribution to the architecture. His bedroom was such a bedroom, situated on another floor from his parent's grander bedroom, to "let the kids make all the noise they want and not disturb us" as his father used to tell guests during tours of the place, winking with that grotesque grimace Reader remembered well. A bedroom a grownup could sneak into in the dead of night and do vile business with the young boy huddled there and no one the wiser. What his father hadn't mentioned on those tours.

Shotgun houses, without the nooks, corners and dark crannies of the house of his youth, suited Reader much more. There wasn't a single corner in which to hide, especially with the Spartan furnishings he always provided whenever he moved into a new place.

He sank down on the couch, on his spine, sipped his drink and began thinking about the job ahead. About the four million dollars that was going to be his in a few days. About the other part. The part that was better than the money.

It felt good to be back home in the Big Easy. Well, Algiers, across the river. Close enough. Motel rooms might be furnished nicer, but they also came equipped with a sensation of being closed in. He just assumed he had a mild case of claustrophobia.

Standing in front of the nurse's desk station reminded Grady Fogarty that he'd logged too much time in hospitals. The people who paint and furnish these places must all go to the same decorating school, he decided. He wondered if he walked into a paint store at random and asked for "Hospital White" or "Hospital Green" whether he'd see the clerk head for a particular shelf with no hesitation.

"Are you injured too?"

It was obviously a doctor who walked up to Grady in the waiting room. He was looking at Grady's stained shirt and at his eye patch as if trying to make a connection between the two. They'd made him leave the operating room despite his protests. The nurse who'd escorted him out was all business, the kind that didn't take shit from anyone.

Grady looked down at his shirt, surprised to see dark crimson. "What? Oh. No. That's not my blood. I'm the one who found Jack. This other thing . . . " He pointed in the direction of his patch, " . . . that happened a long time ago. How—"

"Is he? Well, I think he's going to make it. We should know in a few hours. By morning we'll know more. He's lost a lot of blood, but his pulse is stronger and we've operated to repair as much of the damage as we could. He's getting more plasma. His blood pressure's better. It's come up." He gazed intently at Grady. "There's something . . . " He paused.

Grady noticed his eyes were bloodshot.

The doctor massaged the back of his neck. "You're family, I assume?"

"Fogarty. Grady Fogarty. That's my brother Jack." He wondered if these people ever talked to each other. He'd given the desk nurse all that information earlier. Told her the main thing she wanted to know, which was Jack's insurance carrier.

The doctor nodded and extended his hand. "I'm Doctor Lyons, Mr. Fogarty. If your brother lives . . . and I'm optimistic that he will . . . there's . . . well, there's going to be a problem."

"Doc, there's something I have to know up front. Would Jack be in better shape if he'd gotten here earlier? Say, an hour earlier?"

The doctor studied his face as if trying to figure out the reason for the question.

"No," he said, finally. "Even if he'd been brought in two hours sooner, it wouldn't have made any difference. Most of the real damage was done at the time of the attack."

A nurse stuck her head around the corner and said, "Dr. Lyons? I need—"

"Give me a moment," he said, holding his hand up, irritation in his tone. "I'll be there as soon as I can." The nurse stood with an exasperated expression on her face, shrugged and walked away.

The doctor looked back at Grady, waited and when Grady didn't say anything, he went on. "The thing is, he's suffered serious spinal damage. He won't be the same man you knew. The weapon used, whatever it was—"

"A knife."

"Yes, well, the knife . . . whatever . . . severed part of the spinal cord. We also don't know how much feeling he'll retain."

"What's that mean? He's paralyzed? Are you sure? There's nothing you can do? An operation, a—"

"I'm sorry, Mr. Fogarty. I wish I could tell you more. It's too early.

Nurse!" The doctor turned and addressed a heavyset young man in green scrubs who stopped and raised his eyebrows. "Tell Donovan I need those reports on my desk. *Yesterday*."

He turned back to Grady. "Sorry. It gets . . . Listen, if you want to go in and look in on your brother for a little while, you can. He's at the end of the hall. Intensive care, room 42. He won't be awake for at least twenty-four hours, however. We've got to keep him sedated until he stabilizes. And no, at this point I can't tell you how his injury will manifest itself. I'd prepare for the worst, however. It doesn't look good. There's something else."

Two orderlies came along pushing a gurney with a woman on it and the two men stepped back against the wall. Another body. Most of Grady's life had been spent in places like this, it seemed, watching bodies being pushed or pulled from place to place. White- and green-coated people hauling away broken bodies. He had no doubt that one day it'd be his own smashed or disease-ridden body being transported somewhere. When that time came, if he was semiconscious he'd know where he was. By the smell. When he was a kid he remembered thinking hospital smells were the odor of healing. Probably because somebody had said that to him. At this age, it smelled like death mostly. Death also had a taste. The taste of a copper penny when you held one in your mouth like you did when you were a kid.

Grady waited for the doctor to go on.

"Also, this is all going to be rather expensive." Dr. Lyons hesitated, obviously loath to continue, but he did. "Normally, the business people take care of this, but I assume there's only yourself in Mr. Fogarty's family and . . . well . . . the thing is, the kinds of treatment your brother is going to need aren't usually covered by most health plans. It's not that we'd turn him out of course, but—"

Grady put up his hand. His eyes became dark slits. "It'll be taken care of, whatever it is."

Dr. Lyons looked at Grady Fogarty and anything else he was going to say, he decided to keep to himself. "Well, I thought you should . . . well—" His voice trailed off. He glanced at his watch and murmured something about "sorry" and reached over to put his hand on Grady's arm. Grady turned away and went over and sat down heavily on one of the chairs in the waiting area, directly off the main corridor. The imitation leather squeaked as he slumped forward, his head in his hands. The doctor stood looking at him for the briefest of moments, shrugged and walked briskly down the corridor.

Grady leaned his body back in the chair and closed his eye, settled back into the darkness.

He wished there were someone to call. Someone to share the bad news with. There wasn't a single person he could think of. No relatives. Maybe some distant cousins somewhere, but nobody close. He and Jack were alike in that both of them were pretty much loners. Friends? Grady might meet a girl or two sometimes at a watering hole, but there was no one he was close to. He was fairly certain his brother didn't have a romance going either or he would have known about it. No one in Jack's life since his wife Sharon died five years ago. No children. Jack's only living relative was one sorry younger brother. Him. Thinking about that made Grady sad and the sadness started turning into more of a feeling of anger.

This was bullshit. All their lives, he and Jack followed the rules, played by the book, even when it meant a disadvantage. It was something they learned from their father. Sharon used to accuse both Jack and Grady of seeing life in black and white terms. Sometimes it's gray, you know, she often scolded, but neither of them ever felt comfortable with that concept.

A rage began to grow. Behind his eyes—good one *and* bad one—where he could feel it palpably. Grady gripped the sides of the chair and his face contorted, eyes closed. A woman clicked by on high heels and started to go into the waiting area. She saw the man sitting in the chair and the expression on his face. She turned and walked back the way she'd come.

Grady's mind was a turmoil of memories and emotions. About his brother. About how Jack struggled all his life to make a living. He remembered the many years Jack put every spare dime he could come up with to help keep their mother in a decent nursing home. Grady contributed too, but the difference was he only had himself to worry about and Jack had a wife to support. The real sacrifice was Jack's, the way Grady figured it. Their mom died after a sudden and brief bout with cancer and after the medical expenses stopped there was a period when the Plan looked possible again. A laugh erupted under his breath that wasn't a laugh at all.

For awhile their dream seemed possible again. The deal was to save their money, the two brothers, and in ten years—ten years was what they estimated it would take, figuring and brainstorming for hours on end—in ten years they would do it. Jack would sell the store and Grady would take a lump sum payout of his pension and the two of them would sell their houses and other possessions. Convert everything they had to cash. Pool their money and go to Vermont. The Plan was nothing grandiose. A fishing camp on Lake Champlain on Shelburne Bay outside of Burlington. Nothing fancy. Some cabins, some fishing boats. A main lodge where Sharon would run a dining room for the fishermen. In the winter when the lake froze they'd rent setups for ice fishing and sell bait. Maybe get a couple of those ice sailboats to rent out. Offer classes on fly-tying to help make it through the slow season. If they watched their money, they figured that while they probably wouldn't get rich, they'd do all right. The main thing was they'd be independent and would be doing what they loved the most. Fishing. The family sport.

Then Sharon got sick. One day she was smiling and excited about a new recipe book she'd bought and the next morning she was in the hospital with renal failure. There'd been no warning. It was one of those things, the doctors said. A year of dialysis, medicine, tests. None of that made a difference. Modern science wasn't yet up to Sharon's disease, not without a transplant, which never became available. Neither Jack nor Grady's kidneys were compatible and she died in her sleep one morning, still hoping for a donor.

Jack buried his wife and the bills started to come at him. The medical expenses amounted to over two hundred thousand dollars after the insurance company sent its last check. We're sorry your wife's dead, the hospital told Jack in so many words, but we need our money. They got it, too. Grady sold his house and added what he cleared to Jack's fund. Jack protested furiously, but in the end, red-faced and muttering, he accepted his brother's gift. Jack and Sharon's home was sold a few weeks before. That left Jack short thirty thousand, but he took care of that by getting a loan on the store. Which meant the bank owned that as well. So far he'd knocked off five years' worth of payments on a twenty-year note. Be paid off in fifteen more years when he was sixty-three.

Fuck. Here we go again, Grady thought. Same-o, same-o.

You boys promise me you'll help each other out, their father said, almost the last thing before he died. Family is the most important thing in life. Besides your integrity. It was the family credo. Family, honor.

Yeah. Same old shit, Pops, he thought, bile treacling in his throat.

Wonder if he'd want us to keep our honor now, Grady thought. Well, Dad; Jack and I both have our integrity, but it looks like our bodies have been compromised. Doesn't seem like the proper reward for living the righteous life, does it?

It ended up that Jack rented a one-bedroom apartment while Grady was a bit luckier. He found a small house he could afford to buy on a land contract. Miss a payment and it was gone. Everything changed after Sharon died. Five years of treading water with no land in sight. Life was for all purposes reduced to worrying about how he was going to come up with enough money to fix a leaking roof.

The Plan was never brought up between them after that. And now this.

He thought of something that had happened a long time ago. When he was a kid. Fifteen years old. Jack was in the first year of his Navy hitch and came home on leave. Took his kid brother out, bought him his first drink and got his cherry busted. Took him to a cathouse, sat out in the living room telling jokes to another whore while Grady lay on top of a black girl who said her name was Wanda. The whole act took all of two minutes, but it was ten minutes before he could stop shaking afterwards. The whole time he could hear Jack telling the other girl jokes and he remembered thinking it odd that Jack was the only one laughing.

Afterwards, Jack bought a bottle of flavored vodka—cherry-flavored, Grady seemed to recall—and drove them out into the country where Jack told him Navy war stories. Grady got roaring drunk. Jack must have been lit up himself. On the way back into town, Jack suddenly pulled off on the country road they were on and dared Grady to run at the stop sign twenty yards down the road and hit it with his fist. As hard as he could.

The instant Grady hit it, he sobered up. It was the first time he had ever felt the kind of pain three broken fingers could give you. Jack sobered up almost as quickly, soon as he realized his little brother's hand wasn't right.

After their dad had taken him to the hospital and they put what looked like popsicle sticks on each broken finger and gave him something for the pain, on the ride home in the car his dad yelled at him until he told him what happened. There was a terrible, shouting argument between Jack and their father that began the instant they walked in the house.

Jack went back to his base in Maryland that night, leaving with ten days left on his two-week leave. He not only didn't say goodbye to Grady, he didn't talk to him for over a year. For snitching. It wasn't until close to Grady's seventeenth birthday, when Jack was home for a few days leave—his first spent at home since the broken fingers incident—that Jack came up to him in the back yard and silently stuck out his hand. It was all Grady could do to hold back from bawling as he put his smaller hand into his brother's huge paw.

"Guess I can't blame you after all," Jack said gruffly. He was standing there in his dress whites and looking away from Grady, over at the corner of the house. "I thought about it and I guess if I was in your place I mighta said something to Dad myself. Hell, you were just a kid then."

Since that moment, they'd been inseparable. Something had changed in Grady. In Jack, too.

After a few minutes, Grady got up and walked slowly down the corridor to Room 42 and tried to prepare himself for what he might find there.

10

IT WAS SUNDAY morning and Reader had picked up his partner Eddie. He handed the toll taker his buck through the window and headed across the bridge on Lake Pontchartrain. He gripped the steering wheel and stared ahead through the windshield at the ribbon of causeway that stretched before him and tried to ignore whatever Eddie was saying. The German shepherd in the back seat lifted his head from time to time, but stayed down and didn't bark or whine. Reader felt kind of bad about the dog and what he was going to have to do to him. He liked the dog better than he did the man sitting across from him, but then he usually did like most animals better than people. Animals were honest about their actions. There weren't many humans who could fit that description, certainly not the punk sitting next to him, yakking away about all kinds of stupid bullshit.

This was the best part of the day, Reader thought; hardly anybody was out driving on the Pontchartrain causeway this early on a Sunday morning. He stuck his head out the window and let the wind blow his long black hair, the ends whipping him in his eyes. It felt good, clean. Ninety-two degrees and climbing, but he preferred the windows down, the faintly salt air blowing in, humidity and all, to the air-conditioning. He pushed his hair back with his fingers and settled back behind the wheel.

The only boat out was a small homemade shrimping trawler over to the east on the Gulf side a mile or so away, crawling at a leisurely pace toward the open sea. Some welder who worked in one of the shipyards in East New Orleans, he bet. Out to get a few shrimp for the family to boil later on, plus a few to sell to Deannie's Seafood for money to buy some beer.

That's the life, he thought. Maybe that's what he'd do after this job. Rig him up a little boat with some nets, get a big-ass cooler and fill it up with Pearl beer and go after brown Mexican shrimp. Have him a dog to come along, keep him company, some mutt like the one in the back seat. Better company than a broad. He laughed and Eddie looked sideways at him, his eyes round and wide. Reader could smell the man's fear like it was aftershave. Eau de sweat.

Yeah, that would be the life. Shrimping. Get a big pot boiling, throw in the crab boil and toss the buggers in till they turned red. Heap 'em up on newspapers on a table in the garage so high you couldn't see over it, sit down and pig out on shrimp and Pearl beer till you went cross-eyed. Get the dog drunk and watch him fall down. Run into things. A drunken dog was a sight.

Yeah, that's what he'd do, but first there was the little matter of this job.

Reality said once all this was over he wouldn't be anywhere near New Orleans or the Gulf. He wondered what kind of shrimp were in the Caymans. Warm as it was, warmer than the Gulf, they were probably as big as lobsters what with that long of a growing season. Shit, one shrimp was a whole meal probably.

Reader swung off the causeway into Covington and it wasn't long before they were turning off the main highway and through the town, out in the country, traveling past horse farms and cane fields.

Rolling down a dirt road past one farm they could see a small oval track that came close to the road and a chestnut thoroughbred getting a workout. Astride the horse was a small black boy, shirtless in coveralls and baseball cap turned backward. The horse was coming on, flat-out flying, his tail out straight behind him. The glistening of the animal's sweat was visible from the car. Reader slowed down to watch.

"Jesus!" Eddie exclaimed.

"Yeah. Remember that one. I'll lay odds you'll see him next week at the Fairgrounds. Put serious green on that one."

"We'll have us some green too, won't we, Reader! Shit!"

Reader pressed down on the accelerator. "You know why they raise so many good horses in Louisiana?" He didn't wait for Eddie to reply. "It's the iron in the soil. And the sulfur. Calcium, too, I think. Best-kept secret in the world. Everybody thinks the best horses come out of Kentucky, Virginia. Bullshit. The best horses come from Loozana. It's the dirt. Chock-full of vitamins, minerals, makes the strongest bones in the world. You never see a horse from Loozana have to be put down 'cause of a broken leg. Kentucky horses, yeah, those babies go down like flies. The soil's all worn out in Kentucky. They going on past reputation. The future's here."

Eddie started to say something, but Reader went on, talking more to himself. "The salt air's got something to do with it, too. Toughens 'em up, helps their wind. Yeah, Kentucky's got a lot more horses, but per capita, Loozana rules, horse-wise. More betting money made on horses from here than anywhere else. Loozana horse hates to lose, especially to a Kentucky horse. And don't talk about those sissy horses from Virginia! Those nags are better off in fox hunts, la-de-da crap like that. Racing, they suck swamp water. Your Loozana horse, that's the ticket if you want a runner."

"You know a lot about horses, don't you?"

"Yeah. We had horses when I was a kid. Had one I used to ride all the time. Ended up I got it taken away and they gave it to my sister."

He'd like to have him another horse. One they couldn't take back. Maybe a whole stable full of horses, all running out at the Fairgrounds, maybe over to Arkansas. Good tracks in Arkansas, too. Fuck a bunch of California racetracks and fuck New York and especially fuck Churchill Downs. That was all political, rigged. The real horse races were in the real South. Real men and real horses.

"How far, Reader?"

"'Bout a mile. Relax and enjoy the view. Have another beer. See if the dog wants one. He knew what was coming, he'd get drunk for sure." He laughed until he started choking and Eddie looked at him like he thought he had a screw loose.

The beer was a test. Eddie had all of the signs of a boozer and boozers worried Reader. Juicers got high to get it up for a job, hold a gun on someone's chest. Liquid guts. He'd brought the cooler to see what Eddie'd do. One or two beers this early in the morning wouldn't mean too much. If the man drank much more than that, he'd consider looking for a new partner.

Eddie reminded him of his father without the size. He looked like him. Drank like him, too. He bet Eddie got mean when he drank, beat up on people. People littler than him, weaker. Like his father. An image of his father rose up on the screen of his mind and rolled, like a movie. He saw his polished wingtips and he could feel again the pain of those shoes as they sank into his ribs.

Little kids, he thought. I bet you like to beat up on little kids, don't you, Eddie. Probably makes your dick hard, too. I know you like a book.

"Nah. I'm done." Eddie was saying. "I drink another one I'm gonna be pissin' every five minutes."

Good, Reader thought. You passed the test, bitch.

Up ahead he spotted the turnoff. An old logging road that went back through a swamp and into acres and acres of mostly oak trees they cut down and hauled out so Yankees could have cute little coffee tables. Once in awhile an opening would appear and a flooded rice field would materialize, a deer standing on the edge of it close to the trees. They weren't going that far. Only to a small sugarcane field on the edge of the swamp where the woods began, an isolated spot some coonass probably planted on land he didn't own. He'd searched for several days for the right place and this was it.

Only straight johns called him anything but Reader. *The Reader* was the name they'd pinned on him over in Angola the first time he got sent up, on account of all the time he spent in the prison library. It was his second name change. The first came when he was a kid and decided he didn't like his last name. After awhile, it got to be just *Reader*. That was twenty years plus and two more stretches past, which was pretty good considering. In that space of time most guys he knew spent more time in the joint than out, so his own track record was not bad, not bad at all. It was funny; the only reason he went into that library in the first place was to avoid Camp J and one of the lines, working in the fields. He'd heard it was the best lick in the joint other than working in Identification, I.D. The librarian, an old semi-literate lifer who only read comic books, laughed at him. Said he couldn't afford it. Said the gig cost fifty green 'less he wanted to be his bitch, give him nice blow jobs, access to his young, sweet ass, things like that.

Reader had dwelt on what the librarian said for awhile, sitting in his cell and that week he killed the librarian with a straightened-out laundry pin. He did it during the Saturday morning movie, an Audie Murphy flick, coming up behind him in the darkened theater and reaching around and sticking him in the throat, feeling him choke on his own blood. The next day he put in a chit for the vacancy. The prison guard with the library assignment remembered him coming in all the time and recommended him, so he got the job. They never suspected he was the one who did in the former librarian. He wasn't one of the ones they called in and smacked around trying to find out. The guy they thought did it, a guy sitting next to the librarian when he bought it, was doing flat time and the prison released him the next month when his time was up. Since they couldn't prove anything they couldn't hold him any longer. He was a stand-up guy by the name of Bobby Rodriguez and he kept his mouth shut. Bobby lost three teeth and a lot of blood when they questioned him, but wouldn't give up Reader or snitch on him. His nose got broken, too. It was two brothers, twins, who worked him over. They were on permanent midnight shift on the hole at their request. That way they could have their fun with the inmates since nobody ever went down there voluntarily. To get put in the hole you were obviously a fuckup, so who cared? Sadistic mothers. Their favorite trick was to lay an inmate down, one holding him, while the other one picked up the end of one of the heavy wooden benches and dropped it on the poor slob's head.

The Duren brothers, lifer hacks. There was a joke that Angola got its hacks from the trains that went by in the night, that they were bums who got off in the wrong place. A month after Reader was released, he caught one of the Duren twins coming out of a bar in the nearby town of St. Francisville. It was Anthony Duren, the one who considered himself a ladies' man. Reader "convinced" him to take a ride with him out in the country. Remember Bobby?, Reader said, grinning, enjoying the way Duren's eyes widened.

Two days later, Bobby received a package in the mail. In the package was a newspaper clipping. A story on an Angola prison guard who had been murdered. There were three teeth rattling around in the bottom of the package. The note wasn't signed, but Reader knew Bobby would know where it came from.

Working in the prison library, Reader learned a lot about electronics, among other things. That's when he first got the idea for the perfect crime. He just didn't know where he was going to use it until this last stretch, and then only by accident. If he hadn't stopped to speak to that guard that day and overheard a new prisoner talking to another, he'd still be looking for the spot to use his idea. After that, everything accelerated.

First thing he did when he made parole that other time was pull an armed robbery on a supermarket. Took himself seven grand from the Schweigmann's out in Kenner on Double-Coupon Day and went and looked up Bobby. He handed him half the take in a paper bag and left without saying a word. From then on when Reader did a job, he'd send Bobby a little something. Bobby was a mechanic and fixed up cars for him when he needed one for a job. Bobby knew electronics too. He'd showed Reader a couple of things, mostly about boats and how to make them go where you wanted without your being on board. Matter of fact, he was working on a special boat for Reader at this very minute.

When this job was over, Reader planned to surprise Bobby with another chunk of cash. Show his appreciation for his part in the job. A bonus. He'd paid him in advance for the boat he was working on, but this would be extra. Bobby was probably the nearest thing he'd had to a close friend in his whole life. He was certainly the only person he'd ever trusted to any degree after what he'd done for him in Angola.

Around eight-thirty a.m. on Sunday was when Reader'd picked to have his little demonstration for Eddie. He figured it would be a time when most of the local civilians would be in church and the area would be deserted. They'd been on the back road fifteen minutes and hadn't seen a single car. Hadn't passed a house. They'd seen nothing but swamps and possums crossing the road. Pine woods, too. Lots of pine woods. Once an armadillo.

"Those're good barbecued," Eddie said, pointing at the animal when they went by.

"Yeah, you hillbillies eat anything if it's barbecued."

Eddie hooted. "Hey Reader, you were in Angola, right? I guarantee you ate your share of armadillo and probably loved it—you didn't think that was black Angus in the Friday night stew, did you? Too greasy."

"Down there," Reader said, pointing a finger straight ahead through the windshield. They were pulled off the road onto a little clearing. In front and to the left was the cane field and behind it the edge of the woods, thick-trunked oaks and a few cypress trees remaining from when the swamp reached that far.

Eddie snuffled back phlegm and complained. "Down *there*? That's pure mud, Reader. These are Bruno Magli's, pal. You don't get these fuckers at Payless Shoes. These shoes don't like mud, Reader. All they know is concrete, sidewalks, cool marble hallways. *I* don't like no mud, neither. There's snakes out there, too. Bad-ass snakes. Water moccasins, rattlesnakes. Fucking *coral* snakes. Pretty little cocksuckers. Kill your ass for drill. I ain't ruining these." He thrust his foot up on the driveshaft so Reader could see for himself.

Reader laughed. "Those're leather, Eddie. Leather comes from cows and cows love the mud. Mud to a cow is like a bubble bath to a blonde. This'll be a treat for 'em, make 'em think they're back home down on the farm where the living was easy. Where they lived the dolce vita before they got whacked out and ended up on your smelly feet. C'mon, let's go." He opened the door. "You carry it." Reader jabbed a thumb at the paper bag on the seat.

"Me? Hell, no, I ain't carrying it. It's *your* shit—*you* carry it. Jeezum! I don't even like sitting next to it. I don't know why you couldn'ta left it in the trunk."

Reader sighed and picked up the large grocery sack lying on the seat between them. He'd allow a little insubordination, but the little punk'd pay for it later. When he first decided what he was going to do, he figured to use a gun, make it quick when the time came, but the bastard'd made him mad, acting like a cunt all the time, whining. Wonder what he'd say if he knew his method of execution had changed to a knife? Stuck in the stomach, at the right place, a man is paralyzed and dies slowly. You twist it just so, every so often, keep it up as long as you want and he can't move. There's something to that way of shanking a person that makes them think that if they can only keep completely still they won't die, so they sit stock-still and take it. Somebody knows what they're doing can make it last a long time. Someone like himself.

"C'mon, chickenshit. Let's go."

He wondered if maybe he'd made a mistake bringing Eddie in on this job with him. Little shit, looked like a jockey 'cept for his little pot belly. Only he'd never make the weight a jockey needed less he quit drinking beer. He was your basic punk. Robbed liquor stores, gas stations, chump jobs like that. This would be the man's first real score. His last, too, if things went according to Hoyle. Reader didn't kid himself this would be his own last job. He was too old a pro. Scamming was in his blood. It wasn't the money so much. It was hardly the money at all on this one. This one was personal. Not that the money was totally immaterial. What'd they say, the business guys, the straights? Money was a means of keeping score? The game's the thing? The Donald Trumps, the Bill Gates', they were right. The score would be high, this one. The World Series, the Super Bowl of scores. The Masters. That's the one. This would be the Masters of heists. He caught a picture of himself in a green jacket and golf cap sitting on a pile of money and smiled.

"Get the dog, Eddie. Put the leash on him and be sure you don't let him get loose."

Eddie glared at him, but didn't say anything this time, only opened the door and snapped the leash on the German shepherd. He yanked him out of the car and the dog yelped as his legs splayed and he hit the ground on his chest, then struggled to get up.

"Hurt that dog again and I'll hook this shit up on you instead, Eddie." Reader spoke in a low conversational tone, but cut glass was along the edges of the words. "That's a dumb animal, never did anything to you." Eddie started to say something, but thought better of it and did as Reader ordered, only tugging a little harder than necessary on the leash as he followed Reader down into the muddy cane field.

Reader remembered the little black-and-tan hound puppy he'd brought home the time he was seven years old. Stole him from a yard six blocks over. Took him away from a kid a full head taller than he was. Big, soft-looking kid, but not big enough to cross the kid with the Barlow knife who wanted his pooch.

In his mind, he saw his daddy coming home that night, falling-down drunk and slipping on the wet pile of dog shit in the yard, soiling his Armani suit. He remembered his daddy kicking the dog, lifting it clear in the air to land against the far wall and then fall to the floor. Reader could see his puppy was dead from where he was, and then he was busy trying to protect his own ribs and stomach and head, all the places where his daddy's Italian shoes were trying to connect.

His mom came in and tried to stop the attack. His father turned on her, hitting her in the stomach with his closed fist. He left them both on the floor and stormed out, heading for an uptown club to pick a fight with someone else.

One thing Reader'd learned from his daddy. How to fight. His father gave him quite a few lessons on the right places to punch to inflict the most pain on the human body.

What'd he learn from his mom? Not much, unless it was valuable to know you shouldn't put your faith in a God who never showed up when you needed Him.

"Goddammit!"

Reader looked back and laughed. Eddie was keeping behind him through the rows of cut sugar cane stalks, trying to step in Reader's footsteps to keep the mud off his shoes. He slipped and fell on his side once; slick brown slime covering not only his shoes, but one side of his Perry Ellis trousers as well. To his credit he still held onto the leash. The dog stood patiently to the side.

"Why th' hell we got to do this? I'll take your word it works. Fucking Magli's are ruint. Lookit my pants." He got up, cursing.

"Because. We have to film this. And I want you to see what happens, how this works. I want you to understand this. You can buy a dozen pairs of shoes this time next week. Hundred, two hundred pairs, that's what you want. Get 'em all different colors. 'Sides, I want to see if it works myself. This is the first one I made."

Eddie was a punk, but if he rode him hard enough he'd do. Once the job was over he was history. A zero like Eddie would roll over the first time a cop slapped him hard or squeezed his nuts. In a way it was a good thing Eddie *was* a jive-ass punk. Anybody more hip would have known Reader wasn't going to leave any loose cannons lying around. Eddie was too stupid to think of anything but the broads he was going to be able to buy and the top drawer booze he was going to drown himself in. And maybe the shoes he was going to stock up on. He was whacked over shoes. Reader guessed it was because he'd never had any when he was a kid.

They reached the spot Reader had in mind at the far end of the field. He'd spotted it a month ago, driving around out in the country. An ancient oak stump that went at least twelve feet around, three feet high, its roots sticking out of the ground. Perfect for what he wanted. Anyone who heard the noise while driving by on the main access road would think—no big deal—some farmer getting rid of stumps. Farmers were always blowing up junk in fields. He took the leash from Eddie and tied it around one of the exposed roots.

He knelt down, reached inside the grocery bag and took out the contents.

"What the hell's that, Reader? Looks like something you make in art class in second grade!"

It *did* look weird. A rectangular blob of material with a length of ribbon cable coming out of one side, a connector at its end and the end of another connector peeping out of the other side of the blob.

"It's a plaster of Paris mold, Eddie. All the goodies are in there, the bomb and the circuit. A remote control receiver. It's filled with Bondo to seal it. That way, if things were to go hinky—which they won't—there isn't a bomb squad in the country that would deal with it. They can't see how it's wired. That's the day they'll be calling in sick, got the blue flu. There's all kinds of shit in there, IDC connectors, the pipe and the goodies, radio control switches, batteries, other stuff. All we need to do is hook it around the guy, tight, so he can't get it off without breaking the connection and we're in business. Like this."

He reached over and patted the German shepherd on the head and bent down and let the dog lick his face. He picked up the contraption and strapped it on the dog's back, snaking the cable under his belly and snapping the connectors together on the other side. The dog reached around with his head and tried to bite at the lump that was on his back. He sat down on his haunches and began to scratch at the cable with his hind foot. He couldn't quite reach it.

"There. It's all set. Slick, huh?"

"Jesus, Reader. What if the mutt breaks that thing loose?"

"He goes boom. Us too, if we happen to be too close. Like within twenty yards or so. The wires come loose, get cut or broken, it sets it off, same as if you put the juice to it."

Eddie backed away, his eyes wide. Reader saw red lines in the whites of his partner's eyes and felt nothing but contempt.

"Let's get the fuck up to the car, man! Look at him. He's gonna break that thing. You're crazy, Reader!"

Reader smelled the animal fear coming from him. Good. Eddie needed to get a little respect for this.

"You know, you're right, Eddie. Let's go back. We'll set it off up at the car."

"What's in that mold, that gizmo thing? Dynamite?" Eddie asked, stepping over the drainage ditch alongside the road and walking over to the car.

"You never took high school chemistry, did you, Eddie?"

Eddie fixed his eyes on the dog still digging with his hind foot at the contraption strapped to his back.

"Fuck no. I was a wood shop man. Fuck a bunch of chemistry."

"I would have guessed that, Eddie. I would have picked you to be a wood shop man. Yessir, definitely a wood shop man. No, it's not dynamite. It's saltpeter and some other stuff."

"Saltpeter! Isn't that what they put in the beans in the joint, take away your sex drive?"

Reader laughed. "Cooks always claimed it was in the mashed potatoes. I guess in a way it might take away your sex drive. At least, when it goes off and you happen to be in the neighborhood. Some other things, too. Sulfur, crushed charcoal. You water it down, mix it up, bake it in an oven at two-fifty. You got to be careful. It's packed in a six and a half-inch galvanized pipe, half-inch diameter. Picture something twice the size of your willie, Eddie—"

"Fuck you, Reader."

"—bit more powerful, though. It's got a flashbulb in one end, wires running out a hole in one of the caps, hooked to the circuit. You saw the connectors. Dynamite's not a good idea. Too easy to be traced. They put little pellets in dynamite. Color-coded. They can tell where it came from in six seconds."

Eddie nodded like he understood, but it was plain he wasn't listening. His whole attention was riveted on the dog who was scratching at the cable with his other hind foot.

"Know anything about electronics, Eddie?"

Reader walked around to the back of the car, popped open the trunk, extracted another grocery sack and came back to the front of the car where Eddie stood staring at the dog.

Eddie said, "Yeah. You ever unhook the VCR to take it in to the shop you want to mark the wires so you get it back right. I never remember how to do that. It's easier to go out and steal another one already hooked up to the TV. Get two for one that way, too. I remember one time—"

"Electronics are the future, Eddie. Computers, robotics. You can do anything with electronics. Like this."

"If you say so."

"How would *you* do this job? How would you take out three, four, maybe five, six million from somebody who doesn't want to cooperate? Stick 'em up with a twelve gauge?"

"Works for me. Folks don't argue with a sawed-off." He sucked back phlegm and swallowed. "Look! That mutt's goin' nuts!"

"I guess they don't, Eddie. Only what if they have a twelve gauge too? Tell me this—how many times you been in the joint, Eddie?"

"A few. Who hasn't?"

"That's right. Who hasn't. How many times you using a gun when you got busted?"

"Well, shit . . . *every* time, I guess. So what?"

"Ever do a bank job?"

"Naw. Thought about it though."

"Know what happens on a bank job?"

"Sure. You go in quick, get out quick. Listen to that dog whine, Reader."

"Get caught quick, too. How many people get caught doing bank jobs, do you suppose?"

"I dunno. Some."

Reader reached in the bag and took out the Futaba and extended the antenna to its full length of a foot and a half. Next, he took out a video camera. He folded the bag and threw it through the open window onto the front seat.

"Not some, Eddie. Most of 'em. Most bank robbers get caught. I'd say about all of them. What happens is a couple of guys go in with shotguns, pistolas under their coats. They hand the teller a note or just announce it, hold down on the guard, all the customers. That's when their troubles begin. Electronic shit starts to go down. Shit, electronic shit's *been* going down before they walked in. Cameras, trip alarms set up in cash drawers, you name it. Today's average bank is a fucking electronic wonderland. Before they got the green in their mitts, helicopters are whizzing around outside and every cop in town is standing outside behind squad cars with a donut in one hand, thirty-eight in the other, pissed off cause they were compelled to leave their coffee and it's getting cold and they were halfway to first with Trixie, the waitress. And if you get out quick enough before all that happens they've got a movie of you. Electronics, Eddie. The bank robbers are beat before they start. By technology. See what I mean?"

"I guess, Reader. We gonna do this or what? It's gettin' hot."

Reader handed the Futaba to Eddie, who took it gingerly. He held it by his fingertips like he thought it might explode. The sun was bright, melting away the morning mist, but Reader didn't think it was the heat that made little drops of perspiration pop out on his partner's forehead. Guy truly was a punk.

Reader aimed the video camera at his partner, then found the Futaba in the viewfinder and zeroed in on it. In a smooth, steady shot, he swung the camera around and found the dog at the end of the field and turned the zoom control until the dog looked like it was ten feet away. He switched the camera off and turned and faced Eddie.

"So, bank robbers are Indians, Eddie. You're an Indian. And you don't have to be so careful with that. That's the transmitter. The dog's got the shit that blows up. The dog's the one that ought to be nervous, but then the dog's got balls."

"What the fuck're you talking about Indians t'me, Reader? I'm no Indian. I'm Acadian. Me, I'm Eddie Delahousie. Delahousie, that's French, not Indian. And that dog's got fleas, not guts."

"Just some history, Eddie. History. Indian history. Besides, you're not French-Canadian. You're a coonass. A coonass with an Indian point of view. Indians were in this country thousands of years before the white man came and getting along fine. That all got ruined. Indians tried to fight the white man with bows and arrows. The white man shot muskets."

"Yeah?"

It started to sprinkle lightly. The sun was out, but it was raining. Reader liked that when it happened. It put him in a happy mood.

"The Indians got muskets themselves, took them off the few white men they were able to kill with their fucking Stone Age bow and arrows. They started to hold their own again for awhile. But the white man came up with repeating rifles. The Indians were right back in the soup again. It kept happening, over and over. Once the Indians got their own selves some rifles, the white man said okay, we got to have something else. And they did. They invented Gatling guns. That was the end of the Indians. You see, Eddie, it's technology. Today the technology is electronics. They got it—we don't. That's why we get caught. By we, I mean those of us on the other side of the law. That's why you're an Indian. You and everybody who looks like your sorry ass. You're trying to fight somebody with a bow and arrow and they got a Gatling gun."

"You know what, Reader?" Eddie set the transmitter down on the car hood and reached through the window into the back seat and took out a beer from the cooler. He popped it and took a long pull, beer dribbling off the sides of his mouth. "You're a smart cookie I guess. Me? I'm a simple gangster, don't know that much. Know something else? I don't fucking *care* about all that shit you're talkin'. Tell me what to do and I'll do it. Only don't call me no fucking Indian. I'm French-Canadian, me, Eddie Delahousie. I don't know if you been puttin' me down or what, but don't do it no more."

Reader laughed. "Okay, Eddie, okay. Look, I wasn't putting you down my friend. Explaining some history, that's all. Tell you what. *You* do it." He handed the Futaba back to Eddie.

"Me? Whaddya do?"

"Push the power button. That one. And duck."

"Duck?"

They both looked to where the dog stood. They could see his tail wagging. He'd quit trying to rid himself of the lump on his back and was standing facing them. He barked.

"Yeah. I'm not sure how big a charge that is. Might be pieces of pipe flying around. Be a shame you got your head tore off before you got to buy all them nice new shoes. Wait'll I get the camera set."

Eddie looked at him like he was trying to figure out if he was kidding and shook his head. Quickly, Reader picked up the camera, turned it on and found Eddie with it. As before, he swung the camera around, seeking out the German shepherd. Once in his sight, he held the zoom button down until the dog looked like he was only ten feet away.

"Now," he said to Eddie.

Eddie held the Futaba out away from him at arm's length and closed his eyes and pressed the red button. For a split second nothing happened.

"Holy fuck!"

The dog evaporated. Half his back disappeared. Flat-out disappeared.

The odd thing was, he remained standing. For a second. His back was gone and half his head, the top half, but he remained standing. A frozen millisecond and then the dog collapsed and sank to the ground. Smoke and chips and chunks of metal flew in every direction, but none came as far as the car. They could see small flames sprouting up on the stump the dog had been tied to.

"Hot damn! Would you look at that, Reader! Man!"

"Yeah. Did a number, didn't it? Took out Rover, killed half his family." He turned off the camera, tossed it into the back seat.

"What's the camera for?"

"We're gonna have a private viewing in a few days. You, me, and Mr. Clifford Saint Ives, the Third."

Eddie's forehead wrinkled, making his eyebrows arch.

"That's the mark, huh? Who's—"

"President of Derbigny State Bank. He's going to see what one pipe will do. Being as he's gonna have three wired to his ass, I think we'll have his attention."

"*Three* pipes? Why three? That dog's vaporized. Half that damn stump's gone, too. Only take one to do the job."

"That's right, Eddie."

He opened the car door and got in. Eddie got in his side. Reader started the engine, turned around in the road and began driving slowly back the way they'd come.

"Mr. St. Ives will see what one pipe will do. When he knows he's got three hooked to him we'll have his complete attention. Taped to his back, close to his spine and his kidneys and six dozen major arteries. His suit will hide it. Coats usually hang away from the body there. C'mon, get in. We got things to do, some more stuff to pick up."

"Why we gotta go to all this trouble? You got me running here, there for all this crap when most of it we could pick up in one store."

Reader sighed. He'd told Eddie a few details, enough for most people to grasp the idea, but Eddie didn't seem to get it.

"I told you, Eddie. Every single thing connected to this job has to be gotten separately and in ways they won't remember who they sold it to.

Like our friend out there. You go to the pound and somebody remembers your face. You buy a mutt off some local yokel, nobody knows nothing. Why do you think I drove over a thousand miles to get this Futaba clear up in Ohio? I coulda picked it up in town."

"Well? Why didn't you?"

"Because, moron. Because some of the stuff I got doesn't get sold every day. This job goes down, the Feds, everybody, will be all over the place. They'll know every piece of equipment we used and if they trace it there's a chance they'll get a description. I walk into Radio Shack and buy a fine-ass remote controller like this Futaba and the FBI sends a sheet around to all the dealers in the country. About that time, some citizen out in Metry says, 'Oh, yeah. I sold one of those to a guy looks like this.' They bring one of them computer artists in and they get together and in two hours they have my face on *Unsolved Mysteries* in thirty-six countries. *That's* why, you idiot."

Reader tapped out a cigarette, got it going. "Eddie, I want you to do what I tell you from this point on. I've been planning every inch of this operation for a long time. I haven't left out a single detail. This is going to be the first job you won't have to worry about getting caught."

"I still don't see why we can't just go in with a couple of twelve gauges."

"Okay, Eddie." Reader sighed. He had explained very little of the details of the job to Eddie. He guessed he'd have to show him the whole picture. Eddie thought the way you did a job like this was to go in blasting. Whoever was still standing won. And it was important he understand what was different with this score. Else he'd be sure and find some way to fuck it up. He'd go over it again. Make sure the dummy understood half of what it was he was required to do. And why.

"The money we're taking is in a bank."

"Yeah? So?"

"A *bank*, Eddie. Electronics, remember?"

"Don't pull that Indian shit again, Reader. I got your 'Indian' hanging, mu'fuck."

Reader felt a barely controllable urge to hit the man. "Let's go through this one step at a time, Eddie. Little baby steps."

"You got no call to insult me."

Oh yes I do, thought Reader. You cry out for it. He forced down his anger though and looked over and smiled at the man. "First of all, what is the most critical part of a robbery?"

Eddie's tone was sullen. "Uh, duh. Gee, I don't know. When you're holding up the place, maybe? Get real."

Reader hit the steering wheel with his hand. "Yes! You're right! When you hold up the mark. You get an A, Eddie."

"Fuck you," Eddie said, but his voice brightened.

"You want to watch your mouth, Eddie. With this plan we're not holding the guy up. He holds up his own self."

"How's that? How do you get a guy to do something like that, wiseass?"

"By giving him an incentive."

"What's his incentive other than he gets blown up if he doesn't do what we tell him to do?"

Reader looked at him in amazement. "Why don't you think about what you said, Eddie?"

Eddie's brow furrowed for a couple of seconds before it relaxed. It was as if someone threw a switch inside his head. "Yeah! He doesn't rob his own self . . . we blow him up! He's got incentive up the ass strapped to his back!"

Reader slumped a little in his seat. "That's the plan, Eddie. I'm glad you understand. How long I been going over this stuff?"

"Yeah, but . . . " Reader could see the wheels turning in Eddie's head. He was looking for loopholes he figured Reader might have missed.

"Look all you want, Eddie. You can't find no holes in this plan."

"Why can't he take the thing off? Once he's inside we can't see what he's doing. Smart banker-dude like that, all he's got to do is shuck the gear and call the cops."

"He *can't* take it off, Eddie. All the wires are in a mountain climber's harness type of rig. It not only goes around his arms and his neck, it also goes up and through his crotch. There's no way to get a thing like that off without breaking a wire. He breaks a wire, he goes boom."

"Oh." Eddie lighted a cigarette and cranked the window down to let the smoke out. Reader waited for the next objection, sure it was forthcoming. He didn't have to wait long.

"Hey! What if he decides to light out? Maybe he goes to the cops. They got bomb squads can defuse a thing like that. Or maybe he goes into hiding. Waits until the battery wears out. What about that, Reader? Didja think about that?" He took a big drag on his cigarette and blew a smoke ring and held his cigarette up close to him and blew the end of it gently. "I think I found the flaw in your plan, Reader." In a barely audible voice, he added, turning his head to stare out the window. "Bet it's not the only one, either."

"You dumb fuck!" Reader exploded. He jammed the brakes so hard to the floor that Eddie pitched forward and hit his head on the dash, sending cigarette sparks flying everywhere.

"Motherfuck! Motherfuck!" Eddie started saying, over and over, rocking forward and back in the seat, his hands cupping around his nose.

Reader eased the car off the side of the road. They were alongside a huge field of sugar beets.

A thin stream of blood appeared between Eddie's fingers and his eyes were wide in a combination of fear and wrath. "You broke my nose! Lookit this, you fuck! You broke my fucking nose!"

Reader reached over and grabbed Eddie by the hair, twisting his head savagely around so that he was forced to look at him. Hate vied with fear in Eddie's eyes.

"I'll tear your stupid head off, you little cockroach," Reader said, his voice low and cold, a whisper. "Shut up and listen. And keep your goddamned blood off the seat."

He let go of Eddie's hair and twisted in his seat, scrunching down and pulling his knee up to rest on the console.

"Sit up and listen, Eddie. I'm going to run down the whole entire thing, *one more time*. That's it. Once more. You don't get it this time, I'm going to retire you as my partner."

He didn't wait for a response, but began talking, his voice a flat monotone.

"Most fucks who do a job like this go in with guns drawn, lots of firepower showing. Fucking major mistake. For one thing, we can't go in when the bank's open because of all the problems I went over. The electronic shit. Now. St. Ives gets the money on Friday evening when the bank's closed. Don't ask me how I know this, I just do. It's fucking drug money he launders for this outfit.

"The easiest way to do a job is to let the mark pull it off himself. We agreed that's true, right? How can one do that? Get a guy to rob himself? Well, there's several ways. One, you might kidnap his wife and hold her for ransom. The ransom being he brings you the money. But how many guys you know dig their old ladies enough to hand over four to ten million dollars? You take a chance doing it that way. The guy may hate his wife. So that's out. You following my line of thought, Eddie?"

Eddie nodded. He didn't say a word. He watched Reader, never taking his eyes from the other man's. He kept touching the side of his nose gingerly.

"Good. That's good, Eddie. So what we're going to do is wire Mr. St. Ives like we done the dog. We're going to go to his house before he goes to work and when he lets in two nicely-dressed executive types like we're going to look like to him, we pull out our pieces and take him on into his bedroom. We hold a gun on him and we make him strip. When he's in his skivvies I wire him up with the bomb. The way the bomb's wired to him, there's no way he can get it off. Not without breaking a connection. If he breaks a connection he goes up. Boom. The Fourth of July comes early. Next step, we get him dressed. Have him put on his best suit. We explain the whole layout to him. Make him understand that he's got a bomb in the small of his back, next to the kidneys and other vitals and that if he doesn't do what we ask him to, he's hamburger. We show him the remote control unit, explain to him how that works. We explain that he's got three pipefuls of black powder encased in Bondo and it's sitting next to a sensitive part of the body. That there's wires going into the pipes and that they're attached to a flashbulb, the kind in cameras. That if I push this button it detonates. That there are crystals in this setup that are set to a certain frequency. That there are thousands of frequencies and that there isn't anybody in the world can guess which one I'm on. That the only one can deactivate this thing is me. Not any bomb squad, not any electronics genius, not even God. Me. I'm the only one can save his ass. That he isn't going to know where we are, but that we'll know where he is and if anything looks hinky, why, we'll push the little red button."

"Ain't *no* way to take it off?"

Reader looked at Eddie and the word *moron* went through his mind. "You're not paying attention, are you Eddie? No," he sighed, frustrated at the denseness of the little man, "there is absolutely no way anyone can remove the bomb without setting it off. The best explosives expert in the country can't remove it the way it's set up." He went on, feeling as if he were talking to a third-grader.

"We've got him on a time schedule. He misses any part of the schedule he's red vapor. We explain to him that it's not his money. That he's got no reason to be a hero. Do what the fuck we say and he lives. We explain to him how this thing works. We show him the movie we just made. An object lesson you might say. We also explain to him that if he gets the bright idea of going to the cops, the boys in blue are going to run as far away from him as they can. This is a foolproof setup. There's not a bomb squad in the country would touch something like this. They won't be able to figure out which wires are the right ones to cut. No way in hell. Bomb guys, they take one look at the setup we got on him, they're gonna laugh and ask him what flowers does he want on his grave. While they're running out the back door. But he's not going to the cops. Because he's going to understand very clearly how this whole thing works. It's very simple. Easy to understand. I can see by your eyes that you're grasping this, aren't you, Eddie?"

"Hey!" Reader laughed abruptly. He reached over and took Eddie's package of cigarettes from where he kept them in his front pocket. He tapped one out and lighted it and handed it to Eddie who took it without a word and began smoking. He kept putting the back of his hand to his nose and looking at it for more blood, but it was past the dripping stage.

Reader continued. "You said what if the guy takes off and hides from us? Not a bad idea except for one thing. If he does that he's cooked. Even if he gets out of range before we can detonate the bomb. You see," he leaned in closer to Eddie across the seat, "if the battery fails, the circuit closes automatically and it goes off that way too." He leaned his head back and laughed a full, hard laugh. "He's fucked if he does and he's fucked if he doesn't. This will all be explained to him very carefully. One other part could get hairy and that's when he hands the money over to us. I got that part doped out too. When the time comes you'll see how that works. All I'll say is that we won't even be close to him when he gives us the money. No, the only hope this poor slob has got is that he does the job we want him to. That he gets the money to us and prays like hell that we keep our word and deactivate the bomb. That's the only chance he's got. And he's got to understand this very clearly. My job is to convince him that a single mistake on his part gets him blown to hell and back and I won't blink an eye doing it."

He straightened around in the seat and put the car back in gear. "You think I can convince him of that, Eddie?"

"I guess so," Eddie said, petulantly, his mind suddenly on something else. "I got to pass by my mama's house, Reader. She made sixty, today. We gonna get back pretty soon?"

***

On the drive back to town, Eddie was quiet for a good long time. It wasn't so good when he began talking again. "Where'd you say you got all this shit, Reader? Why can't it be traced?"

Reader reached into his pants pocket and felt around for a bill. They were approaching the toll booth for the Pontchartrain causeway. "Easy. I got the only traceable part from someone who won't talk."

"Bullshit. You can't trust anyone."

"I can trust this guy, I think."

"Oh yeah? How so?"

Reader stared at his partner and smiled.

11

THE MAN READER thought was dead wasn't however. Jack Fogarty lay in a hospital bed with needles in his arms and tubes inserted into every possible orifice, but he still possessed life.

His brother Grady was at his store, which was located in what Dayton residents called the Oregon Historic District. It should have been called the "Oregon Deteriorated District," Grady thought. It was a neighborhood where the local liquor store wouldn't be apt to advertise "Free wine samples," as he'd seen a store out in the suburbs do one time. Jack's store was on Fifth Street, off Patterson and not far from the Great Miami River. Grady was familiar with the Miami. He'd seen more than a few floaters fished from its depths. When he was a kid he swam in it, took home stringers of small-mouth bass from its waters. The Miami still had fish in it, but you didn't eat them, not unless your body was low on its lead or mercury quotient for the day.

It was a day and a half removed from his brother's attack and Jack had passed the crisis during the previous night. Chances were fifty-fifty he'd live, but the doctor still didn't know the extent of his spinal injury and how it would manifest itself. They were running test after test and the bill was mounting. Grady tried to keep his mind off that.

There was one positive about all this. After all the misfortune piled on him and his brother, once again there was a direction to his life. This sounded terrible when Grady considered it, but it was true. He had a mission once again. To find Jack's attacker. A negative positive, if such a thing even existed, but Grady couldn't deny the heightened state he had been in ever since he'd discovered his brother's bloody body. He realized how much he'd missed the surge of adrenaline that came when you were on a case. Especially this case. Doing something useful. That was it. He realized how purposeless he'd come to feel in the past few years since he'd been forced out to pasture. Oh sure, he helped Jack out a lot at the store and he hustled security jobs when they became available, but jobs weren't plentiful for a man with only one good eye, even if the vision in it was still 20-20. He'd had too many days when all he did was go fishing.

Or drinking. A lot of that lately. Booze and women. You hang around the one, you get the other. He'd go into a bar thinking he'd have one quick beer and it seemed like there'd always be an attractive and willing woman in the joint and two hours later he would know more about his new friend than he wanted to. There were times when Grady wasn't sure whether good looks were a blessing or a curse. It was a toss-up. In a bar, with a beautiful woman sitting next to him, it seemed like a good thing, but the next morning staring out a bleary eye at the disheveled form lying next to him and smelling the curdled stink of her breath made him think otherwise. He suspected many of the women that ended up in his bed felt the same and he couldn't much blame them. What he hated most was the morning cup of coffee they both felt obliged to share with the same sense of sober awkwardness. Rarely did he go out with any of them twice and only when he and a former bed partner found themselves next to each other on bar stools. It was a hell of a way to live, he'd thought more than once, but he didn't do much to change it.

Booze was a way to keep from thinking how much he missed police work. Funny—the drunker he got, the more it cropped up in his thoughts. He shook his head the way a dog would in ridding itself of water after a dunking, and forced his mind to go blank.

He'd let himself in Jack's store with his own key and was waiting for Marty to show up. It was the start of the detective's weekend, but he'd only balked a little at Grady's request.

"Well, I don't know, Grady," he'd said into the phone. "It's my day off." After a little silence, Marty said, "What the fuck. My wife is driving me nuts anyway. Give me an excuse to get out for awhile. She's got a bunch of women over for some kind of sex toys party and I can't hear the ballgame for their giggling. If I don't get out, they're going to be asking me to come model some of their shit. Give me half an hour. I gotta make a stop and pick up some butts."

Grady walked through the debris that was strewn everywhere. He consciously avoided looking at the spot where he'd found his brother, but it was hard to miss. The rest of the store looked as though the proverbial tornado had blasted through from door to door.

The more I look at this, Grady decided, the more it stinks. At first he'd figured it was kids maybe or your basic armed robbery gone hinky, but none of the evidence seemed to hold up for that being the case. Yeah, on the surface it did, but not when you started looking at things closer. Things like the shelves that were tipped over. It wasn't done randomly, for one thing. Every single one of them was pitched forward at the same angle. He bet there were no prints on any of them, either.

The front door opened and Marty walked in.

"Your brother has quite a place," he said. "Not exactly a Radio Shack."

They shook hands. "I appreciate your time, Marty," Grady said. "No, Jack's got a pretty special store. He doesn't get things from your usual sources. Most of his customers are serious hobbyists, into more sophisticated stuff than your weekend model airplane buff. I help him out quite a bit. He has some government clients. He's got stuff the CIA could use." He paused. "And does."

"Not your strip center mom and pop operation, eh?" Marty grinned.

"Not at all." A slight smile appeared on his Grady's face.

"How's your—" Marty hesitated.

"Eye?" Grady finished it for him. "It's fine. Messed up my golf game some, but I manage. My depth perception is a bit off at long distances. Under a hundred yards, it's fine."

"I didn't know you were a golfer."

"I'm not. That was supposed to be a joke."

Marty reached down and picked up one of the parts lying on the floor, looked at it a second, then put it back. "We were all sorry you retired, Grady. You were one of the best."

There was a short silence in which Grady could think of nothing to say. He turned his face away from the other cop, self-consciously.

Marty cleared his throat after a moment. "Well, hey, anyway . . . Listen, you know if any of those militia types ever come in? You know, survivalists, doomsdayers, folks like that?"

"Fruitcakes, you mean?" Grady thought a minute. "Well . . . a few, I guess. Jack was pretty careful, though." He paused, eyes narrowing. "Oh—I see where you're going. You think maybe one of those kooks . . . "

"I don't think a goddamn thing at this point. Oh, I've got a couple of theories, but at this point, to be honest, we don't have a line on any suspects at all. It's a possibility though, isn't it?"

Grady considered it a moment. "Sure. *Anything's* a possibility at this point, but for some reason I don't think this guy's your garden-variety crackpot. What I think is that whoever did this is one smart cookie, not your typical neo-Nazi moron. Look at these shelves for instance."

He explained to Marty his take on the shelves and the detective nodded in agreement.

For a moment, both men looked silently at the jumble before them, then Grady asked, "What have you guys got?"

"Well," Marty began, "not a whole helluva lot so far. I got a new partner, young pup who thinks he knows it all. His theory is that it was either kids got surprised in a burglary or else it was an armed robbery went bad."

"New academy graduate?"

"Yeah. Went to college. Believes in the 'likes kittens' theory still."

Both men howled.

"Oh, God! I'd forgotten the 'likes kittens theory'!" Grady said.

"Yeah," Marty said, wheezing as he wiped his eyes and shook with laughter. "This kid even called it that. Said he learned it at the Academy. He didn't know the instructor was pulling his legs. The instructor was Black Jack Parton. You *know* he was shucking them, but this kid never caught on. Listen to this. He quotes Black Jack to me. Musta wrote it down verbatim. Says to me, dead-serious, 'Mr. Sprague, criminals are human beings too. Even the worst criminal has human qualities. He may like kittens, for instance. Now, can a guy like kittens and still be all bad? Deep in the worst criminal's body still beats a human heart. Never forget that.' I swear—" He began laughing again and both men shook silently, tears coming to their eyes.

Grady said, coming up for air, "He needs to meet Charlie Manson."

"Oh, God," Marty said. "Just keep him off the parole board. He'd probably want to take Manson home and rehabilitate him."

"Yeah," Grady said, "and buy him a kitten."

"So Manson could pluck its legs off!"

Both men lost it, roaring and slapping each other. Then, just as abruptly as they'd begun, both sobered, Grady first, looking around the trashed store.

"I wish Jack could help us on this," Grady said, his smile fading.

"Yeah. Once he's conscious and gives us a description of this punk, we got 'im."

"No, I was thinking another way. Even if he wasn't the victim he could probably figure this out in a New York second. Remember the Boroni case?"

"It was before my time, but I heard stuff. Jack helped on that one, did he?"

"Helped? Hell, Jack *solved* it. By himself." The Boroni case was an insurance fraud affair. It was more than that. It was also a way Mr. Boroni figured out not only to collect the insurance on his Chris Craft, but to get rid of a wife who didn't approve of his affairs. There was a bonus there too, in that she was worth half a million dead.

"Wasn't there a bomb in Mrs. Boroni's drink or something? It was something like that, wasn't it? Boroni had one a'them weird old-time Eytalian names, didn't he?"

Marty walked back up to the front of the store poking with his foot at the wreckage on the floor as he went. Grady followed along, recalling the case.

"That's right. Ideal. That was his first name. Ideal Boroni. See, Boroni knew his wife liked her booze. She also had a habit of running out to their yacht when they had a rhubarb. Sit there and get tanked to the gills. Always drank the same thing, this weird fucking shit. Seems she had a sweet tooth, liked Irish coffee. Well, sweet-tooth Irish coffee. She used expresso and dumped two of them packets of Sweet 'N Low in it before she hit it with the booze. A dieting drunk you might say."

Both men laughed. Grady went on.

"The old man set her up, picked a donnybrook with her and off she ran, just like he figured she'd do. Hiked on out to the Mad River. Only thing, when she dumped in the sweetener, it kind of blew up on her. Seems Mr. Boroni had substituted sodium in all the packets, sealed 'em up again."

"Sodium. What the hell's that? The stuff in crackers?"

"It's a chemical. Not soda, *sodium*. Looks kinda like sweetener only more silvery. Sodium hits water, it blows up."

"So there was a chemical reaction, right? To booze? How'd he do it?"

Grady smiled. "The guy soaked charcoal starter fluid into all the woodwork. Really laid it in. Figured when the stuff blew up, the boat would burn and sink and they'd figure it was another boating accident. His luck wasn't so good though. The boat didn't burn enough and didn't sink. He shoulda checked the weather forecast. It called for thunderstorms that day."

"So how'd your brother figure that out?"

"He was with me when the call came in for Arson and Bombs so I asked him to come along. He could always tell more about a crime scene in ten seconds than the lab whizzes could in ten days with their microscopes and college educations. He doped the whole thing out in ten minutes flat."

"So, I ask you again . . . how'd he figure it out?"

"Easy. From fishing with our grandfather."

"You lost me, Fogarty."

Grady reached in his pocket and got out a stick of gum, taking his time to unwrap it. The corners of his mouth turned up. "Our grandfather used to take him fishing when he was a kid. Grandpa used sodium. Quicklime works too. They both explode when combined with water, only sodium has the best explosion. Grandpa would fill up a stone jug with the stuff and cork it. Put two strings on it. One to lower the jug into the lake and the other hooked around the cork. When the jug hit the bottom, he pulled the cork. The jug goes kaboom and you get your limit. Anyway, that's how Jack knew what the guy used. Actually, he *didn't* know that right away. He got suspicious when he smelled the starter fluid. It was pretty strong. I smelled it too and so did every other shield on the boat, but I didn't make any connections."

"So what put Jack onto the deal?"

Grady looked at Marty and grinned. "He noticed there wasn't a barbecue grill around. He thought of Grandpa and his fishing technique. His mind works funny, makes connections like that, connections most of us miss. He looked around and sure enough, found a big jar of the stuff on the bar. Boroni musta left it out like that, figuring once the explosion happened it would help it along in a big way."

"Damn! That was some slick thinking!"

"Jack's smart, for sure. Lot smarter than I am. Got that from our dad."

Grady was more like his mother, he knew. Tenacious. Bullheaded, as his dad always put it. He usually got his man during his time on the police force, but it was more through dogged persistence than flashes of brilliance. Jack was the one with the insights. And now . . . he didn't want to think about what was going on with Jack's brain or his body. Maybe the doctor was wrong. He didn't know how tough Jack was.

Grady shook his head to get back to the present. "Look, did you guys take prints?"

Marty shook his head. "Sure, but not any we could use, looks like. That's why I knew you were right about the shelves. That was the first thing we dusted and the lab guys said whoever'd done that probably used gloves. You could tell where he grabbed each of them by the dust. They were smeared, but not a trace of a fingerprint. I got to tell you Grady, some of the guys think like my partner. That this is a B&E went hinky."

"That what you think, Marty?"

"You know better. I'm old school, same as you. These young guys think everything fits into a category and that's how you solve crimes. Build a profile, feed it into a computer and out comes your criminal all nice and neat. You and me, we know better. The thing is, these new guys we got, they got no respect for the criminal mind."

Grady agreed. Whatever this bastard was, Grady thought, he was no dummy. Marty was right. That was the difference between experience and inexperience. As much as you might hate the bad guys—and in this instance, hate was a mild description of how he felt—you couldn't make the mistake of underestimating them. He said, "I'm glad to hear you say that. This guy is slick, all right. It's good to know we're both on the same wave length. I'm going to need a friend on the force if I have any chance of solving this."

"Now wait, Fogarty. You're retired. Leave this to me. I'll get this fucker. You know what the captain'll do if he finds you messing around on a case. Especially this one."

Grady turned and spit his gum into the trash can behind him. "No, *you* wait, Marty. This is my brother and nobody's going to keep me from working on this case. You're a friend, you'll help. Matter of fact, I'll show you my good faith, share what I know with you. And don't worry. The captain won't know I'm around." Before the detective could reply, Grady began walking toward the darkened back of the store.

"Come here. I want to show you something," Grady said, beckoning.

Marty followed. If he was going to comment further he kept it to himself.

At the front of the store Grady stopped and pointed up at something on the wall near the door. "See that? That's the control box for the burglar alarm."

"Yeah? So?"

"So, whenever we were in the store after he closed, Jack and me—chinnin', stuff like that—Jack always turned the alarm back on. Lifetime habit. In case someone tried to break in while we were there. Jack's deaf. He's got this hearing aid he wears, but it don't do much. He was always afraid somebody'd break in while he was in here alone and he wouldn't hear the guy. It was the way he protected himself. This isn't the best neighborhood, if you haven't noticed. This shoots the B&E-gone-wrong theory. This wasn't some guy who threw a brick through the back door glass like we're supposed to think it was. This guy was in here with Jack. My brother let him in for some reason. It's attempted murder, pure and simple. I don't know why. I don't know what was in the store that this creep wanted, but I'm going to find out. Look around. This place has electronic shit the government spooks don't have. This wasn't some punk after a couple of hundred bucks for his crack habit."

He began walking back to the cash register and Marty followed, keeping quiet and letting Grady talk.

"Listen. Jack did an inventory last week. I helped him on the goddamned thing. Find the inventory, match the receipts of what he sold in the meantime. Take your own inventory, match it against his and you'll have what the guy was after. It'll be a lot of work, but it'll pay off. Give those eager beavers something useful to do."

Marty sighed. "Okay, okay. If there's an inventory list we'll find it. We need to know what was taken anyway so if it gets fenced we've got another angle to work. You need to get out of here. I've done as much as I can, time being. I got to get on home. My old lady thinks I've got some bimbo shacked up. She watches too many cop shows."

Grady didn't argue, followed his friend to the door. Locking it, he asked Marty one last question. "Did the guys get anything from the neighborhood? Anybody see anything?"

Nothing of importance, Marty said, except from one of the waitresses across at Bandy's Grill. One of the girls named Cheryl gave the uniforms a description of someone who might be worth talking to if they could find him. They were circulating the guy's description. He'd get Grady a copy of the flyer.

"Thanks." Grady offered his hand to shake. "I think I'll go over and talk to her myself. You said it was Cheryl? Tall redhead?" Grady knew everyone who worked at the diner, Cheryl especially. Cheryl had been a couple of years behind him when they were in high school.

Back when life was a lot simpler.

12

SITTING ACROSS FROM a criminal in a rundown shotgun house smack in the bowels of New Orleans' Ninth Ward was not Clifford James (C.J.) St. Ives's idea of a great place to be at nine p.m. on a Sunday night or any other time. He didn't have much of a choice, though. The man on the other side of the kitchen table shoving pieces of paper across the dirty oilcloth held the key to his future. St. Ives was keenly aware of the packet of five thousand rubber-banded dollars in his coat pocket. Money he was to hand over once he okayed the merchandise.

Passports, birth certificates, drivers' licenses, social security cards. A marriage license dated two and a half years ago. Amanda's image, as well as his own, stared up at him from several of the documents, but the names were different.

His read Raymond Theodore Broussard and Amanda, well . . . he hoped she'd like her new identity. He'd spent a lot of time choosing it. A long time ago in one of their pillow talks she'd confided to him that she hated her name. Said it always reminded her of some old maiden aunt. Said she especially hated the diminutive form, only she didn't say that; she said *nickname*. There were some things about Amanda he wished he could change. Her lack of education was one of them.

Katina was the name she wished her parents had had enough foresight to give her. Amanda acted as if it were a personal act of meanness on their part.

Katina Broussard was the name on most of the documents. Except for the birth certificate. That read *Katina Hebert*. A real stroke of genius, that was.

Clifford St. Ives didn't like this place at all, particularly the noise: sirens erupting continually, kids screeching, doors slamming. Very different from his own quiet neighborhood. The guy had some kind of bizarre collection of hurricane lamps. They were everywhere, all colors, all sizes. I guess I'll come here, we get a hurricane, lose all the power, C.J. thought, smiling inwardly. And the wallpaper! Mardi Gras colors, all the rooms. Purple, green and gold. It was giving C.J. a headache. He remembered a house just up the block from his on Magazine. Same colors on the frame. Right next to an LSU fan's house, purple and yellow which was supposed to be gold but more resembled baby diarrhea. You can make some people rich, he thought, but you can't teach them taste. He always wondered what the insides of both of those houses looked like. Much like this one, he decided. He ought to ask the man if he had any wealthy relatives.

The man was dark complected. There's some Negro blood there. Trying to pass. What was it they always claimed? They were Indian, Spanish? Right. He was about as Indian as Martin Luther King.

Something was wrong with the man's eye, too. St. Ives studiously avoided looking at it directly, focusing on the other one, the good one, the right eye. The one with the eyelid that didn't droop half over, covering part of the iris. It was a different color too. The color of the inside of a Snicker's Bar, milky brown. The other, the good one, was dark brown. The guy was a frigging mutant.

"This is the first time I've been down in the Ninth Ward in a long time," St. Ives said. "Almost didn't find this place. Your directions aren't the best." He could smell the spicy odor of boiled mudbugs and crab boil and it was making him hungry.

The man merely grunted and waited on St. Ives to finish inspecting the documents. He tapped out a cigarette from the pack before him on the table and lighted it by striking a kitchen match with his thumbnail.

"You know why they call these shotgun houses?" Clifford James said, in another attempt at conversation.

Clifford James, C.J. to his friends, didn't know why he was so nervous.

He went on, not sure why he was being so voluble to this cretin unless it was nerves, understandable given where he was and all that money in his pocket. The man sitting across from him folded his arms and squinted at him with his good eye through the cigarette stuck in his mouth. He didn't reply, only sat back and stared blankly like some damned Buddha. C.J. went on, not sure why he was being so voluble to this cretin unless it was nerves.

"It goes back to the days when there wasn't any air-conditioning. One, two hundred years ago, maybe longer. They made them this way to beat the heat. They built them to catch the prevailing trade winds . . . what is that . . . east and west? I don't know, I always get that confused. Maybe it was north and south. Which direction's that?" He pointed toward the front door.

"Anyway, they faced the houses to catch the breezes. They made them without any room dividers, straight through from the front door to the back. That way, when it got hot they'd open the front door and the back door and the breezes would flow right through."

He watched the man to see if he was getting this. A guy like this guy probably lived in this house or one like it all his life and didn't have the slightest idea of its history. Ignoramus. Manny, that was his name. What the hell kind of a name was Manny? Some Negro thing he bet. Short for Manuel. Trying to act like he was a Spaniard. A conquistador.

C.J. went on, talking and signing papers. He was starting to feel the perspiration collect under his arms.

"They called these houses 'shotguns' because you could stand at the front door and fire a shotgun at the back door and not hit anything in between."

He didn't know why he was telling this Yat all this. Nervousness, he guessed. It was going to be great to be out of this town with all its ignorant coonasses and scum, like this moron.

"I guess you know what a camelback house is. It's a two-story shotgun."

Manny sat there, stolid. He said, "You got the money? You got your merchandise. I want my money."

It was Manny's longest utterance so far in the entire visit.

"Yes. Yes, I do. It's right here."

He extracted the bills and handed them across. Manny didn't look at them. He sat impassively with his arms folded, a cigarette hanging smoldering from his lips.

"Aren't you going to count them or something? Be sure I didn't cheat you?" He giggled and wished he hadn't. He sounded like a kid when he did that.

"It's there. Every dime. You're too much a fucking pussy to try and fuck me. By the way, every motherfuckin' six-year-old in Louisiana knows why a shotgun house is called that."

"Well . . . " St. Ives said, standing up and stretching his arms, trying to ignore the insult. Trying to act nonchalant. He gathered up the documents up and put them in the briefcase he'd brought. "Well . . . laizzez les bon temps rouler." He shined Manny a beatific smile.

The man gave him a dour look and muttered, "Whatever," then added, "Lemme me ask you a question, Jack. I don't usually ask this, but I'm curious. Who you runnin' from, man? The cops after you?"

The cops? The police'll be the least of my worries if I get caught. I should hope all I have to worry about is the law. The thought of the potential danger he was facing and the way he was handling it made him feel a little bigger. Damn! He was doing it! If this nobody spade trying to pass for white only knew what he was up to, he'd have a heart attack. He decided not to answer the question, to ignore it.

"Shut the door on your way out."

"I will," said the banker. "I certainly will. And, Manny? Thank you. Thank you very much."

He clutched his briefcase in both arms as if it were a baby that needed to be held carefully, and walked to the front door. As he was closing it he sneaked a glance at the man sitting at the kitchen table and saw he still wasn't moving or touching the money. Manny was staring at him and St. Ives's pulse quickened.

Asshole, he thought hurrying to the car and looking up and down the street. *I'll be lucky if I don't get mugged in this cesspool.*

He locked the door before he started up the engine, glancing around to be sure the others were still locked.

It wasn't until he was in the CBD on Canal that he let his breath out fully and realized he was freezing. He reached to switch the air-conditioning button to the vent; it felt better. He knew he should go home, but he desperately needed a drink. He wanted to be around people with some class. He decided to go to the Grill Room on Gravier. He had a taste for the wild mushroom connelloni and the grilled venison with whipped sweet potatoes. Stop by afterwards at the Fairmont Hotel, get a drink at Bailey's. He wondered if Busta was still open. Maybe he'd take his drink up and see. Get a haircut. He'd look good, by God, when he and Amanda got on that plane.

Katina, he thought, wryly. *I'd better get used to calling her Katina. I can imagine her face when I tell her. I'll tell her when I show her the money. Two surprises at once.*

He gave the maitre 'd a broad grin as he entered the restaurant. A gorgeous woman in a dress that C.J. figured had to go for at least a thousand, clicked past him on stiletto heels and smiled. He winked at her and followed her into the bar.

God! Life was great! Absolutely grand and glorious!

The next day C.J. told Amanda he was thinking of taking a vacation. He was considering a cruise on the QE2. Go to England maybe. The QE2 is the creme de la creme of ships, he told her. Very impressive setup he said: plush staterooms, Crystal, Beluga caviar, a *real* ship like the kind high society people used to take on the Grand Tour.

"I want you to go with me," he said, reaching across the table for her hand and squeezing it. He was looking into her eyes, but cognizant of her cleavage as he leaned across the table. About one more square inch of exposure and Miss Jane, the head loan officer, would be having a chat with her. He could feel himself becoming aroused and tried to take his mind off her breasts, but it was difficult. All he could think of was how brown and large her nipples were.

"But what about Sarah?" she said. "How can we do that?"

"To hell with my wife!" His face darkened. "Sarah's history. I'm leaving her. I should have done it a long time ago. The first day I met you, I wanted to leave her. I've waited too long to do this as it is. I'm going to do it. I'm going to Europe. I've never seen it as a tourist. Always on business. Might as well have gone to New Jersey for all you see when you're on business. I want to visit cathedrals, drink wine out of your slipper in Montmarte, fuck your brains out in a Swiss chalet. You're going with me. Won't you?"

They were sitting at an outside table at Cafe du Monde in full view of the tourists with their cameras and Bermuda shorts and daiquiris in go-cups and in view of the locals who either worked in the French Quarter or came in from the neighboring parishes to party or hear some music. The locals looked out of place surrounded by Hawaiian shirts and loud children. St. Ives was conscious of the image he cut sitting there. The epitome of wealth and power, Clifford St. Ives wore a dark blue Armani with black wingtips and a Sulka tie. His slender manicured fingers held a Players cigarette and the action he made when he put it to his lips could be described only as a *sip*, a delicate little maneuver he made through pursed lips. C.J. worked hard to cultivate his image, having spent years studying, watching others, how they acted, what fork they picked up, how they held their wine glass. It wasn't the image he was born with. Not an image his mother and father, both Cajuns, would recognize if he ever happened to visit them, which wasn't a remote consideration. Not since college over twenty years ago. No one at the bank, nor any of his business associates, knew he could speak perfect coonass French or that by the age of ten he could field dress a deer. Or that his father trapped alligators and sold the hides and meat on the black market. His *Who's Who* entry read quite differently. A pure piece of fiction that everyone had accepted whole cloth.

Across the table from him, looking as cool as the iced French Roast she was sipping, in the same white silk blouse and navy blue skirt that could be seen in the window at Saks a few blocks over on Canal, was Amanda Villere. Amanda, who worked for him at the bank as an Assistant Loan Officer, was trying to hide her nervousness at their public exposure. She didn't especially like the idea of sitting out where everybody in town could see her and C.J. together.

Before Amanda went to bed for the first time with C.J., she worked in the bank as a teller and worried about keeping her job at Derbigny. She'd made more than a few mistakes in counting out change and more than once was required to stay over to redo the daily count. She knew firsthand the definition of the word probation.

She forced herself to remember C.J.'s logic over a year before when the affair first began: *No matter how hidden the places we go to, someone sometime is bound to see us. New Orleans is a small town especially for a banker. If we go to very public places, no one will think a thing of it. They'll assume we're talking bank business. Besides, this is New Orleans. A guy's got some money, position, he's expected to play around and have a mistress. Look at Governor Edwards.*

She didn't care. It still made her jittery. C.J.'s wife was one scary bitch. Her maiden name was Derbigny. That said it all. They met face to face at the Christmas party last year and Amanda could tell by the way she acted that Mrs. St. Ives knew something. Very proper, very dignified, *very cool.* Mrs. St. Ives didn't have to say anything special. The look in her eyes was enough. Amanda felt like a deer caught in a car's headlights. C.J. laughed when she told him. That was like a man. Take everything at face value. His wife never accused him of anything, therefore she knew nothing.

Mrs. St. Ives said only one thing to Amanda at that meeting. *You certainly got promoted very quickly, my dear. You must be very intelligent.* She flashed a smile without any warmth in it and moved on, her diamonds twinkling.

"Well? You'll go, won't you? You have to go, Amanda. Don't worry about your job. You won't need your job. I'm going to take care of you."

He sat there, waiting for her answer. He felt the heat rise in his groin again. God, what a body! It was hard to think of anything else with a great pair like that staring at him.

"All right. Of course I'll go, sugar. When do we leave?"

He beamed. "Week and a half. There's a few things I have to take care of. Details. Do you have a passport? If not, I can get that taken care of quickly."

Actually, he said, continuing his sentence silently, it's already been taken care of, my sweet.

There's something he's not telling me, Amanda thought as they began to discuss plans. *I'll get it out of him cause I know damn well there's more to this than leaving his wife for a fling with me.. And what happens after Europe? I know. Fucker goes back to his wife and I hit the bricks without a job. Horny bastard keeps looking at my tits. Guess I know what's on his mind. I wonder if we'll go back to work. Shit! He's not the one who gets yelled at if I take another afternoon off. I hate the way everybody looks at me with their goddamned noses in the air.!*

"Italy," he was saying. "Definitely Italy. And of course England and France. Is there anywhere special you've always wanted to go? Switzerland perhaps? Spain? We can go anywhere, anywhere your little heart desires, pumpkin."

I should tell her, he thought. *But I can't. It would spoil the trip, spoil everything. How do you tell your lover that you're going to steal four million dollars from a drug cartel? Plus the million already taken from the bank where you both work? That when you leave the country neither of you will be coming back? How do you tell her she'll have a new identity? Easy! You wait until you're in the islands and she sees the money all spread out on the bed. That's when you tell her.*

"Come on," he said, digging in his wallet for tip money. "Let's go. I want to go to the apartment. I've got some good stuff. The same stuff I used last time. Primo. I'll put it all over you, lick it off."

He was too busy smiling at the Vietnamese waitress who came up to see the look Amanda gave him. It wouldn't have pleased him.

13

"HI, CHERYL."

Grady sat down at a front booth and watched her putting away silverware in the drawer beneath the counter. They were the only two in the diner. He figured Bandy was in the back somewhere like always. He was seldom far away. Grady figured he didn't trust the help all that much.

"Hi, Grady. We heard about Jack. A bunch of us were talking about going up and seeing him. Can he have visitors?"

Grady could see the concern in her eyes. He and Jack spent many hours in Bandy's, drinking cup after cup of coffee, flirting with the girls. Cheryl was nice.

"I don't think so, Cheryl. Not yet anyway. He's in pretty bad shape. He's in and out of consciousness. Not a coma . . . that's what the doctor says . . . but it looks like one to me. When he comes to, he doesn't seem to be aware of much. He doesn't recognize anything or anybody. The doctors say it will take time. They . . . they're not sure if he'll ever be all right again. The impression I get is that if he makes it, he might be able to serve hamburgers at Mickey D's, but he'll need some help if he has to make change."

Cheryl's hand flew to her mouth and she sat down in the seat across from Grady in his booth, brow furrowed in pain. "Are *you* all right?"

"What? Yeah. Compared . . . Sure. Listen, Cheryl, I need some help. The suits tell me you were on duty the night this thing happened."

"You kidding, Grady? I work twelve hour shifts. I'm *always* here. I told the police everything I could think of."

"I know. I'd like you to tell me if you would. You said a guy came in?"

Her brow lifted and she nodded. "A real jerk."

"How so?"

"Well, he kept bitching about the coffee."

Grady snorted. "*That* makes him a jerk? Cheryl, everybody comes in Bandy's trashes the coffee."

She twisted her mouth. "Well, yeah, maybe, but this guy was . . . well, he was *odd*. You guys are joking, but he was like bent out of shape over it. And we know you guys. You're teasing. This guy was different. Nasty-like. That wasn't what got me, though. It was his hair."

"Hair?" Grady leaned forward.

"Yeah. Weird. It was blonde."

"What's weird about blonde hair?" Grady was puzzled.

"It was the wrong color for his eyes. His eyes were brown."

He was thoroughly bewildered. "I don't get it."

"It's a wonder I noticed anything at all. I was running my ass off. There was a mob of people in here. You know, come to think of it, I remember seeing a light on over at Jack's. Nothing unusual. At least I didn't think so at the time. You know Jack. Always coming in at weird hours, messing around with that stuff he has over there. I didn't think anything about it until now. Would that be important?"

"Maybe. What's this stuff about the guy's hair?"

"Well," she sat down on a stool and leaned over, placing her head in her hands and her elbows on the counter. "Like I said, he has blonde hair and brown eyes. Oh—and a beard. And glasses. The beard was blonde, too. Darker, but blonde."

"I still don't get it." He picked up his coffee and sipped. He was getting exasperated, but tried not to let it show.

Cheryl laughed. "I shouldn't wonder! Men never observe things like that."

"Like what? Cheryl—"

"Keep your shorts on. I'll explain." She reached behind her for the coffee pot, turned and poured more into Grady's cup, then put the pot back on the warmer. "Blonde hair and brown eyes are the rarest combination of hair and eye color there is."

"It is?" He didn't know that.

"Cheryl!" It was Bandy. He stood at the rear of the diner, hands on hips, a little martinet of a man, all in white, a cigarette stuck between his lips.

"What?"

"You got those receipts done?"

"Pretty much. I'll bring them back in a minute."

"Ten minutes. I need them. You're supposed to be working you know." He turned and disappeared into the back room again and closed the door.

"Asshole," she said, shaking her head and turning back to Grady. "I went to beauty school for awhile after Dunbar. Wigs were my specialty. I can spot a wig a mile away. This guy was wearing one. Fake beard too would be my guess, although I have to admit this was a decent enough one. I wouldn't have caught it if it wasn't for the color of his eyes. Soon as I saw his brown eyes, I knew he was either wearing a wig or colored his hair. Another thing. I didn't pay much attention to it at the time, but it seems odd, doesn't it? He kept looking over at Jack's place. Like he was studying it."

Grady's stomach muscles tightened.

"Can you describe him any more?"

Cheryl nodded, her eyes widening. "That's easy. Not a real big guy, but one who works out. You could tell. Muscles. He looked . . . hard. Like his suit didn't fit him right, you know? I don't think he needed glasses, either. Don't ask me why I think that. I don't know, something about the way he was wearing them. Like he wasn't used to them. He kept messing with them. Taking them on and off. Maybe he got glasses for the first time, I don't know."

He slid his empty coffee cup over for a refill and asked a couple more questions, but she wasn't able to add much more other than the color of the suit, which was blue. The man's tie was blue as well, but that was the most she could remember. Grady wrote down his home phone number and told her to call him if she remembered anything else, no matter how slight or unimportant she thought it might be.

"Thanks, Cheryl." He put a dollar bill on the counter on top of his card. "I appreciate your help."

"You need anything . . . ," she said as he opened the door. " . . . you call. We all like your brother around here." *You too,* he thought he heard her say as the door closed behind him. A day ago, he'd have been hitting on her, he realized. Not now. Something had changed.

Grady climbed in his car and began the drive home. Along the way he went over in his mind what he knew. What would a guy in a disguise want from Jack? Somehow, he knew Cheryl had described Jack's assailant. There was no hard proof, just a gut feeling, the kind he'd learned to trust over the years.

Sometimes, they were all you had to go on.

14

THE COP WHO answered Grady's call was another new one with a name like Smithers or something. Christ. Three years out to pasture and they'd replaced the whole damned department. Every time he ran into somebody or called down there he was talking to people he'd never heard of. Grady couldn't remember any mass retirement exodus three years ago, but there sure as shit seemed to be a whole new bunch there now and they all seemed to have button-down names. Where the hell were all the micks and eyetalians? What kind of police department was it becoming what with all these kids' names, like Ivy League MBA's?

Come to think of it, he didn't recall seeing any of the noses, that day at Jack's. That's what they called the Macedonians he'd served with. Dayton's Macedonian population was substantial. He'd gone through the academy with a Macedonian who was a cousin of Dayton's most famous native son, Jamie Farr, the guy who dressed in drag on *M*A*S*H*. He'd met Mr. Farr at a smoker one time. Nice guy, although his cousin said Farr always claimed to be Lebanese because nobody knew where Macedonia was. Grady got the idea this pissed off his cousin, one of the countless Bojrabs in the Dayton phone book.

"Lemme speak to Detective Sprague," he said.

" . . . see if he's available," said the voice on the other end, softly, the speaker sounding like he was all of thirteen years old and taking a call for his dad. "Sir."

"He's available, hotshot. Tell him it's Fogarty."

Marty must have been standing a foot away, his raspy voice on the phone in less than two seconds.

"Fogarty! How goes it ol' bud!"

"You tell me, Marty. They get the inventory done?"

"Yeah. Last night."

"I thought you were gonna call me."

"I was getting ready to. It was late when they finished. I got in about two minutes ago. Look, I got a note on my calendar to give you a holler."

Grady waited. He lighted a Marlboro medium and stared at his shoes. He told himself to remember to pick up a can of shine.

"Hey, it turns out your brother keeps good records. I think we got a pretty accurate list of what he sold last week after his inventory. They woulda got it done sooner 'cept they had to put all the shit back on the shelves and count it. You wouldn't believe all the little knickknacks there were!"

Yes, I would, Grady thought. I helped him do that inventory last week.

"All I need is what's missing," Grady said. "Don't worry about what he sold. I don't think whoever hit him bought anything."

"Well, ol' bud, I think you may be partly wrong there. We found something."

"What?"

"We got a pretty sharp gal who did the inventory. Remember Ida? She spotted something."

"I remember Ida. She's a good cop."

Grady took a long drag off his cigarette and felt his lungs ache. He ought to quit smoking. His lungs probably looked like a couple of black walnuts.

He remembered Ida all right. He remembered a night on a stakeout in a van whose lettering said *Smitty's Heating and Air Conditioning* on the outside, and he remembered especially a pair of long, long legs. He remembered a couple of other nights as well, then it wore itself out. Only they remained friends, not enemies as is the usual case. Ida had given out signals that she wanted to move past a casual affair. Cops shouldn't get involved, he'd told her when he saw things were heating up. Especially with other cops. She must have agreed with his logic, as her affection for him soon cooled and a week later she was dating somebody else. A straight guy, somebody who sold insurance. Smart move, Ida, he remembered thinking at the time, but every once in awhile he wondered what would have happened if they had gone on seeing each other. It's all so much ancient history, he thought, and switched focus back to the present.

"What'd Ida find?"

"Well, you're wrong about the perp not buying anything, looks like . . . but we're right, this wasn't a B&E. In fact, I'd say you were right on the money. This looks more like armed robbery."

"How so?"

"Ida figured that out pretty quick with all the records we found. She noticed something missing. A receipt. All his receipts were in perfect order, even the ones he messed up. He'd write a void on them. Well, listen to this . . . she couldn't find the last one he wrote. She knew it was missing cause his sales book was right there on the floor where it'd been knocked off. According to the numbers there was only one not accounted for. The last one used. And she found all the rest. Every single one of them."

"So that one's gone. We don't know what was on it. The inventory'd show what was missing. That's what would be on that receipt, I'll bet. Read me the list of what's missing."

"Don't have to. I told you Ida's a sharp cookie. She took the receipt book to the lab and they got the whole thing. Your brother had written it without taking it out of the book. Came through on the next receipt and the lab boys said it was the easiest thing they did all week. I got it right here. You know I'm not supposed to do this, give you this, but what the hell. I don't think it's gonna help much though. Looks like pretty normal stuff you'd buy in a store like that. One big item. A remote control transmitter. Futaba. You heard of those? Expensive. My guess is that's what the perp killed him for. Cost three grand, but there's something I don't understand. Two hundred of this is for something your brother wrote down as a 'Service Charge', only it doesn't say what the service was. Doesn't look like any big time deal to me. Probably a punk like we figured. Want me to fax it to you?"

"You think I got a fax machine in my shoe, Marty?"

They both laughed.

"Tell you what. If it's not a long list, read it off. Hold on a minute—let me grab a pencil. Marty?"

"Yeah?"

"Did you ask yourself what punk spends three grand on electronic stuff? Doesn't sound like a punk or a kid to me."

"You're right, Grady. I think I got my partner convinced it wasn't, either." The detective read off the items and hung up.

Grady stood for a minute with the receiver in his hand, then he shrugged and put it back on the hook.

The phone rang. It was Marty again.

"Hold on to your hat, partner. We got a break, maybe. Something just came in."

"What?" Grady felt the skin prickle on the back of his neck.

"I told you we circulated a flyer with the description that waitress gave us?"

"Yeah. Cheryl."

"Yeah, the one at that grill. Well, we got a call from a guy that owns the Clark station on White Avenue. You know, a couple of blocks from Jack's?"

"I know the station. Go on."

"Well, this guy took care of a customer that night that matched the description we sent out. This guy was driving a blue or a black Chevy, he thought. That's not the really good news, though."

"What's the good news?" Grady tried not to be impatient.

"The good news is the guy paid for his gas with a hundred dollar bill. The better news is the station guy still had it. And we got prints."

"You got prints!" This time, Grady couldn't contain himself. "Well, fuck it, man. Who the prints belong to? Quit fucking with me and tell me what you've got!"

"Sorry. We may have something and we may not. Anyway, what the lab boys found was two sets of prints, one which was the station owner's, guy by the name of Binford . . . and this other set. This other set is real interesting. Belongs to a guy by the name of Charles Kincaid. This Mr. Kincaid is from New Orleans, his last address according to the NCIC, and . . . listen to this, Grady . . . Kincaid has quite the little record. Nasty cocksucker. Looks like he killed his own father, for starters."

"Only two sets of prints? On a hundred-dollar bill? Doesn't that strike you as odd, Marty?"

"My thoughts exactly," he said. "What's your theory?"

"That's a no-brainer. He wiped down the bill before he spent it. Didn't want any prints on it besides his own."

"I'm with you. That's what I figured, too. Fact is, I did a little experiment. I asked the lab boys to take ten bills out of their own pockets and see how many prints were on them."

"And?"

"Twenty-three sets, on the average."

"You know what else?" Grady asked.

"What?"

"Jack always kept a C-note in the drawer. For emergencies. You didn't find one in the register, did you?"

"No. We sure didn't. Buncha change on the floor was all."

"I'm on my way down." Before Marty could reply, Grady slammed the phone down and was out of his house sprinting for his car.

"Marty!"

"Hey, Grady. Man, you must have flown to get here this quick. I can't fix any tickets you got, you know," he chuckled.

"Never mind the jokes. Tell me what you've got."

"Cool down. Come in here."

Marty motioned for him to follow him into a conference room. "Tactical Room," it said in big letters over the door. It was a room Grady was familiar with. Marty rummaged through some papers on the desk, extracted one from a pile and handed it to Grady. It was a rap sheet on one Charles Kincaid. No middle name. Under "Aliases" he saw only one. *Reader.*

"Interesting nom de plume. You got any art?"

"Yeah." Sprague picked up a 5" by 7" black and white photo and pushed it across the desk to him. Grady studied the features. Black hair—guess Cheryl was right—husky build, as she'd said, but what struck him the most was the guy's eyes. There was no expression in them. As if the guy was there, but he wasn't. Kincaid was a double for the actor Charles Bronson, but Grady had seen movies in which Bronson smiled. Grady couldn't imagine a smile on this creep. He took one more look at the photo and placed it in his jacket pocket. Marty started to say something and changed his mind, waving his hand as if to say go ahead and keep it.

After a slight hesitation, "Yeah, it looks like maybe this is our guy. We got a problem, though."

"What problem?" Grady's brow knitted and his eyes narrowed.

Marty sighed. "Even if this is the perp, we can't do much. There's not enough evidence to convict. We've notified the New Orleans P.D. and gave them what we had and they laughed at us."

"What!" Grady's face twisted into a mask of outrage.

"Calm down. They're right. All we've got is a set of partials that might be this guy's. The prints weren't that clear. They're good enough we're pretty sure this is the guy—at least we know he was in Dayton—but there's not enough points to make it positive far as a court's concerned. All we got is enough to make him a suspect. No court in the world is going to convict a perp on the little we have. The captain talked to the prosecutor. Jerome laughed him out of his office. Said to come back when they could give him something he could use. When we told him we figured Kincaid was gone, probably back to New Orleans, he laughed harder. Said there was no way they could get an extradition order with what little there was. Said to quit wasting his time."

Grady sat down heavily in the chair in front of Marty's desk. He knew Marty was right. He'd dealt with Jerome Higgins, the prosecutor, before. The guy was the supreme conservative. Wouldn't take on a case unless it was airtight.

"You got an address on this creep?" Grady asked.

"Well, yeah. Probably not any good. Some apartment in a town called Algiers. I gather it's across the river from New Orleans. It's two years old though. Here." He wrote on a piece of paper and gave it to Grady, who looked at it for a second and stuck it in his coat pocket with the photo. "What you got in mind?"

"I'm going to get him."

Grady stood and folded Charles Kincaid's rap sheet into four squares and put it in his pocket with the other papers. "I'll get all the proof you need."

"Wait." Marty caught him halfway out the door, grabbed him by the shoulder. "You're not on the force any more. You can't go off like some damned vigilante after this guy."

Grady turned, reached up and removed Marty's hand from where it was gripping his shoulder. "Yes I can, Marty. And I am. I'd appreciate your help, but without it I'm still going after this guy."

"Grady . . . " Marty started to say something and scratched the top of his scalp instead. "Hell, Grady. I'd do the same if I was you. Be careful, man. Tell you what—I've put in a request with the Feds for NCIC info in case they got anything else. I'll see what the FCC and ATF might have too. Be cool, man. You don't want to be the one ends up in jail."

"I won't," he said. "I'll let you know where I'm at. You get anything more, you call me right away."

"New Orleans? That where you're going?"

"I'm halfway there," Grady said, moving through the doorway.

The sun was creeping to the edge of the horizon when Grady threw the last pair of socks in his suitcase and closed it. On the way out of town, he stopped at an Amoco and gassed up. Then, he pointed the car's nose south.

Most of the day was gone when he phoned Marty from a pay phone outside a Popeye's Fried Chicken in Mississippi. A thermometer on the outside of the building read 97° even though the sun was going down. Marty had some more information. He read him a list of names he'd gotten from NCIC, folks that might be interested in electronic gear, but it didn't look as though it would be much help. The list consisted mostly of individuals belonging to political fringe groups and terrorist groups. Sounded pretty much like the same list of names he used to go over back when he was on the bomb squad. Christ, weren't any of these crackpots caught and put away yet? No lone wolf bandits except some safecrackers, but for some reason Grady couldn't explain, he didn't think this was a yegg. Grady asked him to fax the sheet to the Day's Inn anyway and any other info he could get from the other agencies, though both men were sure Kincaid was the right guy. He didn't want to eliminate any possibilities. He went into Popeye's and picked up some red beans and rice before he got back in the car. He drove nonstop the rest of the way to New Orleans, going across the Pontchartrain causeway in the middle of the night. After he checked in and showered, he walked over to the front desk and asked for messages. There was one fax from Marty. They were looking up in Dayton in all the usual places, but Marty figured the same way Grady did. Kincaid was back in New Orleans.

The car rental place he'd passed on the way into town proved very accommodating. They had not only rented him a car, but let him park his own on their back lot for a small fee. At first, they tried to talk him into taking one of the flashy T-birds out front, but he held out for the gray Dodge Dart four-door he'd spotted. It was a twin for his own. No sense in driving all over town in a car with Ohio plates. Who knows when or if he might run into Kincaid and if the guy was this smart, he'd tumble to him in a minute if he spotted plates from the state where he'd just committed a crime.

The motel clerk gave him directions on how to get to Algiers. At the Vallette street address he'd gotten from Marty, he didn't get much of anything useful. All he found was a retired black woman living there. No, she never heard of a Charles or a Reader Kincaid, and no, she'd never seen the person in the photo Grady showed her. The person who lived there before her was a young black man who sold cellular phones. Before that, she didn't know. Folks didn't stay in these apartments long. She was moving out herself soon.

Grady got in the car, drove back over the bridge to New Orleans and headed out to Kenner. He found Veterans Highway and looked for a gas station where he could buy a city map. Driving along Veterans, he had several near misses in traffic when cars pulled out without warning and crossed lanes inches in front of him. A traffic cop could have a field day, he thought. Half the drivers on the road appeared to be drinking something and he bet it wasn't coffee. He wondered what the DUI stats looked like in this town.

There were two guys working at the station, a teenager and an older guy. He waited until the older one walked out to the bays to go up to him and ask, "Where's the best place in town to get a girl?"

If Kincaid liked hookers, this might be the best way to find him.

"Hell, y'ain't gotta go clear inta town," the guy said, grinning. "Do what the preachers do—pick any joint on Airline Highway. They partial to tourists on Airline. Don'tcha watch the news? Say, y'ain't a preacher, are ya? I bet y'all got a TV show and everything, ain'tcha? They gonna love ya over t'Airline! Say, what channel are y'all on?" He guffawed and slapped his knee.

"You might want to try and control yourself, Clyde," Grady said to the man as he opened his car door. "You don't want to end up with a heart attack while you're having so much fun."

Grady made a mental note not to go back to that station.

15

SARAH ST. Ives was on the phone.

Bastard. Bastard, bastard, bastard. *Bastard!*

"Thank you Jane," she said pleasantly, in a voice that belied her anger. She hung up the phone with deliberate care.

That was it. That was enough. Who did that bastard think he was? Didn't he realize it was *her* bank, not his? Her grandfather's present to her, her debutante surprise, her inheritance? She'd earned that bank, in more ways than one. Hers, not his, not that lying, philandering coonass son-of-a-bitch of a husband, who convinced everybody into thinking he came from quality. She knew what he was, where he came from. A long time ago, she helped him create the fiction everyone accepted. Knew all about his working in the cafeteria, when he was putting himself through Ole Miss. Knew all about those movie-star good looks that turned her head—her cheerleader, summa cum laude head—so smart she fell for a low-life coonass with ambition. Smart, but dumb. Dumb little cheerleader with hot pants and a Phi Beta Kappa key.

The ambition. That's what turned her on to him. That and the looks. God! He was a killer back in those days, could have been in movies, in magazines, modeling underwear. Still was. That was the problem. Goddamn coonass movie star! And her. Look at her. Cursing like an Italian waiter or one of those Third-World Catholics, the ones who made her ashamed of her faith. He'd turned her into this coarse person. And what did she do? Only helped make him what he was, the ungrateful bastard. Figured out the lie herself, wrote it, lived it, played it to the hilt, got him in *Who's Who* with a bio that made him look like one of the fucking Kennedys for Christ sakes, the ungrateful bastard.

She recalled the phone call she'd gotten a week and a half ago.

"Sarah," the voice said. *"Your husband's fucking Amanda from the bank. It's time to do something about that."*

I agree, she'd replied. *But that's not why. This is why.* And she told the caller. *Yes,* he said. *That's a good reason.*

C.J. was out with the fucking bimbo right now, no doubt. She listened to the bank's chief teller, her voice calm but her eyes full of fury. "He's away on business, Mrs. St. Ives. He did call in a few minutes ago and said something had come up. He'd run into a client who needed to talk to him about a loan. I think he said it was Mr. Bell. You know, Mr. Bell who has Bell Industries?" In that tone Jane used, that superior, nasal voice. That said, *between you and me, we both know where he's at, honey. That's some husband you got there.*

Sarah St. Ives hung up the phone softly and then picked it up again. She dialed information for the number of Bell Industries.

"J.J.? How are you, J.J.? We don't see much of you and Dorothy. We'll have to have you over soon. Would next week be convenient? Listen, J.J., is my husband there by chance? He mentioned something about seeing you this week, today I thought. No? Well, it's nothing important . . . "

Lying bastard. Reaching for the phone, she dialed the bank again and asked in a voice muffled by a handkerchief held over her mouth, "Is Miss Villere available?"

When she hung up the phone, tears of anger welled up but she forced them back.

Okay, Buster. You asked for it. Let's see how tough you really are, you piece of Bridge City trash. Now you get to play in the big leagues; see if you can hit the curve ball.

What she did was go over to the CD player and put on Pavarotti. She remembered something she'd read about the tenor one time. He owned horses. Wasn't it funny how people of distinction possessed much the same interests? She listened to the opening strains of *Quando Le Sere Al Placido* and smiled, one long graceful finger on the pulse in her neck. It would be nice to see the horses again. Perhaps she'd have a ride. It had been weeks since she'd been on a horse. Blue Boy. She'd take out Blue Boy. Once more she dialed a number.

"Hello? Grandfather? I want to come over and have a talk. I need your advice on something. I'll tell you when I get there."

There. What should she wear? The blue suit, that's the one. Grandfather says it makes my eyes bluer. And my jodhpurs. Better take some jodhpurs. Take Blue Boy out.

She turned the volume as loud as it would go. _Yes,_ she thought. _La donna è mobile. Très mobile._ Luciano Pavarotti's voice filled the room as she busied herself packing.

In a short while, she was walking out to the street where her car was parked. She failed to notice the two men watching her from a midnight-blue Caprice parked halfway down the block.

Reader and Eddie sat in Reader's car and watched the old man making his way up the street, stopping every so often to pick up a can or bottle and place it in his shopping cart.

"That's—"

"Yeah. I've never seen him over on Magazine. Closest he gets usually is maybe Tchoupitoulas. Mostly he's up in the CBD. What's with the cans? I've never seen him pick up cans. I thought he was strictly a paper man."

Both of the men laughed. "Maybe he's diversifying," joked Eddie.

"I'll tell you a story about this guy," Reader said. "You know how he's always going around to the trash bins and picking out newspapers and putting them in his goddamned cart . . . well, one day, Sunday, I was thinking . . . I got this huge-ass bundle of the Times-Picayune I gotta pitch . . . I'll throw it in the car and next time I see the old geezer I'll give it to him.

"Anyway, I got this crap in my car two, three days when I spot him up on the neutral ground on Canal. I pull over and yell at him, 'Hey, old-timer. Here's a drink for you. This'll get y'all some good wine, what?'

And this creep . . . smells like you wouldn't believe, like the underside of a board you find in a vacant lot . . . this asshole says, believe it or not, he says, 'Keep your fucking charity!' He's screamin,' 'Keep your fucking charity, motherfucker! I don't need your fucking handout! I'm working here, motherfucker!' I couldn't fucking believe it! To me, *Reader*, he says this with people standing all around listening to this shit."

"What'd you do?"

"What'd I do? I got out of the goddamned car. I left the goddamned car in the middle of the street and walked over to him, ten pounds of Sunday papers in my mitts, of which five pounds is all about how come the Saints can't win noway, and I stick 'em in his goddamned shopping cart. That's what I did."

"Uh-huh."

"Uh-huh? Uh-huh your ass! Fucking asshole starts throwing my papers outta his greasy cart! Throws 'em all over the street. Fucking polluting motherfucker, throwing my papers all over the goddamned place. I went over to this cocksucker, pulled my gun out and put it on his ear."

Eddie smirked.

"I guess you didn't shoot him, didja Reader? I see him right there, half a block down."

Reader chortled. He'd felt the mad all over again for a minute, but it fell away and his shoulders shook with silent mirth.

"I guess you're right, Eddie. Naw, I didn't shoot him. I was going to, but fuck it, guy wasn't worth that kind of trouble. Man, you talk about a scene! People all running to the other side of the street, women screaming, stuff like that. This guy, this *bum*, he's got *heart*. I got the gun right up alongside his skull and he says to me, 'Take a hike. I want your help, I'll call you on the phone. You don't get no phone call, don't be bringing me your charity bullshit. I'm working here.' He says that. Doesn't look at me the whole time. Keeps throwing papers out of the cart. You've got to admire that. So I didn't shoot him. I tapped him with the gun butt. Not that hard. Knocked him down, shut him up. He's an all right dude."

Somebody came out of the St. Ives house. She was wearing a blue dress that Reader could tell a mile away wasn't bought off the rack at Penney's.

Maison Blanche threads, all the way. She got in the Mercedes parked in front, getting in from the curb side. Slid over and drove off.

Reader could tell by the hunch of her shoulders that she was mad. Good, he thought. Mr. C.J. St. Ives is about to lose his happy home.

Bye, Sarah, he goodbyed in his mind. *I'll be seeing you later. At a little reunion.*

He spoke to his partner. "That's the wife."

"You gonna follow her?" Eddie asked.

"Naw. Looks like St. Ives isn't home. He's the one I want, not her." He'd seen what he wanted but it wasn't information he wanted Eddie to know. It was coming together.

He gunned the engine briefly, let off the gas and eased forward and out into the street. When they passed the street person he honked and waved. The old man never looked up.

"Bet that old fucker's used to people honking at him," he said, heading the car north toward the French Quarter. "You know, that day I braced him, it must have been ninety-five degrees, a hundred percent humidity. He's got on four layers of clothes under that shiny black suit, all the time. Not a drop of sweat on him, either. Go figure."

He pulled up to drop off Eddie back at the Seaport Cafe on Bourbon and leaned across the seat to talk as Eddie stood with the door open, one foot up on the curb. The Quarter bustled. Tourists all over the place with their go-cups in hand, whores out already, even though it was only mid-morning. Barkers stood in front of strip clubs, exhorting visitors from Indiana to come in and see the "real thing—pussy like they ain't got back home." Vietnamese standing in front of the Takee-Outee's and beefy guys with beer bellies on the sidewalk in front of daiquiri places hosing down the sidewalks. Behind him, a guy in a bottled water delivery truck lay on the horn. Reader ignored him.

"Now you know the house where we're going Friday. In suits. With briefcases. You got your briefcase? Tell you what. Get a haircut. Get a decent one this time. Go to Kenneth's out in Metry. You'll like it. Lots of cute girls. Good cutters. Tell them you're going to start working in insurance, want to look professional. Let them do what they want. Get about half that shit cut off. Buy you a blowdryer and get the girl to show you how to use it. I don't get you, Eddie. Spend all that money on shoes and clothes and get your hair cut by Tony the Wop. And no booze Thursday *or* Friday. I don't want a lush on this job. I don't want to see you Friday morning nursing a hangover, either. Get it out of your system today if you have to. Got it?" He pulled away and left Eddie standing on the sidewalk, his hand running through his thin, straggly brown strands like he was saying good-bye to them and wanted one last feel.

Yessir. You'll want to look professional when they lay you out in that coffin, bitch . . . Reader stuck his hand out the window as he pulled back into the traffic and gave the trucker behind him the bird. He was disappointed when the truck slowed and didn't come after him.

Brought up that fight itch a couple of notches.

16

POOR EDDIE, READER thought after dropping his partner off. He didn't have a clue. If Eddie knew who it was they were robbing, there was no doubt the punk'd back out. He'd said it was drug money being laundered, but he hadn't told him whose drug money it was. Yet. Not till he was further in. If he had, Eddie would have run screaming down the street. Grudgingly, Reader thought that might show a bit of sense on his partner's part. He wondered briefly about his own brains. Why not forget it, take some quick money out of another bank? This setup would work anywhere, any bank he chose. It didn't have to be this one.

He sighed. Yes, it did. This is the only bank for the crime he had worked out. For this much money. For not just stinking bank money. What was that? Half a million, a million if they were lucky? If you even got to the vault. Chump change at the teller's drawers. Not this particular bank, though. This bank was good for three million, maybe double that. Maybe seven million. It depended on how good a week Guterez would be having. Discount half of what he'd heard and that was three, four million they brought in, at least. All denominations, all unmarked bills, mainly hundreds.

Besides, that wasn't the real reason he was doing this.

One last check to be made. He headed out to Fat City, out to Houma House Apartments off Veteran's.

Fat City. One of Reader's least favorite places. The locals' "French

Quarter." Thirty-plus nightclubs, bars and funspots, packed into a three or four block area, bounded by Veteran's Highway on one side, Esplanade on the other. Driving down Arnoldt was a bitch, trying to inch through the crowds of drunks that were always walking in the street as they bar hopped, did their pub crawls. It was party time in Fat City, every hour of every day and night of the year, twenty-four hours, three hundred and sixty-five days of the calendar year. New Orleans' best kept secret is the way the locals thought of it. It was an unspoken law to never tell out-of-towners about the area. Who wanted Fat City ruined like the Quarter had been? Their own private party area. Most natives wouldn't be caught dead in the French Quarter unless they worked there. It certainly wasn't a place you'd go to party. That was for the goombahs from the Midwest. Like Mardi Gras. The smart set got out of town during Carnival. Went to San Francisco or skiing in Colorado. Over-priced drinks, tourist traps with the worst music in town, and, except for a few joints, the blandest food in town, dishes watered down in flavor to please the tourist palate during normal times; magnify that ten-fold during Mardi Gras.

The nature of New Orleans pleased Reader, suited him perfectly. It was a town that appeared on the surface to be wide open, the people garrulous and breezy, but the really important stuff they kept close to the vest. Hardly any tourists, for example, knew that New Orleans was the only town in the country where you should never ask a cabbie or a doorman to recommend a restaurant or nightclub. Every time one of those guys steered an unsuspecting tourist to a joint, they got comped a buck or two. The worst places in town were often the busiest because of this . . . and they were mostly all in the French Quarter. Right where the natives wanted to keep outsiders. Let 'em buy overpriced drinks and be amazed they could walk around on the streets with a drink in their hand, get rowdy and play the fool and nobody seemed to care. Why should they? It was only a bunch of chumps and their wives or girlfriends from Iowa and Pennsylvania . . . partying with other suckers from nowhere places, getting ripped off by the hustlers that were everywhere down there, legitimate and otherwise. The town got rich on rubes and they never knew they were missing the best part of the city.

Two sunbathers, both good-lookers, blondes, were sitting out by the pool when he walked through. Both of the women smiled at him and he looked away. When they saw what apartment he went up to, one of the girls said something to the other. *Bastard*, is what he thought he heard when the door opened and he stepped inside.

"Ladies out there friends of yours, amigo?" he said, heading to the kitchen counter and the big bottle of Jack Daniels that Octavio kept behind it. "They don't seem to like you." He hoisted a glass to the man who had opened the apartment door. He poured whiskey into two glasses, ran a little water from the tap in his and handed the other to the grinning Cuban.

"Those girls?" He parted the curtain, peeked out. "Ay, Reader, I know them. We're *muchachos. Compadres.* They *love* Octavio. They know what I got and it makes them ache they want it so bad." He pointed to his crotch. "They maybe a little pissed at the moment. A tiny misunderstanding. We'll fix it up. Tonight, we get married. All three of us. You come by, you can have one. I'll take the ugly one, amigo, you take the *uglier.*" He laughed until his eyes watered at his own joke.

Reader took a long swallow on his drink and ignored him. Octavio never changed. Always thinking with his dick. He decided to humor the man. He had something important for him to do yet. "I could see that, my friend. They seemed very much in love, I think. Now. Any changes I should know about? Friday still the day they do it?"

"Oh, si. Si." Octavio went over to the one easy chair and sat, swung his leg over the side. Reader sat on the couch and set his drink on the glass coffee table. The apartment was decorated in what Reader thought of as Early Jive-Ass Drug Dealer Tacky. Decor of the day down here in Fat City. He'd never seen so much red in all his life. He bet he had red silk sheets on his bed. A waterbed, no doubt.

"I'll be leaving this afternoon," Octavio said. "Tonight and until Friday, I'll be with lots of people, having fun. Miami is nice this time of year. Everything is ready. Your room, your papers, the whole enchilada is ready. I talked to Senór Guterez, this morning—an hour ago. He, personally, will deliver the money. He likes to deliver the money. I've told him many times—Senór Guterez, you shouldn't deliver the money yourself. That's what you have people for, to do these things. But Senór Guterez—that is his pleasure. I think what it is, he doesn't trust anyone. Especially the hombres that work for him. He's gonna be surprised, eh? I'm glad I'll be in Miami when this goes down. I wouldn't want to be near Senór Guterez when he learns his money has been stolen. He's gonna be one pissed off muchacho. It's not going to be healthy to be near that man."

Senór Guterez was Octavio's and a lot of other people's boss. People who made their living selling drugs. Originally from Cuba, then from Miami when he grew up and found the opportunities for financial improvement limited after Fidel Castro came to power. Now he was in New Orleans, head of a drug cartel that was one of the wealthiest in the hemisphere, with tentacles reaching from the jungles of several South American countries clear into the condos and corridors of Washington, D.C.

Fidel Guterez was handy with a machete, like many of his ex-countrymen, only he cut throats instead of sweet sugar cane and he preferred the scent of cocaine in his nostrils to that of Havana gold leaf.

Every Friday evening after regular business hours, Guterez personally oversaw the transportation of the weekly take from his operation to the bank that was pleased to launder it for him, in return for a comfortable commission. A very slick operation that had been in place for over twenty years, even before his present "partner" had taken over his end of the deal. The operation that Reader had overheard the Cuban discussing back at Angola. He'd not only learned all about the operation for his bag of cookies, but arranged an introduction to the man whose apartment he was now in. Octavio will do anything for a buck, the man had said. This had proved to be accurate.

At the Derbigny State Bank on Baronne Street, in the heart of the CBD, Guterez and Clifford St. Ives would sit in leather chairs in St. Ives's lushly appointed offices and snort lines of sweet white powder while Guterez's men brought in bag after bag of greenbacks to be put in the banker's personal office safe. St. Ives enjoyed his own coffee setup, not some prissy cappachino machine made in San Francisco, but a hot plate and coffee maker that emptied into a thermos carafe. He would time the boiling of the milk to coincide with the moment when the coffee finished, and he would pour equal parts of both into huge china cups. Cafe au lait the right way.

"Yes," Octavio had often told Reader, "these two gentlemen have a fine time while we're unloading the money. They have a great time while we break our backs."

Octavio referred to this conversation again. "I'll be thinking of that this coming Friday when you are taking his money from him. Are you going to make Mr. St. Ives carry his own money out?"

"I'll tell you all about it afterward," Reader said. He finished his drink and poured another from the bottle. No water this time. Reader said, "Tell me how it goes. Everything."

"Man, I told you. Ten times, I told you."

"Tell me again."

Octavio shrugged, reached into his shirt pocket, took out a joint and lighted it. He swung the other leg up and sank deeper into the chair.

"First we go to the warehouse. The one in Chalmette, on Parks Road. That's where Senór Guterez has his office, where everything happens. Shit comes in—shit goes out.

"Then we load up the limo. You should see this limo. It's got a false floor, half-inch steel, holds a ton of money. One in front, one in back. Another one under the trunk. Heavy-duty springs, thing looks weird. Nine million dollars, we packed in there before. One time eleven. You know how much eleven million dollars weighs? A lot, amigo, a lot. We pack it in there and we go into N'Awlins on Saint Claude. You want the route again?"

He squinted through the smoke.

"Good. Because they change the route all the time. They not dumb, these fellas. There's two cops, that's their area. They come around, watch for us while we unload at the bank. That's two rich cops, amigo, who ain't gonna be fishing for no sheepshead off a pier when they retire! They watch me and my compadres break our backs unloading and they make more money than we do and we do the hard work. A union is what we need. Maybe the cops' union, eh?"

He laughed and pinched out the end of the joint with his thumb and finger and put it back in his shirt pocket.

"We put it in a safe in C.J.'s office. That's what Senór Guterez calls him, C.J.. They're best friends, these two. It's a special safe that St. Ives has. Then we leave. We don't stay too long. This isn't what you'd call a social occasion. Mr. St. Ives does something with the money after we leave. He gets it in the regular vault or something. That I don't know. It gets to the Caymans. A special bank. That's Mr. St. Ives's department. I know one thing about Mr. St. Ives. He likes his nose candy. Senór Guterez— sure, he likes a toot himself—but Mr. St. Ives—he *really* likes it, you know? It makes the boss nervous, I think. I heard him say something one time."

He swung his legs around and off the chair arm. "How you gon' do it, Senór Reader? I showed you mine, now you show me yours. Eh?"

Reader knocked back a slug of his drink. "You're going to like this, Octavio. I'm wiring St. Ives with a bomb. A bomb I'm controlling by remote control. He doesn't bring the money to us, he gets turned into something you wouldn't recognize. See? He does the robbery himself. Or else."

Octavio was impressed. "Reader, you are a smart man. The smartest man I have ever known. I salute you!" He raised his glass in a toast of admiration. The two men clinked their glasses together.

"Glad you like it, my friend. Now. I'll be seeing you in Miami Saturday morning. Eight sharp. At the Fontainebleau in the coffee shop. For a moment only. I'll give you a key to a locker. I'm thinking Rio, right now. I've heard some good things about Rio. You ever been there? You could help me with the lingo. See what you can do, line up a plane. Get somebody doesn't ask questions."

"A plane's going to be difficult, Reader. Expensive."

"I give a shit about the expense. Can you do it?"

"With enough money, yeah."

"You'll have the money, Octavio. Let me know how much."

Octavio shrugged. "Whatever you say, my friend. Say," he said, grinning broadly, "I think I got a disease, Reader. Polio."

Reader stared at him. You could never tell when Octavio was serious.

"Yes," the Cuban said, his grin widening. "I'm sure I have polio. I have all the symptoms. One of my legs is a tiny bit shorter than the other two." He laughed aloud, slapping his knee at his wit. Reader smiled back at him, even though he didn't think it was that funny.

At the door Reader paused and said, "You be sure and call me if the routine gets changed. You got the number. You know," he added, "you might want to consider adding a couple other colors to this place. Get yourself a black couch or something. The place looks like it's hemorrhaging." He didn't know whether Octavio laughed and he didn't much care.

One of the girls had left the pool, but the other remained behind and smiled as he walked by.

Behind him, he heard Octavio at the door calling out to the girls at the pool. "Suzanne. Are you mad with me, my little bonita seniorita? I'm ashamed of myself. Won't you come and talk? I'd like to show you how sorry I am. I am so worried, Suzanne. I think I have a disease. Come up and I'll tell you my symptoms. You will be *simpatico*, I think."

On the outside wall by the parking lot, Reader spotted a payphone. He got out his little black book and dialed a number. When a voice answered, he asked for Fidel Guterez. When he came on, Reader told the man some interesting things, in a voice so soft that someone standing next to him would've had trouble hearing him even if he knew Spanish, the language Reader was using. He might have heard the name "Octavio." And in a peculiar voice. Like he was trying to disguise his normal one.

This was the chancy part of the job. If the man simply killed Octavio after he'd gotten the information out of him and then killed C.J., it was all over. He was betting on what he'd learned about Guterez. That he was a man who liked to play games, liked to think he was in control. The kind of guy who would have some fun with information like he'd just given him.

After he hung up, Reader glanced back at the pool. The girl was gone. That polio line must have worked.

He wondered if his phone call had. The whole plan depended on it.

17

TRAVEL OUT OF New Orleans to the Pontchartrain Causeway that stretches twenty-six miles over the huge lake, dead from years and years of chemical dumping except for the occasional sand shark that travels up into it from the Gulf. A lake, once beautiful and teeming with whole families swimming and dozens of anglers with lines out along its shores, incredible and lush with trout and bass and blue crabs: now a watery desert. Signs every few hundred yards on the beaches warning of the dangers of swimming in its highly-contaminated waters. A glimpse of an old amusement park, once alive with bright-eyed children, now rusting and abandoned, as barren and sterile as the lake on whose shores it perched.

Louisiana, a state built and maintained with the oily lubricant of graft and bribes. A state with plenty of anti-polluting laws on its books, most of which were easily circumvented with enough money in the right places. Go across the bridge and land on the other side in Mandeville, the home of the state insane asylum and, in the countryside adjacent, the estates of many of the owners of the chemical plants and other industrial concerns whose refuse had murdered with cold, calculating avarice almost all life in Pontchartrain's waters. Their mansions, set back on long, winding lanes, hidden from the public byways, were everywhere, even though passersby rarely glimpsed them.

In one such mansion, possibly the grandest of them all, was a smartly-dressed woman, who at that moment was removing the white lace shoulder wrap she had purchased just the day before at Maison Blanche and placing it on the back of the Queen Anne chair she was sitting on, her legs drawn up and crossed beneath her. Pure Irish lace, imported . . . and such a steal at only six hundred dollars.

Sarah St. Ives looked down the long, black oak table at her wheelchair-bound grandfather. To her left she could see Blue Boy and several other horses grazing in the pasture on the other side of a whitewashed fence. In the other room she could hear Cora, her grandfather's maid, rattling cutlery. A pleasant breeze wafted through the open French doors, bearing the smell of freshly cut hay.

She had just finished telling her grandfather everything. Her anger had overheated her, causing her to remove the wrap. Perspiration could ruin a fine piece of lace like that. Sarah St. Ives always took care of her things.

"That bastard!"

"Calm down, Grandfather. I didn't tell you this to make you have a another stroke. I know what to do. I want to know if you'll help."

They had chosen the drawing room to sip sherry and discuss the state of her marriage. Her grandfather had asked Cora to bring them the bottle and close the doors behind her. Sarah glanced around the room, recalling the times growing up when her grandfather would excuse himself from whatever gathering it was to retreat to this room with expensive men in expensive suits. State senators and even a U.S. Senator had been in this room. The governor, often. Captains of industry. Oil men. Men who made the wheels of commerce turn the way they wanted. Many of the men who had helped destroy the lake she had just driven over. They always closed the doors, and she had always wondered what they talked about. Now it was she who was sitting in the drawing room with the doors closed.

"I'm going to divorce him, Grandfather. My problem is how to get him out of the bank. Without anything. I don't want him to have a dime. Can we do it?"

Titus Fuller Derbigny was in a wheelchair, but his back was straight and strong, his white hair neatly cut and combed. The suit he wore came directly from Bond Street in London and had not a wrinkle in it. The perfectly knotted Sulka tie was the same chocolate color as his eyes.

Although his legs were useless, he still had full use of a razor-sharp mind that was legendary in Louisiana financial and political circles.

"I can't believe that cur!" he thundered. "Fouling his own nest! A decent man would never have a mistress that worked for him. Especially when his own wife owns the bank he and his chippy earn their living from! It's all because of that damned Edwards," speaking of the governor of the state, a man who openly kept mistresses, both in Baton Rouge and New Orleans. Not only was Edwards's own wife aware of his peccadilloes, but the entire state was as well.

He was livid. His granddaughter meant more to him than anyone else, more than his own son had when he was alive. His granddaughter wasn't flawed like her father had been. The fact that his son-in-law kept a mistress was barely worth notice. Most men in his position in New Orleans enjoyed a lady friend or two, but there was an unspoken law that a gentleman kept his affairs separate from his home and family. Private, not public. And since this was his wife's bank, it was the same as her home.

"Of course I'll help you, sugar girl."

"Well, Grandfather . . . " Sarah took a sip of her sherry. "It might not be that easy. Who knows what a judge might do, the way circumstances are today?"

"The circumstances are fine, darlin'. This is still Louisiana. *My* state."

"Well, Grandfather, that's worse. Did you forget about that damned old Napoleonic Code? The man is king. The husband can get everything in a divorce even if he doesn't deserve a penny."

Titus Derbigny stared without expression at his granddaughter. "Hand me that phone, little girl. Quit worryin.' I want you to dial this number for me. My fingers . . . shake a bit nowadays. I'm calling William. I want you to tell him you want to sell me your shares back for a dollar. Don't worry—" He saw the look of consternation that crossed her face.

"It's only temporary, sugar baby. Until we get the divorce behind us. That won't take long. When I get finished talking to William, I want you to dial Judge Foster's number for me. It's in that book over on the sideboard. I want to make sure he gets your case on his docket. You rest easy, Sarah. It'll all be taken care of. There's something else we've got."

"What's that, Grandfather?"

"His background." He looked at her sharply to see how she received that.

"How'd you . . . why . . . I didn't . . . "

"How'd I know about that? Sugar, it's my business to know everything that affects this family. I knew about Mr. St. Ives after your second date with him. Want me to tell you where he took you, what you wore?"

"Well, then, how come . . . "

"Why didn't I say anything? Sugar, your happiness means everything to me. If you wanted this man and that's all there was bad about him, I wasn't going to stand in your way. How do you think he ended up with such a good biography—a complete work of fiction if I do say so—no, darlin' girl, your grandfather has always watched over you and I will again. You can count on it. Now." He patted her knee. "Let's you and I make some phone calls, take care of this contemptible coonass. He needs to know who's in control. Who's always been in control. I'll tell you some other things about your husband you didn't know."

She went over, bent down and put her arms around her grandfather.

"I knew you'd take care of everything, Grandfather."

"Now, you're going to learn how the Derbignys operate, sugar girl. How we got to where we are. It's none too soon to learn, especially since you'll be taking over the bank. That's something you need to do immediately. No use in wasting any more time. Strike before the enemy knows what hits him. That's the secret of success in any war. And don't kid yourself, darlin'—this is a war. This is what you have to do. I want you to do this exactly like I tell you."

She listened, fascinated, as he made a series of calls. One, she wasn't allowed to hear.

"This one," he said, apology in his voice. "Is better that you don't know about. I'll make this call, and then you go home. Once you kick that no-good husband out, you come back here to be with your family for a few days. We'll take good care of you." She left the room dutifully, and only heard her grandfather's greeting as she closed the doors behind her.

"Buenos dias, senòr. We've got a . . . "

When she'd entered the room, Sarah had felt like her grandfather's equal. By the time she left to let him make his phone call, she felt exactly as she had when she was a little girl.

A feeling she hated. A feeling she was not going to have much longer.

18

GRADY WASN'T YET in the mood to start hitting the bars so early in the afternoon. Doing the legwork he planned to do to find out . . . what? He didn't have any kind of special plan. Not much of one, anyway. Try to locate Reader Kincaid, that was the only thing he could think of to do, now that he was in New Orleans. Once he found him, then what? Several scenarios presented themselves, most of which involved beating the motherfucker half to death until he confessed to being the one who had stabbed Jack. Maybe go ahead and cancel his ticket.

That was bullshit and he knew it.

He dug out the bottle of Jim Beam he'd packed and poured himself a shot in one of the plastic cups he found in the bathroom. Three-fourths of the time it was unbearably loud with the noise of airplanes coming in to land. They sounded as if they were ten feet over the roof, for good reason: the Day's Inn was directly across the street from the airport runways, maybe less than a hundred yards from where they touched down. It was no wonder he'd gotten such a good deal on the room.

He had to admit he didn't have much of an idea what he would do even if he could find the man. Beating or torturing someone, even someone like Kincaid, who had almost killed his brother, wasn't an option.

"You got to face that mirror each morning, boys," his father had preached over and over. "Play by the rules, and you can sleep at night."

Well, he'd played by the damn rules, all his life, and what had it gotten him? Broke and half-blind. Some reward. His own father had hardly prospered playing by the rules. Ended up dying of a heart attack and leaving barely enough to bury him. Same with his mother. Even the guy who'd shot Grady in the face—the act that forced him into an early medical retirement—that asshole got out of prison in less than three years. He'd see him every once in awhile, staggering out of a bar usually, and once they met face to face. The guy openly snickered at him. He cocked his thumb and finger like a pistol and pointed it at Grady. "Pow," he said, dropping his thumb, and it was all Grady could do to control himself, keep from punching his lights out, or worse.

No, it wasn't fair. Not fair at all. All his life, his father preached to his sons, "Play by the rules, boys. Keep your integrity. Give up your integrity and you give up who you are. An honest man might not have much in the way of material goods, but he can sure face that mirror every morning with a clear conscience."

Sure. He'd kept his integrity and here he was, your basically unemployable cripple. Great reward. Jack, too, kept his integrity and there he was lying in a hospital bed, probably paralyzed for life. If he lived.

It wasn't the first time he'd questioned his father's credo. But through everything, through all the graft and corruption and the rewards to the practitioners—rewards he saw firsthand every day—he'd held onto that integrity. For what? *So I can face myself in the mirror each morning when I shave? Was it worth it?* He thought of all the money he'd passed up on the job. There'd been plenty of chances. He knew cops who were set up for life. Had swimming pools in the back yard, and not the above-ground kind. Vacations in the Bahamas. All you had to do was look the other way. An envelope full of money every week, as long as you played ball. Not him. Not Mister Honesty. He could sure use some graft money now. He wondered if he would take it if it was still available.

It was hard, sometimes. It was damned hard. Now in particular. With a pile of debts that was growing into Mount Everest every day Jack lay in that hospital bed.

A memory drifted up in his mind. Jack walking a mile home a month after he was discharged from the Navy on a leg broken in three places. He walked a mile on a broken leg! His brother hadn't yet bought a car and had walked to the girl's house he was seeing. Jack told him the story the next day after he'd come back from the doctor with a cast on his leg.

"I get there," he said, laughing. "And there's this other guy there. Larry Fuckface." He laughed again. Grady knew Larry Gifford. A guy about the same age as his brother, but who'd avoided the service by getting married and immediately fathering a child solely for that purpose.

"Her parents were gone and ol' Larry was sitting at the kitchen table with her, drinking beer. When I first went in, it was kind of tense. I knew why he was there and so did she. Trying to get in her pants. Fucker!" Grady remembered Jack laughing as he told the story.

"So, I go up to him and say, 'What's up, Larry? Aren't you supposed to be somewhere else? Like with your wife and little girl maybe?

"Well, this asshole gets up and takes a poke at me and we spar around like a couple of John Waynes. End up on the porch. Fucker surprised me. He didn't have that bad of a punch. Hand me those, Grady." He pointed to the pack of cigarettes on the nightstand. "Well, Janice is squawking and screaming and we're dancing around on the porch and I put everything into it and swung from clear back in center field. I was going to lay him out, little brother." He tapped out a cigarette and Grady reached for the packet of matches on the stand and lit one, holding it over for his brother. Jack took a deep drag, turned the cigarette around and blew smoke at the ember, making it flare.

"Only I didn't." He grinned then winced as he shifted his weight in the bed and a pain reached him from his leg. "Missed him completely. I swung so fucking hard I spun around and fell off the porch. Right away, my damn leg hurt like hell. Took all the fight out of me. Besides, Janice wasn't that big of a deal. Right about then, my leg was killing me and I figured they probably deserved each other, so I took off. Walked all the way home." Grady could tell he was proud of that.

"Remember when I came in last night?" Grady did. He was in bed, but the commotion in the kitchen brought him running. Jack was sitting in a chair and their father was cutting his blue jeans off of him. His leg had swelled so much they couldn't get them off. Their mom was yelling and crying at the same time and Dad was cussing up a blue streak.

"Remember what Dad said? He said my leg couldn't be broken because you couldn't walk on a broken leg."

That was exactly what Dad had said. Grady'd been there, heard him say it. Their father helped Jack into his bed and said if his leg was still hurting in the morning they'd take him to the doctor, but all it was only a bad sprain. It wasn't possible to walk on a broken leg, he kept saying.

They'd all been surprised. By morning, Jack's leg had swollen to twice its size and was all purplish and black around the ankle.

Broken in three places, the doctor said, showing them the x-ray. Two of the bones are small and can't be set, but we'll get this big one here, he said.

That was Jack, Grady thought. Tough all the way. That wasn't the end of it. Six weeks later, the doctor took off the original cast and put on a walking cast and ordered Jack to take it easy. "Only walk to the bathroom," he said. Of course, Jack didn't listen. He went dancing that very night, over at the Methodist where they had Friday night dances in the summer. And rebroke the leg.

This time their father was really smoking. But Grady and Jack had another story to share.

When he left his motel room, he slammed the door shut as hard as he could. An elderly couple coming out of their room a few doors up looked at him and the man stepped in front of the woman as if to shield her.

"Sorry," Grady mumbled at them, getting into his car. He left rubber as he whipped out onto Veterans Highway . . . and swerved the car off the side of the road, braking furiously as the shadow of a 707 passed directly over him, so close he swore he could see the passenger's faces.

"Motherfuck!" he yelled out the window, steering back onto the pavement. Who was the idiot who decided to build a runway this close to a highway? Planes didn't look to be any more than fifty feet off the ground when they passed over the traffic. If you didn't have to worry about somebody shooting you or sticking you in this town, you had to worry about being wiped out by a pilot's miscalculation when you were out for a Sunday drive. He'd be glad to be back in Dayton when this was over, he decided, feeling the thin film of perspiration on his forehead cooling in the air-conditioning.

While he was putting down a restaurant cup of coffee a few minutes later, he studied his map. The prison at Angola looked easy enough to get to. He thought about phoning first, getting permission, but decided to just chance he could find someone in the administration who would be willing to talk to him. It didn't look like all that long of a drive and it was a sunny day. He welcomed the idea of being in the car's air conditioning for an hour or two instead of pounding the pavement in this godawful heat.

He hoped he wasn't setting off on a wild-goose chase, wasting valuable time, but he didn't know quite what else to do. It was a place to start.

19

HALFWAY OVER THE Atchafalyah Swamp on an elevated U.S. Highway 10, Grady had to slam on the brakes. One minute the sky was as blue and clear as a movie starlet's contact lenses then suddenly a dense fog bank appeared. He hadn't been paying attention, enraptured as he was by the swamp scenery on both sides. As far as the eye could see stretched cypress trees draped with Spanish moss, hummocked bayous and stretches of open water dotted with islands of marsh grass. Soaring herons, stalking egrets, brilliant flamingoes, dozens of alligators visible even from the height of the road and a car traveling in excess of eighty-five miles per hour. And still being passed! He was so engrossed in the eerie beauty of the Atchafalyah that he failed to see the solid wall of mist approaching until it was just a few yards in front of him. The thickest fog he'd ever experienced. The moisture in it was so great he had to turn on his windshield wipers. What amazed him were the cars passing him after he braked and slowed to a speed of thirty which still felt too fast for the zero visibility. One after another and they all had to be going at least sixty! And there was no place to pull off. Occasionally, to the right, a ghostly apparition would appear, startling the bejesus out of him until a nanosecond later he would realize he'd seen one of the cypress trees. Fucking Land of the Lost, he thought, his head aching from the intense concentration of watching the siderail and straining to keep in the far right lane without going over the side. Fucking alligators were down there licking their chops, he bet. He wondered how many cars had gone sailing into the swamp in this kind of business.

And then, just as suddenly as it had appeared, the fog vanished and he was driving out of it into brilliant sunlight. A red pickup truck screamed around him, horn blaring, and Grady found himself grinning weakly at the disappearing vehicle and the arm sticking out of the passenger side saluting him, Italian-style.

His watch read a quarter past ten when Grady turned off 10 just past Baton Rouge onto State Highway 61. The fog had cost him at least half an hour, he figured, but since he didn't have an appointment, it didn't really matter. Twenty minutes later, he was cruising through the town of St. Francisville. He stopped at an Amoco station for directions and the attendant started giving them to him before he even opened his mouth.

"Just go to the light at U.S. 61 and state road 10, go north three miles and take a left at Tunica Trace. That's state road 66. Stay right on that and you'll end up at the front gate. You got a relative up at Angola?"

"How'd you know what I wanted?"

There was a definite smirk on the man's face. "You didn't pull in at the pumps so I figured you were after directions. The only directions anyone around here ever asks for are out to the prison. I guess you're one of those Yankees think we're all bubbas, aren't you?"

He thanked the man, even though he didn't much feel like it, and continued out of town, hoping the man hadn't been playing a joke on him.

He hadn't been.

The place was frickin' enormous. Went on as far as the eye could see. He was surprised to see there were no walls, not like the prisons he was used to. Just fences, albeit not your suburban chain-link affair, but heavy-duty steel that had to be twelve feet high, topped off with barbed and razor wire.

At the front gate he explained his business and was led by a uniformed guard to a one-story concrete block building where he was told to wait in the visitor's waiting room. There were upwards of fifty people in the room, mostly families, mostly black. Folks visiting inmates, he guessed. He'd asked permission to see the warden at the gate. No, he didn't have an appointment, he said in answer to the receptionist's question.

It wasn't more than five minutes before an attractive brunette in eyeglasses and a white sweater and slacks entered the room and offered her hand.

"Hi!" she said with a cheerful smile, sticking out her hand. He shook it, admiring her firm grip. This was a woman of personality and warmth, not at all what he would have expected at an institution like this. "I'm Cathy Johns. Warden Burl's not in today. Over at the capital, chasing the impossible dream." Seeing his puzzled face, she explained, "More funds for this place." The corner of her mouth twisted sarcastically. "Perhaps I can be of some assistance?"

He explained why he was there. She murmured sympathetically when he told her about his brother, but didn't interrupt. When he finished, he said, "Look, I know I don't have any jurisdiction down here, but I'm just looking for anything that can help me get this guy."

Her eyes turned serious. "I remember Kincaid vividly," she said. "There's a lot of men in here that should have been cut loose before that man. Truth is, he's one of the few I wouldn't be sorry to see come back. Follow me."

Grady followed her clicking heels back to her office. Inside, she indicated a chair in front of her desk for him to take. She went around and sat in the swivel chair on the other side.

"Coffee?" She reached for a coffee pot on a small stand beside her.

"No, thanks," he said. "This place is huge!"

"Too big," she agreed, nodding solemnly. "Over 5,000 inmates."

"My God. How many staff?"

She picked up a piece of paper on her desk and glanced at it. "Well, we just had a budget cut and had to lay off thirty guards. That leaves us with—" she picked up a pencil and jotted down figures. Looking up, she smiled brightly, and said, "—exactly one thousand four hundred and sixty-six guards. That doesn't count the medical staff, the people who work in the mail room, the chaplains, the clerks and administration folks in this building or the business office. Some other personnel. We have twenty-one administrative officers. I'm not including Warden Burl, his deputy warden and the twelve assistant wardens. Or their assistants."

"Good Lord." The figures astounded him. "This has to be the biggest prison in the country."

"I believe it is," she said. "The sad thing is we keep getting bigger. Louisiana is one of those states that takes being tough on crime to the limit. Over half of these men will die here."

She slid the paper into a side drawer. "Listen, Mr. Fogarty. I'd help you if I could. It's just that I can't allow unauthorized personnel to view any of the inmate's records. Even if they're no longer inmates. I'd need a warrant to do that. Some kind of official order from a judge."

Fuck. The official run-around was the same here as it was everywhere else in the universe. He started to speak when she held up her hand again. On some people, that gesture might have come across as imperious, but on her it didn't seem that way at all. Just a mannerism that said, hey, I don't have time to waste on trivialities.

"Like I said, Kincaid's one man I wouldn't mind seeing back here. And I don't say that often. But he's just a bad one. Very bad. I'm truly sorry about your brother." She looked away, out her window, as if remembering something. She got up. "Come here, please."

Puzzled, Grady did as she asked. He followed her gaze out the window. Her office looked out over an exercise yard. Men in institutional whites, others in jeans and denim shirts, were scattered everywhere in small groups, engaged in various activities. He could see chess boards on picnic tables, a concrete area where men were lifting weights, a basketball court. Two guys in headgear sparring in an outdoor ring. He estimated there were about three hundred convicts in the yard. Typical prison scene. Looked like most he'd seen, except for the lack of walls at this place. Only high fences with razor wire. He wondered what their escape percentage was. Then he noticed the towers and the outlines in the sky of men with rifles. Outside the east fence, he saw a uniformed man riding a horse.

"See those men?" She was staring out into the exercise yard.

He nodded, wondering what she was leading up to.

"I know almost all of them by name. This is the main prison and we have about 2,600 men in here. The rest are housed in the five outlying camps. You know what? A lot of those guys would pose almost no danger to society if released. Oh, sure, there's those that'd be back in here in a week, but I'd bet a year's salary on a whole lot of them. You know why they're not on the street?"

Here it came. He should have recognized a liberal when he saw she didn't come equipped with a snarl. He didn't say anything to her question. What was he supposed to say?

"Louisiana is one of a very few states that gives felons true life. Fifty-two percent of all the men in Angola will die here. I'm not saying all of them should be set free. But a large percentage should be. And they won't. You know why?"

"Tough parole board?" he ventured.

"Ha!" For the first time, there was no warmth in her eyes. "That, and tough politicians. Or at least that's the way they try to come across. Lock 'em up, throw away the key. That's the attitude. And for what? Did you know that crime has gone down in this country? And yet, we're locking more and more people up for longer stretches. It's the media. Politicians. Makes for good theater. At these guys' loss." She waved her hand toward the yard and walked back over and sat down. Grady followed suit, reclaiming the chair he'd sat in earlier.

She went on in that vein for several more minutes, and even as Grady began to see the injustices as real, there wasn't much he could do about them. He wasn't even a citizen of the state, for gosh sakes. Besides, all he wanted was some background information on Reader, maybe something he could find in the records of his incarceration here and she'd already told him to view those would be impossible. Preparing to make his good-byes and leave, he stood. He stuck out his hand. "Well, Ms. Johns, this has been real informative, but I've got to be going."

She looked up from behind her desk but didn't get up to shake his hand. Instead, she made another of her now familiar waves of the hand, indicating he should take his seat. "Hold on," she said. "I can't allow you to look at his records, but there's nothing that says you can't talk to any of Reader's acquaintances."

He sat back down. "But I don't know any of his acquaintances."

Her mouth turned up in an open grin. "Figured that. However, I do." She reached in a desk drawer and pulled out a pad of paper and began writing on it with a pen on the desktop. "Here," she said, sliding the pad across to him. "If you were to request a visit with this man, I believe that could be arranged." She paused. "If he's willing."

He turned the notepad around. *FRANK CABRINI*, it read, printed in all capitals. "He own a housing project in Chicago?" he asked, a slight smile on his own face.

"Not that I know of," she replied. "But he owns half of New Orleans. He's the Mafia don. First one we ever had in here. Usually mob guys this high get federal time but this guy screwed up. Got caught with a little girl, which made it state time. He knows Reader as well as anyone. Reader did a few jobs for him while he was here, is the rumor. Reader didn't have many friends as I recall. This man knows as much as anyone about him. You make an official request for a visit, I'll see what I can do. It probably depends on if he's bored today or not."

She opened another desk drawer and retrieved a form, which she handed across. "Just put his name in the box indicated and fill out the rest. It'll take about a half hour. They're still at breakfast. I wouldn't interrupt him during a meal or he might not want to talk to you." She smiled. "These old capos, they like their food."

She was a gem. He filled out the form, gave it over, and went back out to the waiting room. There seemed to be a whole different set of visitors from the first time he'd been in there. Some little kids running around, a huge black woman screaming at them, which they cheerfully ignored. Half an hour later, a skinny, uniformed guard walked into the office and asked if he was Mr. Fogarty.

"Miz Johns must like you," the guard said, after relieving him of all his possessions except his cigarettes and a book of matches, leading him down a long hallway and then outside. They were headed to a large Quonset hut, looked like. "She's letting you go to Cabrini's work assignment. Usually, you'd have to go to the regular visiting room."

"Where's he work?"

The guard snickered. "He's a barber. Can you imagine? The boss of bosses cutting hair!" They entered the Quonset hut, which turned out to be a gym. It smelled like gyms everywhere. A group of men were playing hoops on the basketball court, traditional shirts versus skins, and in a far corner two men sparred in a boxing ring. Other men were jogging around the perimeter of the large room. On one side, three small offices were partitioned off.

It was true. The godfather was a barber.

Cabrini's "barber shop" was a single office room in the recreation facility just off Ash-1 Dorm. A deep sink which had more rust showing on its surface than white porcelain, an old-timey barrel hydraulic barber chair, the kind Grady vaguely remembered from the barber shop of his youth, and a lime-green cabinet with a razor, shears, some bottles and a couple of combs showing through the little glass window. That was it, furnishings-wise. The chair had definitely seen better days. The brown imitation leather was cracked in a dozen places, gray tape covering the wounds. A razor strop, blackened with age, hung from a clip on the side of the chair.

"Grady Fogarty, Mr. Cabrini," he said, offering his hand to the small, wizened man who sat in his chair, reading the *Times-Picayune* and puffing on a non-filtered Camel which he held daintily between the tips of his forefinger and thumb and sipped on like it was a straw. The way he was smoking the cigarette made Grady think of the way young kids did, first time they lighted up. There was the hugest man Grady had ever seen, clad in a guard's uniform which was straining at the seams across his massive chest, sitting in a chair in the corner, deep in an issue of *True Police Stories*. He'd barely looked up when Grady entered the room, before going back to the article he was deeply intent on. The room smelled like Old Spice and then Grady saw the familiar white bottle up on top of the tool cabinet.

Cabrini was dressed in a starched and pressed white shirt and tight jeans that were creased as well. His prison number was stenciled above the left breast pocket. He wore white socks and highly polished black wingtips, which seemed greatly out of place with the rest of the attire. Captain of Industry in stevedore mode, Grady thought, whimsically. Dapper little dude! The old man folded his newspaper and slipped it between his hip and the side of the chair. He stared intently at Grady for a moment, then turned his head slightly and said out of the corner of his mouth, "You can wait outside, Billy."

"Okay, Mr. Cabrini," the giant said, getting up and bending the corner of the page he was on before he closed the magazine and put it under his arm. He went over to the wall cabinet and removed the razor and pair of shears, slipping them into his pants pocket. The look he gave Grady could only be described as blank. "I'll be right outside."

Once the guard had closed the door behind him, the old man said, "Billy's a laugh-a-minute. Mr. Personality." He laughed, waved his hand to indicate that Grady could take the chair Billy had just vacated. "He played football at LSU. All-American his senior year. Busted his knee in his first pro practice. Which is why he's working here. Plus which he can barely read or write." He laughed again. "So. What's your game? What is it you want from me? You're a cop, they tell me."

He looked frail, but Grady had seen his kind before. You couldn't be fooled by the exterior. This guy was cool as new sheets. You could see it in his eyes. Eyes that never smiled, even when his lips did. Grady pulled the chair close to the barber chair and offered his pack of Marlboros to Cabrini. The old man shook one out, tore off the filter and lit it. He stuck the pack in his shirt pocket.

"Camels are my brand," he said. "It's funny. You tear the filter off a Camel filtertip and it doesn't taste like a Camel. But, you tear the filter off a Marlboro, it does. Tell me, what the fuck does that mean?"

Grady shrugged. "Beats me. Same company makes both, maybe?" He didn't know. "Maybe they put the low-grade in their Camel filtertips and the good stuff in their Marlboros?"

The old man grunted, took a deep drag off the cigarette and began hacking until his eyes watered. He shook out another cigarette and tore off the filter and laid it down in the ashtray in the arm of the chair. Hard-core chain smoker, Grady surmised. Getting the next one ready. Fuck! He was going to quit for sure, once this was all over.

"I understand you're a friend of Reader Kincaid," Grady began. "I'll be honest. I'm not. He almost killed my brother. Maybe he has. My brother's not out of the woods yet. That's why I'm here. I want to find him, talk to him. They tell me you might know where I should look."

The old man stared at him. Grady held his eyes for a moment, then looked away. "Yeah," the mafia don said finally. "I know 'im. Is that it? That all you wanted to know? If I was a friend of Reader's?"

Grady looked back. The guy's stare was relentless. Look like that would shake up the devil himself. "I was hoping you could tell me something about him."

Cabrini picked up the second cigarette from the ashtray, lit it from the first one then mashed the first one out. "You mean, tell you something you can use to bust him with?"

Grady matched his stare and this time it was the old man who looked away first, a slight smile curling up. The kind that said the wearer felt superior. "Yeah. That's exactly what I want you to do. My brother—"

Cabrini snorted. "That supposed to make me cry or something?" He stood up. "Look, Mr. Policeman, I thought this might be a nice little break in my day, but all you're doing is yanking my chain. I give a fuck about your brother." He turned toward the door. "Billy!"

The door opened and the massive guard appeared, filling the entire space with his frame.

"Billy, we're done here. I wanna go to the library. Popeye here wants to go buy some flowers, put 'em on his brother's grave." He laughed, a tittering sound like a car starting. At the door, he turned. "You know, at least you were honest. You didn't give me no bullshit about what you wanted. Tell you what. I feel generous today. Also, I don't think you're smart enough to figure Reader out. He's smarter than ten cops." He walked over, took the pack of Marlboros from his pocket and stuck them in Grady's own shirt pocket. "Plus, this might make it interesting. See if you got what it takes to catch a real genius." He took out his own pack of Camels and lighted up. "Look, Dickless Tracy, I tell you what I'll do. I'll give you one of those clues you guys get all hot and bothered over. Listen up close." He stepped up to Grady, leaned in close and whispered, "The answer's in Shakespeare, my friend. Look it up. The play where the guy says, 'A rose is a rose by any other name.'" Grady's stomach rolled from the sudden stench of garlic.

Cabrini stared at Grady for a minute and Grady thought he'd never in his life seen eyes with so little expression in them. Then he spoke, his words flat and devoid of expression. "You think Reader's a bad guy, don't you?" Grady didn't reply. The answer was obvious.

Cabrini pressed his lips together tightly and shook his head slowly back and forth. "You're wrong, cop. Reader's a good guy. You ever figure all this out, you'll see."

Spryer than Grady would have thought, Cabrini turned, walked away and was out the door before he could ask him what the hell that was supposed to mean. Just as he reached the door himself, the guard who had escorted him to the room appeared.

"Visit's over, sir," he said. Grady could just see the old capo going across the expanse of grass to a low-lying building across the way, jabbering something to Billy, who kept nodding and nodding. A second later, they disappeared inside. Over the door, Grady could just make out a faded wooden sign that read *Library*.

On the way back, two men pushing a stainless steel cart passed them and they had to move off the sidewalk to let them pass. They were both dressed in white smocks and their heads were covered with something that looked like it was made out of white gauze. Grady's escort caught his raised eyebrows and said, "Inmate cooks. They're taking meals over to the hostel. I had that detail once. Fuck that shit! Bunch of old cocksuckers dying, half of them got AIDS. Pays a premium to work that gig, but fuck it. Life's too short."

What a total waste of time this was, Grady thought grimly, following the guard back up to the front of the building. They passed Cathy Johns' office, but he didn't see her anywhere around. He signed out, got back his billfold and loose change and was out the front door of the administration building, into the blinding sunlight, halfway across the parking lot and thinking about where he could get some lunch, when he heard his name called. He turned around to see Johns walking fast toward him. He stopped and waited for her.

"Well?" she said, somewhat breathless when she came up. "Learn anything useful?"

He shook his head. "Guy just screwed around with me. Quoted Shakespeare. Only, I don't think it was Shakespeare. Listen, thanks for your help. I appreciate it. I know your hands are tied."

"What'd he say?"

"Weird stuff. A rose by any other name is still a rose. I ask you, does that make any sense?"

A thoughtful look came into her eyes. "Maybe. I was just looking at Reader's sheet." She looked around, almost as if to see if anyone was listening. "Look, Mr. Fogarty, I think probably Cabrini's known Reader and his family since he was a little boy. I think I know what he was talking about. The thing is, I'm not sure if I can legally tell you what I know. It might amount to the same thing as letting you read his record. It's not that I don't want to help you—" She looked like she was struggling to make a decision. "Oh, hell! Look, let me put it this way. When I was going through Kincaid's sheet, I saw something. It might be what Cabrini was referring to." She looked thoughtful. "Although, I really don't see how it's going to help you."

"What is it!" he snapped. Immediately, he was apologetic. "Sorry," he stammered. "I'm just desperate for anything that can help me. What is it you saw?"

She was quiet for a moment. A pair of men in guard's uniforms got out of a car in the parking lot and walked their way.

"Hi Teddy, Jim," she said as they came abreast. They touched their fingers to their baseball caps as one and said, "Miz Johns. Nice day."

When they'd passed, she looked back at Grady. "Look. I feel uncomfortable telling you this. Tell you what. I'll kind of point you in the right way. If I were you—" she paused and brought her hand up to shade her eyes. "—I'd check Reader's packet through the NCIC. I think if you look hard, you'll see something very interesting. I'd look back. *Way* back." She put down her hand then extended it to Grady. "There. That's all I can say."

She withdrew her hand from his and before he could say anything, she was walking away. He knew better than to go after her. She'd probably stuck her neck out farther than she should have already, telling him what she had. Release of official documents or the information in them without a writ was serious business. He knew it could cost her her job.

"Thanks!" he shouted, when she was almost at the administration building steps. She continued on into the building, holding up her hand and waving behind her in his direction and then she disappeared.

"I hope," he said to no one, heading for his car, feeling like more questions had been raised on this visit than had been answered. Like, what the fuck was that business about a rose supposed to mean?

Grady decided he couldn't wait to get back to New Orleans. He turned off U.S. 10 at Baton Rouge and drove downtown. A guy at a gas station who spoke with what he now recognized as a Cajun accent, gave him change and pointed to the payphone outside at the corner of the lot.

He was in luck.

"Grady! Where the fuck are you, man? I thought maybe you were dead. Haven't heard a word from you since you left. What's up? Catch your guy yet?"

"I'm still down here, Marty. I'm in Baton Rouge, actually. On my way back to New Orleans."

"Baton Rouge? Isn't that the capital or something? Tracked Kincaid there, did you?"

"No. I just came from Angola, the state prison down here. Marty, I might have copped a break. I won't know unless you can do me a favor."

"You're not going to ask me to put my ass on the line, are you?"

Grady frowned. "I don't think so. Marty, this guy is worse news than we thought. I'm running out of time. Unless you help me out, he might get away with everything."

There was silence at the other end for a long second. When Marty Sprague spoke next, his voice was low and tense. "What do you need, Grady."

"It's nothing will get you in trouble. I just need you to wire me some stuff to the New Orleans police station. I don't think they'll give it to me unless you send it. Being as I'm retired." He laughed. "And a Yankee. They don't seem to like Yankees, some of these old boys."

"Go."

"I need everything you can find on Kincaid."

"Grady, you got his rap sheet."

"I got the short version. I need the long form. Probably have to go to NCIC for that. I want to know everything there is on this guy. If he got popped for jaywalking, there's a sheet somewhere. I think what I'm after happened a long time ago."

"Grady, that can take days."

Grady switched the phone to his other hand, fumbled around in his shirt pocket for his cigarettes.

"I don't have days, Marty."

Marty cursed and bitched, but in the end he said he'd see what he could do.

"Thanks, pal," Grady said, just before hanging up. "I'm about an hour away, hour and a half if that damn fog's still there. Don't ask. I'll swing down at the station there on my way home, see if you sent it yet."

When he hung up, he tried to take a drag on his cigarette, but it was soaked with sweat. When he'd held his arm down for a minute, the sweat had just poured down his fingers.

Fucking weather!

Driving back to New Orleans, Grady had the frustrating feeling that visiting the prison maybe hadn't been a total dead end, but might qualify at the least as a cul-de-sac. Metaphorically. And what he needed was a neighborhood map.

Metaphorically.

20

"I THOUGHT I told you to stay sober."

"Reader. Hey, Reader. Where y'at, m'man!"

"Yeah. Where *y'at's* right, Eddie. You are a fucking Yat, aren'tcha? I told you to keep off the sauce, you fucking alky."

"Hey . . . hey, man. I'm not drunk, Reader. I had me a few beers t'clear my head. I'm on top of things."

"Yeah." Reader looked around the room. Beer bottles everywhere, on the floor, in the kitchen sink, one in a potted plant over by the window. He saw another room in his head. A room in his youth. Imported French brocaded curtains on the windows, instead of the cheap blinds on Eddie's. Sheets on the king-sized bed that cost more than a month's rent for this dump. There were bottles in that room, too, only they were imported single-malt bottles and bottles in leather cases with the owner's name engraved on them. Carleton Tower. He remembered the bottles of Carleton Tower.

Remembered a young girl, standing in the doorway, weeping silently. His sister.

"You got any coffee?" Reader asked, going into the living room. "I mean *coffee*, not that other shit."

Eddie stumbled after him, rubbing the stubble on his chin. His hair was greasy and dirty, but short. At least he'd done that right, got it cut like he'd told him, Reader thought.

"Fuck an A, Reader. I made groceries yesterday down at

Schweggmann's. Community Dark Roast. With chicory, like you like. I'll put it on."

He heard Eddie stumble back to the kitchen and thought he heard the word "bastard," but he let it slide.

"Jesus, Reader. You really have thought of everything."

Eddie was reasonably sober after three cups of coffee and Reader burning holes into him with those death-ray eyes. He didn't trust him the least bit, half-figured Reader would try to ice him after the job. Eddie was ready for that. Strapped to his left ankle was a gun in the slickest little holster that fit down inside the new boots he'd bought a week ago. Snakeskin mothers that he'd paid four hundred bucks for. Eddie loved shoes. It dated to his own childhood when there was never enough money for shoes. He didn't get his first pair until high school, which he quit after one year. The year he discovered how much money you could make breaking into places that didn't belong to you.

Let Reader try and fuck with him. He'd learned a thing or two about fuckers like Reader that thought they were so friggin' smart. There were dudes ten times tougher than Reader in the joint and he'd lived through that plenty of times. He wasn't any jailhouse virgin, sure, but who was? It wasn't that bad usually, not if you cooperated, didn't get smartmouthed or try to resist. It was a way of surviving. Some didn't. That was because they weren't as sharp as he was. Stupid fucks, anyway, Eddie thought. They deserved what they got.

Reader's plan *was* smart, though. Eddie could see that. Reader was right—that was one of the weak points of the plan, the pickup.

"See?" Reader explained. "I've got all the bases covered. Most guys, they figure on all the things going as planned. Me, I plan for all the *bad* things that can screw up. Let's say St. Ives goes to the cops—against our express orders—and they follow him to where he makes the drop. Only this ain't a regular drop. This is down on the Mississippi, N'Awlins side, and he doesn't get those instructions until the last phone call from about a block away. He takes the money down to where we tell him and puts it in this boat, which is where we tell him he'll find it. Two boats, actually. One's for you. Only you'll already be gone in ours, waiting out in the middle of the river. He puts the money in the box that's marked like I explained to him during the last phone call."

"Box? What box, Reader? What boat?"

"It's a special box, special boat. I got a guy making it right now. Has a false bottom. It's got a waterproof lining that seals itself once the box is closed. Whatever's in the box stays nice and dry if it happens to land in the water. See? It's in this nice little waterproof bale thing." He laughed. "And it's going to land in the water about halfway across the river. Underneath the boat, where nobody can see it. This guy that's building it, he's a fucking electronic genius. This is a slick box he's fixing up. Sits on the main deck, near the stern right over this false bottom that you can trigger by remote control. You hit the button and a pneumatic doohickey shoots out the bale with the money in it. Fires it out of the bottom of the boat. It snaps closed and the boat keeps truckin' on over to the other side of the Mississippi. Bim, bam. Slick, huh? The bale's in the water where you can pick it up without anybody seeing you."

Eddie's brow furrowed as he struggled to understand. "But won't it float up to the surface?"

"It would if I let it. You're going to be in the middle of that big fucking cesspool of a river in your own little pleasure craft. From where I've been running St. Ives all over town with our cellular phone. You're gonna be steering the thing and I'm going to be bringing the car up as soon as I see St. Ives put the money on the boat and leave, also per my instructions. When the boat passes you, you're going to punch this little button and the money drops out of the bottom of the boat and guess who's there to get it? Ten minutes from then you're back in the car, we're pouring champagne all over each other long before they crash down on poor old Frenchie and they all get a surprise. If St. Ives plays it by the rules, the only one that gets surprised is Frenchie. But, fuck, if Frenchie's halfway smart, he takes the boat. It's worth a lot more than the two grand I promised him. Ha! I can see Frenchie water-skiing on Pontchartrain, dodging those sand sharks that come up in there all the time."

"Frenchie! Who the fuck's this Frenchie you keep talking about?" Fuck this shit, Eddie thought. How many motherfuckers were on this job he didn't know about? Reader must think he was a complete zero, didn't let him in on half what was going down. Eddie couldn't wait to shoot his arrogant ass. He told himself to be cool, stay calm, act like you don't know nothing.

Reader's brow furrowed for a second and smoothed. "Oh, yeah. I guess this is the first you hearda him, isn't it? We got us another guy helping us on this part. Pal of mine named Frenchie Mirabeau. He's a guy I hired for this one little bit. Frenchie is going to be waiting on the other side. His job is to get the money out of the boat, put it in his trunk and deliver it to us."

"I don't get it, Reader. Why would you want to do all that? It sounds like a lot of trouble for nothing. Why don't we have this St. Ives guy hand over the money? I mean, fuck! He's wired up with a bomb. You think he's gonna do something crazy like call the cops?"

"It's for insurance," Reader explained, with a huge sigh, as though he was disgusted. Fuck'm, Eddie thought. He waited for Reader's explanation.

"It's in case St. Ives gets cute. Maybe he wants to be a hero. Maybe he's dying of lung cancer and doesn't give a shit if he croaks. Maybe he calls in the cops for those reasons or half a dozen more. Maybe he tells Guterez what's going down. Who knows what goes through a guy's head? He probably won't, but I'm planning for all the bad things that can go wrong." What he didn't bother to tell Eddie was that he'd already made arrangements for Guterez to know exactly what St. Ives was up to. That Eddie was the wide-eyed rube watching a shell game in progress. It was hard to keep a straight face.

"Why I gotta be the one in this boat? Why not you?"

"Why, Eddie. I had this idea you might not trust me. Which is why I'm letting you pick up the money. You rather we switch places and I pick it up? I'm cool with that." He saw the change of expression in Eddie's face and nodded. "That's what I thought." He decided to hit him with the clincher. "There's another thing. When St. Ives puts that money on the boat, we're done with him. That's when I take him out. Probably shoot him. I don't want an explosion just then. Draw too much attention. You want that job?" Again, Eddie didn't say anything, but Reader could tell from the look in his eyes that he was digesting all this and had come to the conclusion he figured he would.

Reader fired up a cigarette and sucked deeply on it. "Let's say the worst happens and he decides to let the cops in on what's going down. Maybe the cops get a helicopter up, figuring we might do something tricky. They do that, they'll be patting each other on the back at how sharp they are. They're way ahead of us dumb crooks. They'll follow the boat to the other side where they figure the pickup is going down. Only thing is, they won't know we got it. You already picked it up in the middle of the river. All that's gonna be in that box is air."

Eddie hated the way Reader was looking at him. As if he were the stupidest fuck in the universe and just couldn't grasp this complicated shit. I oughta blow his big-shot ass away right this minute, he thought. Only he didn't. He'd wait until a better time. When the money was in their hands. In the car, when they were divvying it up.

Reader was speaking. "You got to understand this is only insurance. I doubt that there'll be any cops, but we got to act like there are, in case. Let's say that there are. We're running St. Ives all over town to different pay phones. We're sitting in our boat, looking like fishermen and we're calling him on a cellular phone. We run him all over until he gets to the last pay phone where we give him the directions to the boat and tell him how he's supposed to put the money in the box. There's a big X marked on the box. Fucker can't miss it. He puts the money in as per instructions. He seals it, engages the clutch and hits the juice like we've told him in his last phone call, and away it goes. It's all programmed to go to the other side as soon as he starts the engine. This shit cost me a fortune. An Autohelm ST 4000W Wheel Autopilot. Kick it on, it goes like a bird-dog to where you want it. Calibrates automatically for current and drift. It'll run right up your nose if you set it for that. Two grand, I'm out for that alone. For the stinking autopilot and to install it. I won't tell you what the boat cost and how much this guy's charging me to fix it up and put it where I told him. Building the box for the money wasn't cheap either. This is one slick boat. It doesn't matter what it cost though. With what we're getting, that's chicken feed."

Reader enjoyed telling this part, Eddie could tell. Fucker has an ego, he thought. He likes everybody to think he's smart. He didn't say anything, only nodded like he was one of the Seven Dwarfs, the one named Dopey.

"If the cops are following him, they got to be going nuts. If they thought to get a helicopter up, they're giving each other high fives. Let's say they do, so what? On the other hand, if St. Ives has told Mr. Fidel Guterez what's going down and Guterez is following him instead, that Cuban *frijole* has got to be going insane. *He* ain't got no helicopter far's I know! He's watching his money cruise over to Algiers and he knows how slow that ferry runs and it's the only way across besides the GNO and with the traffic on that sucker, the ferry's quicker. He knows he hasn't got a prayer to get across in time. He wants wings so he can fly over that sucker.

"Picture this. The money boat is cruising over to the other side like it's the U.S.S. Missouri or something, to where Frenchie's waiting—"

"Yeah, but there ain't going to be any money, Reader. You explained all that."

Reader's upper lip curled the slightest bit.

"You're right, Eddie. There isn't going to be any money on that boat. Only Frenchie doesn't know that. Frenchie's one little part of the insurance policy. A distraction. If all this comes down, if it goes screwy and St. Ives calls in the cops and if they get a helicopter up and if . . . you know, all those *ifs* that probably aren't going to happen . . . well, if they do, Frenchie will be some more bait to buy us time."

"How so? I don't get this at all."

"Cause, stupid. If the cops are on the scene and if they have a chopper up, they're gonna see that there's a guy waiting on the Algiers side and they're gonna figure he's the bad guy."

"So—"

"So, they're gonna be all over Frenchie like fleas on a junkyard dog. It'll take them a half hour minimum to figure out they've been had. Of course, Frenchie's gonna know that in about half that time, but so what? There's nothing they can pin on him, not unless he breaks stupid and says the wrong thing. Anyway, all the time they're giving him the hose and trying to figure out where the money has disappeared to, gives us boocoo time to make our getaway."

Eddie sat and studied what Reader was laying out. This was the first time he knew there were others involved. He knew Frenchie Mirabeau all right. Guy was all right, but a bit of a lush. Fucking Reader was planning to double-cross the guy for sure. He saw how the wind blew. He didn't doubt for a minute he'd do the same to him. He'd have to be on his guard every minute. Maybe he'd better get another gun just in case. He wondered what else Reader had "forgotten" to tell him.

Reader stretched his lips back, teeth and gums showing.

Eddie looked up and jumped.

"What?" Reader stood up, looked around the room.

Eddie stared at him a minute. "Nothin'. I . . . it . . . you . . . you looked like one of those damned rings you usta get in the gum machines. We called them 'Doctor Death' rings. Christ! You shoulda seen your face!"

Reader sat back down and showed his teeth again. He spoke softly.

"Eddie, I *am* Doctor Death." He gave a little snort through his nose.

Eddie made up his mind to get a second gun for sure. Strap it up under his arm. Motherfucker like this, he thought, you needed to be extra sharp yourself. Don't get caught with your pants down.

It'd be hard, but he wasn't going to touch another drop until this deal was done. Reader was smart. Scary smart.

He lifted his arms a little and felt warm drops of perspiration roll down. Fuck me, he thought. What have I got into?

21

EARLY AFTERNOON—IT WAS such a broiler outside that C.J. and Amanda sat inside for the air-conditioning, sipping iced coffee at their usual spot, the Cafe du Monde. Outside at that moment, the Duck Lady roller-skated by on the sidewalk, her pet ducks behind her. Amanda laughed at the sight, but C.J. didn't share her amusement. In his opinion the freak was an embarrassment to the town. Once, she'd been the subject of a Mardi Gras poster. Good God, what was on their minds, putting a lunatic like that on a poster for visitors to gawk at and think this was representative of New Orleans? First thing he'd do if he was mayor would be to get rid of her. Put her in a home somewhere. Second thing he'd do is close all those tacky Takee Outees that littered the Quarter. Eyesores. Third thing—

"C.J.," Amanda was toying with her stirrer, her eyes downcast. "I've been doing a lot of thinking. I don't think it would be a good idea for me to go with you on this Europe thing."

C.J. St. Ives looked at her in amazement. This wasn't in any of the scenarios he'd imagined.

"What're you saying, sweetheart? I thought you were excited about it. You said . . . "

"I know what I said." She pushed her glass away from her and looked up. "I guess it sounded like fun at first, but what happens when we get back?"

C.J. was puzzled. What does she mean?

"I'll lose my job."

"Your job? I don't get it."

"My job, C.J. You don't think I can just take off like that and come back and everything's the way it was? Your wife will have my ass. I won't only lose my position; she'll see to it I never work in another bank in Louisiana. Hell, probably the entire country. You know how her family is. With the clout her family holds in this town, I'll be lucky to be making change at Mickey D's!"

"Sugar, sugar, I told you not to worry about your job. I'm leaving Sarah. I'm going to marry you. We've been through this. Why are you starting this all up again?"

She set her jaw. He knew that look and didn't like it.

"I know what you say, C.J., but I also know how the world works. That woman has you by the short hairs. You think she's going to let you walk away and keep on working at the bank? You're nuts if you think that. No, you go and I'll keep my job thank you. *That*, I can depend on."

He stared out at the sidewalk. The Duck Lady was gone, replaced by a troop of six or seven black kids with a boom box and a big square of cardboard that they were laying down on the sidewalk in front of the outside tables. That's the way the yokels from Missouri see us, he thought. Break dancers and Duck Ladies. Vietnam refugees waiting tables in half the restaurants. He felt his lip curl as he turned to Amanda.

You little idiot, he thought. You wouldn't be a teller if it wasn't for me—they wanted to fire your ass months ago. It won't be Sarah keeps you from another job, it'll be your own sorry ineptitude. He didn't say aloud what he was thinking, but he knew what his face looked like, stony and hard.

He softened. He wanted this woman more than any other woman in his whole life. Hell . . . he wanted her right this minute. She just needed to listen to reason. He reached for her hand, closed his fingers over hers and squeezed.

"Baby, you don't have to worry about your job. Trust me on this—you won't have to worry about anything ever again. I can't tell you any more than that, only that money is going to be the least of your problems."

He'd said too much. But, what else could he do? He needed to convince her to come with him. Once she saw the money she'd thank him for taking her. Thank him? She'd fuck his socks off!

"Come on," he said, helping her up, his hand under her elbow. He'd get her in the sack, give her a good hard fuck. She'd change her mind. He knew what she liked, the way she liked his tongue to move. Nobody eats pussy like you do, C.J., she'd said more than once. He didn't know quite what to make of that—be proud she'd called him the best or be jealous because she was comparing him to others.

"Where?"

"You know."

She hesitated, but only for a moment.

In the car she said, "Miss Jane told me your wife called yesterday looking for you."

"So?" he said, pointing the car for Riverbend and the apartment.

"So, somebody called and asked for me, too, Miss Jane said. The way she said it, I know it was your wife."

"Baby," he said, slightly exasperated. "At this point, I don't care if Sarah comes up and watches us fucking. I tell you, I'm divorcing her. It doesn't matter. You'll see."

Once again, C.J. missed the look in Amanda's eyes.

22

SHE STARTED UP again in the apartment while C.J. was making drinks—Dewars and water for him, Jack and Coke for her. "She made a point of it, C.J. Listen to what I'm saying. Her snooty little nose was up in the air and she gave me that look. She knew and I knew and she knew I knew, who it was calling. Your precious wife Sarah. That goddamn bitch Jane, lording it over me like she was the elder in some church. I hate her, the old bitch, making everybody call her Miss Jane this, Miss Jane that, like we were some field hands back on the plantation. Lawdy, lawdy, Miss Jane," she said in a falsetto voice. "If I be's good, kin I come up to the big house?" She giggled.

"Like I said, so?"

"C.J., I think we better cool it. I don't think I'm going to go with you to Europe. I'll wait for you. You get your divorce, we'll take it from there. I'm scared, honey. I don't have any family, nobody to take care of me if I lose my job. I know you say you love me, but I know men, sweetie. We go to Europe, have some fun, come back and your wife starts to holler, you're gone. You know she controls the purse strings. When it comes right down to it, I wonder which you love more, me or that bank she lets you run."

The rage welled up in him and it was all he could do to keep his face and voice calm. She never talked to him that way. Who the hell did she think she was, talking to him that way! He was the president of the bank for chrissake! A position he'd earned. She made it sound as if the bank was some bone and he was some dog his wife kept for amusement. He tried to get his emotions under control. God! After all he'd done for her, she has to try and emasculate him like that.

Don't lose it, C.J. She doesn't know what she's saying. God. I wonder if the whole bank thinks like that. Do they look at me and think I'm a pet my wife has on a leash? He couldn't stand it. Is that what Amanda really thought of him? Didn't she understand he loved her? That he'd never treated anyone as good as he did her? Anybody else, he'd have gotten rid of long ago. He put up with a lot with her, he thought, wondering if he was becoming too weak. Hell. He loved her, that was the difference. He drained his drink and went over and poured another, no water this time.

"Amanda, you have no right to say something like that. I'm president of Derbigny because I earned it. I'd be president whether it was my wife's bank or not. I've worked every job there, paid my dues. I'm a damn good banker. Thirty-two percent growth in total assets since I took over. You think that's charity? That's good banking. Goddamned good banking."

He was proud of his control. He'd almost blown it. That damned Cajun temper. He must be anglicized now. Completely. If some bitch had said something like that to his father, she'd be spitting out teeth. His mother was proof of that. The only teeth left in her head by the time she was twenty-five were store-bought choppers. From sassing his dad, at least what his father considered sassing. Sometimes he thought the old ways were better. When women knew their place and kept it or suffered the consequences.

In a second his anger ebbed. Control. That was the one thing he always prided himself on. It was the one thing that had gotten him to where he was. That violent temper he'd had as a kid had been successfully sublimated for years, even thought there had been times he'd come close to reverting to the nature of his youth. The beginning of his success had begun long ago when he'd recognized what it took to appear civilized. He'd wanted to hit Amanda, sure, but he held back. He loved her. He must. This proved it. Anybody else—if one of the many tellers he fucked over the years had said something like that to him, she'd be seeing stars. At least be standing in the unemployment line. He'd just proved his love, even if she didn't know it.

"Amanda, put those doubts out of your mind. You're my baby. I'll take good care of you, you'll see." He tried to put his arms around her.

"C.J., I need to think. I don't know . . . I'm a paycheck away from the street. I'm not like you, with money in the bank. I've tried, but I can't seem to hold onto it. I need security, C.J. Try and understand, honey."

She twisted away. "I'm sorry I made that crack about your wife. I didn't mean it, baby. I . . . I mean . . . I can't go. Not till I'm sure you love me. I know I'm not the first you've had a thing with. I heard the talk in the bank long before we went out. 'Go out with C.J. on Friday, look for a job on Monday.' I don't hear that anymore, but I heard it plenty at first."

She went over and sat down on the bed and fished in her purse until she found a cigarette and lighted it. She crossed her legs and looked up at him standing in the middle of the room. She gave him a quick half smile and cupped an arm under her elbow, her index finger at her cheek.

"Look C.J., I'll tell you what. You go to Europe and have a good time. I won't ask you what you did over there. Have a ball. When you come back and get your divorce, I'll be here. It'll give us both time to figure out what we want. You may find I'm not what you're after. There's lots of girls. Of course . . . " she hastened to add, "You'll come back with a great tan and a million stories and you'll get your divorce and we'll get married. We'll go back to Europe on our honeymoon. How's that sound? Baby?"

He looked at her, his mind working.

"We're not going to Europe."

Her eyes widened. Well, hell, he'd done it. There was no turning back. His foot was in the fire.

"What do you mean? You've got tickets, everything. Turn mine in. You're marked out; I saw the schedule. You've got business there. That thing in Bonn. You can't—"

"Amanda, I never meant to go to Europe. That was for everybody else. You too, I guess. We're going to Belize."

"Belize! What's . . . where's . . . I don't—"

"I wasn't going to tell you this, Amanda." He dropped down on one knee in front of her, eyes pleading. Listen to me, please, Amanda, he thought.

"Baby, we're leaving for good. It's all taken care of. I was going to surprise you. You won't believe the surprise I have in store for you." He thought again of the image he'd harbored for months. Showering her with greenbacks, hundred dollar bills, and afterward fucking her on top of all that money while a tropical breeze wafted through the windows over their nude bodies.

"I've got more than a million dollars. In a bank. In our new names. And that's nothing. There's a lot more to come."

He went over to the dresser and pulled out the top drawer and dumped the contents on the floor. Underwear and socks and T-shirts spilled to the floor in a heap. He brought the drawer back over to the bed and put it upside-down on the bed. Ripping the tape that was holding a sheaf of papers and documents, he spread them out on the bed. Amanda's eyes got wider.

This was good. Everything was going to be fine. She'd go nuts, once she knew everything. Imagine what must be going through her mind. From a glorified teller who never made more than five hundred a week in her life to . . . *millions*! He wished he could have waited until they were in Belize to lay all this on her, but this might be better. He felt his cock swell, imagining how she was going to be screwing him once she saw what he'd done for her.

"Here!" he said, shoving a passport at her. "This is you. See the name? It was a surprise. Well, here—surprise!"

She picked up the passport and opened it.

"Who's this?" She said the words slowly, not comprehending. "Who's Katina . . . Broussard? Why's my picture—"

He laughed, throwing his head back, enjoying the moment.

"That's you, sweetheart. You're Katina Broussard. *Mrs.* Katina Broussard. Your maiden name was Katina Hebert. Take it." He handed her the birth certificate. "It's the name you always liked, you said. I wanted to surprise you with it—with everything else, but you couldn't wait, you little minx. There's more."

Now that the dam was open, the waters burst forth. He could see, or thought he could see, the wonderment of all that he was telling her filling her with delight.

"There's much, much more. We're rich, Amanda. Or, I should say—_Katina_—get used to your new name, darling. After Friday, it's yours forever. And we've got more than a mere million. A lot more. Friday, we'll have four million. Five million, maybe. Maybe more. I'm going to tell you everything, sweetheart. Lie back and listen and be happy. We're richer than you could ever believe. I'm going to make you so happy!"

He ran it down, the whole scheme.

He told her about the laundering operation he was involved in. He told her about Friday nights, when he would sit in his office and do coke lines so pure they were iridescent, about how the muchachos would bring in stacks and stacks of money, a bale of money, all hundreds. He told how he was going to miss making that deposit this week, and would Fidel ever be mad. Fidel would want to kill him, he said, but Fidel would never find him. _Them._ He'd planned this very carefully. There wasn't anything he hadn't thought of. The plane right now was being readied for their trip. All the details were worked out.

All but one.

He'd figured the wrong reaction from her.

"You've got to be crazy!" Amanda stood up, her eyes blazing. "You thought I would go along with this insanity? You're talking about _drug_ people, C.J. Drug people _kill_ you. Dead. Dead, dead, dead! They'll find us! There's no place on earth you're safe from these people. Let me out of here. I'm going, C.J. You go to Belize or wherever it is—leave me the hell out of your schemes. I don't care if I have to draw unemployment. Christ! I don't care if I have to become a street hooker. At least I'll be alive. With you, it's only a matter of time before my throat gets cut. You thought I would go along with this? You're a fucking asshole, C.J. A dead, fucking asshole. You're insane. Your little plan is insane. I'm outta this dump, buster. I want as far away from you as I can get." Something dawned behind her eyes. "My God! They'll come looking for me when you go! They'll think—"

She was starting to realize the implications of her predicament.

"Everyone in the whole world knows you're fucking me! You do this and I'm dead. You bastard. You fucking, fucking bastard!" She began to strike at him with her fists, crying and screaming at the same time. At last, he caught her arms, held her wrists. They both stood with chests heaving, tears running down her face, his own features contorted in disbelief.

"Let me go," she said, struggling to regain her composure. "Let me go, fucker. I'm going to the police. That's the only way I'm saving my young ass. God, why did I ever take up with you! You're not even a good lay. God, you know how many times I wanted to tell you that? Let me go, you fucker!" She turned into a madwoman, screaming and pulling and yanking, trying to scratch his wrists with her nails, trying to get away. C.J. was amazed, flat-out stunned by the woman, standing with spittle at the corners of her mouth, pure venom in her blazing eyes, her legs spread apart like some Irish washerwoman.

He didn't think about it. He hit her. Punched her as if she were another man. Put all his weight behind it and watched as she slumped down, soundlessly until her head hit the floor and she let out a little sigh. She lay stone still, her eyes open but unseeing.

His eyes darted around wildly. Did anybody hear? He strained to hear the neighbors doing something in response, listened for the sound of approaching police sirens. Nothing. Most of the neighbors in the building probably worked, he thought.

He stood there a full ten minutes not moving. After awhile, he sat down on the bed and tried to think. He tried not to look at Amanda lying on the floor. He didn't have to look to know she was dead. The instant he'd struck her and saw her head snap back, he'd known that. You can't fall like that, look like that and still be alive.

What was he going to do? At first he thought he'd carry her out to the car. Find some bayou and dump her.

No. That would be stupid. With his luck, some trapper, some poacher like his father would find her, do the right thing for the first time in his life and call the cops. They'd figure out who she was in about a day and then all hell'd break loose. It wasn't much of a secret who she had been seeing these last months.

About the time he should be boarding the plane for Belize, he'd be sitting in some squad room with his only travel opportunity a bus ride to Angola, chained to some 7-Eleven midnight bandit with a do-rag on his head.

In the end he decided to do nothing. A couple of drinks calmed him down and allowed him to think. A line of coke helped more. Leave her where she was. Turn up the air conditioner. It's only two days till Friday. Once he was out of the country, who cared if they figured out who killed her? There was no way they'd ever find him. He'd hidden his tracks too well.

Yes. That was the thing to do. Nothing.

Now that he'd made a decision he visibly relaxed. He fixed himself another drink and drank half before he dragged Amanda's body into the bedroom closet and shoved her deep into the corner. He threw a pile of clothes over her—old shirts, trousers, whatever he could find.

Amanda. For a moment remorse swept over him. What had he done? His poor, sweet baby. The feeling began to disappear, replaced by anger. The idiot! He'd offered her everything, the world. Who did she think she was! In a way he was glad he'd killed her, that she was gone. There were things about her that irritated him, the more he thought about it. Lots of little things. The way she talked, for instance. No education unless you call a high-school diploma education. Always saying Yat shit like she was going to "pass by her mama's," "make groceries at Schweiggman's," "make twenty-four" on her next birthday. She wouldn't have fit in where he was going, with the people he was going to be associating with. Money people. Cultured people. He'd have grown tired of her. He could see that with perfect hindsight. She was pathetic, a pretty, empty-headed bimbo. No, this was for the best. All she would have done was increase the risk for him. The only person who would have known where he was or what he'd done. Who knows what might have happened if she'd gotten pissed at him sometime.

He began to feel better about what he'd done. Probably saved his butt in the long run. Women never could keep a secret. He felt like a drink, like celebrating. He was almost home free. Things that looked like a disaster a minute ago suddenly looked like opportunity.

He made his drink strong, all Dewars with only a splash of water. As it rolled around on his tongue he felt the bite. It made him feel strong, alive. God! He'd killed a human being with one punch! He made a fist and flexed his arm.

Everything was going to be okay. He made another drink, but left out the water this time.

He waited until it was dark before he left the apartment, tried the door from the outside several times, made sure it was locked. Hurriedly backing the car out of the lot, he looked up at the window to be sure he hadn't forgotten the lights.

Heading down St. Charles, he began to consider what he would tell Sarah about coming home so late.

The farther he drove from the apartment, the more his confidence in his plan ebbed. He began to weep quiet tears of frustration. It was getting too complicated. What was he going to do without Amanda? He tried to think of her, tried to think of what he'd felt for her. That was all gone, vanished as if he'd never known her. She'd become a problem. He wiped his sleeve across his eyes. Get it together, C.J., he told himself. You're good at problems. You'll solve this one too. This was Wednesday. Wednesday night. Do what you planned. Keep your head. Keep her in the apartment. Corpses didn't start smelling in two days, did they? Two days was all he needed. Who gives a fuck who finds her body once he was gone? He was going to vanish completely. There could be no trace, not the way he'd planned it. There was only one loose end. The pilot. Even that was taken care of. He was landing in a small private airstrip. Nobody lived on the land it was on. He'd take care of the pilot. The same way he'd taken care of Amanda. It would be easier after killing Amanda. He'd wondered if he could do something like that, kill someone. Well . . . he could.

He started feeling differently about things. Pride. He'd done all right by God. There were plenty of other bimbos. Especially when there was four million dollars for the spending. There was one hell of a lot of bimbos when you could write a check for four million bucks.

He pushed down harder on the gas pedal. Fuck Sarah too. Fuck dreaming up some cock-and-bull story. Tell her he was out having a drink. Fuck her if she didn't like it. Two more days and he'd never see her again anyway.

C.J. was starting to feel downright good. He told himself it was only the heat that was making him sweat. He turned the air conditioning higher.

23

MOSTLY WHAT GRADY found out in the bars he hit along Airline Highway was that the drinks were cheap, for the simple reason that there wasn't much actual booze in them. He also learned that if he wanted to get high or have sex with anything at all, living or dead, animal, vegetable, or mineral, it would be easy to do. A couple of times an attractive woman or two gave him the eye and he knew it wouldn't be hard to end up in the sack with her if he gave half an effort, but he didn't. Getting laid was the farthest thing from his mind. He wanted to stay focused on finding out what he could about Kincaid. A week ago, he was banging everything he could get his hands on and now he barely looked at the opposite sex. He couldn't decide if that was good or bad.

He'd spent most of the afternoon in the *Times-Picayune* newspaper morgue, going over old newspaper articles that appeared under the keyword "Kincaid". At first, they weren't going to allow him access, but a phone call to Marty and a talk he had with the morgue supervisor changed his mind. There were about a dozen stories, ranging back almost thirty years, but nothing that he didn't already know. Now he was ready to hit the bars, see what turned up. He hated to leave the air conditioning of the building, but there didn't seem to be much else he could get there. One thing was really odd. None of the stories filed under Kincaid's name mentioned the murder of his father. He made a note to find out why.

The whole thing might well be a wild goose chase. There was no proof that Kincaid came back to New Orleans just because he was from there originally. He might be living in Canada for all Grady knew, and maybe nothing was going down at all.

No. He was right about this. His instincts told him he was on the right course. Kincaid was back in New Orleans and he was planning something big.

What he did was hit as many spots as possible, showing Kincaid's picture to the bartender and barmaids and customers. He ordered a real drink in about every third bar. The rest of the time he'd drink ginger ale and pass the photo around, ask if anybody knew Kincaid. He offered money several times to no avail. Nobody seemed to know the guy or at least they didn't claim to.

By midnight, he'd exhausted most of the places that looked promising. On the pretext of finding some "action" he was told by a guy in a tittie bar to try the joints closer to New Orleans out on Jefferson Highway. It was while driving past the juke joints and fried chicken and seafood places that lined the highway that he spotted a large red neon beer sign on a building. He could use a beer. Every time he got out of the car he figured he lost a pound, from the sweat that poured from his body.

He'd almost driven by the place. It didn't look like much on the outside. The flat, rust-speckled tin sign read "Sally's," and it resembled one of the countless honky-tonks the cops in Dayton would have referred to as a "bucket o' blood."

When he walked through the door, the worst live music he'd ever heard assaulted his ears. The entire band was off-key, limping through a tortured version of "Faded Love." The bar was directly to his left and every seat seemed to be taken by a cripple. Not a single person sitting there—all men—appeared to have his entire complement of body parts. One was missing an ear, several an eye, as evidenced by eye patches, and at least two were sporting stumps where their hands used to be.

Grady took the only remaining seat, a stool with one leg shorter than the other three. Barroom polio. It was at the end nearest the door. Even the furniture had infirmities. His kind of bar.

He ordered a beer from the bartender, a short, squat tree stump of a man, who took his money without a thank you, just a nod. Grady tipped the bottle back, enjoyed the feel of the cool liquid as it trickled down his throat. He started to say something to the bartender, pull out his picture of Kincaid as he had at the other places, then decided not to. He was tired. He'd done enough for that night. Surly as this bartender looked, he didn't think he'd get much out of him anyway and all he'd accomplish is turning his half-pissed-off mood into a full-fledged one. Fuck it. He'd have a beer or two, look around, see if he spotted any alligator shoes and if not, head back to the motel. Hit it again in the morning.

He was staring straight ahead at the backbar, reading the labels on the liquor bottles, when he felt a guy bump into him. He turned around, half-prepared for an altercation, when he saw the guy was just having trouble getting up on the bar stool next to his. Not only did he have an old-fashioned hook where his right hand used to be, but his right leg didn't seem to be able to bend. Fucking regular Long John Silver! He'd landed in the middle of the cast party for M*A*S*H, he thought, and extended his hand to help the guy up onto his seat.

"Thanks," the guy said, gruffly, squirming around until he was settled. Without asking, the bartender brought him over a bottle of Dixie beer and a shot glass and poured it full from a Wild Turkey bottle. The man reached in his shirt pocket with his good hand and withdrew a roll of bills which he tossed up on the bar, from which the bartender removed what he was owed, putting two quarters back beside the roll. Not a word was exchanged between the two, although the bartender did something that puzzled Grady somewhat. As he slid the quarters over, he glanced at Grady and raised his eyebrows and shrugged. Like he was trying to tell him something. Fucking weird bar, Grady thought.

His new neighbor grabbed the shot glass and downed it in one gulp, and as he put the empty glass back down on the bar, he extended his hook. "Branson," he said. It felt funny, shaking a metal hook, but Grady did, grasping it between two fingers and his thumb.

"Fogarty," he returned, and turned back to his beer. Last thing he wanted right now was to have some rummy bending his ear. He could feel, rather than see, the man staring at the side of his head.

"Quarters?"

Huh? What the hell was he talking about?

"Quarters. Y'all wanna match some quarters?"

It was the last thing Grady wanted to do. He was tired, thirsty, and what he really wanted to do was roll out of this bar and find his bed and crank the air-conditioning as high as it would go. He didn't know why he agreed.

"Buck," the man who'd introduced himself as Branson said as he flipped his quarter. "We play for a buck in here." He caught the spinning quarter and trapped it on the bartop.

Shrugging, Grady picked up a quarter from his own pile of change and flipped, saying, "Match you," while it was still in the air. He won. He just pushed the dollar the man gave him onto his pile of change. They went again. Again, Grady won. Then, he lost a couple, but after that it seemed he couldn't lose. Eleven, twelve in a row he matched.

"Figure the odds on that!" he laughed. He bought the man a beer and another shot and another beer for himself. "How 'bout we call it a day, partner?" he said to Branson.

"Fuck that," the man snarled. "Gi' me a chance to win back my money. Make it twenty."

"I don't think so," Grady said.

"Ten, then."

Grady sighed. Some folks just never learned. To hell with it. It was no skin off his ass if this guy wanted to lose his rent money. He sure wasn't some kid he had to look after.

"Okay. A couple more. That's it, then. I've got to get going."

"Okay, then," Branson said, and he separated a ten from his roll and pushed it out by itself on the bar. He flipped and while it was in the air called, "Match." He showed heads at the same time Grady showed tails. Grady reached for the bill and put it on top of his pile. For a second, Branson didn't say anything, and then he went ballistic.

"You cheatin' bastard!" he said. His face was livid with rage, and spittle had formed at the corners of his mouth. Out of the corner of his eye, Grady saw the bartender start toward them, reaching for something on a shelf behind the bar.

In a split second, a couple of thoughts went through Grady's mind. *This is the part where I call him something and he calls me something else and then he tries to hook me with that weapon on the end of his arm, and the bartender, who's his brother-in-law, cracks me with that sap he's bringing with him, and . . .* He didn't think beyond that, just cocked his right arm back and blasted his forearm across the man's nose, knocking him back off the stool and smack into the table directly behind them. The table flipped up with the force of the impact, scattering beer bottles and ash trays along with the three guys sitting there who went backwards off their chairs, yelling and cursing. The next thing Grady knew, the bartender was leaping over the bar—fucking gymnast, was Grady's half-thought, jumping off the barstool—only the guy didn't take a swing at him, but grabbed his arm and yelled, "C'mon!," taking off on a dead run, pulling Grady's sleeve behind him.

Before he could sort out what was going on—behind him, the band had begun playing louder and even more off-key, and women were screaming and men shouting—he found himself in a small office and the bartender was closing the door behind them. And shaking silently with laughter.

"Man!" he said, getting himself under control. "I thought ol' Branson had you there, my friend!"

"What—" Grady didn't know where to begin, what to even ask.

"—was that?" the bartender finished for him. "That, my boy, was Branson. He pulls this shit all the time." He walked around to the desk that was there, sat down and opened up a drawer and took out a bottle of Wild Turkey. From the same drawer, he came up with two clear plastic glasses, into each of which he poured a generous shot and pushed one across the desk in Grady's direction, leaned back and drank his down in one swallow. He poured another one, about half the original amount and grinned at Grady. "Siddown," he said.

He took a sip of his whiskey. "It's all under control now," he said. "Friend of mine was out there and I already had him call the cops. About a minute before Branson made his little move. We was wondering if Branson would get you. My friend wanted to stop him before he started, but I thought you looked like you could handle yourself."

There was a knock on the door.

"Come in," the bartender called out.

The door opened and a skinny middle-aged man wearing a string tie and a white Stetson walked in. "It's a regular gumbo ya ya out there!" the man said, shaking his head and laughing. "They just picked him up, Sally. Band's taking a break. That okay?"

"Come on in, Rufe," the bartender said. "Here." He reached back into the drawer and got out another cup and poured it half-full of Turkey. Rufe walked over, accepted the cup and hoisted it in a vague kind of toast before drinking it down in three swallows. He never even blinked.

"This here's Rufus Jones," he said to Grady. "He owns the Black Angus up the block. Rufe's smarter than me, gets the hell out of his place early. Me, I'm married to this joint, I guess. Oh." He stood up and extended his hand. "I'm Salvatore Graciano. No relation to the champ. Everybody calls me Sally."

Grady was still in semi-shock over what had just gone down, but Sally must have intuited that, as he began explaining.

"That character you had that little run-in with out there is Charley Branson. Charley used to work at the elevator out on River Road until a few years ago when he caught his arm in a conveyer belt. Tough fucker. Everybody was out to lunch, but he grabs his hand, gets in his car and drives to East Jefferson Hospital. Passes out as he goes in the door. They might have been able to save his hand, but he forgot to take it in with him and nobody knew it was out there sitting in the passenger seat. They found it later. A day later. Bit too late to reattach it by then. Looked like a ripe avocado, I guess, by then. Don't think it smelled that good, though."

He put his feet up on his desk.

"Now, Charley feels like he's not a real man anymore. Crippled, can't work, you know. Drinks too fucking much. Pulls shit like he did on you all the time. Rufe's had to kick him out of his own place a few times, too." Rufus nodded, smiled. Sally went on. "He sidles up to some poor yahoo—'scuse me, *tourist*"—here, he smiled—"gets 'em into matching quarters with him and somewhere along the line calls 'em a cheater. Then, he just whomps the hell out of the poor sap. He's hooked a few guys pretty badly. You're probably lucky he didn't take out your good headlight, my friend. You did the right thing. Nail him before he can nail you."

"You knew this guy was a lunatic and you didn't stop him before he started his little war with me?" Grady was furious.

"Hey!" Sally was up. "Cool down, pal. I don't know you from Adam. I was right about you, wasn't I? You do know how to handle yourself."

"Well . . . " Grady didn't know whether to handle that as a complement or what. The guy was right, though. He wasn't his baby sitter. He began to calm down. "I guess you really couldn't do anything until he started something."

"That's right," Sally said. "Most times, situation like that, there's a lot of barkin' before the dogs go at it. You surprised me. Charley, too, I guess." He and Rufus both began laughing and Grady had to smile himself.

"You're right. Most times, that's what would have happened. I just had a hard day and wasn't in any mood to go through all that. Been in enough fights to know what's coming, so I thought I'd just save us both some time."

Sally gave Grady a hard look, as if he was just realizing something. "You're a cop, aintcha?"

"Not your favorite kind of customer, place like this, is it?" Grady said.

"Relax, man. I'm a cop myself. So's Rufe. Or at least we used to be. Retired. NOPD, twenty and out. Both of us walked the Quarter for our beat most of the time. That's worth thirty years, compared to out in the parishes. Went in in uniform, went out in uniform. Neither of us ever made a suit, though we each had our chances, I guess. Never had much ambition for a shield, myself."

"Me, neither," said Rufus, who had been quiet during this exchange. "Hey, Sally, I got to get going." He gave his friend a little wave of his hand, shook hands again with Grady, and walked out the door, closing it behind him.

"Good guy," Sally said. "Where you a cop at? I can tell you're not from here. I mean Louisiana, not just New Orleans. Chicago? New York?"

"Dayton, Ohio. I'm here because of this guy."

Grady reached in his jacket pocket, pulled out the picture of Reader Kincaid.

Sally turned out to be Grady's first decent break. "Hey, I know this guy. Know who he is, anyway. Matter of fact, a guy I just seen him with uptown a couple of weeks ago comes in. Eddie something. You want, I can ask my wife. She'd know."

They went back out to the bar, which looked much as it had when Grady first walked in. The band was back off their break, cranking up their rendition of "Faded Love" which must have been a local favorite Grady figured, much as they played it. Charley Branson was nowhere to be seen and the table he'd crashed into was back in place. The same three guys were sitting back at it and one of them nodded pleasantly at Grady as he walked by and took his former seat at the bar.

"Always figured the real work got done by the hoofers like me," Sally was saying from his side of the bar, sharing a beer with Grady. He'd refused Grady's money for it. One of the waitresses had been behind the bar when they came back up and she left as soon as the boss came back, to take over her tables. Nobody acted like much of anything significant had happened. Normal night, Grady figured. Jesus.

"Now?" Sally was going on about his police career. "Now, they're all in cars, wondering why the crime stats keep going up. I got no regrets though. I seen it all, brudda. You want an interesting beat, try the Quarter. More perverts per square block than anywhere else in the world. I include the tourists in that assessment, too. Something happens to people when they come down, and I'm not talking just during Mardi Gras. It's something in the air, maybe in the crab boil. Makes your pecker swell and your brain shrink. You uniform or a suit, Grady?"

"Uniform the first nine years, suit the rest. I was late making detective. Made a major fuckup my first case."

"Oh, yeah?" Sally put his foot up on something behind the bar and picked up a toothpick from a little porcelain container on the bartop and began digging around in his mouth. "Me, now, I *never* fucked up." Grady shared in the man's chuckle. "So, what was it you did?"

"Well," Grady began, "I was still in the Academy and one night I was in this bar that happened to get robbed and the bartender shot the perp, only he got away. Dropped his gun though. The perp. The first suit on the scene collared me and told me to collect evidence. That's where I screwed up. Big-time."

"What'd you do?"

"He gave me a couple of bags and asked me if I knew how to collect evidence. Hell, yes, I said, cocky. You know. I'd seen enough TV to know how to do that, even though we were just starting the class on evidence. I was kind of full of myself in those days."

"Yeah," chuckled Sally. "Been there, done that. So, you still haven't told me what you did that was so wrong. I know. You grabbed the gun, wiped out the perp's prints with your own."

Grady's smile was rueful. "Worse. The detective gave me two bags. One paper, one plastic. I picked up the gun all right. With a pencil through the barrel. Told you I'd seen a lot of cop shows."

"Wait! Don't tell me! You put the gun in the plastic bag! Am I right?"

Grady downed his beer, held up the empty bottle and Sally plopped another down in front of him. This time, he took two ones from the stack Grady'd put out, trading him two quarters.

"You got it. It got busy then or the lead detective might have caught it in time. Only he didn't and they didn't find it out until back at the station when they were cataloguing stuff into the evidence room. It—"

"Had sweated and the prints were gone."

"You got it, chief. I didn't realize you didn't put something like that with prints on it in a plastic bag. I shoulda—"

"Used the paper bag! Ha! No wonder you didn't get your shield for nine years. Hey, that's not the worst thing, believe me. Hell, you were just a rookie. The detective should have kept a better eye on you."

"Well, they caught the guy about a half hour later so it wasn't as bad as it could have been. A block away, bleeding all over the place, getting into a cab. That saved my butt from being kicked off the force, but it took a little longer than it should have to cop the gold shield. Live and learn."

"Yeah," Sally agreed, shaking his head in commiseration. "Ain't that the truth, brother." He picked up a bar rag and began wiping down the counter in front of him.

"So you got this bar," Grady said. He decided to relax, have another beer. Sally kept his beer at the perfect temperature, just above freezing. One degree more and it would turn to beer slush. He felt he'd run into a kindred soul. Their initial difficulty over, he decided he liked the guy. There was something about the work, the things they faced, that bonded all cops, no matter how far apart the places where they worked. The scenery might be different, but the human animal was the same everywhere. Missoula, Montana got the same share of excrement as Chicago's Loop.

"Yeah. So I got this bar. I couldn't get out of the Quarter fast enough when my time was done. Liked it when I was there, hated it as soon as I walked away and realized what I'd been swimming in. Never go up there anymore. They got the beat cops on motorscooters these days! Can you imagine! I couldn't do it. Next thing, they'll have 'em wearing those little caps with propellers, handing out gum drops to the bad guys."

Grady told Sally why he was in New Orleans, why he was looking for Charles Kincaid. What he'd learned so far from his trip out to Angola and digging through old newspaper stories. Not much. He even told him what Cabrini had told him and the bar owner couldn't make any more sense out of it than Grady had.

"Man-oh-man! So you think Reader Kincaid tried to kill your brother! Man, I'm sorry. Makes you crazy, don't it? Listen, Fogarty, if I hear anything, I'll let you know. I'll ask Veronica when I go home. Leave me your number, someplace I can reach you. I'll tell you this—you come to the right place. Most of the local outlaws come in some time or other. They know I run a clean bar, something that's hard to get on this end of town. They figure it's a safe place to be, won't be no trouble at Sally's. I keep things in line. Make a few bucks now and again, too. I keep in touch with the boys downtown. A lot of information comes my way so I make a little both ways. Know what I mean?"

When Grady hit the sheets that night at the Day's Inn he did so with a mild buzz, but he felt he'd made some progress and counted the headache worthwhile. At least he'd made a valuable contact, someone connected to the criminal pipeline. Someone who knew Kincaid. What was better, Sally was one of the good guys. He'd been dying to ask the bartender to call his wife, wake her up and ask her right away what she knew about this friend of Kincaid's, but he figured he better not. He didn't think the man would do it anyway and he didn't want to lose the only contact he'd made. He trusted Sally to call him as soon as he talked to his wife in the morning. Sometimes, you have to let things play out naturally.

He tossed and turned for an hour before falling into a fitful sleep. His brother's face kept swimming up in the darkness.

24

EARLY THE NEXT morning, Grady was wakened by the ringing of the phone in his motel room. It was the duty officer at the N.O.P.D.

"We've got some stuff here from the Dayton P.D., Mr. Fogarty. See the desk for it, sir."

Grady was there in half an hour. He took time to brush his teeth and throw some water on his face, but it was an unshaven and breathless man that rushed up to the desk and gave the officer his name and signed the clipboard he handed him.

Back in his motel room, he spread out the materials Sprague had telexed. They more than covered the bed and small desk and overflowed onto the floor. It wasn't until shortly after noon that he finished going over them all. By then, his stomach was making noises and he realized he hadn't eaten. He strolled down to the motel office and poured himself two cups of coffee from the complimentary service and cadged a breakfast roll from the tray on the table and brought them back to his room. Nibbling on the cinnamon bun and sipping coffee, he stacked all the papers together and went back through them, occasionally plucking one from the stack. Marty had been thorough. From the volume of reports, Grady couldn't imagine there was another scrap of paper on Reader Kincaid in existence. Most of it contained information he already knew. There were a couple of interesting reports, however. One was a report from the U.S. Department of Justice. Kincaid showed up in their Homicide Investigation & Tracking System report, known to cops as the HITS sheet. The other was a profile provided by the Violent Criminal Apprehension Program, or VICAP. Both gave a picture of Kincaid that was chilling. They listed crimes Kincaid was suspected of committing. When Grady finished reading them he was impressed. Detailed in each were six deaths of prominent businessmen in the New Orleans area who had died in what were ruled as accidents over a period of twenty years, but were all linked to Reader by an informant who claimed Kincaid had been responsible. The informant was a small-time hood named Yves Mirabeau who was known to most acquaintances as "Frenchie". As best as Grady could determine from the reports, Mirabeau had given up the information a few years ago when he was busted on a morals charge, in an attempt to trade information for a lighter sentence. The info hadn't resulted in anything much as the little Mirabeau had given them wasn't enough to convict Kincaid although he had been questioned on the crimes. Kincaid hadn't been told who had snitched on him, common procedure when police wanted to keep a snitch active.

Interesting, Grady thought, putting the two reports aside. I wonder if this Frenchie is still around.

The other paper he separated and put with the HITS and VICAP reports was Kincaid's complete rap sheet, beginning with a youthful crime against property and concluding with the armed robbery he'd just done time for. Grady read and reread the report, sensing there was something important in it, but he just couldn't find it. He paid particular attention to Kincaid's early arrests, keeping in mind the cryptic "clue" Frank Cabrini had given him, and the advice Cathy Johns had passed on, but even after reading it so many times his eyes began to blur, he could find nothing that related to "a rose by any other name." He stuck the sheet with the others anyway, just in case. Grady knew that sometimes what you were after was right in front of you and you just needed a break from it to bring it into focus.

The next two days brought Grady a lot of scuffed shoe leather and healthy contributions to the gasoline industry, but little to show for it. He began asking around for the man known as Frenchie, but either he was being stonewalled or the man had long departed the New Orleans scene.

He stopped in at Sally's a couple of times, but each time Veronica was out and Sally hadn't had a chance to talk to her. He hadn't heard of Yves Mirabeau either. They'd lost a bartender, it seemed, and husband and wife were splitting the day in half, each working at the bar which was open twenty-four hours a day, seven days a week. Grady was crazy to grab Sally's arm and make him pick the phone up to call her, but knew that would only antagonize the man. On the second night of pounding the bricks, he hit the sheets frustrated and worn to the bone.

The next morning, Grady drove down to a coffee shop named Morning Call in Fat City that the motel clerk recommended. There, he got his second break. He was scanning the morning *Times-Picayune* while stuffing down a beignet and some of the best coffee in his life and was about to turn the page when a small item caught his eye.

It was an article quoting an Animal Control official who was outraged over an incident out at the lake near Covington. A German shepherd was blown up back in the swamps. Probably by a remote control device, the investigating sergeant had theorized. He didn't have a theory why someone would go to all this trouble just to kill a dog unless it was some kind of satanic cult. The report went on to say that the Animal Control officer, a woman named Whitney Farver, was furious that anyone would do something like that to an innocent animal.

He'd dealt with cults before. There were kooks everywhere. Mostly kids who read too many comic books and not enough Mark Twain. That's what piqued his curiosity as he read and made him think there might be something there. Grady'd never heard of an animal being sacrificed by explosion. They usually cut the poor creature's throat. Occasionally they hanged them. Something wasn't right about this. What really caught his eye was the speculation that a remote control device had been used.

Maybe if there was something else to go on he'd have let it go, but any lead was precious. He decided to pay the Animal Control office a visit and see what information he could dig up. Maybe blowing up dogs was common in these parts. It wouldn't surprise him.

"Are you with the New Orleans police? You aren't a native, are you?"

Grady looked at the animals housed in the cages they passed as they walked. Dogs, mostly, but some cats, too, and a monkey.

"Who lost their monkey? Are those legal to keep? No ma'am, I'm a cop . . . well, retired. I'm from Dayton. Ohio. I'm checking into an attempted murder back home." He hesitated. "My brother's."

The woman in khaki looked piercingly at him for a moment. She said softly, "I'm sorry."

"Grady Forgarty," he said, smiling. He offered his hand.

"We can talk while I feed the animals," she said. He followed her through a door that led to a long line of cages on either side of a narrow corridor.

She stopped before a cage full of dogs and slipped the latch open.

"Hold this for me," she said. "Don't let them out."

She reached down to lift up a large bag of dog food that was leaning up against the cage. The bag looked heavy.

"Here," Grady said. "Let me."

When the animals were fed, she walked back to her desk at the front and indicated a chair before it for Grady to sit in. He sat down and watched her as she fiddled with some papers on the desk.

"I'm sorry about your brother," she said, after a silent moment that stretched too long for comfort. "I take it he's alive since you said it was an *attempted* murder. What's a mutilated dog in New Orleans got to do with somebody's attempted murder in Ohio? And yes, monkeys are legal if you purchase them from a licensed dealer and if you apply for a permit and get them shots. Only there're a lot around that aren't legal. They're a big headache. This is a seaport if you haven't noticed. A lot of sailors come through from off the tankers and other ships. This is one of the biggest ports in the country. Maybe the biggest. Most of the grain from the Midwest leaves for overseas from New Orleans. Drive out on River Road sometime. There's an elevator out there you won't believe. Not to mention gas and oil. We're hurting—the oil business isn't what it used to be, but it's still got a pulse."

She got up. "Come on," she said. He followed her back past the animal cages to the end of the corridor where there was a steel door with a small window at the top.

"Our lab," she said, opening the door. Grady followed her in. There was something on the table, a lump covered by a sheet. She walked over, pulled the sheet back. At first, Grady couldn't make out what it was. Some kind of animal, mangled badly, blood pooling in the rubber pad it was resting on, a mass of stiff, matted dark hair. Then, he saw ears and exposed teeth and realized the lump was a dog's head. A German shepherd.

"That's—"

"The dog that was blown up. The one in the article. I'm just getting ready to test him for rabies."

"Rabies?"

She pulled out a pair of surgical gloves from a box on the stainless steel counter next to the table and donned them.

"State law. Whenever a dog gets killed, no matter what—road kill, whatever—the state says I have to test it for rabies. We get a lot of that down here. If this dog is infected, we'll have to put out an alert. My guess is that this dog was healthy, though. I found the owner and he says if it's his dog, he's had his shots."

"The owner?"

"Yes. A man named Pelkerson. Well . . . maybe the owner. He called after he saw the article."

"You have his address?"

"Up front. I'm pretty sure he wasn't the one did this. Not the way he was carrying on."

"I'd like his address."

"Sure." She picked up a box from the counter and set it down next to the dog's head.

He watched as she scraped tissue onto a slide and waited while she peered at it under a microscope.

"Just as I figured," she said, glancing up at him. "Nothing wrong with this dog." She smiled slightly, but there wasn't any humor behind it. "Other than somebody blew him into a million bits."

Grady cleared his throat. "This thing probably hasn't got anything at all to do with the guy I'm looking for," he said, watching her strip off the gloves and throw them into a wastebasket lined with a garbage bag. She began to put things away, the last thing being the dog's head which she deposited in the garbage bag. She lifted it up, wound a twistie around it and placed it near the door.

She turned. "Then what'd you want to see the dog for?"

"The article said the police said they found evidence the dog was hooked up with a pipe bomb. And probably blown up by remote control. That's what got my interest. My brother has an electronics store and whoever attacked him stole stuff like that, remote control equipment. You know, those gizmos that you use to control model airplanes, cars, things like that."

She gave him a quizzical look.

"Look, Miss . . . Whitney, I don't know if there's any connection or not, but I don't have much to go on. And I've had something to do with satanic cults—I could tell you a story or two if you had time—but I never heard of any of 'em blowing up their sacrifices. They usually—"

"I know," she interrupted. "They usually use a knife, cut their throats. Little twisted minds." She shuddered. "Look, I'd like to help you, but I don't know that I can. And I doubt if you can get much from the police who investigated it. They don't put a lot of priority on dog mutilations." Her tone was bitter. She opened the door and they exited the room. Grady waited for her to lock it and they walked back to the front.

"You were going to give me his address?"

"Of course . . . " She rifled through papers on top of her desk. " . . . .here it is."

She fished out a scrap of paper and handed it to Grady.

Grady stared at the small handwriting.

"What's a 'Chef Menteur'?"

She smiled. "It's not a 'what', it's a 'where'. It's a street. Over in East New Orleans."

"Can you give me directions?"

"I'll draw you a map. That's kind of a tough area to find places in."

She was right: Grady had a hell of a time finding the house. It was in one of those subdivisions where all the homes look alike. A ranch, next to a two story colonial, next to a ranch, next to a two-story colonial, next to a ranch. The contractor had only used three colors for maybe a hundred or so houses. White, yellow and a salmon shade of pink. He saw a blue one that must have been repainted, the neighborhood rebel.

The house he was looking for turned out to be one of the standard pink ones. "I knew I shouldn't have sold Fritz to that asshole." The man, Pelkerson—no Mister, no first name—coughed and hacked through his words. That Camel couldn't be helping. Grady instinctively looked down at the pack of Marlboros in his own pocket. He counted six ashtrays—all overflowing—just in the front room. I bet the state of Virginia loves this guy, Grady thought. He took a seat on the couch and Pelkerson sat down heavily in a Lazy Boy, an open, half-empty carton of Camels within easy reach on the floor beside him.

"It's just . . . I . . . well, I don't have long to go and I wanted Fritz to have a good home."

"I'm sorry, Mr. Pelkerson," Grady said. "What's—"

"The big C," he said, anticipating his question. "They give me six months. I'll take six months. I think they're optimistic."

He lighted a new cigarette off the one that had burned down. "Like I said, I'm not long for this earth. All I wanted was for my puppy to have a good home. That's why I ran the ad. I didn't want him to end up in the pound."

Better if you had, Grady thought. "Is there anything you can tell me about the guy who bought your dog?"

"Naw. Wish I could. You on the case?"

Grady nodded. Let him assume what he wanted.

"Yeah, well, like I said, he never introduced himself. I don't think. I don't remember him saying his name. I can describe him though. Imagine a creep."

Grady smiled. "I could use a bit more than that."

Pelkerson went into a minute-long coughing fit that bent him over and brought tears to his eyes. When it subsided he took out another cigarette and lit it off the one he had going. Grady made a mental note to cut down on his own consumption.

"Goddamned lungs." Pelkerson inhaled deeply. "Probably look like a couple of wharf rats got run over by a semi. I'm an organ donor, but I don't think those're the organs they're gonna want."

He took another drag and waved his visitor into the kitchen with his cigarette. There were even more ashtrays there, as well as a nearly empty vodka bottle on the kitchen table.

"He was about medium build, skinny little asshole—brown hair, long, like a hippie." Grady scribbled notes on a pad, wondering as he did how many hippies this man knew from personal experience.

"Oh. One thing might help. I knew this guy wasn't a dog lover . . . I tried to catch him . . . drove off before . . . anyway . . . he wore these fancy shoes. Alligator. You don't see those much. That's when I went after him, only he drove off before . . . when I *think* about those shoes! Guy likes animals don't wear shoes like that. He kicked him."

"Kicked him?" Grady leaned forward.

Pelkerson went into another coughing spasm. When it passed, he lit another cigarette off the one that was burning. Grady felt an overwhelming urge himself and shook out a Marlboro medium, almost asking permission.

"Kicked my baby. Kicked Fritz. That bastard!"

There wasn't much else. He couldn't remember the color of the man's eyes or the make or year of his car, only that it was brown. He was positive about those shoes, though.

Grady worked up an appetite talking to Pelkerson. It was almost noon and he hadn't had anything but an unfinished beignet earlier that morning. A few blocks after leaving Pelkerson's he passed a sign that said *DiNardo's Poboy's*. Plain enough. No subterfuge there. Grady liked the look of the place. He'd seen other poboy places driving through town and wasn't quite sure what they were. Like a hero or submarine sandwich, he guessed, craning his neck to take in the place. There wasn't much to see—a counter, behind which three people rushed around, filling orders, cooking things on an ancient pot-bellied black stove. A walk-in cooler and a couple of large trash cans rounded out the furnishings there. Where Grady stood were four small tables and chairs and an L-shaped counter wrapped around the far wall. An overhead fan stirred hot air lazily around.

"Order?" one of the men behind the counter snapped, looking around the woman who had already ordered an oyster poboy. Besides the woman and himself, all of the other customers were men in yellow hard hats. There was a new office building going up across the street and Grady assumed these were some of the workers on lunch break. He scanned the wall menu again.

"I don't know . . . I like shrimp." He glanced again. "That can't be right!"

"What?" The guy taking orders looked around to see what he was talking about. Grady was looking at the menu.

"Two-ninety for a shrimp poboy? There's gotta be what? Two shrimps on it?"

"It's *shrimp*," he said. "Shrimp is plural *and* singular. Like deer. And we put on a lot more than two shrimp, I promise you. A dozen and a half. You a yankee, aintcha? You gonna be surprised, man. These shrimp will actually have flavor. They're not boiled in salt water and ruined, like they do up north. These are boiled in crab boil. They won't cost a month's pay, either. You wanna order it dressed," he advised.

"Dressed? With the shells on?"

"No." He smirked. "Dressed down here is what you'd call 'with everything' back in Chicago."

"Dayton," he said. "I'm from Dayton. It's a long way from Chicago." He thought about saying something else to this smartass, but decided against it.

Grady picked a table by the front window to eat the sandwich, which was huge. Most of the construction workers just stood at the stoolless counter and leaned over the butcher paper their poboys were wrapped in.

As he was leaving, he decided to take a look at the phone book hanging on a chain by the pay phone over in the corner.

Twenty minutes later, he was driving back to New Orleans proper, feeling fat, sassy and downright refreshed. And ecstatic. At last, he had what might be a bona fide lead. Tucked inside his pocket on a slip of paper was Yves Mirabeau's address.

Grady decided he'd had enough of smelling his own sour perspiration. He wanted a shower and clean clothes before finding his way to the bar the man had suggested. He made a quick U-turn and headed over to Jefferson Highway, nearly sideswiping a beat-up pickup truck. He was getting into the New Orleans driving rhythm. The driver in the pickup didn't slow down a bit.

An idea occurred to him, and he turned the car around again, making a U-turn across lanes, just like the natives. One lead, like the one he'd just gotten, was great. Two would be even better.

"Sally in?" he asked. A huge woman, easily three hundred pounds, was tending bar when he walked in. Her arms looked like giant sausage links. Only one customer was at the bar, head down, apparently napping.

"Who's asking?" she said, wiping a glass and giving him the eye.

Grady was surprised at the softness of her voice, considering her size. "Tell him it's Fogarty. We met the other night."

"My wife," Sally said when he came out from the little office behind the bar. "Veronica, meet Grady Fogarty. Hey, wake Pete up there and tell him it's time to go home." He nodded in the direction of the sleeping drunk and led Grady back to a table. Veronica came over with two beers, set them down and went to stand behind the bar. She stood a minute, then reached out and pushed the sleeping man's head. He fell back, seemingly in slow motion, and landed sprawled in a heap on the floor, his head making a dull thud when it struck the concrete. The man didn't even let out a groan. Veronica looked over the top of the bar, shrugged and went back to polishing glasses. None of the customers even looked around.

"She's Italian," Sally said, turning back to give Grady his attention, eyes twinkling, his voice low so she couldn't hear. "Everybody wonders, I guess. She's a great gal, the apple of my eye. So she gained a few pounds? I love her. What's on your mind."

Grady felt embarrassed. Did it show in his face? "I got a lead on this Frenchie guy. I also got a description of somebody else that might be an acquaintance of the guy I'm looking for." He gave it to him, hair color, eyes, height, what little he had.

"That could be about six hundred guys," Sally said, taking a swig and wiping his mouth with the back of his hand. "Look around, take your pick." It was true. There were maybe four guys in the bar at the moment that loosely fit the description. All of a sudden, the biggest roach Grady ever saw crawled up from Sally's side of the bar and headed straight for Grady's drink. Defensively, he grabbed his glass as Sally swatted the bug away.

"I didn't know those boogers could fly," Grady said, in a tone half-admiring, half-disgusted. The roach whirred and landed on the floor ten feet away and began crawling"There's something else," Grady said, turning back to Sally. "This guy said the man wore alligator shoes. That mean anything? I figure, down here where they grow 'em, about a million people wear alligator shoes."

"No," Sally said. "Only one I know. You're gonna like this. The only guy I know wears alligators is that guy I was telling you about. The guy that was in the other night. What'd I say his name was? Eddie? Yeah, that's it, Eddie something. Hold on a minute."

He signaled for his wife.

"Veronica, tell Grady what you can about that Eddie character. I don't know if I mentioned it, but Grady's a cop too, retired, same as us." Grady's eyebrows shot up. "Oh, yeah. Veronica was a cop, too. Worked vice mostly. Used to pose as a prostie."

Man, thought Grady. _Man._

"Veronica, you know that guy comes in once in awhile, drinks Stingers—remember you were talking about him acting like a tourist or something—guy with the alligator shoes and those other shoes he's always wearing—snakeskin's—shit like that."

"That's easy, sugar. You're talking about Eddie Delahousie." Grady leaned in closer to hear her. The longer Veronica talked the lower and throatier her voice became. "Wears those goddamned shoes pimps wear. Stacy Adams, I think they are. There's a store up on Canal all the pimps go to. Lives over in Fat City in one of those apartments down on Arnoldt.

You know, drug central. Boozer. Punk. I'll get his rap sheet for you tomorrow, if you want. That other guy—Yves Mirabeau? I'll see what I can get on him, too. You want to be careful over in East New Orleans. They're a different breed of cat. New Orleans folks don't mix much with that part of town. They're weird people over there."

Grady had to blink at that. Weirder than here? He didn't say what he was thinking.

She wandered back down the bar, picking up glasses and polishing them.

"Well? There you go, Fogarty. She was a good cop. Never used to miss much. Still doesn't."

When Grady left, the drunk still lay on the floor.

Grady was exhilarated on the drive back to the Day's Inn. Two solid leads, he was getting somewhere.

In the shower he soaped down, then slowly turned the left tap until the water was ice cold. "Fuck it," he said aloud. "I wonder how long it takes to get used to this godawful heat?" He dreaded having to go back outside.

Once dressed, he checked his piece and got two extra clips from the suitcase, slipped them into his pocket. He spread out a city map he'd purchased at the front desk and took out the slip of paper with Mirabeau's address on it.

There it was. Monroe Street. East New Orleans. He penciled in what he thought would be the easiest way to get there.

Forty-five minutes later, he was making a right turn onto Monroe. Mirabeau's house was the second from the corner, one in a row of Queen Anne-style houses turned into boarding houses. It was in need of a paint job. Looked like green was the original color, but in the darkness it looked almost gray, at least where the remaining paint still clung to the wood. You could tell it had been a gorgeous mansion at one time, but at this stage of its history was more down-at-the-heels than dowager. Frenchie had the apartment to the left, according to the number on the sheet of paper.

The front door was wide open, but all the lights were out. Grady eased his gun out of its holster and walked in, finger on the trigger. He tiptoed in, stopped once he was inside to accustom his eyes to the blackness.

"Jimmy?" Grady's heart almost stopped. Not two feet in front of him, a voice came out of the darkness. He stepped forward, barely making out a lump a little bit blacker than the rest, from the faint light coming from the street. The lump spoke again. "That you, Jimmy?" Suddenly, a light switched on, blinding him momentarily. He held his gun in front of him and his vision cleared to show a small man sitting in a lumpy over-stuffed brown chair, his hand on a lamp on the stand beside him. The man squinted up at him. It was clear he was drunk. "You're not Jimmy." He tried to raise up, but didn't quite make it, slumping back into the chair and knocking over the can of beer in his lap at the same time. "Shit! Looky wha' y'all done, cocksucker!"

Grady swiftly walked back to the door and shoved it shut and came back to stand over the man. He made sure he got a good look at his automatic.

"I want you to tell me about Reader Kincaid," he said.

The effect that name had on the man was amazing. He was instantly sober.

"Oh, hell," he said.

Grady thought. He had to be cool here. He put away his piece, making sure Mirabeau saw what he did.

"Reader Kincaid," he repeated. "Talk to me."

"Fug." Mirabeau struggled to sit up, looked around on the floor and found the six-pack sitting there. He tore one off and popped the top, not offering any to Grady. "I ain't gone fug up, man. Shit! Reader ain't got to worry none 'bout dis boy."

"Yeah?" Grady walked over to the couch next to the chair Frenchie was in and sat down. He tried not to show his excitement. He'd hit pay dirt. Mirabeau had been in contact with Kincaid. Sounded like maybe he was involved with whatever he was up to. "Suppose you run it down to me so I can see you got it right," he said, taking the chance he'd guessed right.

"Shit, man. It ain't no big thing. Next Friday, he calls me and I go there and wait."

"So far, so good," Grady said. Damn! What should he ask next? "How about you tell me where you're supposed to go to."

"Wait a minute." Frenchie turned a bleary and suspicious eye toward Grady. "You a damn Yankee. Y'all don't work for Reader!"

Grady was on his feet and jerking the man up before he could say another word. "That's right, punk. You know what I am?" He could feel the man shaking.

"You a cop. Thass it . . . you a cop."

Grady threw him like a rag doll back onto the chair and the man moaned and tried to sink into the fabric. "You're right, Mirabeau. I'm a cop." He reached in his coat pocket, pulled out his badge and flashed it at him. Not long enough to let him see it wasn't a badge from a local law enforcement agency. Not that he could probably tell anyway, as drunk as he was.

"Oh, man," Frenchie moaned. "It ain't nothin'. I'm just supposed to pick up something."

"Pick up what?"

The man's tone turned whiney. Grady could tell he was used to talking to cops. He'd heard the same kind of voice a thousand times. "I don't know, man. Reader didn't say."

"Then I've got no choice but to tell Reader you told me his plan." That was inspired, Grady thought. "You know he knows you talked to us before. How you think he's going to feel if I tell him you talked again? You think he's going to like that?"

The man groaned again and struggled to sit up. He reached for the beer can on the floor, saw it had spilled too, and grabbed another. "You ruint my beer, man," he whined. "Two beers. You gonna buy me a beer, man?"

Grady jerked the can out of his hands and threw it against the far wall. It exploded in foam. He leaned over, got close to the man's face. "I'm not buying you a goddamned thing, Mirabeau. This is what's going to happen. You're going to tell me what job Reader hired you for and I'm going to let you keep walking the streets. You don't tell me what I want to know, I'm making a phone call. To Kincaid. I'm going to tell him you ran his whole scam by me and I'm going to remind him you were the one got him hauled in a few years back. Remember that? Think he's going to be happy about that?"

Grady could see the wheels turning in the man's head. He decided it was a good spot to give the man an out.

"Look," he said. "This is simple. I don't want you. I want Kincaid. You tell me what's going down and you go clean. We do our thing and you walk away. You don't have to worry about Kincaid. We're going to make sure he goes away for a long, long time."

Grady was really stepping over the line with this, but he was done playing by the rules. This creep knew something and he was going to get it out of him. If he couldn't trick him then he'd beat it out of him. He didn't much care at this point. Right now, he'd enjoy hitting someone, especially someone who was a friend of Reader Kincaid's. He didn't think he'd have to, though. This guy was a millimeter away from cracking. Punks down here are pretty much like punks back home, he decided, watching the guy's eyes, darting here and there as if looking for a way out of the fix he thought he'd found himself in.

"Reader won't know?" he said, finally.

"Reader won't know," Grady said. "I want everything. What you're supposed to do. How you get in touch with Reader. Everything you know."

At the end, when Mirabeau had finished with his spiel, Grady was disappointed. He was sure the little worm had told him everything he knew, but it turned out not to be all that much. Reader was going to give him a call, after which he would drive across the GNO bridge to Algiers and wait at a place along the river (which Reader would give him directions to at that time) and wait for a boat. On the boat would be a package.

No, Frenchie didn't know what was going to be in the package, except that Reader had said it would be a large one. Drugs, Frenchie figured, although that didn't make sense. Reader never messed with drugs. Something hot, he figured, shrugging his shoulders. He was to pick up the package and take it home, wait on Reader to call or show up. That was it. And, no, he didn't know how to contact Reader. No phone number, no address, no nothing.

"Okay," Grady said, when he was finished. "I think you're telling me the truth. If you're not . . . " He left the threat unfinished. He shook his head. "Here's the score. You go ahead, business as usual. Reader calls, you do what he says. Call me at—" he pulled out a pad and pen and scribbled a number, tore the sheet off and handed it to Frenchie. "—this number. Comprende?"

He did. He wasn't about to tell Reader any of this. Grady could see the fear in his eyes when he said that and he believed the man.

"Don't do anything stupid," he said in parting, and Frenchie nodded soberly. Grady was sure the man wouldn't. He looked too scared.

Back in his car, Grady smacked the steering wheel in frustration. "Damn!" he exhaled. He'd gotten something, but not a lot. He really didn't have much more information than when he'd begun. He already knew Kincaid was up to some kind of big job. With what Mirabeau had told him, he figured he was only the pickup guy. There was only one thing that could be in that package. Money. And somehow, he didn't think Reader was really going to let this loser pick up his payday. It didn't make sense with what he knew about the man. No, his guess was that Frenchie was designed to be some kind of decoy.

Sighing, he turned the key in the ignition, put the car in gear, and drove off. Maybe he'd have better luck with his other lead. Eddie Delahousie.

Bingo. His luck was holding. One E. Delahousie listed and two Edwards. Checking his map, he found that one was in Metairie. That'd be the one. He decided to wait until the next day to check it out. He was bushed. All he wanted right now was a meal and some shuteye. Maybe sleep was all he needed to fend off the headache he could feel just beginning.

Finding the apartment was easy, but Eddie Delahousie wasn't in. Grady considered picking the lock and looking around, but decided against it. It was enough for the moment to know where the man lived.

As he was leaving, a dark-blue Caprice turned in behind him from the cross street. He just caught a glimpse of the man behind the wheel and something jarred in his mind, but he couldn't figure out why until a few blocks away and the man had turned off. *Reader*. That had been Reader.

He jammed on the brakes and cramped the wheel hard into a tortured turn, going up over somebody's front lawn with his left wheel. Screaming past a stop sign, he was vaguely aware that a car coming from the through street on his left had hit its brakes to avoid hitting him as he flew through, but all that was on his mind was to find the bastard in the Caprice. He was sure now that had been Kincaid.

There! A flash of blue down that side street. He jammed on the brakes, punched reverse, his tires screaming blue smoke as they bit into the pavement. He hit the brakes again, reverse again as he whipped past the street entrance, then crammed it into drive and shot up the street. It ended at Veteran's Highway. Six lanes of speeding cars, going both ways. He eased out into the street with the front nose of his car, looking both ways. A truck, going at least twenty miles faster than the speed limit, narrowly missed him, screeching off to his right, which forced another driver over right as well, and there was a whole progression of horns blasting and curses yelled out of vehicles. Fortunately, nobody crashed into another car.

The Caprice was nowhere in sight. Grady pulled out into the traffic flow and at the next street that led back into Fat City, turned right again. Maybe Kincaid had turned off into one of the back streets.

Up and down streets, criss-crossing back and forth in a matrix to cover every possible way Kincaid might have gone, looking down alleys as he fired down residential streets, all to no avail. The man had disappeared. Acknowledging defeat, Grady pulled over, his hands shaking as he shook out a cigarette. Two deep drags and he could hold his hand up without it trembling.

That was nuts, he told himself. *What if you'd caught him, Grady? Then what? Were you going to shoot him? End up in Angola with that Cabrini guy? That's real smart.*

He eased back onto the street, forcing himself to drive a safe and sedate 30 miles per hour.

You'd a shot the son-of-a-bitch, wouldn't you, you dumb flatfoot! What would that get you? In jail yourself, is where it'd get you. Lot of help to Jack you'd be in the joint. You got to calm down, man, get this guy the right way. Find out what he's up to, bust him with some proof. Do it by the numbers, Grady. Be a cop. Forget it's your brother this asshole tried to kill.

He needed to go back to the motel, get his head straight. Figure out what to do next. Figure out how to keep his emotions in check and do the job right.

See if the front desk would sell him a couple of aspirins.

Reader hadn't noticed Grady, but as it turned out he didn't need to. He received a phone call from his old friend Bobby.

"Reader?"

"Yeah. What's the problem?"

"I thought you might like to know there's a guy asking around town about you. He was out on Airline last night. He's got your picture and everything. Funny thing. This guy's a Yankee."

"A Yankee?" Christ. He should have taken care of that waitress.

"Yeah. I got his license number. Looks like a rental. That help any?"

"That helps more than you know. I owe you, Bobby. I owe you big."

After he got the guy's description, he called another friend.

"Lionel," he said. "I got something I want you to trace."

An hour later, the phone rang again. As soon as he realized who was on the other end, Reader's voice got respectful. "Yes sir," he said and then listened for a long moment, after which he said, "I appreciate the information. Somebody else just told me about him. Don't worry. I'll take care of him." He listened a moment. "It's going just about how I thought it would."

"Mostly." He said the last aloud, softly, after he hung up. He sat there, staring ahead for long moments. After awhile, he picked up the phone again and dialed a number. A female voice answered.

After he returned and took his second shower of the afternoon, Grady lay down on the bed with only a towel around him and enjoyed the delicious frost of the air-conditioning on his moist body. The phone rang.

"Mr. Grady Fogarty, please."

"Dr. Lyons?" He recognized the voice. "How's my . . . " Grady paused as it hit him. He sat up and his towel fell to the floor.

"He didn't make it, did he?"

After he hung up, he sat staring blank-eyed at the floor for long moments. When he finally rose and began to get dressed, he put on each article of clothing slowly, methodically, in a daze.

Of all the memories he could have dredged up, the one picture that kept flashing through his mind was perhaps the oddest. It was the look on Jack's face when it was time to shoot The Cat. The "Cat" was part of the Fogarty family lore. One afternoon, when they were both kids, Jack went out to the shed to get the lawn mower. His turn to mow. He was fooling around inside, killing time before facing the blazing summer sun, when he heard a growl. Up on the worktable was the biggest cat he'd ever seen. Not purring or meowing . . . but growling! He went to grab it by the scruff of its nape—"I was just going to toss him outside," he said later, when the cat lunged at him and bit him savagely on the hand. In the fleshy part between his forefinger and thumb. Ripped it wide open. He had the presence of mind to run for the door and slam it behind him, trapping the animal.

Back in the house, their mother's face went white when she saw the wound. He was bleeding pretty good and they could see the cat's teeth had punctured all the way through. It took seventeen stitches to close it. Their father showed up just as the doctor was giving him a tetanus shot.

It turned out they had two choices. They could either bring the cat into Animal Control where they would kill it and send it downstate to be tested for rabies or they could keep the animal for ten days and see what happened.

"We'll keep it ten days," Wade Fogarty said. "I want the satisfaction of killing this thing." When they got back home, Wade went out to the shed with a quilt and a wooden crate he'd hammered together into a cage and caught the cat by tossing a large quilt over it. The animal was huge.

"Thirty-five pounds if it's an ounce," their dad ventured. "Looks more like a wildcat than a regular cat." It was huge, all right. And growled and hissed at whoever came near its cage. Each night, he had Jack feed it a bowl of milk. No more, no less. "I just want to keep it alive," their dad said. "He gets no more than that."

When the ten days had passed, Wade was waiting for them when they got home from school. He had the cage loaded up in the back of the car, along with Jack's twenty gauge, the one he'd gotten for his twelfth birthday.

"Come along, boys," he said.

He drove out into the country until he found the place he was looking for. A big field of red alfalfa, recently mowed, the sweet smell of fresh-cut hay still hanging in the air. He hauled out the cage and took it out to the center of the field, along with a length of clothesline. Setting down the cage, he tied the clothesline to the top and backed away, feeding out line until he was about twenty feet away.

"Get your gun," Wade ordered his oldest.

Jack came back with the shotgun and Grady saw his face was as pale as the day he'd been bitten.

Jack looked at Wade. "Dad, why don't we just let him go? He doesn't have rabies." He held up his hand. "See? My hand's almost healed. It feels fine." He wiggled his fingers to show him. "Good as new. See?"

Grady stepped up. "Let me shoot him, Dad." He wasn't quite sure what was going on, but he knew for sure Jack didn't want to kill that animal.

"No," Wade said. "This thing bit Jack, so Jack's the one has to kill it." He got that look in his eyes that said this wasn't the time to be defying him. "Just do it, son. I'll pull the top off and you nail him. It'll feel good. Just remember how it felt when he bit you."

Grady remembered Jack swallowing and nodding. He chambered a shell and slipped the safety off. "Okay," he said, his voice barely above a whisper. "Do it. Hurry up."

Their father smiled. "That's my boy. Okay. Here goes." He yanked at the clothesline and the top jerked off. The cat just stood there. Jack drew down, aimed . . . and nothing. For five seconds, then ten. Wade looked at him. "Shoot the damn thing, Jack! He's gonna take off in a minute."

Jack aimed down the barrel again, started to squeeze the trigger, then raised the barrel. The look on his face was a look Grady had never seen on him before. A look of abject misery.

"I . . . can't, Dad."

"Here!" Savagely, Wade Fogarty ripped the gun out of his hands. The cat started to move. First a step, a paw gingerly touching the grass just beyond the cage bottom where he stood, then he stepped off and took another step. He turned his head toward the three people and then began trotting off toward a line of woods to the east.

Kablam! The force of the pellets lifted the cat clear off its feet. Only it wasn't dead. Somehow, it staggered up and began running again. Bam! Bam! Kablam! It took three shots to finish him off.

Afterward, Grady took it upon himself to go fetch the cage. It was heavier than he thought. Lurching back with it, he saw his father and brother both just standing there, not saying anything. Both were looking at the ground. He took the cage over to the car, slid it up on the back seat. In a minute, Jack and Dad joined him. Jack got in the back seat with the cage and Grady got in front with Wade.

No one spoke on the drive home.

A week later, Jack intercepted a pass in the game against Taft High School, which turned out to be the winner, and on the way home he and Wade were laughing and chattering like the cat episode had never happened. After that, they seemed to be almost as close as before. Almost. Every once in awhile, when the family was gathered in the living room to watch TV, Grady would catch his dad looking at Jack and he had a funny look on his face.

But the look Grady remembered most was the one Jack had when he stood in that field, holding a shotgun and said, "I can't, Dad."

Some shit to be remembering now, Grady thought. He tried to pull up another memory, but couldn't. He just kept seeing his brother in that field. And then the magnitude of his loss overcame him. He lay face down on the bed and his throat ached as he tried to keep down the sobs and failed.

25

C.J.'s euphoria remained undimmed until he strode through the door of his house. Walking into the living room, he saw Sarah sitting in his favorite possession, his leather chair. That was something he was going to miss. He wondered what the furniture stores would be like in Belize. Maybe he'd have to order from the States to get what he wanted. Then he noticed the policeman. In full uniform, sitting in a chair in the corner, hat on his knee.

"Hello, Sarah," he began. "What's . . . listen, I'm sorry I'm late. I got tied up in a—"

Her voice was permafrost.

"I don't care where you were, Clifford. Fucking your little tramp I would imagine."

"I—" He started to speak, but she waved an imperious hand.

"It doesn't matter. You can see her all you want. In fact, I'd suggest you go to her right away. You see, you don't have a bed in this house any longer. I want you to leave immediately. You can have ten minutes to pick up your pathetic little personal belongings and I want you out of here. For good. If you don't do as I say, this gentleman will arrest you."

His face drained of color. What was going on? He tried to collect his thoughts, figure out what to say. God! What else could go wrong?

"You're no longer needed at the bank. As of five o'clock this afternoon you've been relieved of your duties. Mr. Savoy is in charge now. Your desk has been cleaned out and all your possessions will be sent to you as soon as we've determined what is yours and what belongs to the bank."

She kept her eyes locked on his. "I'd tell you to turn in your keys, but that won't be necessary. All the locks have been changed. Keep them as a souvenir. You'll be served with the proper papers tomorrow. Give me an address to send them to. Or would your little hideaway on Burthe be satisfactory? Didn't think I knew about that, did you? There's a lot I know, Clifford. That's it, no discussion, no arguing, no pleading, no nothing. I want you out. Immediately. To save you some breath, there's nothing in your name. Not the house, not your bank accounts, not your car. Amend that. I'm going to let you have your car. Temporarily. You might think about making arrangements to apply for credit for a new one. Only don't apply at my bank. What I'm doing, Clifford, is leaving you the same way I found you. Although," her voice dripped with sarcasm, "I don't doubt that with your charm you'll find another meal ticket. I wouldn't look for her in Louisiana, however. The word is being put out about you. I shouldn't imagine you'll find much future in New Orleans."

Sarah stood up, turned her back and began walking toward the dining room. She spoke again without turning around. "Oh, and tell your little whore she's fired as well. She can pick up her check on Friday." She left the room.

"Sarah," he said, in a little voice. He started after her disappearing figure but the policeman stood up.

What was this?

"Sorry, sir. I can't let you go in there. If you want something from the master bedroom and she approves, I'll escort you to get it. Otherwise, you'll have to leave."

"What the hell is this! I'll call the chief! I'll have your—"

"Sir, I'm here on personal orders *from* the chief. Will you leave quietly?"

Upstairs in the master bedroom, he went over to the walk-in closet and peered in. He briefly considered packing at least his suits. Fuck it, he thought; I'll get all new clothes. Clothes that won't have the stench of *her* money on them. He did go over to his dresser and open the bottom drawer. Far in the back he felt beneath a pile of sweaters until his fingers touched the full plastic bag he was after. He hefted the five full grams of cocaine in his hand lovingly and thrust it into his trouser pocket. That was all he took. He glanced once at the dresser she had bought in France and shipped over ten years ago. He picked up a paperweight and stared at the dresser mirror, but one look at the beefy cop standing in the hallway changed his mind.

At the last minute, he changed his mind, grabbed a suitcase and packed a couple changes of clothes. Just until I get new ones, he thought.

As he walked to his car, all he could think about was what he was going to do about Friday. The fucking cunt! Her grandfather was behind this, he realized. Problem, C.J. Big fucking problem. Solve it, big boy. You can do it. Don't panic; think! In his Lincoln he took out the packet from his pocket, rolled a dollar bill up and snuffled back a big hit, not much caring whether the policeman inside the house saw him or not. He thought about his next move.

The coke didn't help like he'd hoped it would.

26

"WE GOT A problem."

Eddie knew this wasn't what Reader wanted to hear. Eddie winced as the cursing came over the receiver, waiting for it to end. When it did he spoke into the silence. "Well, something's happened with St. Ives, Reader. I didn't go over there this morning."

"Why the fuck not? Didn't I tell you . . . "

"I didn't have to. He ain't there no more."

"Meet me at Sally's, Eddie. That place you hang out in Metry. Don't say any more on this phone. Be there in twenty minutes."

Fuck me, Eddie thought. That was the only coherent thought he could muster. Fuck me.

All the windows and doors were open, a coolish breeze blowing through Sally's Bar, clearing out the stale smell of beer. Sally himself was gone downtown to the open-air market in the French Quarter, picking up condiments for the kitchen, but Veronica was at the bar when first Eddie and then Reader came in and took seats at a table in the back. There were no other customers in the place. She walked over to their table.

"Stinger, Eddie?" she asked, smiling. "You?" She turned in Reader's direction.

"Jack and water. Make it a good color. I'd like a clean glass, too. If you have one."

Back at the bar, she found her husband's little black book and thumbed through until she found Grady's name and motel number. She made both drinks stiffer than she usually did and brought them to the table. She set them down and smiled sweetly at Reader, wondering if he was the kind of drinker who appreciated spittle in his drink.

Back at the bar, she dialed the number on the phone kept beneath it. It rang and rang. Every so often she hit the redial button with the same results.

"Tell me," Reader began. His eyes, cold and hard and piercing, never left Eddie's. "What's going on, Eddie?"

"Cool down, Reader." Eddie threw back half his stinger in one gulp and stuck up a match for his cigarette. His hands were shaking. "I went there last night like you said. He got home late. Then he left. Reader, there was a cop there! I think your guy's in some shit with his old lady. That's what it looked like. When I saw the cop car, I got out and walked down to see what I could see. Like I was out for a little stroll, you know?"

That was a genius move, Reader thought. Like you looked like you belonged in that neighborhood, you fucking wharf rat.

"He came out in about a half hour and got in his car. He didn't look too good. Looked worried and pissed off at the same time, you know? He was carrying a suitcase." Eddie downed the rest of his drink and said loudly, "Hey, babe, hit me."

When Veronica brought the drink, she put it down a bit hard so that some of the liquid sloshed over onto the napkin.

"I'm not a 'babe,' sonny. I'm the bartender. And the owner." She turned and walked back.

"That's a big mama!" Eddie said, chortling. "How'd you like to—"

"Shut up," said Reader. "Just tell me."

"Okay, okay. Keep your shirt on. You'll be proud of me, Reader. I did the smart thing."

Yeah, thought Reader. Yeah. You did, only you don't know it. This was turning out just like he figured.

"I followed him. He went to the Fairmont Hotel. I went in and sat where he didn't notice me. Fucker got shitfaced, puttin' 'em down like nobody's business. You could see he was fucked up. I think his old lady kicked him out."

Perfect. The plan was proceeding exactly as Reader had imagined. So St. Ives has lost his happy little home. Eddie should be telling him any minute about his hideaway Uptown. He made an effort to look interested. "Then what happened?"

"Well, he goes out to the pay phones, out in the lobby, y'know, and he makes a call to someone. I went out when he did, not knowing where he was going, thinking maybe he was leaving. I couldn't stand around so I went to the john, then came out. That's when he left."

"Where'd he go?"

"Drove clear out to Riverbend. Fucker's got an apartment on Burthe. Right there, you know, by the Camellia Grill. I figure he takes ladies there. Probably fucking all the little girl tellers at his bank."

"What'd he do at this apartment?"

"Nothing. I mean, I couldn't see in or nothing, but he was going around from room to room, by the lights, and a half hour after he gets there he turns everything off. I waited a good two hours, but he don't come out so it's obvious that's where he's staying."

"You didn't stay all night? You didn't go back in the morning?"

"Naw. What for? Isn't it obvious that's where he's gonna be? Reader, look, I ain't dumb. The guy's wife's kicked him out. He's shacked up with somebody, at least got him a little crib for playtime and that's where he's gonna be when we need him."

"You're an idiot, Eddie."

"Now, wait a minute . . . "

"No." Reader stood up. "_You_ wait a minute. This whole deal may be fucked up. It's his wife owns the bank. Her and her granddaddy. If she kicked him out, it may be he isn't going to be in any position to launder Guterez's money any more. We have us a situation, looks like. I need to figure things out. First thing we do, we go over to this apartment and see if he's there."

"Now? But—"

"Now. This minute. Come on."

Not that he liked Eddie, but it felt a bit weird chewing out the guy since this was only going down the way he'd planned—he snorted and Eddie looked at him funny—but if he didn't, he'd get suspicious.

"I was just thinking of something," he said. "That fat broad there. How'd you like to have her on top?"

"Oh," Eddie said and snickered.

They were halfway to the door when Veronica came around the end of the bar and said, "You gents can't leave. I fixed you another drink. On the house." She smiled and held up two glasses.

"Drink 'em yourself, *babe*," Reader said, and the two men walked out. Veronica went to the door behind them, alert enough to grab a pad and pencil. She was able to get both license plates. As soon as she'd written them down, she picked up the phone and dialed Grady's motel again. After letting it ring, she hung up and dialed another number.

"Hey, Harvey . . . this Harvey? Yeah, great. Listen, Harvey, do me a favor will you? I got some numbers I want you to run for me . . . "

Reader was getting into his car when he heard Eddie yell, "Guterez? Did you say Guterez?" He pretended he didn't hear him.

Turning out onto the highway, Reader allowed himself the slightest smile. He had a pretty good idea who CJ had called. He would've liked to have listened in on that conversation. Especially since he spoke Spanish fluently, could understand all the cuss words.

I hope you were creative, St. Ives. He punched the gas and moved out into the traffic. *I'm counting on it, pardner.*

The cops had let Reader out the day of his parents' funerals. Only he wasn't Reader, not then. He was Charles. The two policemen who took him in the car both called him Chuck, which he hated. "My name's Charles," he said, and both cops laughed, and they talked with each other during the ride there. It was one of those typical hot and sultry New Orleans summer days and the car's air conditioner was turned up, so Charles couldn't have heard them if he'd tried. Mostly he didn't. Mostly he was bored. He was glad to be out of the Orleans Parish jail for awhile. Spent half his time fighting with guys who wanted to make him their punk and half the time walking around puddles of vomit from the drunks that were all tossed into the same large bullpen. After a couple of fights, especially one where he broke a big guy's nose—a really *big* guy—he was left alone. The pools of vomit didn't go away. There was a never-ending supply of drunks in New Orleans who kept coming and going every couple of hours.

The services for his father and mother were scheduled for different times, but at the same cemetery. There wasn't a choice to make. He went to his mother's. Hers was next to his father's already-closed pit. His had been earlier in the day.

They buried them in the St. Louis cemetery. Where else with their money? Probably the single most famous cemetery in the United States other than the one in Washington, D.C. The St. Louis cemetery was the one they sent all the tourists to. It had been in at least a dozen movies. Marie Laveau, the Voodoo Queen, was buried there. Louis Armstrong. Books had been written about it.

His grandfather was there. When he arrived, his grandfather got up and moved to the back of the crowd, as far away from him as he could get. Reader could still remember the snarl that appeared on his lips every time he glanced his way.

There was even a bishop to deliver the funeral ceremony. Not some pink-cheeked parish priest boyo, but a full bishop.

One other thing was weird. The way he felt. He thought he killed his daddy for what he'd done to his mother, but when he got there and sat in the front row between the two uniformed cops, he couldn't feel a thing. He could only vaguely remember what his mother looked like, though it had been a mere three days since the killings took place.

Before they lowered the coffin, he said to one of the policemen, "C'mon, let's go. I want to get out of here. Take me back." It began to drizzle on the walk back to the car. They just beat a Second Line wending its way into the cemetery from off Canal as they drove out the gate. Somebody famous. A musician, had to be, although these days they were starting to see Second Lines at other folks' funerals, too. Famous corpses, usually. The cops pulled off to the side and watched for a minute, commenting on the music.

"Fucking boogies can play, can't they," Frank said. Walter, his partner shook his head admiringly in agreement.

"Let's wait till they leave," Frank said. "They play all that depressing music going in, but on the way back they're gonna get down. They been drinking since they left the Vieux Carre."

They'd been listening to the security communication on their radio.

"I bet we have to pull an extra shift," Walter said. "There's gotta be two hundred people there! All of 'em heading back to the Ninth Ward in about a half hour, drunk as skunks."

"Nah," Frank said. "They'll call out the black officers. The white guys, they'll just keep on the perimeter. Besides, if we take our time, they won't call us. We'll just wait till they leave and then drive slow back to the jail."

On the way back to the parish lockup, he overheard Frank say, in a low voice, to the other, "This is shit, Walter. They shouldn'ta made the kid go if he didn't want to. Poor fucking kid."

He began to giggle in the back seat and both cops turned around to stare at him, the one called Walter saying, knowingly, before they turned back around, "Shock. He's in shock. Think we ought to take him by the hospital?"

That got Charles to laughing more. He didn't know why he was crying at the same time. It didn't make sense. He didn't feel sad.

He hated the way his father's face wouldn't go away. He hated it worse that his mother's did. From that day on, she completely vanished from his memory and the only way he could recall her features was to pull out her picture. As soon as he put it away, it was as though he'd never seen it. It was the oddest thing. It bothered him, but he never told anyone.

The other face he couldn't get out of his mind was his grandfather's. Only it was a face he didn't want to forget. Ever.

27

IN AN HOUR C.J. had put down three drinks. Twenty minutes more and a scheme began to form itself in his mind.

The bar at the Fairmont was full of boisterous drinkers, mostly professionals in business suits and tailored outfits, many of whom he knew. They kept coming up to him, saying hi, C.J., how's business, trying to tell him banker jokes, business gossip. For once he didn't smile, didn't crack jokes, just sat staring at them until they shrugged their shoulders and walked away, looking for more lively conversation.

He liked the Fairmont. It was his favorite hotel and his favorite bar. It was its history that he admired. It represented the kind of elegant patina he had tried to create for himself. The Fairmont was the hotel the book *Hotel* had been written about. When they made the film and then the TV series, they changed the setting to the San Francisco Fairmont, which was part of the same chain.

Phone call. He'd make a phone call. He squinted at the bar phone but thought better. Privacy. There were booths in the lobby, he recalled.

He ordered another dirty martini and took the drink out with him. He failed to notice the man with long oily hair who came out of the shadows of the room behind him, stood staring at his back as if in indecision, then sauntered slowly over toward the restrooms.

"I got a problem," C.J. said as soon as he heard the voice on the other end.

"I don't like problems, C.J."

Now that C.J. was actually talking to Guterez, he found he was scared. A minute ago it seemed crystal clear what he would say and how the drug dealer would react. A minute ago though he was sitting in the bar slugging down glass after glass of courage. All of a sudden he was sober and wondering if he could make the man believe him. If he couldn't he'd be dead. One thing men like Guterez didn't tolerate and that was somebody fucking them over.

He took a deep breath and plunged ahead. There was no choice.

"It's not a big one, Fidel. Nothing to worry about. Probably my imagination, but I wanted to let you know."

There was a silence.

"Well?"

"Listen, I don't know for sure, but I think maybe somebody's been watching us."

"Like who?"

"How do I know who? Just somebody . . . probably nothing. Maybe it's my overactive imagination. No, that's not it—I know who it is. At least I think I know who it is."

"Then *who*, goddammit!" The receiver felt as if it had exploded. Fidel never talked to him like that. Must have his nose in the coke.

"Hey, there's no need for . . . "

"No need for what, St. Ives? You call me up—you're not supposed to call me up at this number—and you tell me somebody's watching you—us—whatever—and you fuck around and don't tell me who you think it is. What am I supposed to do—use fucking ESP? Tell me what the deal is. *Dio*!"

"I think it's my wife."

"Your wife! What the fuck?"

"Yeah. It's my wife. I'm sure of it. She's suspicious, thinks I have a girlfriend. I think she's checking up on me."

"You *do* have a girlfriend. You *always* have a girlfriend. I've never known you when you *didn't* have a girlfriend. She never worried about it before, did she?"

"Yeah, well . . . I know. I think that's it. I think she's got some detective on me, trying to dig up something. Maybe for a divorce. You know?"

"What's that got to do with us? With our deal?"

"Well, nothing really. Except if he—this detective—whoever—is snooping around and sees something, tumbles to what's going on, *that* could be trouble. Hey, that *would* be trouble. Trouble we don't need, eh?"

"So what do you suggest we do, C.J.?" The tone was sarcastic.

"Well . . . to be on the safe side . . . probably nothing. Like I said, I thought this week at least . . . maybe it's not a good idea for you to bring the money to my office. I thought maybe we could make the drop someplace else. I'll make sure nobody's following me. This guy—if there *is* a guy—hell, I'm not sure there is, well, another week, things'll be back to normal. This isn't the first time Sarah's gotten bitchy. Probably make me drop Amanda, tell her I'm sorry. You know. So I lose a teller. Glorified teller. So what. I know how to handle Sarah. It's just that if there's a guy snooping around trying to take keyhole photos it could mean trouble. Easy to avoid it. Do it different this one week." Then, like he'd just thought of this, "Hey, maybe I could pick it up out there?"

There was a lengthy silence.

"Fidel?"

"Si, si. I'm thinking. Yeah. You know that might not be a bad idea. Come at nine. I'll have a couple of the boys watch. If you're being followed we'll get him. Yeah. That's good. Do that. Nine. What's his car look like? What's this guy look like?"

Look like?

"Well . . . he's easy to spot. Drives a brown car. A Camaro, maybe. Has a big hook nose. Guy's got short, black, stringy hair. Tries to hide the fact he's going bald, starts his part above his ear. Greasy black hair." He blamed the booze for his snicker and tried to assume a sober face.

"Like us Mexicans, eh senor?"

"No, Fidel, that isn't what I meant."

"Good. Because I'm Cuban. Between you and me I don't like Mexicans either. Tell me more. How tall is he? How much does he weigh?"

C.J. gave him a complete description. Of Fred Touschoupe, one of the bank clerks.

"I don't like this, St. Ives. If this is a setup, something funny, you're in trouble. Very big trouble. You know that, eh senòr?"

C.J. was sweating when he put down the phone and it wasn't the drinks. For a minute he thought he was going to get sick right in the lobby of the Fairmont, but the feeling passed and he drained the glass he'd brought with him.

You're a slick son-of-a-bitch, he told himself. This is going to work out perfectly. Absolutely.

He thought about the place where he was going to have to spend the night and wondered if he could do it. Maybe he should get a room here in the hotel. Thinking about that, he decided against it. All his stuff— passports, clothes—were at the apartment.

As he left the hotel he passed by the man who'd followed him out of the bar.

Out in Chalmette, a Cuban-American picked up his ringing phone and listened to a friend of his. A very powerful friend.

"Yes sir," he said, his head nodding vigorously. "You were right. I just got a call from St. Ives. I told him to come out here." He listened some more, nodding occasionally, but not speaking.

After the other party was done, Guterez said, "Si. I understand. That's what I was thinking also. Besides, this is very amusing. I've already thought up a surprise for him. I think maybe I'll let him go . . . only not with what he thinks. I'm already having one of my boys load up the suitcases for him."

He listened again for a moment. "No. Of course not. You think I'm stupid? The money's already in the car." He laughed. "No, just a little surprise for him and Mr. Kincaid. You'll see. You're going to love this."

28

THE WINTER BEFORE, when C.J. was driving around with one of those real estate booklets on the car seat looking for an apartment to rent, he fell in love right away with the duplex on Burthe. Smack on Riverbend, the place where the streetcar makes its only turn from St. Charles onto Carrollton, the area was New Orleans at its best. Just off the mansions on St. Charles near Tulane and Loyola Universities. Scattered for blocks around were arty little shops, dress designers and intimate tiny cabarets, along with the student bars and bookstores. Lines of students, their visiting parents, and tourists waited on street corners for the streetcar.

"Charming," he said to Amanda the first time he'd brought her to the apartment. "I like this area better than any place in town. *This* is New Orleans. No fucking tourist traps like The Court of Two Sisters all the doormen steer the tourist suckers to down in the Quarter. Well, sure, some stumble down here, just not the same ones you get in the Quarter. It's . . . well . . . *charming*." Amanda wasn't the first girl he'd brought to the apartment, but it looked as though she'd certainly be the last.

He felt queasy, trying to sleep with Amanda's corpse in the closet in the same room. It was hard enough to sleep as cold as it was. The air-conditioning was up as far as it would go to keep her body from smelling. He slept with every blanket on in the place except the one he had thrown over Amanda's rapidly decomposing flesh. He'd shuddered when he'd seen how white her skin had become.

He awoke out of habit at six the next morning, but couldn't force himself to get up. With the covers pulled up to his chin he tried to consolidate his thoughts, but he just couldn't concentrate. Four hours later, he was still in bed.

When the doorbell rang he almost jumped out of his skin.

He tiptoed to the front door and looked out through the peephole. Blue uniform. His heart stopped. It was a cop, coming to arrest him for killing Amanda. He looked again. It was only a mailman. He exhaled and opened the door.

It was a special delivery. A signature was required for what turned out to be a bulky package from Sarah's lawyer, William S. Bottoms, Jr., LL.D., Attorney-at-Law. Lots of raised black letters on the cover letter. He hated the button-down asshole with his ceaseless, boring fucking cocktail party stories. C.J. laughed out loud. No more of those goddamned cocktail parties! No more sucking up to monied assholes with more money than they could ever get rid of if they stood at the door of a furnace shoveling it in all day. Standing around talking about which Mardi Gras balls were the best and which Krewes were for the nouveau riche and not worthy of anything but disdain.

He gave the old man grudging credit. Sarah's grandfather was good. There was no doubt in C.J.'s mind as to who was running the show. How'd he find out about this place so soon? Of course. He remembered Sarah's mentioning it the night before. Maybe she *did* have a detective on him.

He opened the packet. The bitch sure didn't waste any time. Notice of decree of divorcement, notice of dismissal from Derbigny State Bank and injunction against entering same. He tossed it on the dresser.

Fucking old man Derbigny. Always fucking with him. He knew beyond any doubt that this wasn't Sarah. It was her grandfather. Fucker thought he ran everything. Not this time.

Maybe he should light out. Call the pilot and tell him he wanted to leave a day early. Christ, there was a Cayman bank account with over a million dollars free and clear waiting for him. But, how far would a million dollars go in today's world? In *his* world? No, he was going to be more than comfortable. He was going to be rich. All he had to do was wait one more day, keep his nerve and he'd be like one of those assholes at those cocktail parties, have more *dinero* than he could shovel in a lifetime. He knew the investments he'd put it into that would double his money.

He got back in bed still clothed, pulled up the covers and thought about the money he was going to make, at the same time wondering if he needed to stock up on Cafe du Monde Coffee. Every so often he gave a sniff to see if he could detect any stench coming from the closet.

Veronica figured that if she didn't get an answer this time she probably wouldn't get another chance to try again until later on, when the after work rush died down. The bar was packed, blue-collar types for the most part with a few suits sprinkled among the crowd, and the only good thing about Sally not being available to help out was that it was mostly beer and shots this crowd wanted. Anybody who yelled out anything that required a blender, she ignored. The women would be along in a little bit, she knew. Most of 'em wanted to make an entrance, wiggle their asses, collect whistles. Damn that Sally! He knew to be at work this time of day. She was about to hang up when there was a click on the other end and a male voice. "Yeah?"

Veronica shouted into the phone. "Fogarty!"

"Who's this?"

"Veronica. Sally's wife. Where the hell you been?"

Grady held the phone away from his ear. It was mid-morning and he must have been asleep ever since he'd talked to the doctor.

"You don't have to yell," he said.

"It's loud in here. I can't hear you. Listen, I've been trying to reach you for hours."

"My brother died," he said. "I was out last night most of the night. Passed out, I mean. I guess I drank too much."

"I'm sorry, Grady. That sucks."

"Yeah," he replied. "It sure does."

"Well, *hell.*"

"Yeah, I know. What's going on?"

"Listen, they were here. Eddie Delahousie and his friend Kincaid. I remember him. Bad customer, that one. I got their plates. Got you an address. Kincaid lives over in Algiers, across the river. Got a reputation as some half-ass master criminal. People think he's a genius, something. I knew him as soon as he walked in the door. This guy's something else, Fogarty, but I guess you knew that. Armed robbery, banks, supermarkets, stuff like that. He likes violence. I talked to a friend of mine downtown, he read me his rap sheet. Two suspicions of murder besides his father, but nothing ever proved. He's done a couple of major stretches at Angola, some smaller bits. This guy's a psycho. Enjoys killing. Loves to use a knife. He's very creative with something sharp."

"I know," said Grady. "That's what he used on Jack. That fits with everything I know about the guy. Thanks."

"Yeah, this is a bad dude for sure. Listen Fogarty—you want him pulled in? I got friends on the force that owe me favors. I can make a call, have him picked up, use a little persuasion, open him up. We got some good interrogators. Very professional. If he killed your brother, I know some guys who can get it out of him. You give me the word. We know how to take care of punks like that down here."

Grady nixed that idea right away. He thought differently. This guy was too together to open up from a little hose job, no matter how expertly applied. He didn't want the slightest mistake made in this. There was no way he was going to do something to cause this fuck to walk. "What for? He hasn't done anything we can pin on him. No. Let him go, see what he does. I want this guy cold. I don't want him slipping through the cracks in the system. You got an address? I've been by Eddie Delahousie's place, seen where he lives. I saw what you meant when you said it was drug central. I walked around, musta got offered every illegal substance there is inside of two minutes by people coming out of apartments. That's a zoo. Where's the address you got on Kincaid? That's a funny name, Reader." He reached in his pocket for a pad and pen.

"That's what he goes by. Does a lot of reading, I guess. Bad guys consider him an intellectual. Right. You know his real name's Charles, but if you were to say Charles to him, he wouldn't turn around. Last address we got on him is an old one, over in Algiers. Vallette Street. I don't think that's where he lives. I'll give it to you, but it's two years old.

These guys don't stay in one place that long. I'll do some checking though. Maybe I can turn up a current address."

Grady didn't bother to write it down. It was the same one Marty had given him, he told her. She said she was sorry, she'd try and see if she could get something more current.

"Where's Sally? He there?"

"No. Son-of-a-bitch! You don't know how to bartend, do you?" She laughed. "He called awhile ago. He's over to Bucktown, heard about a deal on some oysters over to Deannie's. We serve free oysters on Thursdays. It's our lagniappe. You like oysters, drop by. Sally's got the best recipe for hot sauce you ever tasted. Better'n Commander's Palace. He uses garlic butter, tabasco, some other stuff. Burn the bark off your throat. Sally won't be back until later. Try around seven. Keep me posted. You want any help, say it." There was a brief silence. "And, hey. You want to stop by and try these oysters. You do, you'll want to come down here to live. Listen, I got to go. This is getting ugly. The zoo just arrived. You want to schlep some beer, play bartender for me, then stop on by. And Grady?" She hesitated for a second. "Grady, I'm really sorry about your brother. Whatever we can do to help, just say the word."

Grady thanked her and hung up. It was a great fraternity. Retired cops. Closest knit bunch in the world. He was beginning to see what Sally saw in his wife. She was a no-bullshit woman, the kind you liked on your side.

Now. What to do. He could drive over to Algiers and ask around the neighborhoods to see if Kincaid was still in town, only he agreed with Veronica. Guys like this don't stay in one place too long. No, a bird in the hand . . . he knew where Delahousie lived. Besides, with what he'd learned about Kincaid, it looked like Eddie Delahousie was only the hired hand, which meant he would be easier to track. He was pretty sure that whatever Kincaid was up to, Delahousie was involved.

I'll get this guy, Jack. I promise you.

He could see the two of them, working a case, Jack Fogarty the sharper of the two in some areas. Hell, to be honest, in a lot of areas.

"Don't put yourself down," he recalled Jack saying, right after the Boroni case, sitting in Friendly's Tavern as they hoisted a few celebratory brews. "You woulda got him sooner or later. I happened to remember our grandpap's fishing technique and what sodium looked like. But he was done for as soon's they put you on the case. You're a bulldog, Grady. A detail man. The best cops are detail men. Kind that pays attention to the little things. You would have made a good archeologist. You figure out how things are put together from practically nothing. It takes you awhile longer, is all."

Once in awhile there was an argument. Jack would comment on his lack of a meaningful social life. Ask him why he didn't get a regular girlfriend, instead of picking up a different floozy every night. Maybe even break down and get married. He'd be kidding, but Grady knew that underneath his sarcasms, Jack was concerned about a lifestyle he saw as barren.

"Why don't you go out, get a regular girlfriend, have a social life?"

"I *got* a social life, Jack."

At the time, he felt only resentment. Like it was any of Jack's business. He was a cop, for crissakes! What girl wanted a life with a cop? The ones who thought they did usually found out otherwise once they were married. He felt like saying; why don't you join the force, Jack, and see how long Elizabeth stays with *you*, sitting up night after night when you're out there, wondering if the next time she sees you you're going to be on your feet or in a body bag.

An hour after arguing, they were both drunk as losing pols on election day and laughing about the whole thing.

He smiled slightly at the memory. He hadn't wanted to admit it then, but Jack was right. His social life was pretty grim. He thought of the last time he'd seen his brother alive, lying in a hospital bed with a hole in his neck and the smile faded. He sighed and picked up the phone and dialed Dayton information for the number of McCullough's Funeral Home. After speaking with Mr. McCullough himself and taking his suggestions for the service and price of the casket, he hung up and decided what to do next. They'd set the services for four days from then. Monday. Didn't give him much time to nail Reader. Maybe he should swing by Eddie Delahousie's place, see if anything was going on. Maybe come up with an idea that would get him somewhere on this.

A few minutes later, he was gassed up and heading for Metairie and Eddie Delahousie's apartment. His watch read two-thirty on the nose.

On Veteran's Highway, Grady saw the street sign flash by as he straightened the wheel back. Arnoldt.

He found the address easy enough. It was an apartment building. *The Arnoldt Street Arms*, it said on the weathered sign. Except the *A* in *Arnoldt* was faded so as to be barely visible. The apartment complex exterior matched the sign. An old upright washer stood next to the dumpster, which was overflowing. And smelled. To avoid the stench, Grady pulled across the street where he'd have a good view and put the transmission in park. If he got low on gas, tough, he thought. He wasn't going to sit in this oven without air conditioning.

C'mon, Grady thought, looking up at the sky. *Send me some luck, willya?*

29

ST. Ives turned out to be a simple-minded chump, at least as far as guarding the security of his apartment. Getting in was simple. Reader told him through the door he was there to collect for the Sunday paper, for his kid who was quitting the route. When C.J. made the mistake of opening the door a tiny crack to protest that he didn't take the paper, Reader shoved the door back hard with his shoulder, sent the man to the floor. Eddie followed.

"You broke my nose," C.J. whined, lying on the floor and looking up, his eyes shining with fear, blood trickling down his lip onto his chin.

"Check it out, see if the girl's in one of the bedrooms," Reader said to Stet Eddie. "See if he's got a gun anywhere around." He bent over the fallen man, his face inches from C.J.'s. He could smell the fear on the man.

"Your nose isn't broken," he said, staring until the other man looked down. "It's not even bleeding that much. You oughta be more hospitable when guests come around. Invite the paper boy in for milk and cookies." He sniggered and grabbed St. Ives' hair, jerking him up. He pushed him against the wall and patted him down. "Christ! You an Eskimo?" The apartment was freezing. He went over and flipped the air conditioner off. "Sit down, Mr. St. Ives." He motioned toward the couch.

"Where's your warrant?" C.J. said. He retrieved a handkerchief from his jacket pocket and held it to his nose, taking it away from time to time to see how much blood was on it. The bleeding had about stopped. "You . . . you look familiar. I've seen you someplace." The corners of Reader's mouth turned up the tiniest bit. Think about it, cocksucker, he thought. I'll give you a clue. Ever look through any old family albums? He didn't tell the man what he was thinking, saying only, "Warrant?" Reader crossed over, pulled the easy chair directly in front of the couch and sat down facing the banker. "Oh, you think we're cops. That's rich."

Eddie appeared in the bedroom doorway.

"She's not here, huh? Probably out shopping. You give her her own charge card, St. Ives? Payday for your fucking?" Reader grinned.

"She's here all right, Reader," Eddie said, still standing in the doorway. "In there." He made a hitchhiking motion with his thumb, jacking it behind him to the bedroom. "She's in the closet. I was you, I'd turn the air-conditioning back up."

Reader stood up. "Well, get her in here. You crazy? Let her alone in there? What if she's got a piece hidden someplace and comes out and wants to play O.K. Corral?"

"She don't have no gun, Reader. Wouldn't matter if she did." He looked over at St. Ives and showed his teeth. "You want to tell him? Y'all have a lover's quarrel, St. Ives?"

C.J. put his head in his hands and moaned.

"You might want to turn the air back up, Reader," Eddie said again, this time with an unmistakably brazen leer.

The way it turned out, C.J. St. Ives was a pushover for a head slap or two. His nose seemed especially tender and was obviously linked directly to his vocal cords. Reader thought about that again and told himself to remember the joke, tell it sometime. He tried it out on Eddie.

"Here's a biology lesson for you, Eddie. Notice how the tongue of the banker species is connected directly to the nose. You want to know something, tap the nose a little." He demonstrated, enjoying the way the cartilage cracked.

C.J. moaned. He began rocking back and forth, his hands cupped protectively around his face.

"You don't have to do that," he said. "I've told you everything."

That was not quite true. One thing Reader was sure of was that either

St. Ives was neglecting to fill in the whole picture or was misleading him on several important parts. He went through the papers that were lying on the dresser. This was something he hadn't counted on—St. Ives killing his little girlfriend—but it was a plus he had. One less person to keep an eye on.

"So this is the deal, eh? Your old lady kicked you out, you and your girlfriend there had an argument and you iced her. Just an accident, is that it?"

"Yes." C.J. put his hands down tentatively and peered at Reader. "That's precisely what it was."

"Okay," said Reader. "I believe you, Mr. St. Ives. The problem is, Eddie's a skeptic. And since he's my partner I got to humor him. Eddie, look in that box you brought in and get me those pliers. The needle-nosed ones. And see if there's a pair of scissors in there. Don't worry, Eddie. I know Mr. St. Ives is the truthful sort. He wouldn't mislead us intentionally, but to set your mind at ease, I'll ask him again."

Eddie was one big grin. He didn't know what was on Reader's mind, but it was going to be fun. He was sure of it.

C.J.'s eyes grew wide as Reader went over and foraged around in the box himself, coming out with two pairs of handcuffs and a roll of two-inch gray tape. "What are you doing?"

Reader silently cuffed St. Ives' ankles together and then his wrists.

"Mr. St. Ives is the noisy type, I think." Eddie watched over his shoulder as Reader tore a piece of tape from the roll and pressed it over C.J.'s mouth.

"Come here, Eddie," he said. "I think you better hold Mr. St. Ives' arms. He's liable to get a little twitchy."

"Nice manicure," he said, holding up the banker's hands.

The whole time Reader worked, C.J. screamed, only it sounded more like a turbine warming up, what with the tape over his mouth. When Reader was done, he held up the fingernail from C.J.'s right forefinger in front of the sweat-drenched man's face. A single drop of blood hung suspended from it. There was a lot more on the finger itself.

"I'm sorry, Mr. St. Ives," he said. "I do believe I've chipped a nail. It's these pliers. I probably don't have the right kind for a delicate job like this.

I think I've got the hang of it, though. The next one'll be perfect. You'll see. You know, Eddie, I suspect you may be right. Mr. St. Ives might be holding out on us. I believe if he is, we'll find out though. I mean, looky here. We've got nine more nails to get at the whole story. Oh. I almost forgot. There's ten toenails, too. Unless he's one of those odd ones and has more. How many did your mother count the day you were born, Mr. St. Ives?"

That's when C.J. fainted, the first time.

Grady wondered if he was making the right move. Maybe he should have gone across the river instead and checked out the neighborhood at Kincaid's last address some more to see if he still lived in the area.

No, Eddie was the one. Wait on him on Arnoldt by his apartment. He'd show. He'd be easier to follow. Kincaid was the brains of this operation, whatever it was. He'd get farther faster sticking to Eddie. See where he went, what he did.

If he showed up at all. Grady got one of those hunches old cops get from an instinct born of years of dealing with punks and perverts, that the timetable for whatever the two were scheming was drawing close.

From time to time he turned on the engine and ran the air conditioner. This place was too godawful hot for humans to live in.

The traffic to and from Eddie's apartment complex was amazing. Nobody stayed long—ten, fifteen minutes at the most. Fat City was drug central, Veronica'd told him, and she was right about that. The action was identical to the last time he'd been here. He bet it never stopped. There seemed to be a lot of hookers around as well. He could see into the complex, which was centered around a pool, and every once in awhile a guy would pull in and go up to one of the four or five girls around the pool and they'd disappear into an apartment. Watching all the action made him want a shower. A cesspool is the way he'd describe where Eddie lived. He must feel right at home.

Whatever they were planning looked like it was going to be done with a pipe bomb. Why did they blow up a dog? *If* they did, but it was pretty clear at least that this Eddie'd been the one to blow up the German shepherd across the lake. It didn't make any sense. The dog wasn't worth anything. Hell, they *bought* the damn thing so it wasn't some dognapping from some rich animal lover gone hinky. So what was the purpose of that? Some kind of trial run? What the hell was it Mirabeau was supposed to pick up?

What did he know about this Reader? What was it Veronica said? A genius. She said he was a genius. He liked killing and he liked supermarkets, banks, places with big numbers. What did all that have to do with bombs and dogs?

Grady felt another headache coming on. The whole thing was screwy. Go through it again, he told himself. It connects somehow, some way. You've got to put the details together in the right way. Try to make some sense of it. He recalled an old movie with James Garner where they used these dogs to hold up a bank. Dobermans trained to rob banks. Maybe this Kincaid has figured out a new twist where he hooked them up with pipe bombs. But then, why would he blow up the dog? As an object lesson to the other dogs? It just didn't compute.

Maybe some variation on the idea in the Garner movie was possible, but he didn't think so the more he thought about it. He saw the picture of Reader in his mind. There was a huge ego involved. Genius type. Geniuses, especially pathological criminals like this guy, wouldn't use someone else's plan no matter how clever it might be. No, this would have to be an original thing, something nobody else could have thought of. The money probably wasn't that important to a guy like this. The money would be a way of illustrating his importance, show how smart he was. A control freak, Grady was sure. Probably didn't drink, at least to excess and despised those who did, figured them for weaklings. He kept turning what little he knew about the guy over in his head, trying to get a handle on him.

The criminal mind, particularly the *superior* criminal mind—fascinated him even as it repelled him. The ultimate challenge, especially for a plodder like himself. He had to admit that as much as he abhorred what Reader had done to his brother, in a way, he was enjoying the chase. He'd been up against some pretty slick operators in his time, but he had a feeling this Reader made them all look second-rate.

He wondered how much money was at stake.

I wish Jack was alive, he thought. I wish he was alive and sitting right here with me. He'd have this figured out in no time. How would you approach this, Jack? Think like a genius criminal? That'd be easy if I happened to be a genius criminal; however, I am just a dumb schmuck cop.

He shook out his fifth Marlboro medium in the last hour and lit it. I need to come up with some self-discipline, he thought ruefully, feeling the ache in his lungs as he inhaled deeply.

He turned the key in the ignition again and winced at the warm air that blasted out of the vents. How can anybody think in all this heat? It was a miracle anything ever got solved. He glanced at the gas gauge. It might be a long wait.

Reader was talking about Indians again. He, Eddie and C.J. St. Ives sat in the living room. St. Ives had come to, but he looked none too good. His color was mostly gray.

"See, Eddie, this guy's an Indian, too," Reader said. "He's a little more advanced Indian than you are, but he's for sure an Indian."

Eddie put down the TV Guide. "Why you goin' off about the goddamned fucking Indians again? I told you, I'm French-Canadian, not no goddamned Indian. You know what, Reader? I'm your fucking partner. Why don't you treat me like a partner? I might not be as smart as you, but I'm not a complete idiot, either. I've done a few things. Why'd you pick me if you think I'm so dumb? This is bullshit, your always raggin' on me."

Reader ignored him. They'd made a search of the apartment after C.J. came to and told them what they wanted to know. Eddie found the papers taped up under a dresser drawer. "See?" Reader said. "He's got part of the package, thinks he's got it all, thinks he's in the twentieth century with both feet. Only he doesn't realize this is almost the twenty-first century. See these passports, birth certificates? This is rich. He's planning on robbing Guterez himself, I bet. Aren't you, St. Ives? Can you believe that, Eddie? What an amazing coincidence." It was, too. Reader couldn't get over it. St. Ives planning to rob *his* money. That was rich. Wait'll he told

. . . It was just lucky Reader'd picked this week for his own plan. A week later and he would've been fucked. Man! Reader didn't like this surprise at all. The dead girl was one thing, but this . . . this was serious. He wondered if there was anything else he didn't know. If there was, he was going to find out.

Eddie whistled. "You think so?"

Reader's lip curled in scorn. "He's got a pretty good plan, shows intelligence. Only notice I said a 'pretty good plan'? Shows no matter how much he thinks he's on top of the game, he's still thinking like an Indian. He's been thinking about all the good things that were going to happen with his scheme and not enough about things that could go wrong. That's the way the Indians would do it. Sit around the bonfire, whooping and hollering and counting in advance all the scalps they were gonna collect, all the white men they were gonna erase. Never thought too much about what if there were more white men than Indians or if their guns were bigger. Or if maybe the white man was sitting around *their* campfire planning to do something to the Indians.

"The smart guys," he continued, "spend more time figuring out what to do when things go bad than they do in thinking about how they're going to celebrate when they win. I'll bet that's what you do, isn't it, Eddie? I'll bet you thought a whole lot about how many shoes you're going to buy when this deal's done, how many different women you're going to screw. I bet you haven't thought once about what might go wrong and how to fix it if it does. Am I right?"

Eddie didn't answer.

"Water." St. Ives croaked from the couch. Can I have some water?"

"Sure," Reader said. "Give him a drink, Eddie. See if there's any popcorn, too. Got to have popcorn at the movies."

He reached over and turned on the TV.

"This thing work all right?" The picture was fuzzy at first, then it began to clear. "Sally Jessy," he said, smirking. "You watch this crap? This is nice." He didn't expect an answer. "I'm glad to see you've got a VCR. Saves us the cost of buying one. I've got a little tape you're gonna get a kick out of."

He turned the volume down and watched the picture for a moment. Sally Jessy Raphael was talking to two young black men on both sides of an older black woman. She walked over to the black woman and hugged her. The camera showed a close-up of Sally and the tear rolling down her cheek.

Eddie came back in and handed a glass of water to St. Ives who sat up and took it in both hands. "There ain't no popcorn, Reader."

Eddie looked like he'd lost his best friend. Maybe he ought to ease up on him before he went south on him, Reader thought.

"Eddie, I guess I been hard on you, haven't I? Hey, partner, sorry about that." He could see Eddie was approaching the point where his attitude could fuck up the job. The last thing he needed now was the guy pulling some shitfit and walking off the job. There were still things he needed him for. Cool him off, make him feel good was what he needed to do. Fuck his ass up later, when he'd gotten enough mileage out of him. He forced a grin. "I was kidding about that Indian stuff. Take a joke, Eddie. Cool down. I don't think you're so dumb. Would I have taken you on if I thought you were a fuck?"

Eddie visibly relaxed. He gave a tentative smile. "Well, shit, Reader, you been treatin' me like a broke-dick dog, whaddya expect? How you think I'm gonna feel? We're supposed t'be partners, this thing."

Reader walked over and slapped him on the back. "Hey, take it easy. I've got job nerves. Couple things been going different than I wanted was all. Like this dead bitch in the closet. Ol' CJ here surprised me, is all. It's under control. We're fine, Eddie. We're about to become rich. One more day. Say, why don't you go out, get some more food? Get yourself a six-pack. Hell, pick up a case, bring it back. We'll all hoist a few. I bet Mr. St. Ives could use a beer. Couldn't you, Mr. St. Ives? Here." He handed Eddie a fifty-dollar bill. "Get some chow, maybe some mudbugs, some cold boiled shrimp, hot sauce. Sounds good, huh? Get back in two hours, Eddie. Tell you what—you got time-go home and pack your shit, get what you need for when we blow this burg. Also," he reached into his pocket and took out a single key and handed it to Eddie. "This is my apartment key. I want you to stop by and get some stuff we're going to need. I got two boxes up on the closet shelf. All the shit we need's there. There's a garment bag, too. Get that. I need fresh clothes."

As soon as Eddie left, Reader went over and grabbed St. Ives by the arms and pulled him up to a sitting position on the couch. He sat down beside him and pulled the man's hands to him.

"I think you maybe forgot a few little details, Mr. St. Ives. We're going to have us a little chat. I need to know about these passports. Although I got a pretty good idea what they're for. I just need you to tell me. There's something else."

He took the man's hand and forced the middle finger out. He grabbed the nail with the pliers and tore, ripping it across the quick, ignoring the screams in his ear. He didn't bother this time to cut down the sides with the scissors. Reader waited until St. Ives came to, his face drenched with sweat, moisture showing all the way through his suit coat. He'd broken the finger, too. That was pretty obvious the way it was twisted and already swollen. He felt the sweat on his own face from the exertion. He looked at the bloody little object and flipped it across the room and set the pliers down on the coffee table. He didn't have to pick them up this time: the things the banker was saying in a high, reedy voice told Reader he spoke the truth.

"Now," Reader said, pleased at his work. "What kind of story did you run on Guterez?"

St. Ives started to open his mouth and say something, but Reader interrupted.

"You got to know I'm way ahead of you, my friend. You can't even see my smoke I'm so far ahead. You want to be very careful here and tell me the truth. I'll know when you're lying. You already surprised me once. It won't happen again."

There wasn't a drop of blood in St. Ives' face. His voice was low and husky when he began talking.

When he finished, Reader said, "That's a little more like it, Mr. St. Ives. Let's you and me hop into the bedroom, let me make you all snug. I've got a few phone calls to make. You can go keep your girlfriend company. Here." He stuck the dish cloth he'd been using to mop up the blood into St. Ives' handcuffed hands. "Keep this tight around those fingers. They feel better already, don't they?"

On their way to the bedroom, Reader nodded approvingly. "Say, Mr. St. Ives, you'd make a good con. You got lockstep down pat. Most guys fall down the first time they try it. You want to be careful when we get to that rug."

One of the calls turned up some interesting information. Reader's friend Lionel had traced the license plate he'd given him to a rental agency. For a fifty-dollar bill, Lionel said he got a copy of the rental agreement from the bozo salesman, which not only gave the guy's name but where he was staying. As soon as Reader heard the name, he made the connection.

"Thanks, buddy," he said, replacing the phone.

He sat there a long time, thinking. Too much shit was happening he hadn't planned on. He breathed deeply. Figure it out, big boy, he told himself. Adjust. It's what you're good at.

After a while, he picked up the phone again.

"Octavio? I want you to tell your boss something. I want you to tell him you got a tip there's a DEA agent nosing around his business. Tell him you got it from a cop you know. Tell him the guy's a lone wolf kind of dude. He's doing this on his own. Let him know you tracked the guy down and he's staying out at the Day's Inn in Kenner. Guy's name is Fogarty." He spelled it.

There, he thought, satisfied. The guy's no longer a problem. Guterez would take care of him.

He leaned back and clasped his hands together behind his head. *I needed a challenge,* he thought. This was getting boring, it was going so good. The slight uneasiness he'd felt a short time before had turned into rosy optimism. This was going to work out even better. More fog and mirrors for the show he was putting on. That was nice.

He made one more phone call. "We had a problem, but I've fixed it," he said. "Settle down," he ordered, listening to the voice on the other end. "I said I fixed it. Here's what I want you to do."

30

GRADY TURNED THE car and the air on for maybe the tenth time since he'd been there and fired up the last of the pack of cigarettes he'd opened when he parked. He thought of the carton on the back seat and was glad he'd bought it. The stakeout on Eddie's apartment was going on longer than expected.

With nothing much else to do, he considered his financial situation. Not good, especially with his brother's unpaid hospital bills and the cost of the funeral three days away. With all that, it was doubtful he'd be able to afford much more than a room somewhere for the rest of his life. He was already deep into what little savings he had on his little jaunt down here. There was a little over three thousand dollars left and if need be he could maybe sell some stuff—his shotguns and the diamond ring his uncle left him, but after that he'd have to return home. He'd have to go back in a few days anyway, for Jack's funeral.

Just as he was settling into some deep-down sorrowful self-pity, a car turned into the street.

He quickly slid down beneath the seat. He knew at once it was Eddie in the brown Cavalier, from Veronica's description, which had pretty much matched up with Pelkerson's.

The Cavalier went past his car and turned into the complex parking lot. Eddie emerged from the car a second later and went into an apartment on the ground floor.

When the man came out with two suitcases ten minutes later, Grady knew he'd made the right decision to wait at his place instead of trying to find Kincaid. The suitcases were a good sign something was up. Eddie was going on a trip and he'd bet the itinerary would begin right after whatever it was those two were planning went down.

All right, Grady thought. I'm on him. Let's see where a dog-killer punk like this likes to go. He turned the key in the ignition.

He followed Eddie, keeping at least two cars behind him, not that he felt he needed to be that careful. The guy seemed to be oblivious to the possibility of someone tailing him.

As he followed, the neighborhood changed, houses thinned out, became bigger, more expensive. Then, just ahead, the Cavalier slowed and pulled off and parked by what looked like a restaurant. *Deannie's*, the sign said.

Eddie came out ten minutes later, his arms under a huge paper sack. Some kind of food, most likely.

It looked like Eddie had enough for ten people, whatever it was.

Looks like he's going to party, Grady thought, waiting until Eddie went by before he turned around and slowly began catching up.

Eddie's car headed back into Metairie, but instead of turning on Veteran's he kept straight, ending up turning left on another highway. Grady recognized it as Jefferson Highway. He was beginning to know the geography, at least of the main streets.

For the next twenty minutes, Grady followed the Cavalier. Up to St. Charles with its row after row of regal mansions, through a seedy part of the city, past the Super Dome and then to the Greater New Orleans bridge. Then they were coming down off the bridge into the city of Algiers.

Grady recognized the bridge and the turnoff when they came off it. He was glad his gun was nestled in the small of his back. Coming off the bridge, the place looked like a war zone. He'd been to Stony Island in Chicago once, but the Cabrini-Green projects had nothing on this dump.

The apartment projects immediately to their left as they came off the bridge looked like the pictures he'd seen of the riots in Brooklyn some years before, the ones President Reagan had visited and were everywhere on the evening news. The look on the faces of the few people he passed looked as hopeless as the deteriorated buildings they were crammed into. Then he was leaving the projects and entering a more respectable neighborhood. The lawns were small and neat and many homes sported flower boxes.

He was so busy watching for derelicts he almost missed Eddie's turn down a side street. He barely made the corner, prayed silently that Eddie hadn't heard the scream of his tires. The Cavalier had disappeared, but at the first intersection Grady's eyes caught a glimpse of it to the right about a hundred yards down the side street. He backed up and turned, noting the street name as he flashed by. Thurman. Eddie was a block and a half ahead by that time, pulling the Cavalier over to the curb. He was getting out by the time Grady could pull his own car over, only half a block away. Grady killed the engine and waited to see what the man would do next.

Eddie went up to a house and let himself in. Grady noted that he took the key from his pocket, not from the ring in his other hand. This isn't his house, Grady thought.

Who the hell's place is it then? *Kincaid's*. That's it. It must be Kincaid's. Maybe they were having a meeting. The guy he wanted could be inside right that minute. Briefly, he thought about busting in, shooting the both of them, then disappearing back up north. He held onto the thought for a moment then let go of it, knowing it was unrealistic. It was nice to imagine, though. Putting a bullet through this guy's brain would be something that would be hard to top, pleasure-wise. One day.

When Eddie reappeared, he was carrying a couple of big boxes in his arms, a garment bag on top of them. He walked to his car and popped the trunk. Grady watched as he placed them inside. After he closed the lid, he stood a minute staring at the house and scratching his cheek as if trying to remember something. He stood for a minute, then shook his head and got in his car.

As soon as Eddie pulled away, Grady drove up to the house and stopped. He reached under the seat, grabbed the pad and pencil he kept there and hurriedly wrote down the address. He squinted at the house then pulled out after Eddie.

He barreled around the corner just in time to see his quarry take a left a block up. He was back up behind him in less than a minute. Luckily, there wasn't much traffic.

Grady followed him back across the bridge and in a few minutes they were back on St. Charles Avenue. He kept close behind as the street curved right and became Carrollton. Grady saw a sign that said Riverbend. That made sense. This was the same street he'd been at not much earlier. Eddie was backtracking. Grady wondered why he hadn't stopped here the first time through.

Eddie was pulling into a Winn Dixie parking lot a block up on the left.

Grady pulled over to the side of the street and watched. At first, he figured Eddie'd forgotten something for the party since there was a grocery store there, but no, he got out with one of the cases of beer—long-necks by the size of them, the old-fashioned big brown ones—and started walking up the street.

Grady moved the car over into the same shopping center at the opposite end, parked, and watched Eddie cross the street. As soon as he was across, Grady got out and followed him. He strolled up to the corner and watched Eddie cross Carrollton and head for the opposite side of the street. He stood on the sidewalk and pretended to be lighting a cigarette as Eddie walked up to the second house from the corner, went around to the side and let himself in at a gate Grady could just see from where he stood. He took his notebook out and pretended to be studying it.

There was a little bookstore on Carrollton directly across from where Eddie had gone. Little Professor. There was a Little Professor bookstore in Dayton, but it was huge. This looked like a boutique. Same chain? He took note of the street the house was on—the intersection of Burthe and Carrollton, and he went into the bookstore.

It gave him a good vantage point. He could see the house through the front window. Pretty soon, sure enough, along came Eddie and another man, husky, with longish black hair, who looked to be in his fifties. Kincaid.

Grady could feel his heart beat faster. Settle down. Take care of business.

Right away he could see Kincaid was the guy in charge by the way he walked, and the way Eddie followed along slightly behind him. Kincaid looked like he was chewing Eddie out, probably for parking so far away, and Eddie was jawing back, but Grady could see it was a losing battle. Kincaid was pretty much ignoring him. He came out of the bookstore in time to see both men jump into Eddie's car.

Shit, he thought. Here I am, way the fuck down here and there they go. He debated whether to sprint for his own car, but decided against it. He'd have to pass right in front of them and he didn't want either of the men to get a look at him.

Lucky thing, as it turned out. They were only driving the car over to the house. He shot back inside the bookstore, ignored the curious glance of the clerk. Grady picked up one of the books in the front window and began to thumb through it, one eye on the house.

Eddie didn't appear to be any too bright. It looked as though if it were up to him, he'd make six trips to unload all his stuff, a block and a half each way. Kincaid was definitely the brains of this pair, he realized.

And this is it. Grady knew that whatever was going down was drawing near. He couldn't figure out where this house fit in, unless this was where Kincaid was staying. If that was the situation, what was the other house, the one in Algiers? Whose house was this? Somebody else in on the job with them? Whatever the fuck the job was.

He watched the two men unload Eddie's car. Then Eddie came out alone, started up the car and pulled out on the street heading west. Grady left the bookstore, uncertain what to do. Run for his car and tail Eddie or stay put, keep his eye on the house? He was in luck once more: he saw that Eddie was just going to park the car back in the shopping center parking lot.

Why the hell is he doing that? There were plenty of parking spaces on the street by the house. He went back inside the bookstore for the third time. This time he'd better do something or the clerk was going to call the police.

"Police," he said, flipping open his wallet and flashing his shield at the young man. He didn't bother to mention that he was retired, and from Ohio. "Surveillance. We got a tip there might be a drug transaction taking place up the street." The clerk nodded blankly, shrugged, and went back to stacking.

Grady knew he was taking a risk. It wasn't that either man knew of his existence, but if he kept showing up in their lives . . . He left the bookstore after nodding to the clerk, crossed the street and walked down Burthe. When he went past the house where Eddie and the other man were, he noted the street address. He continued past until he reached the corner, turned west and went around the block, coming out across from the shopping center by a high school. He watched a streetcar make the turn from St. Charles onto Carrollton, waited until it passed so he could cross back over to the shopping center and his car. Just as he took a step to go across, he felt a hand on his arm and turned quickly. It was a policeman in uniform. Shorts. The word "cute" came to Grady's mind and he struggled not to smile.

"You got business here?" the cop asked.

"Am I doing something wrong, officer?" Grady asked. What the fuck?

"I didn't say that, sir. May I see some I.D.?"

Grady shrugged, pulled out his wallet and flipped it open. His shield glinted in the sunlight.

"Oh," the policeman said. "Visiting fireman, eh??

"Yeah," Grady closed his wallet and put it away. "Pleasure, not business. Just visiting. Can I ask why the roust? Hope I don't look like the bad guys."

The officer smiled. "Actually . . . yes. The, uh . . . "

Grady's hand went to his eye. "Oh, yeah. The patch."

"Sorry, sir," the policeman said, suddenly embarrassed.

"Hey, no problem. Just doing your job. I understand."

The officer seemed relieved Grady wasn't mad. "It's drugs. These dealers are all the time around here. We keep a full-time guy here during school hours, but it doesn't help much. While we're at one side of the building, somebody's at the back. I swear there's more drugs around here than out in Kenner." He shook his head. "Well, sir, have a nice stay while you're here."

Grady turned and walked quickly across the street, stepping around a crowd of tourists waiting for the next streetcar. He locked his car and looked around. There was a bar on the corner, *Madigan's,* that looked like it gave a view of the house the two men had gone into.

Nice-looking place, wide open doors and the cheery look of a neighborhood favorite. Grady picked a table in the front. A large plate-glass window afforded a full view of the house down on Burthe. He ordered a beer and got change for the phone. The bartender pointed to the back, by a pinball machine.

"Sally."

"You got 'im."

"Can you find out who owns a house if I give you an address? Maybe check out a Polk directory, you got one?"

He was on his second beer when the phone rang and the bartender asked if there was anybody named Fogarty there.

"Fogarty, that was easy. The owner is a Melvin Davis. It's listed as a duplex. Is that right?"

"That's what it looks like. Upstairs and down. Separate entrances, way it looks."

"Yeah, well, I got the info from a friend down at the station who looked it up for me, said it's one of those investment properties, the owner doesn't live there. He's got a bunch of these things, rents 'em out. Has a company called Breakwater Management."

"You got a number for them? Never mind, they're probably in the phone book."

"I'm ahead of you, Fogarty. Already called them. The top unit's vacant. The bottom one's rented out. Interesting who it's rented to."

"Who?"

"Clifford St. Ives."

"Should that mean something to me? One of Reader's criminal friends?"

"I guess it wouldn't. Caught my attention, though. Mr. St. Ives, or C.J. as he's known around town, is quite the big shot. Married, got a big place Uptown off Magazine near Flagon's. Within walking distance of Commander's Palace, the toniest restaurant in town. His place is worth a cool million, at least. In his wife's name. Actually, her grandfather's the real big shot. One of the biggest names in the state. He's all hooked up with the governor and all the other big deals."

"Big shot in what way, Sally?"

"Banker. He's the president of Derbigny State Bank. Kinda funny, isn't it? I mean the president of a bank and all, married, and he's got this little place over on Riverbend. That's mostly students in that part of town. Tulane undergrads. Professors, long-time locals, old money. It's a nice neighborhood. What would a guy like St. Ives be doing with a little crib like that, you suppose?" He laughed.

"A girlfriend."

"Yep. You're pretty sharp for a Yankee." He laughed again. "Ol' C.J.'s quite the guy, you know. Lot of talk about him around town. There was talk of him running for governor a few years back, but something about his background kept him from doing it. I think the wife's grandfather put the kibosh to that. There's lots of rumors, but nothing concrete. Something about he's not who he pretends to be. I've heard talk ol' C.J. comes from cracker stock, but nothing for sure. I know one thing. His wife is the hammer in that family. Her granddaddy is one powerful pistol, one of the old coonass Mafia, that's all cleaned up these days, respectable. He's one of a handful of people can decide who the governor's gonna be. It's his bank, one of them anyway. He gave it to her when she came out. Now that guy's a guy to watch out for. Titus Derbigny. He's the real deal. Not like this piss-ant who married his granddaughter."

Grady paused from writing down the names Sally was giving him.

"Came out? She's gay? I don't understand . . . "

"Debutante. Guess they don't have debutantes where you're from. It's a big deal with some folks. Not me. I came out in the back seat of a Plymouth. Anyway, it looks like this is C.J.'s love nest. Any of this help?"

Grady thought a minute. "Yeah. I think so. It's interesting, him being a banker. Things are starting to make some sense. I'll keep you posted. Thanks."

"Hey!" Grady put the phone back to his ear. He'd almost hung up.

"Why'd you mention Reader?"

"Cause Reader's in this apartment. The one you say belongs to this C.J."

"Jesus."

"Yeah," Grady said, after a silence. "Two and two are starting to make four."

"I read you. Starting to look like an inside bank job, isn't it?"

"That's the way I see it. Say, Sally, one more favor. Can you see if Kincaid has a phone in his name? Maybe a cellphone? If he does, can you get me a copy of his phone calls for say the last month?"

He could and he would.

He hung up and took his beer to the front. He couldn't see all of the house itself from there, but he could see the street directly in front and part of the building. If any of them came out this way, he'd be able to see them.

It sure looked as though it was going to be an inside bank job. Probably this C.J. was in on it. But what did they need electronic gear for?

"What time you close?" he said, going up to the bar, laying a five on the bartop and sliding his empty bottle over.

"Close? You're in New Orleans, mister." The whole bar laughed, and Grady thought he heard the word "Yankee."

31

READER MADE HIMSELF a drink from C.J.'s stock and peeked in on the banker in the bedroom. Sleeping. He sat down on the couch in the living room and took inventory. He was proud of how he'd handled the Fogarty thing. Once Octavio told Guterez the guy was a DEA agent, in town with a mission to bring him down, that little problem would be eliminated. He chuckled aloud, visualizing how his plan was moving along, in spite of the unexpected arrival of the cop from Ohio. All the players were jumping through the right hoops.

And Guterez. The thought of the man made Reader laugh aloud. Such a cocky little rooster. Always thinking he was on top of his game. *Just wait*, he mused. *Whole lotta shit's in this ball game, Fidel.* He knew exactly how the guy'd react. Hadn't he learned volumes about the guy from Frank Cabrini and hadn't he been studying the man for months and months? I know when you're gonna take a shit, Guterez, he thought and smiled. Cabrini had your number all right. A vision of a notebook swam up in his mind. A page with Guterez's name on it and the word *ambitious* scrawled underneath.

It was proceeding just as he'd figured. Soon, Mr. Banker C.J. would be taking a trip out to see Senor Guterez. Senor Guterez would, of course, know all about the bomb St. Ives was wired with, long before he showed up, thanks to the information he'd fed Octavio. Information Guterez was sure to get out of him pretty soon if he hadn't already. Reader wished he could be there to witness *that* little scene. He wondered what Guterez would do. That was the *X* factor. Although it wasn't. Not really. He figured the Cuban for one of two moves. Maybe he'd just blow St. Ives up, zip him right there. Reader didn't think so, though. An explosion at his warehouse would bring unwanted visitors in blue uniforms. No, he'd send him away, only not with the money. He bet he'd make C.J. think he had the money though. He was counting on that. Reader wondered what Guterez would put in the suitcases if he did what he figured. Toilet paper, maybe? He'd figure Reader to take care of the banker once he showed up without the money. It was delicious, imagining the suave drug dealer making chess moves in his head. Not knowing he, Reader, had already placed his own pawns in such a way that any move he made was preordained. Guterez would think himself the slickest dude in the Big Easy. There was no doubt he'd send somebody with C.J. or have him followed. To take care of Reader. One less guy to deal with at the final showdown.

Yeah. It was like being the director of a play. You did this and then that and then it all fell together on opening night. Everything that happened, that looked happenstance, deriving from the expediency of the moment, had been arranged for. It was all built on Reader's knowledge of the psychological makeup of each of the principals. His only regret was that he couldn't be in several places at once to see each act played out.

Reader got up and went into the kitchen. He deserved another drink. He poured two fingers from a bottle of rum into a water glass and raised it in a toast.

"I'm coming, Grandfather," he said aloud. He drank the liquid down in one smooth gulp. At the same time, he heard a loud moan from the man in the other room.

An hour passed, and the bartender at Madigan's and one or two patrons at the bar saw the one-eyed man sitting by the front window smack his forehead with the back of his hand, push back from his table and walk out.

"Tourist," explained the bartender to one of his regulars sitting at the bar. The regular shook his head in agreement.

Crossing the street toward the apartment he'd seen Reader and Eddie go into, Grady was struck by the serenity and beauty of the neighborhood. Manicured lawns, brightly-colored flowerbeds, women out with babies in strollers, Tulane students walking by with books in their arms.

The lock to the upstairs apartment was easy. Once inside, Grady tiptoed through each of the rooms. There were only four. A huge living room area, a fairly-good-sized bedroom, a bathroom, and a kitchen nook just off the living room. The best thing was that it was empty. Going back into the living room, he dropped to the floor and put his ear to the hardwood. He could hear voices below, but they were too muffled to be understood, except for an occasional word or two which didn't make much sense, heard out of context. He was within a few feet of his prey, but he might as well have been a hundred miles away.

Discouraged by the failure of what he'd thought was going to be a good idea, Grady slipped back out.

He started to walk back to his car when he thought of something. He walked back to the apartment building. There were no windows on the north side and from his knowledge of the upstairs apartment he figured the layout was probably the same in the lower. He was right. Edging around the corner, he saw there was a large picture window in the back, exactly like the one in the upstairs apartment. He crept to the edge and lifted his head up slowly until he could see in.

It was the living room. Toward the rear of the room stood two men, their backs to him. Reader and Eddie. Eddie turned suddenly and walked toward what Grady knew was the kitchen, from the way the rooms were laid out upstairs. As soon as he stepped away from Reader, a remarkable scene revealed itself. There was a man sitting in a chair. He'd been hidden until Eddie moved. And he was handcuffed.

Must be St. Ives. But what was he doing in handcuffs? Even from the distance of the far window, Grady could see the man was in pain. Just then, he lifted his hands to brush his cheek and Grady saw the blood on his fingers. What the hell?

"Sir!"

The voice was so unexpected, Grady jumped straight back, luckily out of sight of the window. It was a woman, standing in the yard next door.

"What are you doing?" she yelled. She had a hoe in her hand and was wearing a wide-brimmed hat, the kind older women favored when working in their flower gardens. "I'm calling the police!"

"Lady," Grady said, motioning to her with his hand to keep it down. "I *am* the police." He whipped out his badge, flashed it at her. "Go back inside," he said, keeping his voice down.

She glared at him a long second, then brandished her hoe at him like a spear. "So you say. I'm calling the police anyway." She stomped toward her own house.

Time to book, Grady thought, striding quickly around the house. He was amazed the men inside the house hadn't already heard her, but he was in luck. He turned the corner of the house and trotted across the street and back toward Madigan's. Looking back as he reached the corner, he breathed a sigh of relief. No one had come out.

Cruising back toward his motel room, he tried to figure out what in the hell what he'd just seen meant.

Obviously, if it was C.J.'s bank Reader was planning on robbing, it wasn't an inside job like Grady initially thought. Reader wouldn't've handcuffed his partner. Grady went over what he knew. Slowly, a picture of what Reader was up to began to shape itself in his mind: Reader blew up the dog and stole the Futaba from Jack so he could wire St. Ives up with some kind of bomb and send him in to rob his own bank.

Was that enough to convict the man? He'd seen convictions under the RICO act for far less. But that was Ohio and this was New Orleans. Would it be enough down here? Would the police even bother arresting Kincaid on Grady's theory, even with the latitude RICO offered? The more he considered it, the more he knew he couldn't take the chance. No, he'd have to come up with more than what he had.

Twenty minutes later, he was pulling up to the house Eddie'd gone to. The one in Algiers. The lock was easy. When he slipped inside, he didn't see a sign of life around except a sleeping wino across and down the street. Most of the houses along the block were dark.

The place was tiny. Two rooms, three counting the bathroom. A small bedroom and a smaller kitchen area. As he began searching through the rooms and the only closet, two things became evident to Grady. This was Reader's place all right. A stack of bills and junk mail was on the kitchen table, all addressed to Charles Kincaid or "Occupant" at this address. He didn't see any personal letters. It was evident Reader didn't plan to return. The place was essentially bare. No luggage and no toilet articles. Oh, there were sheets on the bed and a few clothes hanging in the closet, but it looked to Grady like a house essentially abandoned. Eddie must have been cleaning it out for him the day before. Getting all his personal shit. What convinced him of that was when he was going through a small desk in the bedroom. The side drawers were clean as a whistle, but in the main drawer were scraps of paper. Things you mean to throw away and don't get around to, the stuff you clean out of your pockets at the end of the day. One of the items was significant. It was a receipt from a photography studio and the notation said the twenty-dollar charge was for a passport photo. Only there wasn't any passport in the drawer. Or anywhere else in the house.

That's what he sent Eddie for, he bet. To pick up his passport and other papers. It made sense. Whatever he was planning, Reader wasn't going to return to his apartment.

It was time for a little old-fashioned detective work, Grady decided.

The kind he was good at. He locked the front door to Reader's apartment before closing it behind him. Go back to the _Times_-Picayune morgue, look at old newspapers again, see if he'd missed anything the first time.

First, he wanted a change of clothes. He was starting to smell sour. And he felt like he smelled. A little too ripe for this kind of work anymore. He wished he possessed more of his brother's intuition.

32

AT ALMOST THE precise minute Grady was going over the Mississippi River on the GNO Bridge, his motel room was being approached by two swarthy Latinos with suspicious bulges under their sport jackets, speaking Spanish to each other in Cuban accents and low voices.

Unknown to either of them—under instructions from Senor Guterez to kill the man they found inside—the person inside at that moment wasn't Grady Fogarty, but his new friend Sally Graziano. Sally was there doing a favor for Grady, delivering a neighborhood parking sticker, the kind good for any place in town. New Orleans is a town that is short on parking space and all the neighborhoods require residents to have their cars stickered for the area they park in or the police would cheerfully either boot or tow their car. Knowing Fogarty didn't realize this and knowing he ran a good chance of running afoul of the parking laws, Sally had taken it upon himself to twist the arm of an old friend down at parish headquarters for one of the stickers usually reserved for big shots. Politicians, lawyers, prominent businessmen, those with an "in" with the police. With the kind of sticker he was bringing the cop from Ohio, Fogarty would be able to park anywhere in town and not be bothered. He had something else for him. A computer printout of all the calls Kincaid had made. Turned out he did have a cellphone. When Sally'd knocked at his door and found Grady wasn't there, he'd gotten a key for the room by flashing his badge at the clerk, quickly, so the guy couldn't see it was just an auxiliary badge. He planned to drop off the parking decal and phone call sheet and call Grady later. Tell him to look on top of the desk in the room and put the sticker he'd find there on the inside back window of his car.

Also unknown to the two assassins as they entered the room, was that Veronica Graziano was sitting out in the parking lot, working on a particularly bad hangnail that had been pestering her all morning. She was listening to Annie Ross and her gravelly execution of Doc Pomus's "To Hell With Love".

Veronica wasn't so engrossed in her sore finger or the music that she failed to see the two men get out of their car, walk up and slip inside the same room her husband had just gone into. She reached beside her for the sawed-off Remington .12 gauge she kept loaded under the front seat and shoved the car door open. With a swiftness that belied her massive bulk, she ran quickly to the motel door.

At the same time that she reached the open door, a Delta 707 coming in from Atlanta passed low over the motel as it came in for a landing on the runway a few hundred yards away. The ground trembled and the roar of the aircraft's jets drowned out the swish of tires and din of horns and other traffic noise from the highway, but even with all the jangle of sounds, Veronica's ears caught the distinct pop-pop-pop that might have sounded like firecrackers to the uninitiated, but to her policewoman's experience meant only one thing. Gunfire.

She drew back a tree stump of a leg and kicked the slightly open door in, a new series of gunshots going off at the same instant the door was ruptured from its hinges.

It was lucky that both men were standing together or else one of them might have gotten a shot off at her. The twelve gauge had enough of the barrel shortened that it created a wide enough pattern to nail both of the men as they turned toward her, killing the one on the left instantly, and disabling the second man long enough for her to chamber another shell before he could react and bring his own gun up. Her second shot caught him full in the chest and lifted him off his feet, depositing him on top of Sally two feet away where he slumped in a sitting position, little bubbles of blood trickling down from both corners of his mouth. Instantly snuffed, only his eyes remained wide open in a walleyed stare of surprise. She dropped the shotgun and with amazing agility and strength was standing over the fallen man, yanking him off her husband like he was a large rag doll. Her first concern was that Sally had caught some of the pellets. She needn't have worried. He was already shot. Veronica was five seconds too late.

In twenty years on the force, Sally'd never had a bullet sent his way. That was what Veronica thought of as she fell to her knees, lifted up her husband and carried him tenderly over to the bed. He looked like a child almost in her massive arms.

"Oh, baby," she sobbed. She kissed him softly on the lips and felt the warmth of his blood on her own chin. His eyelids were fluttering rapidly. Veronica had seen this before. He was going. She fought to regain control, drawing back deep breaths into her lungs.

"It's . . . it's . . . " he struggled to talk. "Shh," she whispered, but he struggled to get it out. Unsuccessfully. His eyes rolled back and he was dead.

When the cops arrived twenty minutes later, Veronica's eyes were red but bone-dry. The chief officer on the scene was an old friend, a guy she and Sally had both served with.

She'd had time to come up with a good story.

"I understand, Ronnie," he said, clicking his tongue in commiseration. "We'll take care of this. Like you said, looks to me like these guys just came after the wrong cops. An old grudge, you say? They been following you for weeks? Some guys you had a run-in with at the bar?" He looked at her, staring hard. "And the guy who's staying here? You were just coming to visit him? I get all this right? An old friend from up north?"

She was nodding when Grady pulled into the motel parking light and screeched to a halt, leaving his car in the middle of the lot, door wide-open, as he ran toward the crowd of blue gathered around his motel room door.

"Let him through," Veronica cried, hearing the commotion at the door and getting a glimpse of Grady. "This is his room."

Suddenly freed from the two uniforms who were holding him back,

Grady rushed into the room and stopped short at the sight of the carnage before him.

33

C.J. St. Ives caught himself thinking about something that hadn't entered his mind in years. Alligator hides. He was seeing himself at ten years of age, rubbing salt on a hide, working it in with the leg bone of a cow, probably from one of the Brahmas that roamed wild in the scrub pines around the swamp. His father, sitting in the corner of their shack, nipping on a jug of 'shine, eyes steady on him the whole time, watching to see he didn't slack off. C.J., then known to his family as Jimmy LeBarre, was aware of his father's eyes on him and especially aware of his leather boots that caught him in the slats more than once when his father thought he was slacking off. His mother too, washing out clothes by hand on the back porch, eyeing her husband from time to time, estimating the times it was safe to take a breather without incurring his wrath.

Bad as that was, right now he wished he was back out in the swamp packing gator tails for the trader that came by. The trader gave them ten bucks apiece for the big ones and sent them off, packed in dry ice, to restaurants, mostly in Louisiana, but some in odd places like New York City and Boston—restaurants that proudly served such exotic foodstuffs as barbecued alligator, elk steaks, delicacies like that for adventuresome gourmets to try.

For once, he was in a situation that he had no control over with no way out. Tears spilled down his cheeks and he wiped his face with the back of his hand, the good one, the one without the broken finger and missing nails. A hand that was handcuffed to its mate. The smell from the closet was beginning to get worse and he swallowed hard to keep from throwing up.

What was he going to do? Guterez was going to kill him. He couldn't dream of going to the cops to get the bomb defused, the way this Kincaid explained it . . . and he believed him. God that was awful. That dog . . . half its body disappearing . . .

C.J. harbored no illusions about Kincaid. He wasn't going to disarm the bomb no matter what he said. This guy enjoyed killing. He could see it in his eyes, read it in his voice. Eyes like his father's. He'd seen eyes like those before, knew the cruelty that lay behind them. He'd seen this man somewhere, but he just couldn't remember where or when.

God, what was he going to do? He put his head in his hands and sobbed, tried to keep the sound muffled lest the two men hear him and come in.

Amanda, he said, silently. Amanda, I'm sorry. I'm sorry you're dead, I'm sorry I didn't get the divorce and leave with you months ago.

His mind whirled. He should have gone with the million in his possession. If only there were some way to still do that. He'd even leave without the million, go work in the cane fields down there, whatever they raised. Anything to keep his life.

He tried to think, but couldn't. He kept seeing that dog and picturing that happening to him. He wondered what it felt like to be blown up. He shuddered, started shaking and couldn't stop. It was like a fever. He hunched over in the bed, his knees up to his chin, shaking and shivering and sweating. The pain in his fingers had died down to a dull ache for a while, but they were on fire again. The stink of his own fear and the smell from the closet hit him and he couldn't help it, it all came up and there was *that*, right in front of his nose and this time he didn't bother to keep his weeping silent, only let it go, not much caring when he heard the bedroom door open.

"Fuck it, *you* clean him up." Eddie was mad. And inches away from pulling out. Reader was at it again, ordering him around like he was some broke-dick dog. Like he needed this shit or something. "All I do is what you tell me. You think I'm your nigger? Get yourself another nigger."

"No, Eddie, you're not my nigger. You're my *associate*. You're my *associate* on a job that's going to make you a millionaire. Go ahead, you want to clear out, quit on me. That's okay. I can do it by myself. I'll be thinking of you when I'm sitting in a cabana, got me a movie star with the sex drive of a president on each side."

Reader stood at the doorway, looking at the banker lying in his mess on the bed and Eddie standing beside him, his face all wrinkled up from the smell. He turned and went back to the other room knowing Eddie would grumble and bitch and cuss him out under his breath, but that he would think about the money and how close they were. In the end he'd clean up the man. Just like he'd do everything else he made him do.

"Keep that door closed," Reader said, walking away. "You can smell that shit out here." He giggled. "Man! You got one stinky girlfriend, St. Ives!"

Later on, he sent Eddie out for something for lunch and he didn't make a peep.

"Get something besides chicken," he said. "I'm turning into a fucking chicken. Get me a poboy. Crawfish. Dressed."

Grady was amazed the woman hadn't shed a single tear.

He was sitting with Veronica at a back table, the only two people in the bar. For the first time in twelve years, Sally's was closed. Veronica had stuck a chair in front of the door. No lock, she said. We never thought we'd close. From time to time, someone banged on the front door, but neither Veronica nor Grady even looked around. After awhile and some muffled cursing the thirsty patron left, presumably to search for a more accessible place to get shitfaced in.

He'd said all the platitudes he could muster and now the pair just sat in silence. From time to time, one of them refilled their glasses from the bottle of Jim Beam sitting between them on the table. The guilt Grady felt was beating down on his sorry ass . . . and that's exactly what he was feeling . . . sorry for his sorry ass. Veronica had told him, emphatically, that he wasn't to blame . . . but he knew he was. If not for him, Sally would be behind the bar that minute, filling glasses, telling jokes, answering the phone. But he wasn't. Sally Graziano was lying in the city morgue, awaiting the autopsy the state law required in deaths resulting from a felony. Probably alongside the two men who had killed him.

He'd been dumbfounded when he heard who the assassins were.

"They were a couple of Fidel Guterez's men," Veronica had said. "How the hell you think Guterez knows about you? And what would he want you dead for?"

Grady thought hard. Then he remembered. The midnight blue Caprice that had come up behind him at Eddie's. Maybe Reader had made him after all. It was the only explanation he could come up with. But what connection would Reader have with Guterez?

He decided to test the theory that had been tumbling around in his mind for the past day or two on Veronica. First, he outlined everything he'd learned, step-by-step, then told her what his idea of what Kincaid was up to. "I think St. Ives does some business with Guterez—probably launders drug money through his bank. I think that's what Reader's after." He told her about the dog that had been blown up and that it looked like the explosion had been triggered by the device Kincaid stole from his brother. "I think he's going to hook this banker up with some kind of explosive, make him bring him the money from the bank's vault," he said. "I don't have all the pieces yet, but that makes as much sense as anything else I could come up with."

"Motherfuck!" was all Veronica could say at first. She poured a large shot and drank half of it, studying what Grady had laid on her.

"What're you gonna do?" she said.

Grady sketched out his plan and Veronica shook her head. "If you're wrong, you're fucked."

"I know," he said. "If I overestimated him, he gets away, scot-free."

"You don't think I oughta just have the locals pick him up?" Veronica asked. "We got enough on him now, maybe. What about RICO?"

"No," Grady said. "I thought of that, but how many creeps you seen walk in your time, Veronica? With more than this on them?"

"Yeah," she said, knocking back the rest of the whiskey and pouring another half a glass. "Yeah. Do it your way, pal. Whatever you need, just ask. I'm in this war all the way. Don't even think about leaving me out. Not now."

"I'm sorry Sally got into this," he said. "If it wasn't for me . . . "

"Hey!" Three hundred plus pounds of mad woman stood up, eyes smoldering. "*You* didn't kill him. Those creeps did. And Reader's behind this somehow. I don't know how, but I know he is." She swayed and Grady realized she was drunk. He wasn't all that sober himself. "Get the motherfucker, Grady. Just get him." She collapsed back into her chair, the wood squeaking in protest. Grady jumped up, went quickly over to her, put his arms around her massive shoulders and just held her as the sobs poured out.

She didn't cry long. This was one tough woman. After she was done, she smiled through her tears and blew her nose. "You know how I feel, Grady?" she said. He shook his head. "Like I'm the Q in a Scrabble game. Without my U, I'm fucked."

He got from her the name of a friend and her phone number and made the call. He waited till the woman, a tiny middle-aged black woman named Thelma, arrived. Satisfied she was in good hands, Grady made his goodbyes and promised to keep her informed.

"Anything you want, you call. You get this sonofabitch." was the last thing Veronica said as he went out the door.

He was just getting in his car when he heard his name being shouted from the back door of the bar. It was Veronica.

"I almost forgot," she said, coming up, breathing slightly heavily from the exertion. "Here."

She stuck an envelope and a stack of perforated computer sheets into his hand.

"What's this?"

"The stuff Sally was bringing you. In the envelope's a parking sticker. Put it in your rear window. That other's the list of phone calls made from Kincaid's phone."

A break . . .

"It's got—"

"Yeah," Veronica said, grinning. "I borrowed a Cross-Reference Directory from a friend downtown and just went ahead and wrote down all the names next to the numbers. Figured it would save you some trouble. Luckily, they were all in the reference."

She went back inside the bar. Grady slipped into his car, cranked over the engine and opened the air conditioning full blast. He began scanning the printout. Most of the numbers belonged to bars, and Eddie Delahousie's number also appeared frequently. Two numbers were very interesting. One belonged to the prison at Angola. The other . . . He couldn't figure out why Kincaid was calling this number, but according to the sheet, he'd phoned it twenty-three times in the last week and a half. He stared at the sheet, tried to figure out its significance.

555-1231. It was a residential phone. The name beside the number was C.J. St. Ives.

An hour after he began, Grady came across an article that made him sit straight up. He was in the basement of *The Times-Picayune*, doing the only thing he could think of. Boring-as-dust, old-fashioned police work. It may have paid off. He opened the folder he'd brought with him and pulled out a sheet of paper and scanned it.

"Shit!" He said it aloud before he could think. The woman at the front, the employee who'd allowed him access to the paper's morgue, looked at him and gave a disapproving frown.

It was right there in front of him.

What he'd just read in the microfiche file was the account of Charles Kincaid's trial as a juvenile for killing his father. Only his name wasn't Charles Kincaid then. It was Charles *Derbigny*.

And Reader's rap sheet confirmed that. It was under Charles "Reader" Kincaid, but sure enough, the murder victims' names were listed as Bradford Wayne and Mary *Derbigny*. He had to have read the damn sheet twenty times, but he'd never caught it. It was just something his eye had skipped over. And registered in his subconscious. That's why he'd read it so many times. Each time, there had been something not right, something he should have caught but hadn't.

It was what Frank Cabrini had hinted at with his "clue." He must have figured Grady'd never guess what he was talking about. The old capo was almost right. Indeed, Grady nearly finished the article before his eye was drawn back and he spotted the name.

The more Grady thought about it, the more logical it became. Guy kills his father, it's reasonable to want to get rid of the name, too. It was getting clearer in some parts, murkier in others. Okay, Grady told himself. Settle down. Don't try so hard. It'll come. It's Derbigny's bank. But the man he was holding was St. Ives. Was the old man in it somehow? That didn't make sense. And why was Kincaid calling C.J. St. Ives, the son-in-law? That made no sense whatsoever. Grady had assumed they didn't even know each other. What was going on here?

There was something else in the article that was interesting. A brief mention of the dead man's sister-in-law who'd caused a disturbance during the last day of the trial. She'd been in the courtroom and had created a bit of a stir, according to the article, having to be forcibly restrained and removed.

Grady wrote down the name of the reporter's byline and went quickly up to the desk where the woman sat, the frown still on her face.

"This guy," he said, "Is he still with the paper?"

She glanced at it. "He was. He's retired. Used to be an editor, I think. Off writing his novel, I suppose." She sniffed, as if she didn't have much use for novels or their creators. Or maybe the gesture was directed at newsmen.

She was reluctant, but Grady was insistent, and she made a phone call to Personnel.

"Seventy-Six, Seventy-Two St. Ann," she said after hanging up, sighing like the effort had really pained her. "It's on the edge of the Quarter, just across from Armstrong Park."

The man was home.

"Mr. Noles? Donald Noles?"

He was indeed Donald Noles, and he was a bit drunk but handling it well, as if it was a condition he was used to. And yes, he remembered the Derbigny case very well. He'd written several stories on it and a couple of them had been picked up by the wire services. "Got me a job as an editor," he said through the screen door. "I was up for a couple of awards for that series, but nothing ever happened there, unfortunately." Grady told him what he was after and what his connection was. The man murmured something that sounded like sympathy, standard-issue.

"Come on out to the porch," he invited, bringing along a bottle of wine and two glasses. "Damn air conditioning's on the fritz. Cooler out there." He poured each a glass of something red and motioned Grady into a wrought-iron chair around a matching table. The retired editor took one across from him. Across the street, the park was a huge expanse of manicured grass and huge oak trees.

"That the one named after Louis Armstrong?" Grady asked.

"The same," the man said. He was already starting on his second glass and Grady had only reduced the volume in his own by a sip or two. Good wine. "Snake country," Noles added, and Grady didn't know what he was talking about.

"The park? There's snakes in there?"

Noles smiled. "Sorry. I was just remembering. There was a lady from your state down here years ago. You may remember it. The story made all the national media, even the Today Show. She was killed over there."

Grady tried to follow what the newspaperman was saying. He couldn't figure out what snakes had to do with it, but he seemed to remember something along those lines.

"She was shot and there was some kind of fuss about her name, if I remember right," he said, trying to recall the incident.

"Yes! That's the one!" The man sounded downright gleeful over the woman's murder. "A drug dealer shot her. She was walking in the park, snapping pictures. Not that unusual that she was shot over there. I've seen four shootings right from this porch in the past three years."

"Wasn't there something about her name that made it big news?" The details were coming back to Grady, but they were sketchy.

"Exactly." Noles poured his third glass. "What happened was the mayor sent a telegram to her family, expressing his sympathy on behalf of New Orleans. Only he misspelled her name. She was from some little town in Ohio and some TV reporter got hold of it and blew it up into a big deal. The gist of it being that New Orleans was such a cold, lawless town that they couldn't even bother to get a murdered tourist's name right. Shit!" He was so disgusted at the thought that he downed his glass in one long gulp. He went on. "What they didn't say was that most mayors wouldn't've even bothered sending a damn telegram. I mean, hell, we get probably five murders a week here on a slow week. The Saints never do much, but we're always in the top five in murders. The mayor was just trying to be a nice guy. He didn't send telegrams to every victim's family, I'll guarantee you. City budget wouldn't cover it." When he said "guarantee" he drew out each syllable.

"Damn fool woman asked for it."

"Pardon me?" Grady didn't remember this part.

"That's what I meant about 'snake country'." He must have noted Grady's quizzical look. "You ever been where there's a lot of poisonous snakes, son?"

Grady said that, yes, he had. In boot camp, in Virginia.

"And what do you do when you're in snake country?" he said.

"I don't know. Watch for them, I guess."

"You're damn right!" The man exploded, slamming his glass down on the table so that it splashed, narrowly missing Grady. "You watch for snakes!" He seemed to realize he was a bit overdrawn and calmed down. "Well, that gal was in snake country and didn't watch for snakes."

He ran down the facts of the incident. "First of all, she was walking around in a park that's maybe the biggest drug scene in New Orleans. She was walking around in August, on a day that hit the high nineties, and the only other people in the park were young black men . . . " he paused and winked, conspiratorially, " . . . wearing full-length leather coats. Now, sir, wouldn't that tell a reasonably observant person something?" Grady started to say something, to even agree, but the man waved his hand. "Hell, yes, it would. She must have been from the smallest town in America. Fucking Mayberry!" He gave a bitter snort. "She's walking around, taking pictures with her Leica and there's hypes every ten feet. Never opened her eyes, I guess. Even then she was all right. Nobody bothered her. Until she went up to a young buck and handed him her camera and asked him to take her picture." He looked at Grady, eyes narrowing. "Now, you're a detective, or so you say. What do you think a drug dealer is doing to do when a young white woman hands him a thousand dollar camera?" Again, he didn't wait for the answer. "Fuck, you *know* what he'd do. Just what this guy did. He saw a month's worth of smack in his hand and he did what any addict with any sense would do. He started walking off with it. Six pawn shops are a block away. And what'd this lady do? She starts screaming at him. What choice did he have? He turned around and shot her. Fuck. I'd done the same thing myself, somebody that stupid."

He poured the last of the bottle into his glass. It came to just half a glass. "So," he said. "Are all the people in Ohio that dumb?"

No sense in getting this guy all riled up, Grady thought. He was an asshole, but he did have a point. He'd seen individuals in Dayton do the same thing, only with lesser consequences. Go in the wrong neighborhood and get messed up. It happens. He shrugged. "Not all of us," he said. "Some of my best friends are half-bright."

"I hope not." Noles looked at him as if to see if he was putting him on, decided he wasn't and grinned. "What was it you wanted to know?"

"I was doing some research and in one of your articles, you said something about a woman creating a disturbance during the trial. A—" He reached in his pocket and withdrew a scrap of paper. "—Sally Truesdale. Remember that?'

The man chuckled. "Crazy Sally. Hell, yes. A nutcase with a big mouth. Had a summer place on Mars if you know what I mean. Kept squawking to everyone who would listen that her poor little nephew was innocent. Screeching at the top of her lungs in court. Innocent! Little fucker clobbered his dad with a baseball bat. Over twenty times. Didn't have a tooth left in his head or a bone that hadn't been turned to pulp. His own mama wouldn't've been able to recognize him. The kid was going after his grandfather when they caught him. That sound innocent to you?"

He leaned back in his chair and stared across at the park. "There was some evidence that maybe the father had killed the mother, but in the end the prosecutor proved that the kid had killed both of them. Sally Truesdale wouldn't accept it. Kept saying the father abused everyone, her sister and the kids—there was a little girl, too, Charles' sister, Sarah, I think her name was—and Crazy Sally was convinced her sister had been killed by the husband and Charles was just protecting himself. It was all checked out. Nothing to it. Charles cut his own throat, driving clear across Pontchartrain to the grandfather's house. Said up front he'd come to do grandpa in."

"How'd the mother die?" Grady was starting to get a different picture than he'd started with.

"Broken neck. Snapped clear in two."

"If Charles did it, why didn't he use the same bat?"

"Who knows? Maybe he figured he didn't need it on a woman."

There wasn't much more he could tell Grady. If Sally Truesdale was still alive, she'd be in the loony bin over in Mandeville.

The ceilings were enormously high and were painted the same white as the walls. Everything was white, even the plastic cubed furniture in the deserted waiting area, only the patina of age gave everything a dirty ivory cast. The cheap futuristic-style plastic chairs were totally out of place in the former mansion. The barred windows were curtainless and looked out on an expanse of lawn in the back that could have used a serious shot of nitrogen.

Yes, Miz Truesdale was a "guest," and certainly, she could have a visitor. Are you a relative, sir? No? Well, okay. I guess. She hasn't had anyone come by in years. Don't know as you'll get much out of her, though. She's . . . you know . . . The squat, busty nurse at the reception desk made the universal sign for the mentally impaired by tapping her finger on the side of her head.

Compassion, thought Grady, following her down a long corridor. *You've got it in buckets, lady. Hope I don't draw your twin if I ever find my sorry butt in a place like this.*

The first impression Grady received when he entered the cell-like room the nurse pointed at was the overwhelming stench of urine. It was so heavy it burned his eyes and tickled his nose. The nurse clicked her heels and returned to her station.

"Atchoo!" He sneezed loudly.

"Bless you." The words were uttered in a quavery voice by a tiny figure slumped in a wheelchair in the far corner of the room.

"Mrs. Truesdale?" Grady approached the woman. It was difficult to see. The shades were drawn tightly and the lights were out. Everything was in dark shadow.

"Who's asking?" There was movement as the figure in the chair straightened up a bit and began wheeling toward him.

"My name's Grady Fogarty. I'd like to ask you some questions if you don't mind. About your nephew."

"Which one?" the woman cackled. "I've got twelve. At least, I used to. They might all be dead now, far as I know. They're not falling all over themselves to come visit their old aunt, I'll guarantee you!" She said "guarantee" with the same inflection as Noles had, but it sounded nicer when she said it. Grady could see her much clearer now, his eyes becoming accustomed to the dim light.

"Charles."

She stopped wheeling toward him. "Oh!" she said, her mouth flying to her mouth. "You know Charles? Oh, how is he?"

"Not exactly," he said. "I'm just doing some research on his case. He recently got released from prison and seems to . . . " He stopped. How to tell his aunt that Reader was up to no good?

"Seems to what?"

Grady sighed. What the hell. "Well, ma'am, it looks like he might be up to something."

"You mean, up to something no good, don't you? Why don't you say what you mean, young man? I'm old, not stupid. And I don't live in a fantasy world. I know what my nephew's become. It's not his fault, but it doesn't change what's real."

Grady decided to be straight with her. "I'm a cop, Mrs. Truesdale. Well, a retired cop. I think your nephew killed my brother." He hated the way her face looked when he said that, but he plunged ahead anyway, telling her everything. He finished and said, "I don't know where he is. I was hoping—"

"That I might tell you. Okay. I understand. What you have to understand is that I don't know. Haven't seen Charles since the trial. Even if I did know where he was, I'm not sure I'd tell you. I am his aunt, you know."

Before he could reply, she asked, "Would you turn on the light? Open those blinds, too, would you? I ask the nurse every chance I get to do that, but she's always too busy. Damned lazy twit!"

Grady smiled at her outburst. She might be related to Reader, but he instantly liked her. She didn't seem all that crazy to him either.

He walked over and pulled the blinds up, brilliant sunlight instantly flooding the room, which he now saw was the same dingy white as the rest of the place. A bed, which could more accurately be termed a cot—hell, it *was* a cot—he could see that, now—a nightstand with a lamp sans lampshade—a bare bulb that he could see was speckled with fly shit—and a cheaply-made chest of drawers and that was the furniture inventory. It was bright enough with the sunlight he didn't need to turn the light on. Probably start smoking anyway, with all that crap on the bulb. He turned and got a good look at Sally Truesdale. Long, white, matted hair hung down past her shoulders and she was the most wrinkled person he'd ever seen. Fierce, blue eyes stared out at him and he was struck by her hands. Probably the longest fingers he'd ever seen. Gnarled and twisted with arthritis now, he could see at one time they had probably been graceful, even patrician. Beyond her, he caught a look at her bed. The blanket was thrown back, exposing the sheet, which was blotted by a large bright yellow stain, superimposed over at least two older, more faded yellow Rorschach blots.

"When was the last time they changed your sheets, ma'am?" he asked.

A faint blush on the woman's cheeks was visible in the new light.

"I'm sorry," he hastened to say, aware he had embarrassed her terribly. "It's just—"

"I know," she interjected. "The whole damn room smells like piss. I suffer from . . . my bladder . . . " She lowered her head, looked at her hands.

"You wait right here," he said, and hurried out the door. *That was a stupid thing to say,* he thought as he strode toward the nurse's station. *Where in the hell was she going to go?*

At the desk, a different nurse was on duty than the one who'd led him to Mrs. Truesdale's room.

"I want fresh sheets," he told her. "And I want them now."

As he was making her bed, he began talking to Sally Truesdale. "A reporter gave me your name," he said.

"Noles," she said. "That the one? Call me Crazy Sally, did he?"

When he confirmed her guess was right on both counts, she said, venom in her words, "May his black soul rest in hell. He's the one got my nephew sent to prison. Him and that prosecutor. They were both in league. Did he tell you he got promoted to an editorship after the trial? That the prosecutor got himself a judgeship? Derbignys carry a lot of weight around here. You catch Charles, they'll probably get you your own casino."

No, Grady said, tucking in the top sheet. "Noles didn't tell me any of that. And I don't gamble, so what would I do with a casino?"

"Leave that out," she said, lifting a quavery finger to point at the bedsheet he was pulling tight. "My feet cramp up if the sheet's tight. Please."

He did as she requested. That done, he went over to the window and forced it open. Instantly, the room smelled better, the foul air sucked outside. Probably what killed the grass, Grady thought. Opening these windows. He took the dirty linen and tossed it out into the hall, closed the door and came back to sit on the bed, faced her wheelchair.

Sally Truesdale told Grady an interesting story over the next three-quarters of an hour. About a wealthy and powerful man, Charles' grandfather, Titus Fuller Derbigny, who, according to her account, railroaded her dead sister Mary's son straight into prison. About a man who controlled newspapers and what went in their stories. How he got an assistant prosecutor to bring the full force of his office to bear on a teenaged boy. How he'd paid for the boy's lawyer . . . selecting the most inept drunken attorney in New Orleans for that chore. How he'd fixed it so Sally herself had ended up in this hellhole when she wasn't any more crazy than the Queen of England, simply because she'd defied him. About a man who was the personification of evil.

"Titus abused the kids from the time they were babies," she said. "Charles' father, Bradford, too. Although, I don't feel so bad about that. Bradford was just like the old man. Both of them were sexually abusing Charles and his sister. Not to mention Mary. You wouldn't believe the things that went on! It was an evil house, just purely evil. Those poor kids never had a chance. My sister was going to leave him. She'd phoned me that morning to tell me that and ask if she and the kids could stay with me until she figured out what she was going to do. She was scared to death. It was for sure the Derbignys weren't going to help support them. That's when he killed her."

"Who? Charles?"

"No, you idiot. Haven't you been listening? Bradford killed her. Charles' father. Broke her neck. All Charles was doing was protecting himself. And avenging his mother. And his sister. That one!"

"What's the sister's name?"

By now, he had out his pad and pen.

"Sarah. But I think she's married, so I don't know what her last name is. Nobody visits me or tells me anything but I still hear things. I've got my ways. Sarah now, she was a strange one. She got the same abuse Charles did, even more from the grandfather, but you think she'd say anything against either of them? Not that one. Odd girl. Testified against her own brother, when all he was doing was trying to save her ungrateful butt! She's the one who called the police on him." She softened. "Of course, she was just a little girl then, and confused. I think she actually believed Charles had killed both her parents. I tried to talk to her during the trial, but they wouldn't let me anywhere near her. I wanted to take both her and Charles home with me. Ha! They might have had a chance."

"Why would a grandfather do that to his grandson?"

The look she gave him was one of pure incredulity. "Isn't it obvious? He was scared to death of him! If Charles had been found innocent, a lot of stuff would have come out. Things Titus didn't want exposed. Things the Derbignys are good at. Terrible things. You don't think his own son

Bradford just learned his behavior from a book, do you? My God, man! The Derbigny's are just plain depraved. Always have been, always will be. Besides," she paused and looked out the window, "Charles would have killed him and he knew it. Titus is powerful, has lots of resources, lots of *friends*" —she spat out the word— "but Charles was too smart for him. He would have found a way, no matter what Titus did to protect himself. If they'd only have let me take the boy and his sister. He could have been turned around. He was just a boy!"

She told him about the trial. "His lawyer didn't even let Charles take the stand."

"That's odd."

The old woman laughed bitterly. "No, it isn't. You really don't listen very well do you, young man? Poor Charles didn't know any better. Christ! He was only fourteen. They put his sister up there, though. The lies she said! That's when I got removed from the courtroom. Not without a fight, I might say! Titus didn't care for that at all."

She couldn't stand what they were doing to her nephew, she said. "They'd had time with Sarah. Time to convince her of things. That Charles had killed their mother as well as their father. Maybe they just scared her half to death. Who knows? That old man is capable of anything. The clincher was when she testified that Charles left the house that morning with but one purpose—to kill Grandfather. That's how the prosecutor was able to convince the jury that this was a case of premeditated murder. Charles' attorney didn't make a single objection during the whole trial, even when this charade was going on. It didn't matter. The judge, jury, everybody involved had been hand-picked by Titus. That's a man who doesn't take chances. Did you know the jury foreman worked for Titus?"

Southern justice. Grady had heard stories, but this was amazing.

"White trash sharecropper who had a section of Titus' land. Not far from here, actually. Everywhere Charles looked in that courtroom, he saw people he knew. Except they were all arrayed against him. Most were on Titus's payroll or owed him favors. Or were scared to death of him. What'd the boy know? He was a kid. Only he knew. Charles is no dummy. Only thing he ever did that wasn't smart was choosing his father." Her mouth twisted into a grimace. "My sister was smart, too. Only stupid thing she ever did was who she picked to be the father of her children. I tried to tell her, but she was bull-headed. Got fooled by that Yale education and all that money, I guess. When she finally figured out that it was only going to get worse and decided to leave and get her children out of that hellhole, you see what happened to her."

They talked some more, but Grady could see she was rapidly tiring. He helped her into her bed. There wasn't much more she could tell him. What he had was . . . well, it was plenty. He almost felt sorry for Reader until he remembered the way his brother had looked when he found him on the floor of his own store.

He thought of one last thing. "You said you'd heard Sarah had married. That's true. She's married to a guy named C.J. St. Ives." He told her what he knew about the man. "What I don't get," he said, "is why Charles would be calling his brother-in-law. I had the idea he didn't even know he had one. For some reason, I guess I just figured he hadn't anything at all to do with his family after . . . you know . . . " His voice trailed off.

"Maybe Charles wasn't calling Sarah's husband," she said. "Maybe he was calling Sarah. Did you think of that? They're brother and sister, you know," she said, somewhat snappishly. "Why wouldn't Charles be in contact with her? They were very close as children. Although . . . I couldn't really tell you. Haven't seen either of the kids since the trial."

He could see he wasn't going to get much more out of the woman. Besides, what she'd said made a lot of sense. Charles calling his sister . . . He wondered what that meant. There was something there. Something important. He'd have to figure it out.

"Young man," she said, pressing his hand into both of hers when he rose to say goodbye, "I'm sorry about your brother. I hope when you get to the bottom of this you find Charles had nothing to do with that." Grady looked into the shrewd gaze of her blue eyes and felt guilty. *She knows more than she's letting on,* he thought. *I don't believe she doesn't know the kind of monster Charles has become. Not for a minute. She's definitely not crazy. She just loves her nephew. That's not really so bad . . .* On a sudden impulse, he leaned over and brushed her cheek with a kiss at which her cheeks pinked.

He stumbled out the door, and mumbled something about maybe coming back and visiting her sometime. *Well, hell,* he thought, striding down the hallway. *She reminds me of Mom, somehow. Not her fault Charles is her nephew.* On the way out, he stopped at the desk.

"Put this on Mrs. Truesdale's account," he said, writing a check for $250 and sliding it across the counter. He wished it could have been for more, but his funds were getting dangerously low. "For incidentals." He flipped his wallet open, exposing his badge. He liked the way the woman's eyes widened. "I want her goddamned sheets changed every day from now on. Twice a day if they need it. I'll be checking back. If she's not given better care than she has so far, expect a visit from the federal authorities. You won't even see us coming, but you'll know it when we get here. You can't pay us off like the state boys." The nurse who took his check didn't appear very happy and he could have cared less. He was glad she hadn't gotten a good look at his shield, but then, he hadn't really given her a chance to.

Driving back across Lake Pontchartrain, he couldn't help but think of the old woman. It was obvious she wasn't any crazier than he was. Probably a lot saner. He knew she was Reader's aunt, but he still couldn't keep from feeling sorry for her. He wished there was something he could do. Mostly, he kept thinking about what the old woman had said. That Charles might have been calling his sister and not C.J. But why? What was going on there?

He shook his head violently back and forth to rid himself of Sally Truesdale's face. That old lady blush . . . that was dirty pool. Concentrate on Kincaid, he reminded himself. That's all you need to think about. He decided to head back to the apartment on Burthe, see if he could learn anything more. An irresistible, gnawing feeling that time was growing short crept through him.

34

WHILE EDDIE WAS gone, Reader got busy. He uncuffed St. Ives.

"Go on," he said, indicating the bathroom. "Get yourself cleaned up. Shave, shower, shit, you know. I want you to look good. When you get done, we're going to get you dressed in clean clothes. I'll lay them out for you. Don't put on anything but your underwear yet. I got a new corset I want you to wear."

He went back out into the living room, not too worried the man would try anything. For one thing it was plain all the spirit was gone out of him; for another, there was no way out except past him and if he couldn't handle an out-of-shape, middle-aged banker, well, he didn't deserve to score on this job.

When he came out, Reader said, "You didn't shave none too well, Mr. St. Ives."

"I tried," St. Ives said, his eyes downcast. "My fingers hurt too bad. I . . . I couldn't hold the razor good."

"Well, Mr. St. Ives, it's important you look sharp. Why don't you go back in and try again? Here's an incentive for you. Think about how much more it will hurt if you was to lose another fingernail. Be harder to hold that razor, wouldn't it? You think about that and let's see how good you can do this time. Be careful—don't nick yourself. You know how nasty those razor cuts can be."

When he came out the second time, Reader nodded his head in satisfaction. He looked the nude man over coldly. "Well, there, see? You can do a good job. Get these shorts on and I want you to lie down on the bed." He looked at the man's crotch and smirked at what he saw. "I guess we know why your girlfriend liked you so much, don't we? Money's better than Spanish fly, eh? Enough money, stretches out your dick, makes it look like you got something there. Is that the way it was? I bet when your little girlfriend sucked your cock she thought she was chewing on a c-note."

As he snaked the connector cables around the man's neck, middle, and crotch he talked.

"This is what we call a foolproof setup, Mr. St. Ives. See, the way it works, the wires go through these cables. Some of 'em are live, some are dummies. Like Eddie!" St. Ives didn't laugh along. He stared lifelessly at the far wall.

"Your bomb squad, they'll go nuts, they see a layout like this."

When he got all the connector cables where he wanted them, he snapped them into place and picked up a can of Bondo and applied the sealant. When he was finished he addressed the man who looked like he was about to piss his pants. "Sit up and get your shirt on. Pull your pants up. I want to see how it looks."

St. Ives tried to button his shirt, but couldn't. Reader tsk-tsked and went over and buttoned it for him. He helped him with his trousers and the zipper as well. Then his socks and shoes.

He eyed his work and nodded approval.

"Come over and put on your suitcoat. We'll save the tie for later. Might as well be comfortable, eh? You can't say I'm not concerned for your comfort, can you?"

He checked the way the coat hung, satisfied the bomb couldn't be seen.

"Good thing you're not fat, wear one of those jackets too small for you."

"What do I have to do?" St. Ives spoke for the first time, in a lifeless voice.

"We're getting to that, Mr. St. Ives. By and by. First, I've got to make sure you understand the situation completely. Come on. Let's you and me go in the living room. It's getting pretty ripe in here. Good thing we're pulling out in a little bit, eh? You sure pick some smelly girlfriends!" He was having a wonderful time, making jokes. He got some towels from the bathroom, soaked them down and put them at the foot of the bedroom door to help keep the odor from wafting out to the living room.

Back in the living room he motioned St. Ives over to a chair and cuffed his ankles together. He didn't bother with his hands yet. Himself, he stretched out on the couch, hands behind his head.

"You do everything I tell you just like I say—don't get cute—and we all get out of this alive. You understand?"

He swung his legs down and leaned over right in front of St. Ives' face, head in hands and elbows on his knees. He was grinning.

"You explained all this yesterday," the banker said dully, his eyes downcast. "I understand how it works. I saw . . . the . . . dog. How do . . . . how do I know you'll deactivate it?" he croaked, his voice near to breaking.

"Why, Mr. St. Ives," Reader said, a smile returning to his lips. "I guess you'll have to trust me to do the right thing, won't you?" He got up and walked into the kitchen. "Would you like a beer? I believe I'll have one. This is right thirsty work."

He presented his back to St. Ives, bending over to retrieve a couple of beers in the refrigerator, and said, "Oh. If you have some idea about grabbing that transmitter before I get back in there, I wouldn't if I were you. You don't know which button to hit, do you? Course," he straightened up and turned around, six-pack of cans in his hands, "you might want to take a chance. You a gambler, Mr. St. Ives? I mean, a *real* gambler? I didn't think so." He sauntered back into the room and over to the man, handing him a beer which St. Ives took and drank half down in one long gulp.

"Me, I'm a pure gambler, Mr. St. Ives. You don't want to play poker with me, I don't think."

As he worked another beer loose from the plastic holder, his lips parted in a huge grin. He had another piece of information he wasn't going to share with Mr. St. Ives. A private joke. Thinking about it, he tried to keep from it, but couldn't keep from chuckling. He turned, opening the beer.

"Yeah," he smirked. "You want to stay away from gambling with me. A good gambler always has an ace up his sleeve."

He walked over and patted the plaster of Paris mold strapped to St.

Ives' back. A giggle escaped his lips, then another, and then he threw back his head and guffawed until he had to wipe his eyes with his sleeve.

"I've got one hell of an ace."

There was just a few more things to do. He led St. Ives back to the bedroom and shoved him down on the bed. When he left, he replaced the towels around the closet door and closed the door to the bedroom.

When Eddie returned, he stuck his head in the bedroom door, took one look at St. Ives and said, "Jesus Christ. He's got the bomb on, don't he?"

"You can see it?"

He looked at Reader, his eyes round. "No. I can tell, way he looks. Stupid fucker looks like he's lost all his blood, gonna piss his pants. Reader, why'd you put it on him *now* for? We got hours yet. What if—"

"What if he decides to try and rip it off? Blow all of us up? That what you're wondering, Eddie?"

"Well . . . yeah. Holy fucking Christ, Reader, what if he figures he's gonna get blown up anyway, might as well take us with him? You ever think of that?" He backed toward the front door, not taking his eyes off St. Ives.

Reader wondered what made a guy that big a punk.

"He might, Eddie. He might. This is fun, isn't it? Wondering if he will, if he won't. Kinda on the edge isn't it? You don't like that stuff, do you? I bet when you were a kid, you were the one wouldn't jump off the garage roof when the other kids did."

He took a long drink of his beer and stretched out his legs, planted his heels on the coffee table.

"Relax. I don't think Mr. St. Ives would do that, Eddie. He's not much of a gambler. He's been a banker too long, I think. 'Sides, I promised him we'd deactivate it as long as he does what he's supposed to. I think he sees the wisdom in following instructions, not being a maverick. This is what Mr. St. Ives would call 'taking the conservative position.' It's a banking term. He can explain it to you, you want to know."

"Rise and shine, sunshine." Reader shook St. Ives, who'd fallen asleep in the chair. He'd brought him out to the living room a couple of hours before. Mostly to watch Eddie's reaction. It was amusing to watch the whites of his partner's eyes. Eyes that never left the banker.

During the time Eddie'd been gone, Reader had not only wired up St. Ives but had been busy making phone calls. One to Bobby, making sure the boats were where they were supposed to be and were all set up. Another to a number registered to an apartment in Metairie.

"Is this Octavio?"

"Si, how you?"

"We're fine. It's all set. How about your end? You tell your boss about this Fogarty guy?"

"Si. Everything is ready. Senòr Guterez, he's sent somebody to take care of that guy. I've also taken care of the plane, everything you wanted."

"Good. I'll see you tomorrow night."

"Bueno, Senor Reader. I'm leaving in a few minutes myself. Senor Guterez wants me to come by for a minute and then I'm out of here."

He hung up. It was all in place. He had an idea what Guterez wanted with Octavio and he grinned at the thought. A minute later, he got Bobby on the phone and Bobby said, "They're all set, Reader, all gassed up, like you wanted. Your gear is below in a compartment, keys topside, under a mat by the steering wheel."

"It's time," Reader said to St. Ives, grabbing him under the elbow and hoisting him up to his feet. "You got it all straight in your mind? Once more—you pick up the money, then come back here. Wait for my phone call. I'll tell you where to bring it. Remember—you call the cops or tell Guterez what's going on, you're gonna go boom. Capiche?"

The banker nodded his head slowly. His movements were lifeless, numb, his head hung down like a puppy that had been kicked in the slats.

"Get it together, St. Ives. You've got to fool Guterez, make him think everything's copacetic. You can't do that, I might as well hit this button and save us all a lot of trouble."

St. Ives tried to stand more erect, hold his head up.

Reader said, cheerfully, "That's better. You keep thinking about what's on your back and you'll do fine. Here." He handed him a set of keys. The banker's own set.

"You got an hour and a half to get back," Reader instructed. "That's when I'll be calling. You don't answer, I push this button." He held up the Futaba. "Get going. Your car's outside."

St. Ives stumbled to the door and opened it. He looked back at the two men briefly, as if he weren't sure they were letting him go by himself. Reader held up the Futaba and smiled. His grin widened as he pointed to his watch.

When the door closed behind him, Reader said, "Eddie, I don't trust him. You follow him. Don't let him see you. I don't think he's going to be paying much attention, but be careful anyway. Once you see him go into Guterez's warehouse, come on out to the boat. I'll be waiting."

Eddie didn't argue. Reader didn't think he would. He knew Eddie would figure that as long as he could trail the guy who's getting the money, he couldn't be double-crossed. He might even conceivably think that there might arise an opportunity where he could take the money from CJ himself.

Nah, went through Reader's mind, the words pregnant with sarcasm. *Not Eddie! Asshole thinks I don't know about the gun in his boot. That bulge is either a gun or the biggest, longest hard-on I've ever seen. Have I got a surprise for him.*

When Eddie closed the door behind him, Reader gave a last look around, checking to see if he'd forgotten anything.

Time to see if his hand was playing out the way he'd planned.

35

GRADY HAD JUST turned the corner on Burthe when he saw a man come from the downstairs apartment and get into the Lincoln parked in front. He wheeled over to the curb and watched. It was the man in the chair, the one who'd been handcuffed. St. Ives. What the fuck? The man didn't leave right away, though; just sat in his car and leaned his head up against the steering wheel. Then another man walked out. Eddie. What the fuck? Grady watched him trot up the street to Carrollton, passing by on the opposite side of the street. Eddie didn't seem to notice the man sitting in the car. Strange. St. Ives just sat there and then he raised his head, started up the Lincoln and wheeled slowly out onto the street. Follow the money, Grady decided quickly. Forget Reader and Eddie. Just follow the money and it'll all work out.

Grady waited until St. Ives was at the corner before pulling out himself. As he went by the duplex he saw Reader come out of the apartment. He swore the man looked right at him and he thought he saw a look of astonishment pass over his features.

Not dead like you figured, eh, fucker? Grady turned the corner behind the banker. *Good. I like that. Now I got you off-balance, just maybe. I like the fact you're not so sure about everything.* He had to fight the urge to stop, pull out his .45 and just cap the murdering sonofabitch. *No,* he told himself. Be cool, Grady. You want him and you want everybody else. You shoot him and not only will you end up in jail yourself, all the others responsible for Sally's murder would walk away, untouched. As hard as it was, he had to put revenge on hold. He wanted every single bastard involved in this thing to pay for what they'd done. For a second, he was tempted to turn around and at least follow Reader, but he quickly reasoned that St. Ives was the money man and if he followed him, eventually Reader would turn up and he'd nail the whole crowd with enough evidence to put them all away. Also, Reader was sharp enough he might see a tail, while he doubted St. Ives would even notice a white elephant bearing down on his ass. He suspected the man had a lot on his mind.

They were two blocks down on St. Charles when Grady saw Eddie's car coming up fast behind him. He slowed and watched the Cavalier whiz past, coming up almost on St. Ives' bumper.

What an asshole, Grady thought. It's a good thing St. Ives has other things on his mind.

It's going down, he thought. This is it, sports fans. For a minute, he'd had the sinking feeling that he was following the wrong person. Until Eddie showed up. That would fit his theory. When in doubt, follow the money. If he'd guessed right, that was the only way he was going to win.

Following St. Ives and Eddie was a breeze. He could see St. Ives' white Lincoln from time to time ahead of Eddie's car. Good thing neither of these clowns know they've got a rearview mirror.

Soon, they were turning onto a street marked Parks Road and Grady closed the distance a bit. Dusk slowly overcame the city as he followed the two cars up ahead.

It was only by pure luck that Grady dropped a bit behind to light a cigarette. He slowed for a second to search for a book of matches he dropped on the floor, his head popping back up just in time to watch the Lincoln turn into a drive leading to a huge warehouse. Eddie's Corvair braked immediately, pulling over to the side of the road about a hundred yards farther back. If Grady's car had been closer, he might have struck the two men that ran out of the darkness up to Eddie's car and jumped in, one in the front seat and the other in the back. He continued on past, hoping like hell that he looked like any other one-eyed schmuck on his way home from work. Passing Eddie's car, he thought he caught a glimpse of a gun in one of the men's hands. He kept on going, trying to keep the car on the road while keeping an eye on the rearview mirror.

What the hell was going on?

The boats were where Bobby'd said they would be. A quick study of the smaller one, a white bass boat, showed him everything was in place; the compartment in the stern where St. Ives was to place the money, the rudder calibrated and the key in the ignition.

That chore completed, Reader jumped off and boarded the second boat, a bright blue Chris Craft. He had a couple of things to do here and then he was gone. He didn't plan to be within miles of there when St. Ives arrived. And Eddie, if he was still alive. Reader got the keys from under the mat where Eddie'd said they'd be and went down below. In the locker was a Magic Marker and a pad of paper. He tore off a sheet and scribbled, *Plan's changed, Eddie. Take the boat and head straight across. Don't worry about the cops. There aren't any. Won't have to do the pickup in the river after all. I drove over. You'll see me when you get there. We'll wait on the money together. Get ready to celebrate, partner!* That done, he picked up the cellular phone and tested it, dialing the weather number.

Good. No fucking rain, he said to himself, punching off the recording. He went to the small refrigerator, retrieved a can of beer and popped it open. Going topside, he sat in one of the deck chairs, drank the beer slowly and watched as the stars came out one by one. From time to time he glanced at his watch. When the hands showed nine-thirty he went below, got another beer, picked up the phone and dialed one of the numbers on the sheet.

He could hear music in the background and a voice that said, "Yeah? This is Frenchie."

"Hour and a half, Frenchie. You all set? You're not drinking, are you?"

"Beer. Don't worry, I'm not fucked up. I'll be there, like you said."

"Go home. Right now. I know you can handle your shit, but I don't want to take the chance you get in a fight in that joint—something stupid happens. I haven't got time to be bailing you out of jail. Understand?"

"Yeah, okay. I'll get something to go. And don't worry, I won't get wasted. I'm drinking beer, my friend. I never get drunk on beer."

"Just be there by eleven. You know what to do. I'll call you an hour later."

"See you at midnight, Reader. Your boat comes, like you said, I'll be there, I'll get it. Hey, I'll even be there early. Say, ten thirty. That okay?"

"That's perfect, Frenchie. It should be coming your way right about eleven. Gives you an hour to get it and get back home. Remember, keep your mitts off it."

"Uh, Reader? There was—"

"Yeah?"

There was a couple of seconds of silence.

"Nothing. I'll see you." The line went dead.

It was almost over. Now the best part to come.

He was covered both ways. If something went wrong, he knew St. Ives would do what he told him. At the very worst, Frenchie would pick up the money, if there actually was any, and he would get it later. But if all went according to Hoyle, the money was heading someplace else, the place he'd wanted it to all along.

There was still that wild card, that fucking cop. He was sure that was Fogarty who had passed by him back at C.J.'s apartment. Fuck him. He was sure the guy didn't have a clue what was up. Following C.J. proved that. He came into the picture again, Reader'd just take him out. If he'd been prepared for seeing him at the apartment driving by, he would have done it then. The guy surprised him. He was supposed to be dead. Fuck it, he thought. Guy's so far out of the game it isn't funny. Don't waste time worrying about a stupid flatfoot with a grudge. Let him follow St. Ives all he wants. He wasn't heading any place Reader was going to be.

He had the biggest smile on his face, wondering what would be going through St. Ives' mind as the hours passed. Assuming that he went back to his apartment once he got the money and waited for Reader to call as he'd promised. If he even had the money. By now, Guterez should have squeezed sufficient information out of Octavio to make sure he wouldn't be giving up any cash to the banker.

He was curious about a couple of other things that he'd never know. Like if Guterez would send any of his men to follow St. Ives. He bet he would. Like it mattered! He laughed aloud so hard he began to cough.

It was just too bad he wouldn't be around to see all that.

36

GRADY CREPT AS quietly as he could around to the back of the warehouse. From the ventilation windows at the top of the building, he could see a faint glow of light coming from the north end. He looked for a way in on the opposite end, hoped it'd be dark enough he could get in unnoticed. There was no way of knowing how many were in there, but even if there were only a couple, he figured they'd be heavily armed. He only wanted information, not confrontation. See what was going on.

He went swiftly across the open space to the shelter of the building and its shadows.

Yes. There was a door on this end. It was locked, but looked easy enough to pick. He worked quickly, cursed softly beneath his breath when he dropped his picks once. At first he couldn't find them in the dark. Feeling with both hands he felt the bits of metal after a minute, picked them up and began trying the lock again. He didn't know whether it was the heat or tension that was making the sweat run down into his good eye making it burn. The fucking heat he decided. Why doesn't it cool off when it gets dark! If he lived here, he'd never go outside. He'd stay in air conditioning all the time.

He kept working the lock and then he was in. He crept in darkness toward the office light, glad there was a cloud cover tonight. Made it easier to move around inside the building without moonlight coming through the windows. Good, if he didn't trip on something in the dark and give himself away. He made it all the way to just outside the office without any accidents. He could hear the voices inside clearly, see where everyone was. He hunkered down.

"Mr. St. Ives. Good evening, Senor. You look very warm tonight."

The warehouse office they entered was small and cramped, what with St. Ives, Fidel Guterez, and one of his men inside, but the air was on and St. Ives was the only one of the trio who was sweating. C.J. could see the suitcases Guterez always transported the money in, sitting beside the desk. Over in the corner were piled kilo upon kilo—dozens it appeared—of what he knew to be product. Coke. Looked like they'd gotten a major shipment.

"Yes. I am. Think I caught something, a bug maybe." He tried to laugh, but only managed a weak smile. "The money ready? I'll get it and go. Got to get it to the bank before it gets too late and somebody sees me and gets suspicious." He looked at the Cuban, then looked away nervously.

Guterez smiled. St. Ives felt a chill. He saw no mirth in the man's eyes.

"Oh yes, the bank. Would that be the bank where you said I shouldn't be seen? The bank you're the president of? Is that the bank you speak of, senor?"

C.J. St. Ives didn't like this at all. Now, the sweat began to roll in earnest and he could feel the pressure of the cables and the package on his back.

"Yes. The bank."

"You know, Senor St. Ives, I been meaning to talk to you about the bank. *Your* bank. It is your bank, is it not?"

"Well . . . sure. Our family's bank. What are you talking about?"

He tried to go on the offensive, but couldn't quite make it. God, this was not going right. Something was up. Guterez suspected something. He was going to die. If not by the bomb strapped to his body, then by this fucking animal. Let me have the money, Fidel. Let me get out of here!

He stood up and C.J. watched the Cuban's smile vanish, replaced by a look that froze the moisture on C.J.'s forehead.

"I am sorry I did not believe your story about this detective. I am sorry that men such as ourselves cannot have trust between us. This is a sad state of affairs, senor, very sad indeed. But perhaps essential to one's safety. Yes, I think it is absolutely essential. Do you know what has happened?"

C.J. managed to shake his head. God, he wanted to pee!

"I received a phone call. From someone you and I both know. Maybe you didn't know I knew him. Your father-in-law. Senòr Derbigny. We've been friends for a very long time. Even longer than you and I have been. Interesting, no? Have you spoken with him lately? He had a very interesting story to tell me."

Oh, God, oh, God. I'm fucked. I'm dead. What do I do? What can I do? C.J. looked at the chair and sat down. "Fidel, I need to go to the bathroom. Could I please use the bathroom?"

Guterez's smile returned. "Oh, surely, Senor. Please forgive my manners. But if you could wait a minute or two, *por favor*. I have a little bit more to talk with you about and you can go relieve yourself. This is muy important. You will want to hear this."

He stepped over in front of St. Ives and bent down, putting his hands on the banker's knees and staring directly at him, his eyes inches from the banker's. C.J. could smell his breath and his stomach roiled at the sweetness of it.

"Senor, I do not think you remember our talk. Do you know why? Because you are no longer *el presidente*, it would seem."

"Fidel, I have to go to the bathroom. *Now.*" C.J. stood up, terror visible in his expression. "If I don't go to the bathroom *right now* I am going to piss all over your floor. Let me go to the bathroom and I'll explain everything."

Guterez took his hands and put them on the banker's shoulders and pushed him back down into the chair.

"I'm afraid you'll have to piss on my floor, senòr." He turned to the other man, a short, swarthy man who remained silent during the conversation. "Felipe, go bring them in."

The office door opened and two men came in—another of Guterez's men St. Ives thought was named Octavio . . . and Eddie. Felipe held a gun on the other two. Octavio looked sick. C.J. could see both of his eyes were almost closed and there was blood on his shirt.

"Is this the detective your wife set on you?" Guterez gestured toward Eddie.

C.J. looked up at Guterez. He couldn't stop the shudder at the look in the man's eyes.

"Maybe. No. I don't know."

Guterez reached over and slapped C.J. The way he slapped him looked like it was in slow motion, casual-like, but it knocked out one of his front teeth. C.J. felt his mouth fill with blood. All his strength drained from him and he felt himself growing faint. And then, from somewhere deep inside, the adrenaline kicked in and he felt the energy return, more energy than he'd ever experienced and he stood up, ripped his coat off and tore his shirt open, buttons flying. In the same instant, so quickly that no one had time to react, C.J. ran to the door, but instead of opening it and attempting to flee, he stood in front of it and hooked his fingers behind the connector cable that went around his waist.

"Eddie," he said, new-found savagery in his voice. "Eddie, tell them what will happen if I pull this cable apart. Explain it to these greasers, Eddie. Tell them we'll all blow up. That I'm wired with a bomb." The man called Felipe made a move with his hand to the inside of his jacket, but Guterez held a restraining hand up and the man lowered his hand.

When Eddie finished confirming his story, Felipe aimed his pistol at C.J. He said, "*Patron*, how 'bout I shoot this piece'a shit."

Fidel Guterez, drug baron and one of the toughest and most ruthless mothers in all of the Southeast, was enjoying all this, although you couldn't tell from the way he acted. Felipe was doing a fine job of theatrics himself. There wasn't the remotest possibility he was going to shoot the banker and they both knew it.

That St. Ives showed up to steal his money was no surprise. That, he'd been expecting. Two days ago, a familiar voice had told him all kinds of amazing things. That St. Ives was no longer connected to the bank in any way. That phone call had come a couple of hours before C.J.'s call from the Fairmont.

He might have been surprised that the man was wired with explosives, except that he knew about that, too. Another valuable phone call, one telling him about his employee's treachery, led him to that information.

He'd admired the way Octavio had hung tough, for many hours even, but nobody could hold out forever against the kind of torture a Cuban with experience in The Revolution could administer.

He forced down the smile that threatened to emerge. He'd love to be there when Kincaid opened up those suitcases and found they weren't filled with stacks of hundred dollar bills. He wondered if he'd appreciate the joke.

He thought about playing out the little drama a bit longer but grew tired of the idea. It was time to get on with business. A powerful man awaited him and he didn't like to be kept waiting. It was time to play out the charade.

"No, Felipe," said Guterez, slowly, getting back to the moment. "Put your gun away. I believe this man speaks the truth. What is it you want, Senor C.J.? You want to leave, I think? Go ahead, leave, puta. I'll find you."

C.J. was feeling the glow of authority and power returning. His Cajun upbringing was coming back, memories of the days when he hunted alligators in the swamp with his father, fearless boyhood days spent in the swamp wresting a hard living from the bayou. "Yes, Guterez. I want to leave. I want the money. If I don't show up with the money, I'm dead. So, I'm not leaving without it. You don't give me the money, I'm pulling this right now."

Guterez hesitated, but only momentarily when C.J. lifted his elbow away from his side in an exaggerated gesture, to show him he would pull the connector cable if he didn't do as he'd ordered.

"Now," C.J. said, once the suitcases were placed on the floor beside him. "Lie down. All of you." He looked at his former partner in crime and for the first time his features relaxed somewhat. "Give me your gun." Guterez shrugged, reached to his back holster and complied. He'd already unloaded it in anticipation of what C.J. would do. He nodded to his men and they dropped to the floor on their stomachs and he did the same.

Except Eddie. "Hey, you gotta take me with you, St. Ives. You don't take me with you, Reader'll kill you. I'm his partner."

C.J. smiled. "I don't think so, asshole. I think maybe your boss will thank me. Saves him the trouble of having to kill you himself. You don't really think he planned to split this with you, do you?"

Eddie stood there, his body trembling with a mixture of rage and fear. He took a step toward C.J. and the banker pointed the gun at him.

"Lie down, you slimy fucker. I'd love to shoot you."

Eddie's face darkened, but he did as C.J. ordered.

As soon as Eddie hit the floor, C.J. was gone, running through the door out into the warehouse, adrenaline making the suitcases lighter than they would be normally.

Immediately, Guterez's men jumped up, Guterez himself rising more slowly, brushing off his clothes, holding up his hand to his men. "No. Let him go. It's all right."

He turned to Felipe, "Give him a few seconds and then tail him. Don't let him know he's being followed. Take Orlando with you. Meet me across the lake afterwards. I want to know everything. Remember Reader Kincaid's face. I want to know what his face looked like."

Felipe nodded, gestured to Orlando and the two men went out the door at a trot.

Grady saw the two men rush out of the office, just a few feet from where he was hidden in the darkness. He'd witnessed the whole scene, from when C.J. had entered the office until this moment.

"Now," Guterez was saying, "Octavio and our friend here. What shall we do?" To answer his own question, he walked over, put his hand inside one of his men's jackets and pulled out a gun. Weapon in hand, he walked up to Octavio and shot him three times in the stomach, his hand on the man's shoulder almost in a friendly manner. As Octavio slumped to the floor, Eddie jumped up. In his hand was the gun he'd hidden in his boot.

"Now, you fuckin' spic," he said to Guterez, bringing the gun up to the Cuban's head. "I'm walking out of here. You and me, cowboy."

Guterez's response was to bring his own gun around to bear on Eddie's face. Toe-to-toe, they stood in a classic Mexican standoff.

Eddie's face went white, but he said, "You shoot me and I'll still have time to—"

Kabam!

Guterez's gun erupted and Eddie stood there, his gun arm slumping a split second before he did, surprise in his already dead eyes.

"Shoot me?" Guterez finished for him. "Maybe. If you don't take so much time talking about it, maracon." He turned to his men and laughed aloud. "This cucaracha has seen too many movies, I think. That's the trouble with Mexicans and their famous standoffs. All you need to do is just shoot the fucker. Nobody's reflexes are that good. A Cubano just shoots, my friends. Remember that."

His demeanor changed to a more sober one. "Juan, you bring the limo around. The money's already on board." He ordered the other men to put the cocaine in the trunk.

Grady waited until they had gone out the front door then raced to the same door and watched them pull away. In seconds, he was starting his own car and speeding back the way he'd come originally. Two blocks later, he spotted St. Ives.

We'll see how slick you are now, Reader, he whispered fiercely to himself, keeping behind the limo just far enough not to be spotted. *I got your ass now.* He picked up the cell phone on the seat next to him and dialed a number. Two rings later, he was delighted to hear Veronica's gravelly voice.

"Got something here you might be interested in," he said.

"What's that?"

"You're gonna be a hero. Call your friends downtown and tell them if they get to . . . " he reached in his pocket for the address he'd hurriedly jotted down " . . . to 27123 Parks Road in Chalmette, they can be on the eleven o'clock news."

"Something big?" Veronica said.

"I'd say so," said Grady, chuckling. "The DEA's gonna be mad your guys made this find."

"And what's that?"

"Guterez's warehouse. There's no coke here now, but I saw a safe that I'll bet has some interesting contents. There's also some dead bodies here. I think if your friends arrest Guterez you'll find the gun he's carrying is the one who killed them. They should get enough evidence to nail a murder charge on him at the very least. Guterez and his boys are gone, but they may be back. One way or the other, they're going to be in a bad way, if what I think happens does."

"Gotcha. It's going down the way you thought?" Veronica said. Grady could hear the smile in her voice when he replied in the affirmative. "That's a start. Now. Get that bastard Kincaid. For Sally. And your brother. And Grady?" There was a pause. "Take care of yourself. I don't want to bury two of my brothers in blue."

"I will, sweetheart. You, too."

This one's for you, Jack, he thought, hanging up. *And you, Sally. Payback.*

37

A BLOCK PAST the Audubon Zoo on St. Charles, Grady's car got sideswiped by a car running a crossing street stop sign.

The damage to the car itself wasn't much, a scrape along the front passenger side. Grady would have liked to have chased down the asshole who'd hit him, some middle-aged slob who gave one sobering glance at what he'd done and put the hammer down, leaving the scene like he had nitro in the gas tank. Only he couldn't. All he could do was shake his fist at the fleeing miscreant and deliver a few choice cuss words. The right front tire was punctured and settling to the pavement, flatter than a soufflé after a California earthquake. People walking by, mostly drunks stumbling out of the bars that lined the sidestreets, kept on going after staring briefly.

"Fucking drunk!" Grady screamed after the departing hit-and-runner. "Fucking New Orleans drivers!" That, plus a kick at the useless tire got some of the mad out of his system and he tried to figure out what to do. Briefly, he considered calling Veronica again and, more briefly, the NOPD, but he dismissed both ideas as soon as they occurred. Veronica wouldn't get there in time, not from clear out on Jefferson and the cops? . . . Well, there'd be too much explaining to do, and by the time he'd convinced someone what was going down, it'd be too late to do anything.

He changed the flat as fast as he could, cursing the heat and the mosquitoes that descended on him in droves. Finished in just under ten minutes, he hopped back in the car.

Please, he begged to the black night as he hurtled down the street, hoping desperately that St. Ives was headed back to his apartment and might still be there.

He wasn't. No one was. Grady put his shoulder to the door, burst through. A horrible stench smote his nostrils. He quickly ran through the rooms. Empty. The smell was overpowering. Breathe it in, he told himself. A long time ago a coroner had told him if you breathed a bad odor for two minutes, the nose shut down.

He found the source of the smell in the bedroom closet. Gagging, he turned away, but not in time to keep from losing the entire contents of his stomach.

Must be St. Ives' girlfriend, he thought, fighting the returning nausea. He stumbled to the apartment door and staggered out, the cooler night air helping revive him as he gulped huge lungfuls. He got to his car and leaned up against it, wiping his mouth and chin with the back of his jacket sleeve.

Now what? Who knows where the hell St. Ives was. With the suitcases, but where the hell would Reader have him go? He opened the car door and climbed in, slumping against the steering wheel in abject and utter misery. Even the knowledge that there was nothing in those suitcases failed to cheer him up.

Wait a minute. He struggled to collect his thoughts, get them in order. Back at the warehouse . . . He pursued the thought that tried to form in his mind, chased it, fought to pin it down, concentrate. *Derbigny*. The drug dealer, Guterez. He'd said *Derbigny*. Somehow Derbigny was connected to all of this. What? Guterez worked for him? Well, sure! Words, bits of information, snatches of conversations all tumbled about in his mind. Reader was Derbigny's grandson. It was Derbigny who had made sure his grandson was convicted twenty-four years ago. Derbigny owned the bank C.J. was president of. Guterez worked for Derbigny somehow. And Guterez had the money. He'd heard him clearly. *"Juan, you bring the limo around. The money's already on board."*

Help me, Jack. Grady thought the words, but it was more of a prayer. *Give me your marvelous intuition. I'm close here, but I don't quite get it. Give me some help, brother.*

Grady never knew if it was a miracle or not, even later, thinking about it. All he knew was that as soon as he'd silently uttered the words, it all came at him in a rush. Reader was stealing his grandfather's money, *that* was the scam. It wasn't just any bank he was after, it was his grandfather's. But why? Stealing the old man's money—that wouldn't be that big of a deal. It didn't qualify as much revenge. Not *serious* revenge. What's the most it could be? A week, a month's take? A guy like Reader wouldn't settle for just that. What revenge was that? An irritation, at most. No. There was more going on here. Grady shook his head to clear the cobwebs. Clearer. It was getting clearer. The key was Derbigny. It all connected to the grandfather. And he knew where the man lived. He'd marked it plainly on the map. Across the lake. Past the town of Abita Springs.

It was a family thing, pure and simple. He knew why Reader had made so many calls to the St. Ives home. Grady realized he'd thought himself smack into the middle of a dilemma. He could follow the money, where he was sure it was headed . . . or he could trust his instinct and go to where he thought the final destination of the money would be. The problem with the first idea was that Derbigny's place was clear across the lake, at least forty-five minutes away, more if he had trouble finding the place. It wasn't like he'd be heading for a street, with clearly marked numbers on the houses. This place would be in the country, hard to find even if it was daylight for someone who'd never been there. The other possibility, just realized, where Reader *might* go . . . and that was an awfully big "might," was right here in town. But if he guessed wrong, he was fucked. His brother's killer would go free, probably never be found.

God, I wish you were here, Jack, he groaned. *I need your intuition.*

Instantly, the answer popped into his head. *Family. This is all about family. Nothing else.* With a flash of insight that stunned him, he knew without a doubt where Reader's final destination was.

Grady swung his legs around, closed the door, started the ignition.

If he was wrong, he was screwed. Kincaid would have won. He'd be too far away to ever find if Grady's guess was wrong. As if he'd even know where to look for him. But he wasn't wrong. He punched the gas and his car shot forward.

Thanks, Jack, he breathed, pushing the vehicle as fast as he dared. *We're not done yet, brother.*

As he hurtled down the streets, the surety of a minute ago began to fade. Trust the hunch, he told himself desperately. It came from the right place.

Out in the middle of the Mississippi, the coolish breeze didn't prevent C.J. from sweating like a hooker during Mass. In the seat behind him sat Felipe and Orlando. After Reader had phoned with directions and he'd driven to the river and found the boat, the two had jumped him.

He'd tried the breaking the cable bluff again but it hadn't worked. They'd jumped in the boat with him.

After an argument. Between the two Cubans.

"The boss said to shoot Senor C.J. And Kincaid," Orlando said.

"The boss didn't know St. Ives was going in a boat," Felipe said, sneering. "And how you think we're going to shoot Kincaid if he's across the river? We'll go with him, do it when Kincaid shows up. Just before we get there, we'll jump out. It'll be all right."

C.J. didn't know what to do. He was fucked whatever he did. The best he could do was go along, try and figure out something along the way.

Hope for a miracle.

"You're not Reader."

"Me? No, I'm Frenchie. You got something for me? Who are you guys? There's only supposed to be a boat."

Frenchie saw the tiny burst of fire from Felipe's gun just before the bullet smote his brain.

"Hey, you're good, nice shot. But, where the fuck's Reader?" Orlando said, wading in with Felipe. "Now what?" He looked at the banker who stood in the boat a few feet away.

"Who knows?" Felipe said. "He'll turn up. Now, we show Mr. St. Ives what's in his suitcases. The best part." He couldn't hold back a laugh. "Open one up, señor," he said, to the man still standing in the boat. "Surprise!"

C.J. looked at the two men and down at the suitcases, then bent over and unlatched one of the suitcases. When it fell open, he stared at the contents.

He looked back up at the men, knowing in that instant there was only one possibility left. "I'll see you both in Hell," he said in a husky whisper, and reached for the cable.

"No!" screamed Felipe, trying to scramble back.

38

FIDEL GUTEREZ ENJOYED rum. Especially Cuban rum, not that gasoline you bought in most liquor stores. For him, *Methusalem* was the only label he'd deign to let pass his lips. From a bottle of that Cuban nectar he poured a healthy portion into a crystal goblet.

Life was good. Life was particularly good this evening. He'd disposed of a nettlesome problem and beaten a rather clever man. And enjoyed every minute of it. Some genius Reader Kincaid turned out to be! Trusting a punk like Octavia wasn't the mark of any genius. And St. Ives. He'd never liked St. Ives from the first time he'd met him. The man had money, dressed well, talked in a cultivated manner, but from the start Guterez had seen through all that, seen the man for what he really was. A pig. A pig all prettied up, but still a pig.

A dead pig. Barbecued.

He leaned back his head and laughed heartily. The two employees that were riding with him in the back of his limousine glanced at each other and smiled. *El patron* laughed like that much of the time. Whenever he did, they usually benefited, for he was a generous man with those who labored for him, and when he was in a good mood, there were usually bonuses and other gifts. For instance, he was sharing his good Cuban elixir with them already, filling their own glasses whenever they got low.

"Senòr Guterez," one of them, a small, pockmarked Cuban from Miami said to his employer. "You got that gringo good, eh?"

"Si, muy bueno!" They all laughed. "Vasta macoule," he said, and pretended to spit and they burst out laughing even harder.

El patron was half in the bag from the rum. And as high as he could get from the Columbian marching powder. All the way from New Orleans he and his men had snorted thick lines on the solid silver serving tray he kept in the limo for just that purpose. This was the good stuff, the uncut product. As his driver turned up the lane, he wiped off the last of the powder and ran his finger with it inside his gums, smacking his lips in satisfaction.

"Ah," he said, a big, fat, satisfied sigh. Life was indeed good.

And there was the Big Boss, trundling down the paved incline from the house. The one who'd called him several days before to tell him their old arrangement was back in place, that C.J. St. Ives was no longer in charge of anything. Not his bank, not his wife, not even his life. It was unsaid during their conversation, but Guterez knew it was his duty to eliminate the man for the boss. That should be accomplished right about now, he thought as the limo braked in the drive before the main house.

His driver ran around and held open the door and Guterez swung his feet out. Ah, there was the good senòr now. He was spinning down the walk from the mansion in his wheelchair, his hand lifted in welcome.

Wait till he hears how I have performed, Guterez thought, standing and stepping forward to greet his long-time powerful friend and ally, Senòr Titus Fuller Derbigny.

If his brain hadn't been slowed by the recent effects of at least a half-gram of top-grade cocaine . . . if the buzz born of swilling almost a full bottle of the best Cuban rum in less than an hour hadn't obscured his thinking . . . or if the glow of self-satisfaction wasn't clouding his vision, the sight of the crippled man in the wheelchair swiftly rising to stand might have registered on Fidel Guterez's consciousness a little bit quicker than it did. His reflexes and reaction time might have been sufficient to speed up the synapses and electrical connections slogging through his brain and he might have been able to make the movie that was unfolding in slow-motion before his redlined eyes speed up enough to bring his own gun up to answer the problem of the machine pistol that magically appeared in the other man's hands.

Or maybe not.

The Cuban drug lord's last mortal act was to throw his hands up in front of his face and cry out a word so queer and out-of-place that it seemed to hang in the air long seconds after the last burst of .45-caliber bullets had torn through his and then his stupefied associate's brains.

Mama!

Guterez's mouth froze forever in the last syllable of his cry and Reader Kincaid tore off the white wig that was beginning to itch, walked over and poured another fusillade of lead into the dead drug czar's and his men's bodies, his teeth bared in what Eddie Delahousie had called his "Dr. Death" face.

39

READER TOOK A moment to enjoy the fruits of his labor. Ten years of planning had gone into this and he was going to savor it.

But not too long. There was no telling if someone had heard the gunfire, even way out here in the boonies.

He shoved Guterez's body out of the way and leaned into the limo.

"I thought so," he said, talking to himself and reaching for one of the cigars in the special humidor by the wet bar. He drew in the rich aroma then licked it all over. Lighting a match, he inhaled deeply, savoring the feel of the smoke as it reached deep into his mouth.

"Nothing like a good Cuban cigar, eh, Fidel?" He looked down at his dead foe.

He took another slow drag and quickly got to work. The money was right where it was supposed to be, in the false bottom. He walked swiftly behind the house where his Caprice was parked and drove it back, parked it next to the limousine. Working fast but methodically, he transferred the bundles of greenbacks. They were all hundreds. He'd hit the jackpot. There was even more than he'd counted on. More than six million, it appeared, by his quick estimate. Five of the millions took up the whole of his back seat where he had his own false bottom rigged. The back seat lifted out easily. It should have—all it consisted of was a balsa frame with a seat cover stitched over it. Not something you could sit on. A piece of art, courtesy of Bobby, just another of his gifts. He'd switched the regular one for it just before driving over from New Orleans. It was a tight fit, but he was able to get all the money in and get the seat back in place. Looking at it, no one would ever guess that there was a king's ransom beneath it.

The remaining million was going to remain here. It wouldn't look like much of a drug deal without the money.

The next thing he did was pop open the trunk of the limo. It would have been a chore to get at the jack if someone needed to fix a flat. First, they'd have to move over fifty bags of cocaine.

It wasn't even tempting. Reader stared at the coke for long seconds and shut the trunk. It was a gift to his grandfather. He grinned broadly at the thought.

The very last thing he did was go back into the house and bring out a body, cradling the slight form in his arms. Titus Fuller Derbnigy. Dead an hour and a half. That had been the truly satisfying part of the evening. He put his grandfather's body in the wheelchair he had minutes before been sitting in himself. He took the machine pistol he'd used to kill the Cubans and, with his handkerchief, wiped off any surface that might have his prints on it. He took Titus's fingers and pressed them onto various smooth surfaces of the weapon then placed the weapon in Titus's hands, making sure his dead fingers left an impression on the trigger as well. He aimed the weapon at the sky and fired off a burst. There. That would leave powder marks. He lowered the dead man's arm and the gun fell from his hand to the ground. No problem. His prints were on it.

He selected the smallest of the Cubans, carried him over and laid him down next to the wheelchair. When he got him where he wanted, the last thing he did was pull the knife sticking in his grandfather's chest out, wipe it down, and place it in the other man's hand, which was still flexible enough to get the man's fingers around the handle. A knife he'd chosen especially for this, one with a smooth steel handle, ideal for leaving a person's prints on.

There. He surveyed the scene. Everything was perfectly in place. It was evident at a glance what had taken place here. A gun battle between Titus and the Cubans. One of them had somehow gotten close enough to the old man to stab him before he died of his own wounds.

He took a last puff of the cigar he'd kept clenched between his teeth the whole time and knocked off the ember with his thumb, grinding the live ash under his foot. The cigar he placed in his pocket. The only bit of evidence that could have been used to prove he'd ever been there. He stepped back.

It was over. For some reason, he'd always imagined a different feeling when this time came. He was surprised to see that he felt very little at all. Even when he'd stepped up to the old man, saw the slow light of recognition dawn in his eyes as he realized it was his grandson standing there before him in his living room, a recognition arriving a sliver of a second before Reader plunged the knife into his stomach just below the sternum and stood there, face-to-face with the bogeyman from his childhood. And twisted. Slowly, ever so slowly. Until the light in the old man's eyes, bright and sparkly and more alive at the onset of his death than it had ever been in life . . . until that pinpoint in his eyes changed, almost imperceptibly, then faded, the luster going and Reader knew it was finally over . . . even though his grandfather still stared at him through pupils which would from that moment be forever sightless. What was unexpected was that Reader felt nothing at all. There was too much emotion, over too many years, to get out in something so silly as tears or laughter. Maybe it never would. Maybe the hatred he'd carried around like a hard, cancerous tumor around his heart, was too deeply imbedded to ever work its way out.

Standing there, staring down at his grandfather, remembering the moment, Reader felt just the way he had during one of his armed robberies, at that moment when the store clerk went for his gun and his own finger squeezed the trigger. Like he was underwater. In a kind of out-of-body trance where everything, all conscious thought faded away. It was as if he'd dove off into unknown water from a great height. You dove, shot into the water and that's where he was, from that second on. In the water. Everything, sound, motion, all else was muffled, distorted, leaving only instinct.

In the water. That's where he was now. He didn't know if he'd ever surface. He turned slowly, walked to his car, turning back around, his hand on the door handle.

"Goodbye, Grandfather," he said. As he drove down the lane there was only one thought in his head. The piece of advice all inmates received when they left prison. Don't look back, they were always told. If you look back, you'll come back. An almost overpowering urge to do just that came over him and he had to fight the urge every foot of the way until he reached the road. But he didn't. Look back.

40

IN THE TWO hours he'd spent parked outside the St. Ives house, Grady had run the gamut of emotions, vacillating back and forth between the certainty with which he'd driven here and the growing black cloud of doubt that he'd figured the whole thing out wrong.

When he first pulled up he thought the house deserted, but a minute or so after he parked the car, a light went on inside one of the upstairs rooms. *She was here.*

That fueled his optimism for a while, but as the minutes ticked by and became one hour then another, the first flush of hope was being bled dry.

Just as he was about to get out of the car and go up to the house, knock on the door, a midnight blue Caprice pulled up directly in front of the house.

Heart thumping, Grady slid down out of sight and watched as Reader got out of the car, walked up to the house and pushed the doorbell. A second later, light spilled out as the door opened and Kincaid disappeared inside. Grady slipped out of the car, pulled out his automatic, jacked a shell into the chamber and crept to the house. He tiptoed around the side of the mansion, softly, like a housecat after a sparrow, until he was at the back door. He leaned over and took off his shoes. He tried the doorknob, winced when it squeaked. He was in luck. It was unlocked. He eased inside, and inched toward the light just ahead in the living room. Two figures sat at a large dining room table. Facing him was Sarah Derbigny. Across from her, back to Grady, was the man who'd killed his brother. He stepped into the room and just as he did a polished oak board in the floor groaned beneath his foot.

Reader Kincaid whipped around, snaking his pistol out of its shoulder holster at the same time . . . and found himself staring into the barrel of a .45 automatic. Held by both hands, the way they taught new cadets in the police academy. Grady Fogarty's two hands.

"You!"

"Surprise, Kincaid. Thought I was dead, didn't you?"

Reader's lips drew back in a snarl. His Dr. Death look. "Seems like what we got here is a Mexican stand—"

Kincaid's sentence was interrupted by the flash and retort of the gun in Grady's hands. The force not only punched him backwards onto the floor, but his hand came up empty, his trigger finger closing on air, his sister's scream frozen in the air. Somehow, he'd dropped his own gun. That wasn't supposed to happen. The pain in his chest seemed far away, like it belonged to someone else. He put his hand to his breast then held his fingers out in front of him, seeing the blood. "You've killed me," he said. *All this way and now this . . .* "You've killed me," he said again, in disbelief.

"And you killed my brother." Grady walked slowly up and stood over the man. "Little trick I learned from your friend Guterez this evening," he said, looking down. The thought that there ought to be more passed through his mind. All the times he'd daydreamed about killing his brother's assassin, he'd figured it would be different than this. The truth was, he didn't feel much of anything. Maybe later . . . He kicked Kincaid's gun away from his body, then stepped over and picked it up. He looked at Sarah Derbigny, who was standing, a look in her eyes. Smiling, but like she was somewhere else. Had gone away from the scene before her.

"Sit down and keep your hands on the table where I can see them." She did as he ordered. Reader started to push himself up then fell back, his eyes rolling back and closing.

Grady knelt and felt along the side of the man's throat. He was gone.

Grady sat in the chair across from Sarah and smoked.

We got 'im, he thought. *You and me. We got 'im, Jack.*

The thing was, it was later and he still didn't feel that great about it, the way things had turned out. He almost felt sorry for the man. Father and grandfather like that . . . Fuck that shit, he decided, dragging deeply on his Marlboro.

"You want to tell me about this?" he said, finally looking over at the woman across from him. Tears rolled down her cheeks, but she hadn't made a sound.

"You're the cop, aren't you? From Ohio," she said at last, talking, the words starting to come. "Charles told me about you. I'm sorry about your brother. It probably doesn't matter, but that wasn't supposed to happen. It was a mistake. No one was supposed to get hurt except the ones that deserved it."

He laughed bitterly. "Yeah. Well, lot of good that does Jack. You call it a mistake. I call it cold-blooded murder."

She began coughing. Now that he got a look at her up close, he saw she didn't look right somehow. Her skin was heavily coated with makeup, but even so he could see her color wasn't right. Looked like she was trying to cover up a bad case of acne. At a distance, she'd looked younger, more beautiful, but now, up close, she just looked old. Sick, like she had jaundice or something.

"What's the matter with you?" he said. Maybe she was a juicer, had liver problems.

"AIDS," she said, her voice flat, emotionless. "My dear sweet husband gave it to me. Got it from one of his bimbos, I imagine. I just found out a few months ago. He hasn't showed the symptoms yet, I don't think. I don't think he knows he has it. Is he dead?"

My God, Grady thought. AIDS. "I don't know," he said, collecting himself. "I think probably so. Your brother would know."

"No, he wouldn't," she said. "If that part of the plan went right he is, but we don't know yet. May I have a cigarette?"

Grady rolled one across the table to her, tossed her his book of matches. She lit up and inhaled deeply.

She began talking but more to herself than him. Grady wasn't sure if she even realized he was in the room. "We'd been married three months when I first realized what C.J. was. I woke up one morning and he was pressed against me. He seemed to be sleeping, but he was hunching me. I reached down and he was hard as a rock and he woke up and we made love. Best sex we ever had, before or after that." She seemed to come awake, realize Grady was there and where she was. Her lower lip trembled. "That night we were at a party and C.J. was talking to some guy about a girl he'd dated in college before me. He was telling him about the dream he'd had about her that morning. That's when I realized it wasn't his bride he'd been dreaming about and that's when I realized what our marriage was going to be like, what he'd married me for. He never knew I heard him tell his little story. From then on, it was all mostly downhill." She shook her head as if to clear it. "So. How'd you figure it out?" she asked.

"Divine intervention," he said, feeling a twinge of amusement at her puzzled glance. "Never mind. So you were in this all the way." It wasn't a question.

"From the start. Charles just wanted to go and kill the bastard. The minute he got out of prison the first time, years ago. That wouldn't have done any good. Grandfather would have been lionized. The governor would have been there, throwing flowers on his casket. This was my idea. Charles came up with the execution. He took a long time to think it up, although we decided to speed things up when I learned . . . " She took a drag on the cigarette, exhaled. "Brilliant, don't you think?"

"You're talking about your grandfather?" He wanted confirmation.

"Of course." She stubbed out her cigarette. "If we're going to be chatting here, do you mind if I get us a drink? They say I'm not supposed to drink with my meds, but I don't think it matters much now, do you?"

He followed her into the kitchen, gun in hand.

Back at the table, they sat back down in the same chairs and she poured them both a drink. Midleton. Grady couldn't remember ever drinking that brand. It was good stuff. From now on, Jim Beam was going to taste like lighter fluid.

She had some story.

"This whole thing was set up to expose your grandfather?" he said, halfway into her account.

"Why else?" she said. "I've got plenty of money. And Charles did all right. He was pretty successful, you know." With her eyes, she asked for another cigarette and he slid the pack over to her, reaching inside his jacket for another one. "When they find Grandfather and Mr. Guterez, it's going to look like they killed each other over a drug deal. Same with C.J. It'll all connect up in the police's minds. They'll finally be exposed for what they really are. That's all this whole thing's about. Surely, you knew that. Why else would you have come here?"

Before he could say anything, she continued. "Except it won't happen that way, will it? Not now. We did all this for nothing. More than thirty years . . . " She looked away, to hide the tears that suddenly started. "You'll see to that, won't you!" She spat the words. "Sure." She was going on, talking more to herself. "Grandfather'll be buried with a stain on his name . . . maybe . . . but there'll always be those who think he was simply a victim of Charles's revenge and was the honorable Titus Fuller Derbigny he's always been." Now her tears started in earnest. She made no effort to hide them, nor the sobs that shook her body. Uncomfortably, and because he didn't know what else to do, Grady just sat there and waited for her grief to subside. In a few minutes, it seemed to and she brought herself under control. She sniffed, pulled a handkerchief out from the bodice of her blouse and wiped her eyes and nose with it. She peeked up at him from lowered head. "Unless . . . The money's out in Charles's car," she said. "A lot of money. And," she closed her eyes, almost in a way that made Grady think of a person praying, "there's a well." She opened her eyes and stared directly into Grady's. "Out back."

"Your grandfather abused you, too. Is that what you're saying?"

She looked at him and the tears had ended. "He never stopped. I was out there two days ago and he wanted to fuck me then. Kept forgetting he was paralyzed. It just never ended." She looked away. Grady followed her line of sight. She was staring at her brother's body. "Until now."

41

"SHE KILLED HERSELF? My God!" Veronica's eyes shone luminously in the near-dark.

Grady nodded. "I didn't have a clue. All she said was she had to use the bathroom. How was I to know she had a gun in there?" He paused. "I don't know if I would have stopped her even if I'd known."

It was dark in the bar. All the lights were extinguished save one in the very back, near a table where Grady Fogarty and Veronica Graziano sat across from each other.

He had her complete attention.

"So the whole thing was one gigantic scam," she said. "And now they're all dead. My God. And Sarah Derbigny killing herself. They won't have a big enough paper to hold all the headlines tomorrow."

Grady nodded again and sipped on the whiskey Veronica had brought out from her private stock in the back room. Jack Daniels. He found himself comparing it to the whiskey he'd been drinking a couple of hours before. In telling the story to her, he felt the amazement he'd felt then all over again. "The whole thing," he said, "was all designed to discredit Reader's grandfather and expose him for the criminal he was. And," he took another sip, "to render the old man dead, of course."

"Criminals." Veronica shook her head slowly, in a gesture of grudging respect.

"Criminals." Grady hoisted his glass, in the manner of a toast. "People like us, but with better clothes."

Veronica giggled, a bit tipsy with the booze. "I'm still not quite clear on how Kincaid knew all this was going to happen the way he did. Wasn't he counting a lot on the way others were going to react? Seems kind of a stretch, doesn't it. I still can't get over the fact that he was a Derbigny."

"He was completely counting on that," Grady agreed, "but take a look at this."

He flipped open the notebook he'd brought in with him and pushed it across the table for her to get a look at.

"I found this in his car. Which," he added, thinking about the blue Caprice. "I'm going to have to figure out how to get rid of. Right now it's sitting outside in your parking lot. I towed it over here. Guess I forgot to tell you that. I couldn't very well leave it there. Would've ruined a perfect ending. I've got to tell you, that was a tense drive. Especially going through the heart of town. If I'd gotten stopped . . . " He let the implication drift up in the smoke from his cigarette.

"Is that all you're worried about, sugar? I'll make a phone call and your problem's solved. You wiped it down, I assume?"

"Of course. And, thanks, Ronny. I was hoping you'd say that."

She reached over and opened the notebook, one of those cheap ones with lined paper. The pages were filled with a tiny scrawl. Every square inch of space had been filled. She flipped through the pages. It was the same on all of them, both sides of each sheet.

"It's Reader's plan," Grady said. "He had help. His sister. Between the two of them, they cooked up a pretty amazing scheme. It should be. They'd worked on it for years."

Veronica picked the notebook up and held it close to her face, trying to decipher the minuscule scribblings. She read a bit and glanced up at Grady. "Doesn't say anything here about a plan. This looks like all it is is character sketches. Look at this." She shoved the book across, placed her finger on a line. "Ambitious, blind spot is uncontrollable arrogance." There was a name circled just before the line. *Fidel Guterez.* There were other names she saw as she turned the pages. C.J. St. Ives, Eddie Delahousie, Frank Cabrini, Titus Derbigny. Other names. Other, similar assessments. "This is a *plan*? Looks like a Psych 101 term paper."

Grady picked the notebook up, closed it. "That's exactly what it is. Kincaid's got everybody in here. All the players. Except me, of course. But I'd call it a graduate study, not Psych 101. You wouldn't believe the detail he has. The section on Titus alone must have taken years to compile. This is a doctoral thesis. It's brilliant. I've just read some of this, but I can tell from what I've seen so far that he knew when any of these characters were going to sneeze next."

"So he just moved people around . . . by what he thought their behavior was going to be?"

Grady nodded. "Exactly right. Him and Sarah. It was a chess game. Gave him something to do when he was in the joint. Kept her from going crazy, holding onto what they were going to do some day. I think what Reader did is leak information to this guy, then this guy, knowing where the information would end up. Sarah helped some here, but that part was mostly Reader's job. He played all of them against each other and while they all had their eyes on what they thought was the pea he already had it in his hand. Old-fashioned shell game. Fooled everybody. Fooled me."

"Almost," Veronica said, replenishing both their glasses from the bottle of J.D.

"Yeah," Grady said. "Almost." He tossed back the liquor.

"So, tell me," Veronica said. "What's the situation? Abita Springs cops are going to find all these bodies at Derbigny's, right? They're going to figure Reader was robbing Guterez and somehow got the guy out to Derbigny's where he killed them all. Right?"

"Not quite."

"Whaddya mean, 'not quite'?"

Grady drained his glass, set it down and pushed his chair back from the table. "That's it for me. I'm going on the wagon. Think I'll quit smoking, too. Might as well get rid of all the vices. I've pretty much given up women. Doesn't hurt as bad as I thought it would. My next girlfriend's going to be someone like you. A U for my Q." He smiled at her. "Back to your question, what I mean is, the cops are going to find a lot of bodies out there at Titus's place, but they're not going to find Reader's. Won't find it anywhere. Lots of stuff is going to come out, but I don't think

Reader's name will come up. It ends pretty much the way he wanted it. The way he and his sister both wanted it."

"I don't understand," she said, genuine puzzlement clouding her face. "Where's Reader? He's not at his sister's?"

He grinned. "In a well just behind the St. Ives' house. An old abandoned well. I doubt if anyone is going to have any reason to ever look in there. Must be sixty feet deep. Maybe deeper. A well Sarah told me about, just before she went into the bathroom and killed herself. At first, I blamed myself for letting her go in there by herself, but it worked out best that way. She didn't have long to go. She had medication, but she wasn't taking it. Told me she wasn't interested in dragging out the inevitable. She'd planned to kill herself all along. There was a note, told all about her grandfather and father. I wouldn't be surprised that if they did an autopsy on Titus, they wouldn't find that he was infected, too. He was still up to his old tricks, according to what she told me. The old guy thought she liked what he was doing to her. She told me a lot of other stuff. Get this. All along, St. Ives was planning to rob Guterez and his father-in-law his own self!" He paused. "She also asked me for a favor. I decided it wasn't a bad favor to ask."

Grady stood up, stretched. "I'm not excusing the guy," he said, "or his sister. But I kind of understand the both of them. The way he ended up wasn't all his fault and it sure wasn't hers. Hell," he looked at her sheepishly, "same circumstances, I might have turned out the same way. That was a pretty horrible grandfather those two had. Father, too."

He sat back down. "After Sarah blew her brains out, I sat there for a long time, me and the music. Just before Sarah went into the bathroom, she put on this album. Opera stuff. Not too bad, actually. I just sat there and thought about everything. The life these two people'd had, the upbringing, the way they'd gotten fucked over way back then. I thought about Jack, too. But, hell, Kincaid was dead. His sister, too. I'd gotten my vengeance. I couldn't bring Jack back. I wondered what my brother would do, happen he was in my shoes. Jack had a wonderful sense of compassion. Not to mention a streak of black humor. I think I did exactly what he would. I dumped Reader down the well, boarded it back up. He fell a long way before he hit the bottom. I doubt he'll ever be found. Sarah, well she left this note and everything. Talked about what her grandfather and her father had done to her. Said her husband had given her AIDS and she didn't want to go on to some horrible, lingering death. I figure like she did, or at least like I think she did. That the police'll think her suicide was just a coincidence—had nothing to do with the shit out at her grandfather's. Get this. In the note she left, she left everything to her brother. Guess that'll sit in an account for a long time. Should draw a lot of interest."

He paused, looked at her with a beseeching look, almost as if he was pleading for understanding, like he wasn't quite 100 percent sure she was going to approve of what he'd done. "I sat there and had a few belts and I started to see it like Reader and Sarah had, I guess. If I'd left his body there, let the police discover him with his sister, there was a good chance Derbigny's good name might have been left intact. I just didn't think that was right, more I thought about it. A week ago, I don't know if I'd felt the same. A week's a long time. A guy can change a lot in a week. I guarantee you I have."

There was a long silence. Veronica reached over, put her hand on Grady's. "Grady," she said, softly. "You're just a big softy." She sighed, patted his hand and withdrew hers. "If it means anything, I think you did the right thing."

"You think so?" He got up. "That's good. Makes the next part work. Wait here. I've got something for you."

He walked to the front door, opened it and went out. A few minutes later, he reentered, lugging a large suitcase. He carried it over to the table and hoisted it up. When he opened it, Veronica gasped. It was filled with stacks of bills. All hundreds.

"You took the money!" She picked up one of the stacks, rifled through it with her fingers. "You said you did, but I didn't really believe it! My God! How much is in here?"

"I'd say about three million," he said. "It's yours."

"Mine! Grady, I can't take this. I'm a cop, for crissake!"

"Ex-cop," he corrected. "And I won't take no. This is yours. You lost a husband over this, remember? This is drug money. Doesn't belong to anybody except some scumbags. The state gets it, you know what'll happen. End up in some politician's hands. I think you could find a better use for it. I *insist* you find a better use for it. The state'll get theirs. Kincaid left a million out at the Derbigny place, according to his sister. Put it in Derbigny's lap, according to what she said." He hesitated. "I only have one request."

"What?" She looked at him, a series of conflicting emotions registering in her eyes.

"There's a woman over in the state mental institution in Mandeville. Name's Sally Truesdale. They say she's crazy, but the only crazy thing she's ever done was to be truthful in a room full of liars. I want you to hire a lawyer, get her the hell out of there, give her some of this money. Enough to make her comfortable, get her a nice place. She's pretty old. I'd like her to end her days in a decent way."

"I can do that," she said, almost shyly, fingering the bills in her hand. "You don't think . . . " she looked at him, " . . . that this would be wrong? I mean—"

They both began laughing. Suddenly, Veronica's hand flew to her mouth. "Sally? You said her name was Sally?"

Grady realized what she was saying. "My gosh! I didn't even think of that!"

Veronica smiled. "Looks like there's another Sally in my life, doesn't it? Well, I've had good things happen in my life with people named Sally. I think we're going to hit it off just fine. I think this is one of those kismet things, don't you?"

Grady leaned toward her and kissed her full on the mouth. She was some woman, was this lady. He stood up. "I gotta be going."

"Grady, this isn't all of the money, is it?"

He smiled. "Nope. I've got a suitcase just a little bit smaller than that one."

She stared at him a minute. "Good," she said, at last. "You're leaving?"

"Yeah," he said. "I see this as one of those situations in life where you've spent all your currency and don't have any change coming. Best to get out quick before you run up a debt. I've run this horse called luck just about long enough. My moral code might not be dead, but it's pulled a hamstring at least."

"No, it hasn't," Veronica said, her eyes soft. "This is one of the most righteous things I've seen in a lifetime. You sleep sound, you hear? You don't have a single, blessed reason not to."

He appreciated the words.

His hand was on the doorknob when she spoke again. "Will I ever see you again, Grady? You going to tell me what beach you're going to be on?"

Grady looked back. "No beach, Ronny. Not the kind you're thinking, anyway. I'll send you a postcard one of these days."

He opened the door, took a deep breath of the night air. Christ, it was hot. Didn't it ever cool down here? He heard Veronica's voice behind him as he closed the door, telling him goodbye, but he didn't look back. Instead, he looked north, saw a place in his mind. Huge globs of snow were falling from a gunmetal gray sky and he could almost feel the wind biting into his face, whipping across the lake from Canada. He stuck out his tongue. Damn! He could almost taste that snow. Tasted good. Christmas in Vermont. What could be better than that?